UNDER THE
PIPAL TREE

ANJANA CHOWDHURY

INDEPENDENT INNOVATIVE INTERNATIONAL

Published by Cinnamon Press
Meirion House, Tanygrisiau, Blaenau Ffestiniog
Gwynedd LL41 3SU
www.cinnamonpress.com

The right of Anjana Chowdhury to be identified as author of this work has been asserted by her in accordance with the Copyright, Designs and Patent Act, 1988. © 2017 Anjana Chowdhury. ISBN 978-1-910836-55-2
British Library Cataloguing in Publication Data. A CIP record for this book can be obtained from the British Library.

Designed and typeset in Garamond by Cinnamon Press. Cover design by Adam Craig © Adam Craig.
Cinnamon Press is represented by Inpress and by the Welsh Books Council in Wales. Printed in Poland.
The publisher gratefully acknowledges the support of the Welsh Books Council.

Acknowledgements

To Vivek, Rishi and Tuhin—Thank you for supporting my dreams.
Sincere thanks to my friends, Ann Wickens, Jane Riddell and Joy Hoppenot for making me believe I could do it and offering valuable feedback. Thanks to Amit and Julie Sinha, Damayanti and Sanjoy Bhattacharya for putting me up in their lovely homes in Mumbai which inspired the setting. Thank you to Jan and Rowan Fortune at Cinnamon Press for their stimulating mentoring service where this book got the tough love it needed.

UNDER THE PIPAL TREE

Prologue

It is not so much the pitch of Rohini's whimper that bothers Maria, but the tone. She detects discontent rising from the infant's navel and dissipating into the night air. The cry resonates with the Imam's call to prayer *Allah hu Akbar, God is great*. In the gathering dusk, the melancholic voice rises and falls like a snake charmer's flute. Beyond the walls of the courtyard, a blackened minaret pokes above the cluster of ramshackle houses. Scurrying to the cradle Maria knocks over a basket of wool—a splash of colour, on monochrome tiles.

'Slowly, slowly,' clucks Indira.

Maria pulls a threadbare shawl over her head and crouches by the cot while Indira knits a coat for the newborn. The instructions from Indira are clear: to wait for a hungry wail. Glass bangles tinkle as she rocks the cradle and croons —*The moon is up, the flowers are blooming/ who hides under the Kadam tree?*

The orange sun slips behind the mosque, its stealth catching them unawares. There is a sharp clash of needles as Indira's fingers work faster in the fading light. She clicks her tongue, dropping yet another stitch. It is a complex pattern and she is determined to finish the garment by Kali Puja festival. Every autumn, when Hindus worship the divine avatars, Durga and Kali, a *mela* is held in the big field with fireworks and a giant *nakardalna*, ferris wheel—just like the ones in Rajgarh.

The saffron sky is etched with an elongated V of birds. A raven's dismal croak, *kaa, kaa, kaa*, jars with the somnolent mood. Roy sahib puts his newspaper down and leans forward to pluck a dead bloom from a potted plant.

'Assiduous pruning is the key. Hybrid tea roses my dears, need tender care like high society ladies.' His short guffaw ends in a long wheeze.

Neither his wife Indira, engrossed in knitting, nor her impoverished companion, responds.

There is a shout in the neighbourhood as the street lamps

go off. At his mistress's command Bibhuti brings in a kerosene lamp. He has been with the Roy household ever since he was a little boy and would leave the house feet first he often says. The flickering flame lights up pockets of the balcony, so that faces and objects appear in random out of the darkness as shadows plunge beyond the railings on to the courtyard below.

Conch shells are blown from Hindu households where women light joss sticks and say their evening prayers by the shrine. Fresh flowers are arranged at the feet of deities— flame marigolds, sweet jasmines and a *rakta jaba,* blood-red hibiscus for Goddess Kali, destroyer and saviour. They bow their heads in *pranam* and ring a brass bell to mark the end of the *puja* ceremony. Through open windows, the scent of wild roses permeates, as heady as incense. The women of 'Shanti Niwas,' Home of Peace sit on the veranda and watch over the baby.

The child tosses in her sleep—her mouth twisted in pain. Maria too has such dreams. Ignoring Indira's directives, she picks up Rohini swathed in primrose blanket and breathes in her scent.

'Sleep well my little princess. I will guard you from the demons,' Maria whispers.

'There are no such things as demons or ghosts.' Indira snips off a piece of wool with her teeth.

Maria blows on the baby's right temple, chasing away her mother's defiant words. Like the Hindus she too believes that a child's fate is written on his forehead. But she does not protest aloud for she owes Indira everything.

Maria places the infant on a patchwork quilt spread on her lap, embroidered with colourful peacocks, elephants and tigers; her gift to the new-born. She waves a corner of her sari at unseen spirits, feeling their presence hovering over the baby. Every morning, just before their walk to the park, she draws a black spot on Rohini's forehead to protect her from the evil eye and blesses her baby mistress with holy water from the Ganges, uttering the name of Jesus and, sometimes Lord Krishna's for extra luck. Following Devi the cleaner's advice, she ties an iron key on a string round Rohini's waist to deflect

6

malevolent forces.

'For a Catholic, you are as superstitious as your Hindu forefathers,' remarks Indira.

Maria ignores the taunt. She believes that the world is an illusion, Maya. If only she had the power of blackmagic to fight the demons.

'It's time for a feed, Maria. Give Rohini to me now and heat up her bottle.'

'Yes Sister.' Maria grimaces at a twinge in her breast as she passes the baby over to the new mother.

The moon hangs low in the indigo sky and the night is cool. November fog swirls around the crumbling house, entering its womb through cracks and crevices. Its fingers slip through railings, sweep around armchairs and claw at the cradle. Rohini sighs and turns her head on the pillow, dreaming, while Maria sings a lullaby softly in her ear. *Elephants dancing, horses dancing, at Sonamuni's wedding.*

Sometimes when the night is still and all is quiet Rohini can hear Maria's voice singing to her in the dark, across the vast plains to her home by the Arabian Sea.

So many stories Maria had told her, which ones were real?

Part 1

Chapter 1 Rohini

Mumbai, India. 2011

Naissance. Janam. Rohini turned these words in her mouth like sweetmeats, trying to conjure a taste of home. Her forty-fifth birthday brought with it deep nostalgia, a longing for childhood treats: twenty paisa worth of hot salted peanuts wrapped in tiny newspaper cones, plump *rasgullas* dipped in syrup, and *payash*—thick creamy rice pudding served up in a silver bowl. She could close her eyes and summon a pretty tableau; Ma and Aunty Maria standing by her, singing '*Happy Birthday to you*' in lilting harmony, Baba watching with a smile.

The memory of food brought Rohini back to the present. She felt faint, not having eaten since breakfast. But the unease in her stomach was more than just emptiness. Something else had occurred that birthday, if only she could remember; she must focus. An ant crawled across her hand. Rohini suppressed the urge to squash it with the tip of her pen.

Memories of that day swirled around her brain, twisting and turning, raveling and unraveling. How old was she then? Seven or eight? Her laughter echoed around the large sitting room, bouncing off walls lined with ancestral portraits. But like the approach of a *Kalbaishaki* storm, the atmosphere changed; and all because of Aunty Maria's rosary beads.

The events were stacked up inside her head. She remembered how the white organza dress scratched at the waist. Hands gripping the table, she leaned forward, dark curls dangling precariously over flames. Pink wax had melted over the white frosted cake. Rohini made a hurried wish for a puppy as she blew out candles. She was not sure of the breed, but prayed for a tan coloured one with long ears.

The gift from her parents, a large doll's house, stood on the table. She wanted to play with it straightaway, but Ma said no, they must do the *ashirvad* first. Indira placed *durba*, auspicious three-forked grass on her head, along with grains of rice, blessing her. They fed her *payash*, thick milk dessert sweetened with *jaggery*. The ceremony completed, Baba walked off to the study. At a signal from Ma, Maria stepped forward to kiss Rohini's forehead and placed a gift in her hand. Rohini ripped the package open, feeling a necklace. She stared instead at a string of rosary beads. Maria was smiling, her teeth black from chewing betel leaves.

Rohini fingered the beads. Her tongue felt rough metal braces on her teeth—another unwanted birthday gift. A new pencil box filled with yellow HB pencils, a scented rubber, or a colourful necklace bought from the market—any of those would have sufficed. She knew Maria was poor.

The day had begun well enough with six hours of school. Rohini loved the lessons. Competitive, she thrust her hand up when it came to spellings and Mathematics. Mrs. Ghosh reprimanded her twice for talking in class. Next time she would be marched to the Principal's office. At break, Rohini distributed a bag of sweets among her classmates. Diya, her best friend, shared her lunch of spicy *parathas*. Rohini's lunch box contained soggy cheese and tomato sandwiches with a lollipop to make it special.

After school Ma and Maria picked her up, stopping at an old *girja* on the way home. Dark walls smelt of mould and incense. Chunks of plaster were missing as if an animal had attacked the bricks at night. Rohini tilted her head back to study the vaulted ceiling, until her neck hurt.

'Frescoes,' said Ma.

For a moment Rohini forgot her resentment at being dragged into this un-birthday like tomb. Blue-red light shone through stained glass. It was like looking through her kaleidoscope, the one Ma had bought for her at the spring *mela*. A large gold cross towered above the altar. Maria's God looked down at Rohini in pity.

She had almost forgiven Maria for the spiritual detour until the gift was unwrapped.

'This is the worst birthday, ever! First we had to go to church because Aunty Maria wanted to go to her *maass*. You made me eat Christ's body. All the other girls there were Catholics. Now I get rosary beads? I'm not even a Christian,' she shouted at Ma, throwing the beads on the floor.

'Hush, it's a blessing. Keep it in your room,' said Ma.

'But I'll be punished by our Hindu gods.'

'God will understand. We celebrate everyone's faith in this house.' Indira squeezed Rohini's shoulder. 'Our driver is a Sikh and he gives me sweets on Guru Nanak's Day. Do I refuse? It would offend him. Hinduism isn't the only path to God.'

'Devi is filling the child's head with too much mythology,' Indira said to Maria who had shrunk into a corner.

Ma never spoke about Hindu deities: blue-skinned Krishna and elephant-headed Ganesh. Devi told her tales while sweeping the floor: how Krishna, the shepherd God, stole milk from flirtatious milkmaids, and how Ganesh lost his human head. Rohini had a stash of comic books full of such tales—glorious battles fought between Gods and demons. Pot-bellied Ganesh was the remover of obstacles. Rohini did not know what *obstacle* meant.

Rohini tried to read an English translation of Gita, but Krishna's wise words spoken to Arjuna the night before a battle was too difficult for her to understand. Baba said to wait a few years before searching for 'wisdom'. Last month, following a trip to the Ras Leela festival with Devi, Rohini had created a shrine in her bedroom.

Infuriated by Ma's random attack on Devi, Rohini unleashed her other grievances.

'Why does Aunty Maria kiss me in front of my friends? Lila says she is a maid and she should not touch me like that.'

Ma's hands shook as she picked up her best china tea plates from the table.

'*Chchee Chchee! Shame on you.* Don't ever call Aunty Maria a maid! Beg her pardon, immediately. Don't you know she has lived with me since we were girls? She took care of me, through bad times and good.'

Maria's shadow flitted across the room, the end of her sari covering her mouth. Rohini stared at the cake, lopsided in the heat of a sultry autumn evening. She resisted blinking; to back down now would be to let her mother win by her wall of silence.

'But you don't allow Devi and Bibhuti to be in the room all the time like her! They are poor too!'

'Rohini, Maria is like family. You call her Aunty, no?'

'Then why doesn't she go to family events with us, like cousin Mita's wedding in Jamshedpur? And why do you pay her Wages? I've seen her name in your account book. I know what it means because I looked it up. You put Pocket Money under my name and Baba's.' Rohini crossed her arms.

'All these questions, you would make a fine lawyer like your grandfather. I said she is *like* family, but she clearly isn't to others. And *never* look in my account book. It's Private. Look that up if you don't know what it means.'

Rohini sniffed, picking up her doll, Tara. Indira put the uneaten cake in a box and put it in the fridge.

'I hope you are satisfied now, Rohini. Maria has gone to her room crying and I'll have to clear up this mess you've made with your angry words. I'll tell her you didn't mean it. You were just repeating what your friends said. Now get out of that nice dress and go to bed. Maria will come up soon to kiss you goodnight. And don't be insolent to her. I don't know what has got into your head today.'

Ma went downstairs, her sandals slapping the tiles.

Until that day, Rohini had never been disrespectful to Maria. Even now when she was in the throes of a nasty migraine, she imagined Maria's soft hands pressing her forehead, her fragile body smelling of sandalwood soap. She could hear Maria's voice singing English songs she had learnt in missionary school or telling her stories till she fell asleep.

But that dark night in October, Maria did not come to her bedside. Rohini waited until the house was completely silent except for hushed voices downstairs. They must be talking about her, how badly she had behaved earlier. Her pillow was wet. Shadows across her room darkened, black sentinels watching. If she closed her eyes, the nightmare would start again.

Bad dreams came to her in the night. *He* came. *M-a-r-i-a!* Rohini was screaming as she fell from the balcony into his arms. He was waiting in the shadows, teeth bared in an

11

oblique smile, face invisible, murmuring to her softly, softly.

After that, there was nothing. Every time Rohini tried to remember, the fragments from the past ended in a grey haze. Memories were twisted with time, the insignificant becoming significant, grand events diminishing to the merely trivial.

On her way to school Rohini received a call from Aunty Maria. Travelling through Mumbai traffic in rush hour, she strained to hear the voice at the other end.

'I just wanted to *wish*-you. Happy birthday my dear! May you have a long life!'

Maria's Anglo-Indian accent made Rohini smile.

'Thank you Aunty. Is Ma there?'

'No, she is out already. At the women's hostel, you-know. She told she will call you tonight. But I can't wait, no? Don't tell your *muthther*. She might get upset to hear I am calling you first. I've been up since five and I thought *ki* I must call Rohini *beti*. All day I am thinking of you.'

She missed listening to Maria talking in short spurts, stressing at unexpected places in her speech, so different to Indira's dulcet tones ladling out a mixture of sophisticated convent school English and languid, alliterative Bengali.

Maria continued listing her mother's various charitable duties and her full week.

'Tomorrow she is giving a speech at a function. She will be bizzy preparing tonight.'

'I am surprised she will have time to talk to me then. I'll speak to you later, Aunty Maria. Traffic is bad. I can hardly hear you.'

Rohini snapped her phone shut and leaned forward to speak to her driver.

'*Jaldi chalo,*' Hurry up. 'How long have you been driving through Mumbai roads? Can't you get through any faster?'

Breach Candy High appeared at the end of an avenue, away from traffic clogged roads. Her chiffon *dupatta* snagged on camellia bushes as Rohini rushed up fake marble stairs. It was five past nine and the assembly had already begun in the main hall. She slunk into a seat nearest to the door hoping to be out of range of Mrs. Bhojraj's line of vision. Some of her colleagues gave her a sidelong look—finely threaded eyebrows raised, *late again*. She would talk to the Principal at St. Theresa's in Bandra for a post, even if it was temporary. It was practically walking distance. Right now, the amount of petrol devoured by their air conditioned Honda was staggering.

'Enunciate. Feel the words on your tongues,' Rohini told her Class Twelve.

> *Seasons of mists and mellow fruitfulness,*
> *Close bosom-friend of the maturing sun.*

'Think about the images Keats is trying to paint with these words. *Mellow, maturing.* What is the theme that resonates throughout the poem?'

Thirty blank faces stared back.

'Anyone?'

'Old age?' Kumar threw up his hands.

By four o'clock Rohini decided to call Shiv to pick her up. She would finish the rest of her work at home. She had barely crossed the threshold laden with an intimidating tower of papers to mark, when Kavita flung herself on to her mother. Birthday greeting was followed by a Tea party. The coffee table was laid out with china cups, triangular sandwiches and a heavily iced cake.

'I baked it myself.' Kavita turned to the maid standing behind a sofa. 'With Paru's help,' she added.

'Then she must join us,' said Rohini.

Paru, not much older than Kavita, disappeared into the kitchen with alacrity and brought back her stainless steel cup and saucer. She drew up a plastic stool she sat on when watching TV with the family. Rohini smiled to see the change in the young cook's habitual shyness. She talked about her village and how her mother would marvel at her having tea at the coffee table.

Rohini received a book of *shayari poems* from her daughter. *I was in such despair/ passing my days in solitude/ It is well that we met. Tanhai*, the Urdu word for solitude, resonated in her soul like the sadness that lingers when a maestro plucks a sitar string.

The sound of the telephone broke up the tea party. Rohini meandered her way past the Kashmiri bookcase to the walnut table where the pistachio handset rested alongside a brass statue of Lord Ganesh.

'Happy Birthday,' said Ma, clearing her throat loudly.

Rohini sat on a plump leather chair, cradling the receiver in one hand and looking through a fashion magazine with the other.

'How are you?'

'Fine,' said Rohini flicking away a fly.

'Everything okay at work? Not too much pressure?' Ma persisted.

'The children don't want to learn. Abha-di is retiring. We'll miss her.'

'Good good.' Ma's reply sounded faint as if she had moved the handset away from her mouth.

Rohini could hear someone else in the background. Probably Baba.

'Are you all right, Ma? You sound distracted!'

'*Na, na* just tired. I had meetings all day at the hostel. They have a security problem there. A burglary took place last week and the girls don't feel safe. We've been talking to the police.'

Rohini yawned, glancing down at the chipped varnish on her fingernails; she must repaint them before going out.

'Well, I guess you should rest then. Take it easy. We're going out to dinner when Shourav comes home. Kavita threw me a lovely tea party with cakes and sandwiches.'

'*Accha*, sounds good. Here talk to Maria and have a good evening.'

Ma passed the phone to Aunty Maria saying *she sounds all right*. Rohini smiled, her mother had never mastered the art of whispering.

'Hello my dear, Happy Birthday. How was your day?'

'Fine. Kavita made me some tea with sandwiches and cake. Shourav is taking me out to dinner. How are you?'

She hoped Maria would not notice the ennui in her voice. She was born on this day and yet she could not feel less alive.

'Fine, fine, just aches and pains. Two ladies growing old

together.'

Soon it was Baba's turn to wish her. This time Rohini left out the tea and sandwiches event. Kavita was motioning with her hand to wind up the conversation. Rohini promised her father she would visit Kolkata soon.

'You always say that dear, but you never do. It's not so far. We have not seen you for over a year. We're not getting any younger. Last year when I was in hospital you only came for three days.'

It was a long speech for Baba. Rohini blinked thinking if Raja was here it would have been easier—both of them taking care of their parents. How dare he leave her so early? Reckless child. But she would not dwell on that now, not on her birthday.

Shourav came home as they were clearing up. He was on the phone, mostly listening and nodding. Only a few years ago he used to bring her a bouquet of Rajanigandhas, fragrance of the night, wedding flowers.

'How are you?' he asked, tucking the phone into his breast pocket.

He glanced at his daughter while asking the question, but Rohini knew the enquiry was directed at her.

'Fine.'

She waited for him to wish her happy birthday, but the moment had passed. Shourav and Kavita were discussing what restaurant they would go to.

'I hear Pratik Sarkar has opened a branch of Kohinoor here. The food is supposed to be excellent.'

Kavita agreed and she called the restaurant, booking a table for eight. Rohini went through her evening sari collection and chose a mustard Ikat sari.

'Is that what you are wearing?' asked Shourav, putting on a tie.

Smart maroon silk with little gold swallows embroidered all over. She did not remember buying it for him.

Kavita intervened before her mother could reply.

'Mummy, why don't you put on the pale blue one with navy border instead? It's very elegant. I'll help you find it.'

'I wish I could wear any colour, like Ma,' Rohini said to

Kavita, going through her wardrobe.

'Nonsense. Dida says *kalo jagater alo*, black is the light of the world,' said Kavita, pressing the pleats of the sari.

Their table for three was by the window. Rohini gazed at the shimmering waters of the Arabian Sea flecked by moonlight. This was one of the moments she was glad of their move to Mumbai. The table was laid out the way she liked—pristine white cloth, silver candlesticks, and pale pink napkins. As she sipped a glass of chilled Chardonnay she was drawn to the far corner of the restaurant where a man sang a *gazal*, 'What sadness do you hide with your smile?'

'Hope this brings a smile to your lips,' said Shourav on cue, pulling out a red box from his trouser pocket.

Surprise robbed her of suitable words as Rohini flicked the lid open. She could not picture Shourav in a jewellery shop alone. Normally he asked her what she wanted. A Swarovski pendant winked back at her.

'It's beautiful. Thank you.'

'Don't have to be so formal,' Shourav replied, picking up his beer glass.

'Did Kavita help you?'

'No.'

Rohini was unable to read her husband's expression as he was studying the menu. He could be as remote as a s*adhu* sometimes, meditating on a mountain top. Kavita put the chain around her mother's neck, admiring the result.

'It goes much better with your blue sari.'

Half way through the meal Rohini asked, 'Where did we go for my birthday last year? I can't seem to remember at all.'

This idle enquiry was interrupted by her daughter's predicament. Kavita had turned a deep shade of red, coughing into a napkin. Rohini slapped her back a few times.

'Why did you order Smoked Hilsa, sweetheart? It's full of bones. Here, swallow this ball of rice.'

Rohini coaxed her daughter to open her mouth while the victim shook her head vigorously, clutching her throat. Shourav waved the waiter away and told Rohini not to fuss. Kavita would soon recover. A mango *kulfi* dessert mended matters instantly.

Rohini sat back at last. *Adieu Tristesse, goodbye sadness.* She thanked Ma Kali for protecting her and asked for this inexplicable burden in her heart to be lifted. A solid marriage and a beautiful daughter—she had a lot to be thankful for.

Chapter 2 Maria

Rajgarh 1966

Maria would always remember the day the monsoon rains had swollen the Kangsabati River and the roads were thick with mud. Nagbabu's bullock cart was embedded in grey silt in the middle of a narrow lane. She stepped carefully around the abandoned vehicle, balancing a large confectionery box in one hand. The unctuous mire reminded her of the cake she had baked that morning for Indira's twenty-first birthday—four inches high, slathered with thick chocolate butter icing, the top sprinkled with silver balls. The expensive English ingredients bought from a Jewish bakery in Kharagpur had cost a quarter of her wages that month. Maria had hidden the money from her father; if he knew it was being wasted on a cake there would be trouble. Indira's mother was throwing a party that night with fifty guests, marking her daughter's coming of age. A chocolate cake was special and Maria knew her carrot *halwa* wouldn't do for this occasion.

Half way through the long walk to Indira's house Maria noticed that the hem of her silk sari was streaked with muck. It was one of Indira's almost new hand-me-downs from last year's festival. The bottle green colour failed to make a contrast on her dark skin. It would have suited Indira better, but Maria made sure she thanked Indira for the kind gift. Peter insisted his daughter behave like a lady, even though his colourful language made the fisherwomen blush.

Maria lifted up her sari as high as she dared, stepping across numerous rivulets down *Chor Gully*. The alley, named after thieves, was the route she took to her night school against her mother's warnings. It was dimly lit, but it saved her a quarter of an hour avoiding the main road through town. Maria walked past the Pipal tree and the Shiv temple, cut through Chor Gully to arrive at New Road railway junction, where she crossed the bridge to enter Pahargung. Indira lived in this new part of town in a large white villa with a garden. It took Maria twenty-five minutes if she did not dawdle.

Progress was slow, holding on to a box and clutching her

sari. It was Rakhi purnima, the night of the full moon in the month of Shravan when a sister ties a holy thread, *rakhi*, on a brother's wrist, to show her love and pray for his well-being. Brothers in turn vow to protect their sisters.

The festive air was thick with anticipation and the young strutted around in bright *kurta-pajamas*. Maria increased her pace, eager to be on the main road. Soon she felt herself skidding and grabbed a lamp post with one hand. Her left foot was deeply entrenched in mud. As a group of young men appeared around the corner, whistling and singing, Maria wished she had not taken the short cut.

What name shall I call you by to tell you how you've ruined my mind?

They encircled her, a pack of jackals surrounding its prey. *Piyarey, khubsurat,* their compliments were tinged with such wanton desire that Maria recoiled, inhaling the alcohol on their breaths. Even a monkey in a sari would be attractive to them. She stumbled, dropping the box on the ground, which sank swiftly into the mud, her precious gift for Indira ruined. Maria steadied her nerves by remembering the Lord's name. She looked for a gap in the sweaty bodies to escape the groping hands pulling at her clothes.

'Look at our memsahib in a mini sari! Show us more of your legs pretty *shishter!*' they slurred, arms flailing, trying to capture their prisoner.

Maria heard the rip as her blouse was torn. By now her sari was half unravelled and her dark breasts exposed in the moonlight. Her body sagged; losing the courage to fight back. Their babble sounded far away. She was shouting for help, but couldn't hear her voice. The smell of *bhang* and country liquor was nauseating.

Maria begged, 'Let me go brothers.' Her voice was drowned by their laughter.

'Get away, *bhag!* Leave the lady alone you *nemekharams,* you pigs!'

A man in uniform lumbered towards them, waving a baton and blowing his whistle. Despite a limp he managed to cover the distance in seconds. The stranger plucked off one of the attackers as easily as a delicate flower. A quick swing of his left fist felled the youth. The gang dispersed, staggering down narrow lanes.

'Are you all right, sister?' Maria's saviour asked, casting his shadow over her.

A luminous globe silhouetted his head. *This must be what the Reverend means when he talks of angels.* Maria recognised his railway guard's uniform and nodded, pulling at her clothes, covering her breasts with the loose end of her sari. She hoped she would never meet him again and be reminded of her nakedness.

'My name is John d'Souza,' he wheezed.

Hat askew, one hand on his hip, he leaned against the bullock cart, which groaned and shifted deeper into the ground. '*Saala*, this thing is broken. Sorry sister.' No one had apologised to her before for swearing.

Maria took John's outstretched hand and stood, still shaky. He kept an arm around her. The nearby trees swayed in the breeze and she was afraid that the men were back. Rather than be glad of the helping hand she wanted to be free of his unyielding clasp, to fall to the ground and let it all wash over her. She felt faint and her body shuddered like the time she had malaria rigor as a child. For a while the world went quiet. When she came round, John's face was inches away from her. For a moment she thought she was in a play as voices reverberated.

'Sister, wake up, can you hear me?'

'Fetch a doctor.'

'What happened brother?'

'Nothing', replied John, protecting her honour. 'She will be all right in a minute.'

He pulled her up and held her close, walking her home as she pointed the way with trembling fingers.

Maria hoped her father would not scold her for being foolish and taking a short cut. But Peter was smiling at the young man who had saved his girl. He bragged about the time he was John's age and had carried a boy out of a burning house. Maria knew the story—the fire was small, but still, it was a heroic act; he had lost an eye that night. She sipped a cup of tea and felt the shivering stop. In their sitting room, weakly lit by one light bulb, she was able to see her new acquaintance better. He had a kind face, a scar on his left cheek and holes in his socks. His hands were what fascinated her most. If she had to guess she would have him down as a butcher.

Maria told her father to send a message to Indira that she would not be able to attend the lavish birthday party. Peter made the call from the pharmacy. He told Maria that Indira was very shocked and wanted to see her as soon as possible.

One afternoon during Puja vacation in autumn, Maria and Indira were in the kitchen making *puris*. Indira's aunt was coming to visit and she only ate food made by the family, not servants. Maria wondered if Tripti Aunty would eat if she knew Maria had helped.

'You are obsessed with your hero,' Indira remarked, stirring potatoes in a skillet.

'I'm not obsessed. I like him. He did save my life, after all.' Maria pummelled the dough to pliancy.

'You were not going to die, they were just making a bit of mischief. The same happened to the milkman's daughter. They ran away with her scarf, just for fun.' Indira rolled out a pancake, with slow circular motions.

She laughed. 'I guess they think if Lord Krishna can steal the milkmaids' clothes, so can they.'

'You don't know Sister, the way those men looked at me and touched me here and there. They would have surely...' Maria stopped kneading.

A clock ticked loudly in the hall. The oil bubbled in the pan. The pancakes would dry out if they did not start frying soon.

'I am so sorry,' whispered Maria turning towards her friend. 'Forgive me.'

Maria could cut out her tongue for reminding Indira of the horror she tried so hard to forget each day spent in this cursed house. Seven years had passed and still neither of them ever set foot in the roof garden. Indira was right; Maria's attackers were just debauched youths, but the dacoits who had entered Palash Villa were evil, brutally stripping the house of jewels and a young girl's honour. Maria was about to say something; admit her guilt about how she could have saved her friend that day if only her wretched brain had not frozen in fear. If only she had picked up the phone in the study. But Indira spoke again, coming to life like a rusted clockwork toy.

'Bad things happen, Maria. You have to move on,' she said, her voice hoarse.

'God will look after you, Sister.'

'Where was God that day?'

Keeping her head bent Indira picked up the rolling pin again, the shaky grip creating oblong *puris*.

Maria was glad Indira went to college in Calcutta. In the past year, she had made new friends and even laughed from time to time. After the night of the circus, Maria thought Indira would never smile again.

By the time the rains ended the neighbours were asking Peter when their daughter would get married. Maria promised her father of John's intentions. There was a tremor in her voice as she insisted it was too soon for him to approach his future son-in-law, but she knew Peter would not be put off for long.

John took Maria out for a walk every day. Little cousin Jenny skipped along behind the couple. On Fridays John went to see Mr Sarkar, the chief station master in Jamshedpur. He preferred to spend the night there. Often they would have a whisky together. Maria did not like Sarkar-*babu* and told John so.

She was busy on Fridays though; it was her laundry day. There was a square slab of cement under the outside tap where the locals came to wash their clothes. Maria rose early to beat the clothes against cold tiles, and hang them out in the sun. Her slim arms were stronger than people expected. It was liberating to raise her right arm up high and slam down the wet laundry on the floor.

'This shirt was almost new, Maria. Look at the sleeve now, it's torn. I've seen you with the washing, throwing it about like a peasant woman. Be more gentle, girl!' her father grumbled.

Lately she beat the clothes harder than necessary. Her mother's sari was another matter. The fragile *kota* material was easily burnt with a hot iron. Frankly, she was tired of her father's household, his complaints. Nothing she did pleased him. She was blamed for being idle and incompetent. If her father thought Maria would remain passive forever like her mother, he was mistaken.

When John came back on a Saturday, Maria said, 'Take me with you.'

'Are you crazy? What would people say?'

Maria did not care. She wished she could run away with John, somewhere far from Rajgarh, as far as the Express train would take them. She had only been to Calcutta once and remembered Howrah Bridge spanning across the Ganges and the crowd jostling her. No one knew who she was in that teeming city.

They were sitting outside the bungalow under the Pipal tree, in full view of the neighbours, at least a foot away from each other. The monkey man walked past shaking his rattle, dragging behind his animal performer. John passed Maria a bar of Cadbury's. Her father watched from inside.

'Just because I only have one good eye doesn't mean you can fool me Maria,' he warned her as she crossed the threshold.

A month later, when the winter days were getting longer, John asked Maria to take a walk down to the river, away from prying eyes. They strolled up and down the crowded bank for an hour, mostly in silence. John bought a plate of spicy fritters from a stall. The man whistled while pouring tamarind sauce and yogurt over crispy battered potatoes. Maria's fingers accidentally touched John's and she felt a spark. She longed to be alone with him, but there were too many people around. It was getting dark.

'Let's go back,' said Maria, 'They will be waiting to serve dinner.'

'No wait.' John took Maria's hand and led her to a frangipani bush.

He dipped into his breast pocket and held out a little package.

'I bought this, nothing fancy just a simple thing.'

Maria looked down at the rolled gold ring, a promise of a new life as an adult. She clasped John's hand, biting down on her lower lip. His hand felt cold. She thought it was nerves.

It occurred to her much later when telling Indira that John had not asked her the question, 'Maria, will you be my wife?'

'Shall we think about our future? I have spoken to your father,' was what he had said.

Maria nodded and squeezed his hand, transmitting some of the warmth from her blood pumping through her veins to his. John plucked a fragrant bloom nestled in the glossy leaves and tucked it in her hair. She wondered if her father had gone to see him.

That night, when Maria stood in the shadowy porch to say good night to her young beloved, he kissed her. This time it was different. His tongue was inside her mouth and his hand on her hips. She told herself she must not fear his passion, but embrace it as a natural act of love. After all, there was more to come, grinding, nauseating motions she had witnessed in stray dogs and human beasts. Maria went inside and locked herself in the bathroom, scrupulously washing her face and hands. That night she knelt by the nightstand where she kept a picture of Jesus and her rosary beads. 'Forgive me my Lord,' she prayed.

Chapter 3 Rohini

He is laughing, shoulders shaking, teeth bared, arms folded. He is waiting for her by the gate. She is standing by the door. A cold wind is blowing her skirt this way and that. There are tiles missing on the path. She doesn't want to leave the house. But a gust of wind whips her up, swirls her in the air and then she is falling, falling. M-a-r-i-a!

Rohini was being shaken like a rat. Jagged rays of summer sun slashed her face and Kavita's face came into view, misshapen like a Dali painting. Rohini blinked away the remaining vestiges of her dream.

'What time is it?' Her question came out in a croak.

'It's past ten o'clock. I have been calling you and calling you.'

'Sweetheart, fetch me a cup of tea and some aspirins. A Valium as well please.'

Kavita checked her bedside unit drawers before walking to the en-suite bathroom. She opened the cabinet.

'There are only Crocins left here.'

'They'll have to do. Can you get me something stronger from the Pharmacy? Ask for paracetamol and codeine, if you can.'

'Don't you need a prescription for those?'

'Tell Patel babu it's for me and your father said yes. The pain is killing me.'

'Is it just a headache then?' Kavita placed a soft hand on her forehead.

'Yes, just a migraine.' She did not like to lie to her daughter, but it was essential on certain days.

It was normal for Rohini to stay in bed all day with a migraine—close the shutters, turn the AC on and withdraw under the covers. Her head was leaden, her body weighed down by chains. *It would require a Herculean effort to get up today. She was worthless, worthless. She would be swallowed by the darkness and then it would be a relief.*

'Did you ring the school?' Rohini addressed Kavita's back, half inside the large armoire.

'Yes. Your sick leave has run out so she is putting it down

as casual leave,' replied Kavita, folding away her uniform.

'I don't care what leave she puts down in her stupid book. I am not well.'

'I know. I'll be in the sitting room if you need anything.'

'Is your school closed today?' Rohini asked swimming back to shore for a minute before drifting away again.

'No Mummy. I didn't go. Who's going to look after you if I'm gone?'

'Silly girl, such a fuss you make.' Her words slurred as Kavita's shadow disappeared slowly into the fog.

Rohini could hear the *nariyal-wallah* passing under their window. The shrill voice of the coconut vendor enticed the neighbourhood with his ware, *n-a-r-i-y-a-l p-a-n-i!* She could do with some green coconut juice to quench her thirst. In the heat of the summer, when she came home from school with her shirt sticking to her back, Maria was always there to greet her with a refreshing coconut drink. She could not summon the energy to wake the maid. Paru would be sleeping in the kitchen. Rohini removed the crochet cover on her glass; beads tinkled, every little sound amplified in her head.

As she slowly woke, she wondered if she had imagined the nariyal-wallah's voice. They were on the eighteenth floor. Sounds rarely travelled up so high. *Auditory hallucinations?* No, she must have dreamt it, she reasoned. After all, she frequently thought of their first rented flat in Mumbai where the honking of cars and vendors' shouts had bothered her daily. Now she missed the human touch.

Kavita's voice filtered in through the door left ajar. The words were muffled. Rohini heard *tablets*. A thin ray of late afternoon sun penetrated through a crack in the curtains creating a pool of light on her bedside table. Rohini noticed that the foil sheet of six Valiums was missing. Earlier, she had found them under her pillow. She stretched out her right hand, carefully feeling around the objects on the bedside table. Where were her asprins? A fat plastic bottle could not be etherised away. The jar of Nice biscuits left for her by Kavita was still there.

She could see the clock, ten past four. Rohini's head still throbbed. Her scarf was missing too, the one she tied around

26

her head. It must have come off in her sleep, while she tossed and turned in the hot bed. Her nightie was soaked with sweat.

Where were her tablets? The girl was constantly tidying. She would have to shout to get Kavita's attention.

'Munni! Darling? Come here please.' Some sweet spiced tea might clear her throat.

'Shall I open the shutters now? The sun is not so strong anymore.' Kavita looked thin, washed by the mellow sunshine. Behind her, Paru hovered, a question on her lips.

'What do you want?' demanded Rohini. 'Don't bother me now.'

'Yes, memsahib.' Paru slipped behind the door like a mouse.

'She only wanted to know how many *chappaties* to make tonight and what *bhajies* you would prefer. I'll tell her to make some *bhindi.*'

'Can't people cope just for one day? Does she have to ask me everything? I can't think. My head hurts so. Give me those aspirins Kavita. Where have you hidden them? It's the maid's job to tidy up not yours.'

'You had your tablets only two hours ago, remember? You called me just after I had lunch. You haven't even eaten anything today. It's not good to have these on an empty stomach. Papa said to…'

'Why do you have to tell your father everything? He is in hospital dealing with real patients. As if I don't know what I am doing. It's a simple headache. All this talking is making it worse. I can't find the Valium either. I think it's rolled under the bed. Look for it. *Jaldi, Kavita-ma*, please,' Rohini cajoled.

She could only motion with her forefinger. Her body was still too weak to be lifted up from the bed. Kavita stood there like a block of stone, *pashan*. No sympathy for her mother at all. Rohini knew she would have to beg.

Rohini had planned to leave the bed and freshen up before Shourav got home. But it was nearly eight when she heard the two of them talking in the other room over the clink of china. A dull emptiness gnawed at her stomach.

The door opened a crack and Shourav's head appeared.

'Rohu?'

'*Ki?*'

'Aren't going to eat at all today?'

'Tell Paru to bring me some soup. A pack of Knorr will do and some bread.'

It was Shourav who eventually came with her supper. He helped her up to a sitting position and placed the tray on her lap.

'How many times have I told you not to call me Rohu? It's the name of a big fish, mister.'

'Didn't I catch the biggest fish in Calcutta?'

Rohini felt her blood seeping back into her veins while they acted out their old wordplay. As she reached out and touched his hand, she noticed that his forehead was lined.

'I'll be better tomorrow,' she promised.

'It's time to see the doctor again Rohu. He won't renew the prescription without seeing you.'

'*You* can do it.'

'You know I'm not a psychiatrist.'

'I'm not seeing Dr. Bose. He will tell everyone what's wrong with me,' said Rohini pushing aside the tray of food. The powdery soup had gone cold.

How could she trust her psychological wellbeing to her husband's college friend and a Bengali? Anything she told the doctor would be circulating in the Bengali gossip network.

'You're being irrational,' said Shourav. 'And a bit paranoid. Doctors follow the confidentiality rule.'

'Yes, in theory. In private, everyone talks. Besides, there is nothing wrong with me.'

'Let the doctor decide that Rohini. He is very senior in his field. Dr Agrawal has retired so we have to find someone new. I know Bose. He has a good reputation.'

Shourav changed into his twenty year old pyjamas, and sank into bed next to her. Rohini watched as he slid under the covers. He took less and less of his side these days. The space between them had widened over the years.

Resigned to the fact that she was going to have to see the doctor soon Rohini compiled a mental list of what she would discuss with him. Psychiatrists liked to analyse things. She would give him something to chew over.

Rohini fiddled with her maroon *dupatta* tugging it first to the left and then to the right in order for it to fall evenly down her back. She pulled her navy tunic over the baggy knees of her *salwar*. Her long black hair was plaited. Loose strands trailed her cheeks. Streaks of grey were starting to appear at her temples, but she was not ready to dye her hair just yet.

'Mrs. Chatterjee,' the receptionist beckoned.

Shourav touched the lower end of her back. 'I'll wait out here,' he said.

Rohini wanted to ask her husband if it was normal to have palpitations, but she could not cancel the appointment again. She knocked and entered. The air-conditioned room smelt faintly of tobacco and cologne.

'Namaskar,' said Dr. Bose with folded hands.

He looked younger than Shourav. She imagined him playing tennis.

'Namaskar.' Her voice was a whisper.

Rohini straightened her back and looked the doctor in the eye, remembering what Ma used to say—*Sit up, speak up. Say what is on your mind.*

'What's been troubling you recently?'

'Nothing in particular: feeling low, having nightmares, recurrent dreams.'

She willed him to pick up on that. He would offer a Freudian explanation. She would nod. He would name a syndrome and write out a prescription. It was as simple as that. Rohini glanced at the clock, ten past six. She would spin her story out, take up the full hour. After all, he was charging enough. Shourav insisted on paying his friend.

'Tell me about your dream,' said Dr. Bose, folding his hands on his lap.

Rohini was reminded of the astrologer Ma had taken her to see just before the wedding. The doctor looked at her as if he too had second sight, *'Saturn is in your path.'* Under the desk, she made a circle with her left forefinger and thumb, and crossed it with her right forefinger three times, to bring good luck.

'It's always the same,' she began, 'this man in the shadows, waiting for me. I am terrified.' She twisted her white and red marriage bangles, *shanka* and *paula*. They were in fashion again.

'Who is the man you are so afraid of?'

Dr. Bose directed his gaze just to the right of her as if he could see someone standing there. Rohini shivered. The AC was on rather low.

'I don't know.'

'Is he your father?' His pen sped across the notepad.

'I don't think so. My father is a gentle man, salt of the earth.'

'Anyone you used to know? An authoritative figure? A teacher, for instance.'

Rohini shifted in her seat.

'I hated my Maths teacher, but that was because of the subject. I never think of him.'

'Is he a character in a book? I know you are an English teacher so you must have lots of stories in your head. Heathcliffe types!'

His eyes twinkled. Rohini uncrossed her legs.

'Stories… Maria used to tell me stories about her childhood and mine. There was a man, an evil man. We used to act it out.'

They are jasmine-scented summer days when Ma is away helping the young mothers. Rohini knows that having a baby without getting married is bad. Ma says the young girls were in trouble. Their families had given them up. Rohini hugs her doll, Tara, and strokes her black hair. She goes to the kitchen to find Maria.

'Tell me a story, about the night the demon came.'

Maria crouches by her little mistress, letting her voice drop.

'The evil man, the badmash came in the night. Three times he circled around your cot, pretending to be a crow.' She flaps her arms like a bird, her black shawl fanning out like Satan's cape. 'Then he swooped, and with one mighty croak he flew away with you in his mouth. Your tatti-filled nappies fell on the floor with a thunk!'

Rohini squeals.

Maria tucks the end of her sari into her waistband.

'But Maria Aunty! What then? How did you save me?' She jumps up and down.

'How I saved you? I didn't save you. He did.'

'Who?'

'A Rajkumar in a princely suit and a turban came up to our house and stood underneath the balcony.'

'And the horse.' Rohini has her hands in the imaginary bridle, feet ready to gallop.

'The horse shook his head, like this and said neighhhhh and off went the prince and ghhora to rescue you! The demon took you to the top of a mountain. He had grown into a huuuuge beast, and was waiting to eat you.' Maria snarls showing her red paan-stained teeth.

'The prince rode up, brandishing his sword and said let go of the princess or I'll kill you. The beast just roared. So the prince had no choice. He said,' Maria pauses to look around the kitchen shelves, 'gamaxine-zarda-castoroil-tejpatta and pointed his sword at the angry beast. In a flash the beast turned into a rabbit and ran off to the woods. The prince brought you home, wrapped in a quilt. I gave him my jewels and he rode away, whistling.'

Maria picks up the thumb-sucking Rohini, saying, 'Chalo! It's bath time for Rohini baby and Tara.' She pauses in the hallway outside the kitchen, looking at the shadows. She whispers in Rohini's ear 'Never answer when the bad man calls you, not even when he calls you by your name.'

Rohini stood by the window; she wanted to throw open the shutters, let the sultry air in. Massaging her chest helped a little, opening up her lungs. She longed to hear the evening song of the birds flying back to their nests. The noise of Mumbai traffic was preferable to the choking silence inside. She tried to count all one-hundred-and-eight names of Lord Krishna, in her head, *Om Sri Krishna namah, om Kamala nathaya namah om Vasudevayah namah.* By the time she counted ten, her breathing evened; her grip loosened on the brass Buddha resting on the window sill. The glittering lights of Marine Drive came back into focus. She noticed then that her scarf was on the floor. Rohini draped the *dupatta* back over her shoulders and returned to her seat.

Dr. Bose looked up from his notepad.

'Who is Maria?'

'My nanny, she brought me up.'

'This man—was she talking about a real person?'

'I'm not sure. As a child she used to tell me lots of fairy tales and this character was the villain. He would chase me and the prince would rescue me; you know how it is.'

Dr. Bose took his glasses off to polish them. His eyes rested on her face. Rohini broke the eye contact and looked down at her tunic. The silver thread had frayed in certain places. The navy colour was looking a bit dull. She must speak to the laundry man. The leather armrests felt clammy against her palms. A vein in her head pulsated. She wished the session would end so she could lie down and organise her thoughts. Disjointed memories danced before her inner eye. She had stepped into a world she had not consciously visited for many years. Part of her searched desperately for the door to bring her back into the present. The other wanted to remain amongst broken toys, tears and Maria's warm lap.

'Would you like a drink?'

Rohini nodded. Bose called the receptionist and the young lady appeared with a glass of cool filtered water. Rohini sipped the drink, taking her time. The image of Shanti Niwas faded, walls collapsing, doors melting, black and white tiles twisting into a black void.

'Aunty Maria always warned me never to say yes if he asked me to go with him. Even in my dreams, I was not to answer. I was terrified of him when I was young. Then in later life I forgot all about him. It's only recently that I've started having those nightmares again.'

'Interesting. I think we've uncovered something there. Let's continue this next time Mrs. Chatterjee.'

Rohini looked up at the silver clock on the wall. Her hour was indeed up. She joined her hands in *Namaste* and left the room feeling strangely light. Next time she would bring the doctor a plant for his desk.

It was only when they were in the car that she realised Dr. Bose had not prescribed anything new. She was to carry on taking the current medication. He also recommended a daily half hour walk.

'When's my next appointment?' she asked Shourav who had been talking to the receptionist.

'In a month.'

'He gave me this notebook to write down my thoughts. We discuss that in the next session,' Rohini told him.

'Homework?' Shourav took Rohini's shanka-clad hand and gave it a squeeze.

Chapter 4 Maria

Maria's news was not really a surprise to anyone. Her father slapped John on the back, making him cough. He bellowed at Pamela, sleeping in her room, to wake up and greet the affianced couple. When eventually she drifted into the room, Peter paused in the middle of a lengthy discourse on health and safety issues in the Indian Railways. His wife's unruly mass of curls had been hastily tamed with thick scented hibiscus oil, the faded kaftan shed for an orange printed skirt, sweeping her ankles. Maria wanted to hug her silent mother; it was so long since she had seen her smile.

Peter bustled about the room trying to find glasses. He fished out a bottle of whisky from a dusty cupboard in the kitchen. All the while he talked, his moustache quivering in bursts of spray exhaling from his mouth.

'The first time I met Maria's mother, three cousins and two aunties came with us to the cinema. My mother had met Pamela at the church and she said *Peter, she will make you a good wife.* She was never wrong and so I believed her. In twenty seven years your mother has touched the broom only a few times and visited the stove now and then. I am too kind, that's the trouble. People take advantage. But Maria's a good girl, hard-working like me.'

Peter poured whisky for John and Coca Cola for the ladies. *Decent women don't drink,* was his dictum. They toasted the happy couple. Pamela did not look at anyone when raising her glass.

After Maria said goodbye to her fiancé that night, her father drew her aside. She turned her head to avoid the s*harab* on his breath. His fingers dug into her shoulder.

'Now just because you are engaged, it doesn't mean you forget your modesty, my girl. None of that.' He made a rude gesture, 'You know what I mean.'

Maria nodded. She was not like the other girls, kissing in cinemas, letting their male friends touch them in private places. Frankly, she didn't even like being held, but she did want marriage, a home and perhaps babies someday—if God was kind.

'I can't afford to pay for the wedding. So make it clear to your man. If he has some savings, fine. If not, I'll have to ask the Bannerjees.'

'Papa, no! I get a good salary being Bannerjee babu's assistant. Indira's mother also pays me for extra jobs. I eat lunch there every day *and* she gives me her old saries, shawls and-all. I can't ask for anymore.'

'You are a naïve little girl, Maria. They make you do the work of two people and give you money for one. You know how much real secretaries earn? With your typing certificate you can get an office job in Kharagpur without working as a servant in the Bannerjee house.'

Maria admitted she did more than her required duties—measuring out Mrs. Bannerjee's medicine, going to the pharmacy and doing the grocery shopping. Indira's mother did not trust the judgement of other domestics when it came to choosing fresh fish or bargaining for the right price. As most of the servants knew, Memsahib was frail and often took to her bed with arthritis. Maria willingly assisted Mrs. Bannerjee in running the house. Even so, she knew she was not indispensable. A household like that could easily hire another servant and she would not be missed if she left.

'Besides, it's like my second home. When you sent me there to look after Indira, I was there from morning till night. It is important for me to keep ties with the family. They pay me a salary, and extras. I can't ask them to fund my wedding as well. That would be taking advantage. Bannerjee Ma will probably contribute to the wedding anyway, so let's see what they give. Don't ask them, Papa, please, I am begging you.'

'As you wish. You are a stubborn girl and not very clever. But it's your life and if you want a shabby wedding, that's what you'll get.' Peter walked out of their cottage, banging the door behind him. The picture of Mother Mary, pinned to the back of the door, trembled.

Pamela walked in. 'What's got your father so upset?'

'Nothing,' replied Maria, putting on her sandals.

She wandered around the village for hours, visiting stalls, looking at coloured glass bangles, long earrings and saries in shades of ruby and rose—bridal colours. She pictured herself in a white satin wedding dress. Perhaps she would wear a tiara. Her friend Diana from the typist school got married last year in the same church. Maria thought her lacy wedding dress a little risqué.

'The neck was so low it showed everything right down to here.' Maria pointed to her flat chest when recounting the event to Indira.

Spring was short and sharp. Summer was upon them, oppressive days without a sniff of rain. Maria attended a double wedding of two sisters she knew. The marriages were arranged by a proper *ghatak*, a matchmaker. Kajal was to wed a man who owned a cycle repair shop, Krishna, a sweet-maker. It was a noisy Hindu affair with swarms of people in the village hall. The sound of conch shells, ululation and constant babble of guests was unlike anything Maria had seen at Christian weddings. She stood alone in a corner and watched the happiness on the brides' faces.

Soon after, she asked John, 'When shall we get married?'

He sprayed the pavement with crimson betel juice before replying.

'I don't know. There is no rush.'

John claimed he did not have any savings. With the money he earned the three of them wouldn't have enough to live on. Maria thought she would give it six months before asking again. She busied herself with John's household, helping his mother. Joy was a widow; her husband had died of TB a long time ago. Maria thought it strange that there was not a single picture of John's father in their cottage. When asked for details, John was brief.

'When Father died we left East Pakistan. We came with nothing. The bastard landowner took all. *Baas,* what else do you want to know? I don't ask for your family's *kahini.*'

Maria kept quiet. Like many other things, it was not her business. For instance, she did not ask John where his mother went every afternoon. 'I'm going to the *girja,*' Joy mumbled before leaving. Maria had stopped at St. Mary's Church several times on her way home and not once seen the lady there.

John was used to his mother's absences, but Maria could

see they needed help. The stove was rarely lit, the floor hardly ever swept. As well as cooking lunch, Maria did the grocery shopping for them. She did not like to ask John for the money. Soon she would be part of their household and be expected to contribute financially.

'You know I don't eat meat!' Joy complained one morning. 'Why have you bought mince?'

Maria sat on a chair, her ankles hurt. She cooled her face with a palm leaf fan.

'Sorry, Aunty Joy. I got confused with shopping for the Bannerjees, our family and yours. I'll take the pack home and make you some eggs.'

Joy dragged her slipper-clad feet into the bedroom and shut the door. John was due to come home soon and Maria would have to hurry if she wanted to put lunch on for them and then race back home to cook the mince for her father. But she would sit for a while first. A gentle breeze drifting in through the open door fanned her face. Maria felt her eyes close. When John walked in he shook her by the shoulders.

'Maria! Why are you sleeping at this time of the day? I'll have to go back to work in an hour. Have you made any lunch?'

Maria swayed as she rose from the sofa. She clung to the edge of the wooden table for support. She had seen one magpie that morning and that was a sure sign of trouble brewing. Maria quickly made a two egg omelette with extra green chillies and onions. There was some stale bread left from the day before. She toasted a few slices on a wire rack over the kerosene stove. John grumbled at the meagre fare saying he would have to stop at a roadside shack to buy *parathas* and spiced potatoes. Maria kept her head down. She could tell by the heat of the sun that she was late for her father's house. She would have to run through narrow alleyways between tightly packed brick dwellings to get in through their back door.

But it was too late. Her father had seen her coming.

'Where the hell have you been young lady?' her father greeted her at the door. *Memsahib*, rich English lady, he taunted her, whenever he thought she was being impertinent.

Maria unwound her long scarf protecting her head and shoulders from the blistering sun. Slowly, she took her sandals off and placed them on the shoe rack at the entrance. The dust on the unmade road had turned her brown feet to beige. Maria held out first one foot, then another, under the outside tap. She brushed past her father at the doorway.

'What, so you are ignoring me now? Spending all day at your fiancé's house! Why don't you just move in, making it easier for me to throw you out?' he pursued her into the kitchen, his boots pounding the tiled floor.

'Papa, please,' Maria raised her right hand. Her new status as John's affianced wife gave her some protection. 'John's mother is not well and I went there to help her out. It is my duty now. How will you manage when I leave? Ma will have to come out of her room and run this place. I'll light the stove while you rest.'

She had underestimated her father's rage. It sounded like an egg being broken, when his thick palm swiped her face.

Maria's legs shook and she sank into the sofa. Her jute bag full of groceries landed on the cement floor, the contents scattering in every direction. A potato rolled under the table. Maria thought she would have to coax it out with a long broom. They were not cheap, twenty *naya paisa* a kilo. The door slammed. Maria knew Peter would stop at Ram-babu's liquor store on his way back to work. Last year the station master gave him a warning after a near miss. If he turned up drunk again, he would lose his job. 'Fuck him,' said Peter.

Maria rubbed her jaw. She must tell John. He would come marching up to her father and tell him to leave her alone. John was shorter than Peter, but she knew he was capable of tackling difficult people. Only the other day he was telling her how he had to ask a couple of Third class passengers sitting in First to leave or he would throw them out of the running train.

Sometimes, she too was a little afraid of him. Earlier that day John had towered over Maria, the light in his eyes shining into hers, trapping her in the armchair. For a moment she saw the beast in him. She would mix *tulsi* leaves, holy basil in his tea to calm his anger.

Soon it was May and time for Indira to come home for her college vacations. Maria began to spend more time at the Bannerjees. She rushed through her day's chores to be at her friend's side.

'All in all, he is a good man,' Maria declared, checking the length of the shawl she was crocheting for Indira's mother. A sweet southern breeze blew in the scent of wild roses from the garden.

'Do you love him?' asked Indira, looking up from her magazine.

'I don't know, sister. What is love in my station of life? Love is for *baroloks*, upper class people like you. I just want to have a home, a family to look after and a good man to take care of me,' said Maria looping her crochet needle to create a design as fine as a spider's web. 'Isn't that what we all want?'

Indira shook her head, braiding her long hair. She was staring now at the darkening sky.

'I don't want a home or children. I want to go abroad, have a job, a career.'

'Really, sister. You are always daydreaming. Your parents are looking for a good match and you talk of going to *bidesh*. Maybe your husband will take you to England, no?'

Indira paused long to answer. Maria was reminded of the capricious tube light in their sitting room. Every time you switched it on, it flickered and stayed dim for a while, bursting into life just when you thought it had finally died.

'I met someone last year.'

'Really? Who?'

'No one *you* know. A doctor. Kokila introduced us.'

Maria blinked. Indira had a proper friend now, someone who belonged to her educated world, someone who was not paid for her services. She watched as Indira paced the veranda straightening cane chairs, pulling away at dry twigs from the hanging bougainvillea. There was a raspberry tinge on her neck.

'You know how I am shy with men?' Indira turned to Maria, not really seeing her there. 'I don't feel comfortable around them. Most men look over women like goods in a shop window.'

Maria nodded. She felt the same.

'I can't make flirtatious conversations like Kokila. Anyway, somehow with Kamal it was different. We went for walks every lunch time. The girls watched me. *So she's a dark one*, they thought.'

Indira picked up a rusty watering can and showered her pots of hibiscus. There were five of them, all different colours, bordering the porch. She bent low to reach the ones on the steps. Her long hair swung like a drawn curtain. After a while she sat heavily on the steps, rubbing a mud stain on the cement floor with the end of her sari. Maria cleared her throat, gently urging Indira to continue.

'Kokila warned me to take it slowly saying I hardly knew him. I thought she was jealous that a man was falling in love with me. *You are making too much of it, I told Kokila. Til ke taal, turning a sesame seed into a palm fruit.* He was going to England for further studies. He hinted he would take me. Six months on, there have been no letters. So be careful who you give your heart to.'

Indira threw a broken branch into the garden. Genghis Khan, their German shepherd bounded up to catch it, tail wagging, his tongue hanging out. But Indira was not in the mood to play. She leaned against a pillar; her sari whipped up by an early *mausami* breeze.

Maria recognised the bitter edge in Indira's voice, sharp as an unripe berry in early winter. The orange sun dipping behind the charcoal lines of the horizon, reminded Maria of *kamalabhog*, juicy, tangerine-scented balls swimming in syrup. She would have to light the incense soon to ward away the mosquitoes, but not just yet. Let Sister recover. Maria would sit here by the porch, waiting.

Chapter 5 Rohini

Rohini ambled into the lounge, dressed in a soft cotton nightgown. She had woken by nine, an improvement after her last spell in bed. For the first time in months she felt calm and was even looking forward to the day, a blue and gold morning. The flat was quiet. Rohini liked it when it was just the girls at home. She found Kavita dusting a bookshelf, reaching Austen and Dickens at the top with some effort.

'Is that my *salwar kameez* you are wearing, Munni?' Rohini pulled at Kavita's baggy tunic.

'No, it's mine.' Kavita hugged her body with her arms. 'I wish you wouldn't call me by that childish nickname.'

'Sorry, but I think Munni suits you. Sweetheart, are you eating enough? Don't worry about your figure. You've always been slim.'

'I'm eating enough.'

'Then what is it? Boyfriend trouble?' Rohini pinched her daughter's cheek.

'No*thing*, just leave me alone,' Kavita knocked over a wooden Buddha on her way out.

Rohini shook her head at her teenage daughter's mood swings. It hadn't always been like that. Kavita was a sweet docile child without a hint of a rebellion in her blood, but since last year she had changed into a capricious creature, friendly one minute, stormy the next. She would have to sit with the young girl and find out what was eating into her. But right now there was just too much to do. A surge of energy rejuvenated her. She would tidy the flat, cook dinner, polish the brass objects—the list was endless.

Rohini went to her god room tucked away next to the study, far away from the toilet and kitchen; no bigger than a large cupboard. The walls were lined with shelves where her *thakurs* were carefully placed in hierarchical order: Lord Vishnu reigned Supreme in the middle, alongside Him was Radha and Krishna, the eternal couple. The ash smeared Shiva, destroyer of ego, sat next to Kali, the ebony goddess of *shakti*.

The shrine had not been cleaned in days. Rohini hummed a

devotional song whilst picking up shriveled flowers around brass deities. She would do a full puja today. Perhaps make a *prasad*, offer a bowl of rice pudding. With her illness and Kavita having her period no one had fed or watered her gods. Shourav had long before excused himself from these services. He healed people—that was his *dharma*.

Rohini would not let Paru touch the shrine; not because her caste was an issue. The girl was a devout Hindu and kept herself clean. Still, her prayers would not be the same, as pure. It was just not done, servants doing puja for the *babus*. Rohini shelved the thought for a moment, it made her feel mean. Prejudiced.

'Paru, can you put some milk on to boil? I'll make *payash*. Did you bathe this morning and change your clothes?'

'Of course Ma. I do the same every morning.'

'*Accha*, first clean the stove. Remember *any*thing non-vegetarian touches the *payash* pot, it's ruined!'

'Yes Ma, I know. I do it at home too. I get up at five in the morning and take a bath in the village pond and then start the puja. The gardener in the big house lets me pick some flowers and…'

'*Baas* enough. *Chaal*, start the payash now. It's nearly midday. I'll go and take a bath and then finish the pudding.'

'Make sure it doesn't burn,' shouted Rohini at Paru who was already in the kitchen washing the pot.

That afternoon she skipped her nap and tidied the lounge. Shourav's medical journals had piled up into several wonky towers. She would give them to the recycling lady in exchange for stainless steel pots. The bed sheets needed stripping. She sorted out the following week's clothes for Paru to take down to the ironing man.

Rohini munched through an entire packet of biscuits as she sat to update her blog. She had been up all night creating one. At three, Shourav had begged her to go to sleep. Soon after, she heard him talking to someone on the phone for a long time. Perhaps it was his sister. When she woke on the sofa, he was gone.

Shourav came back at teatime.

'I've been busy all day,' she said.

'So I see,' he answered. 'Everything okay?'

'Yes, of course. I wanted to tackle all the tasks I had neglected for so long. Sit down. I'll make a cup of tea. Paru! Put the kettle on. You'll never guess what I found under the bed. My bangle you gave me years ago. See? I love the designs painted on gold. I've been looking online for some beautiful sets of jewellery for Kavita's wedding.'

'She's only seventeen.'

Rohini waved away his doubts. 'It's *nevver* too early to prepare for a wedding. Gold is cheap now if you exchange. I've got all my big-big earrings. They are so old-fashioned. I'll trade them for a sleeker design in twenty-four carat gold, no impurities. Maybe a diamond set too. I'll order them both.'

'Rohini, stop! Don't spend all our savings on Kavita's wedding. That could be years away. Listen to me. You are thinking too fast. You need to calm down and take things slowly. Read a book!' Shourav advised, taking off his shirt and retiring to the bedroom while his wife continued to shout out her grandiose plans.

When Rohini returned to work the following week, the summer semester had already begun. The cover teacher had left her with piles of assignments to mark. Rohini flicked through the mostly-uninspired essays hoping to find a lotus in the mud. Hardy's Tess had failed to impress her class. She may as well teach astronomy, one could not find a world more alien to the Mumbai youngsters.

'Your earrings don't match, Ma'am,' said Karishma handing over her work to Rohini. It was two o'clock in the afternoon. How many others had noticed?

'It's the latest fashion,' she told the young pupil with modeling aspirations.

Karishma lifted up a well-shaped eyebrow. 'Really?'

'It's supposed to be quirky and whimsical.'

Rohini hoped humour would absolve her of a fashion faux-pas. She had no desire to be a laughing stock amongst her pupils and in the staffroom. The headmistress was questioning her frequent absences and her colleagues' fake concern for her health, barely hid their curiosity.

Rohini waited until the classroom was empty before peering into her compact mirror to spot any sign of madness. She was wearing a pearl earring in one ear and a ruby in the other. Luckily her long hair had disguised the error for most of the day. It was only after lunch when she tied up her hair that her mismatched earrings were visible. She pulled out two long strands on either side of her head to cover her earlobes.

That afternoon Rohini raced through the afternoon lessons beginning with a mini-biography of Hardy and then went on to explain the social classes of Victorian England.

'Is it that different from the class system and prejudices that exist in India today?'

Rohini drew on examples of maids being seduced by rich men, and unmarried mothers shunned by polite society. The pupils nodded with vigour. She continued her lecture above the hum of voices. Her fingers sped across the blackboard, drawing a table of social classes and writing key words. At the sound of the bell, the students left in a noisy shuffle: scraping desks and chairs, picking up books and schoolbags.

Kumar stopped by his teacher's desk.

'Madam, we had a lot to say on the matter, but didn't get a chance today.'

'Good point. Let's discuss this next week, *everybody!*' Rohini shouted after the departing class, their gaggle of voices echoing down the corridor.

Rohini's next appointment with Dr. Bose was on Thursday night at six o'clock. She knew the address by heart, forty-two Marine Drive, third floor, first door to the left. Abandoning the lift, she resolutely climbed the stairs, stopping only once.

'Chatterjee,' she panted, before collapsing into a plump white chair.

It was twenty minutes before she was called in. By then she had drunk three glasses of water and flicked through all the magazines. Rohini carried a large silver bag into Bose's room. Like a magician she produced a cactus and placed it on the wooden desk.

'Voila! It would remind you of prickly patients like me,' she said. 'Actually, maybe you should put this on the window sill.

The man at the nursery said it needs light. Don't water it too much.'

Rohini walked around the desk, holding the plant aloft. She went to the window and yanked the blind open. It was several moments before she was satisfied with its position.

Dr. Bose thanked her and motioned to his patient to sit on her allocated chair. Rohini perched on the edge of the seat, shaking a leg. There were pictures on the walls she had not noticed before—Grand Canyon, Ooti, a Matisse, and an art-deco metal clock. The room was quiet except for the humming of the air conditioner. She fiddled with the pen stand, rearranging the pens and pencils, dropping a few. Bose took out his full-scape notepad and clicked his Mont Blanc pen.

Oddly a tune kept going round and round in her head - Tchaikovsky's Swan Lake. *La la la hm hm hm hm*. Rohini pictured the grace of the ballerinas swaying this way and that, diving across the imaginary lake. The music rose as the black swan entered the group.

Dr. Bose cleared his throat. Rohini stopped, her head cocked to one side.

'Did you sleep all right last night?' asked Bose, his forehead wrinkling.

Rohini shook both her legs under the table. The chair squeaked with the motion.

'I need a lot less sleep these days. Did you know Margaret Thatcher only slept for five hours a day? My head is full of ideas and plans. I was up until early morning, making lists. I went on the internet and bought some curtain materials. I need a sewing machine. I've seen a nice Singer machine that will do the job. Ma used to make all our curtains and clothes. I'm going to teach myself. There must be lessons on Youtube I could watch. I have also started a blog. I'm going to put all my recipes on it, some book reviews and maybe my thoughts. You told me to write them down.'

Rohini picked up her fake crocodile skin handbag.

'I've started a diary.'

She started to rummage frantically amongst the contents.

'Where is it? Where is my purple notebook with the sari

print on it? I put it in my handbag, I know I did. Kavita must have taken it out. She snoops you know, she goes through my things.' Rohini emptied out her large handbag.

Dr. Bose came over and touched her shoulder. He started to pick up some of the items that were scattered all over his oak desk.

'Let's put these back in your bag. You can show me the notebook later.'

Dr. Bose wrote on his prescription pad. Rohini felt flushed and patted her face with a tissue. Her heart was beating very fast. She barely heard Bose's monotonic diagnosis.

'Mrs. Chatterjee, you need to slow down. You are not getting enough sleep. You are entering another phase. You are on a high. I'll prescribe some medication for that. Otherwise you will burn yourself out and crash. There are some excellent mood stabilisers that will help you through these extreme phases. Of course psychotherapy is most beneficial and we will continue to tackle your triggers factors during these sessions.'

There was a pause. Rohini put her lipstick and mirror away. It wasn't perfect, but she looked normal. The cracks in her foundation would have to remain.

'Did you hear what I just said? You need medication for your condition and therapy, Mrs. Chatterjee.'

Rohini shook her head. 'All this time I was low. I couldn't do anything. I had to drag myself out of bed every day. I lacked motivation. I've changed. It is working, doctor. Your treatment is working. I didn't believe in this psychotherapy nonsense, but now I see the benefit. I feel I can do anything I want. I can write a book, learn to swim. All the things I have always wanted to do. I feel I have the energy at last.'

'And you will do all those things, but slowly, one at a time. You have what we call a bi-polar disorder. In the olden days it was known as manic-depression—periods of depression followed by periods of exaltation. Neither phase is healthy. We want you to be in a more neutral phase. That's possible with modern medicine. You are in fine company, Mrs. Chatterjee. Quite often these mental disorders go hand in hand with creativity. We believe Vincent Van Gogh for example suffered from bi-polar disorder.'

'And Van Gogh committed suicide, I think. Is that what's in store for me?' asked Rohini, a dimple appearing on her left cheek.

'Ah! But he didn't have the benefit of modern treatment with medicine and psychotherapy. It's nothing to worry about, okay? Let's carry on where we left off last time.'

Rohini settled into her chair and tried to breathe deeply. He was a good doctor. He would rescue her from this confusing jungle, where she kept getting lost.

'We spoke about your dreams last time. Would you like to tell me about Maria?'

Rohini drummed her fingers on the polished desk. She had painted her nails a rich bronze, Revlon number twenty-one African Sunset.

'My mother did not want me,' Rohini answered.

Dr. Bose's gaze scorched her face, but she would not be intimidated, she would tell the story her way. She would start with her mother.

'Why do you say that?' asked her doctor.

'She was always out, working for charities. I was left with Maria. It was Aunty Maria who fed me, put me to sleep, gave me a bath, and showed me how to use a sanitary towel when my periods started. My mother never had time for me.'

'Surely this is common in wealthy middle classes?'

'Just because it's common, it doesn't make it right, doctor. As I grew older I felt I was beneath her notice, I wasn't important enough. I made sure my daughter always had me around. I started to work when Kavita went to school. Now she looks after me.'

'Tell me how you feel when you are depressed.'

'Worthless. Unhappy. I keep telling myself I am so lucky to have a loving husband and a caring daughter and yet I snap at them. The feelings implode. Everything comes crashing down inside me.'

'Do you feel angry or sad?'

'Angry. Then the sadness comes, dark waves, until I don't want to live anymore.'

'Is that what happened last year?'

'I had a nervous breakdown. Stress at work. I was in Dr. Agarwal's care for six months. Then Shourav mentioned you. It's just maintenance now, really. I am a lot better.'

'Is there anything else you remember? Anything else you'd like to talk about?'

'No, that's it.'

Dr. Bose wrote out a prescription for her. Rohini glanced at the paper. She did not understand what they were. She would ask Shourav. Dr. Agarwal had prescribed anti-depressants like Amitryptylene Hydrocholride, but the new names scribbled almost illegibly across the prescription frightened her—Lithex 300, Desval ER 500, Clonotryl. Some would help her with this particular disorder, others with side effects.

For the first time since she was diagnosed with mental health problems, Rohini wondered if she should consult her father. He was a psychiatrist after all. She had never been comfortable discussing her personal problems with him. Her mother had always acted as a go-between. Sometimes it was Shourav who would take his father-in-law's advice or at least keep him in the picture. Medical treatment had changed so much since Ray sahib had practiced that it was hard for him to make a judgment. He merely requested they avoid giving her an electric shock unless it was absolutely necessary, for instance if she sunk into a deep uncommunicative depression. He had seen many patients undergoing the treatment and it wasn't pleasant.

Rohini folded the paper into her bag. She walked to the door and then turned back.

'Am I going mad?'

'No. Lots of people suffer from this illness and with treatment they are able to carry on with their jobs and lives. You have a great support network, use it. Don't fight it alone.'

Bose walked over to her. There was a foot of space between them. She wanted him to put his arms round her, but he was her doctor. She swallowed.

'I can't remember where Shourav took me on my birthday last year. Is that of any significance or is it just old age?'

Dr. Bose touched her left shoulder, covered with her

blouse and the *pallu* end of her sari. Rohini felt the warmth of his hand through the silk. It would be all right.

'Let's see if we can remember that in our next session. But you can't cheat and ask anyone else, okay? You've got to explore your psyche by yourself. Some memories can hurt like a decaying tooth, but you have to pull it out to be free of the pain.'

It was only afterwards that she remembered the superstition. *You must touch both my shoulders or my mother will die.* She could not tell the pragmatic doctor that.

A flirtatious breeze from the Arabian Sea played with Rohini's hair sweeping it across her face like a veil. Rohini and Shourav walked side by side in silence letting the evening air blow away the cobwebs. After her consultation she had wanted to escape the air-conditioned room, at once a place for interrogation and confidence. Either way it was not always comfortable. With the act of unburdening came confronting ghosts.

'Let's have a *pau bhaji* here by the sea,' suggested Rohini, 'like we used to do, when we first came to Mumbai.'

Hot sautéed bread filled with spicy potatoes lit their tongues alight and in that moment Rohini felt blessed. She could see the crinkle in the corner of Shourav's eyes amidst the myriad of lines crisscrossing the map of his face.

'*Ki?*' Shourav asked. *What?*

'Nothing,' replied Rohini wiping away a turmeric smear on her husband's chin. *Petuk thakur* she teased, greedy god.

She would show him the prescription later. There was time enough to tell him about her disorder. She did not want to think about it just now. There was a knot in her stomach, a feeling that in simple language the doctor had said she was going mad. She was racing towards a black hole, but she would not fall in. She would not let the evil forces draw her into nothingness. A gust of cool wind pulled at her sari.

A dog of uncertain breed wandered over to them and sat next to Rohini's feet. She was reminded of Cassius in Julius Caesar. The beast had the same 'lean and hungry look.' Whether he was just after her leftover food or he was trying to communicate, she was not sure. Maria believed that spirits often made contact through animals. Rohini looked at the canine's liquid brown eyes. Who was he? What was he trying to tell her? Was it a warning of darker times to come? She shivered and wrapped her sari end around her shoulders. She threw the dog a piece of bread. He gobbled it down.

Chapter 6 Maria

The first time it happened it caught Maria off guard. Her periods were over and the last of the soiled napkins were wrung out to dry. She never mentioned such things to John; he was a man. Hindus did not touch holy idols at such times and even though it was not forbidden in her faith, Maria also abstained from visiting the church when she was menstruating.

Washing her hair after a week made her feel clean again. She plucked a marigold from the Duttas' flower pot, making sure the old gardener was not watching. Tucking the gay bloom in her braid she hummed her way to the hundred year old *girja* swinging her beaded jute bag.

A stray dog came limping round the corner with a rat in his teeth. He was a mongrel, a street fighter. Spotting her he paused in his tracks, sounding a warning with a low growl. Maria stopped as an old fear resurfaced. The scar on her right leg was from a nasty canine bite in childhood. Saliva dripped from the animal's mouth. After keeping still for a couple of minutes she took a tentative step forward. The beast snarled, then began a slow elongated circuit around her.

His emaciated belly rose and fell in uneven waves. Maria shivered, feeling his dead eyes rake her body. She shrunk into herself, flailing courage coiled tightly into a knot in her stomach. The dog dropped his bloodied prey and with tongue hanging out he paced across the dirt track towards his new victim.

Maria grabbed a branch from a wild rose bush and waved the stick at him. The dog took unhurried steps towards her. *Bhag!* This time her squeak came out in a higher octave. Putrid odour stung her nostrils. Eyes, dull brown marbles, set in milky white, pierced hers. She lowered her body and picked up a sharp stone. *Hut, go away,* she spat, aiming at his belly. He refused to budge, adding a loud bark. Cornered, Maria lifted a brick, broken in half, its edges still sharp and raw. The weapon landed just short of his left leg, mangled in a previous accident. He turned at last, lifting his head in a defiant howl.

Maria waited until the dog had completely disappeared and

51

her heart was beating at a slower rhythm. The sun had risen above the palm tree. The church bells struck twelve. Maria remembered which way she was heading before the inauspicious encounter with the dog. She was convinced it was a bad omen. Jyoti, the fishmonger had told her that spirits communicated through animals. Someone was trying to warn her.

Maria was glad when she could see the steeples at last. There was no one in the church. The cool darkness soothed her a little. She knelt before the altar, lit a candle and crossed herself three times. The reverend came in from the vestry; his soft footfalls making her look up. She liked the feel of his palm on her head.

It was almost half a mile to John's bungalow. He was asleep on the couch when she arrived. Maria tiptoed into the kitchen hoping John wouldn't notice she was late and that the stove wasn't lit. She had dawdled too much earlier and the morning had gone in a blink of an eye. It would have to be rice and lentils cooked together into a *kitchuri* as she hadn't been to the market. Bending over the clay oven, she blew on the coals, gently coaxing the flames to rise higher. By the time she had cut the vegetables to add to the stew bubbling on the stove, John was up.

Rubber sandals beat the cement floor coming nearer. His cold hand on her bare upper back, where the tailor had cut the sari blouse too low, sent a shock of current up her spine. Maria covered the pot and straightened up to face him. Caught in his gaze, she shifted the *anchal* of her sari higher to cover her breasts. John took a step towards her and grasped her chin. He smiled and shook her face left and right. His eyes were on her, but she knew he was far away.

'My shy bride-to-be,' he murmured.

Her blouse felt tight. She longed to be out in the sunshine away from the cottage full of shadows.

'John,' she rasped.

'Shsh.' He put a finger on his lips and led her to the divan in the sitting room.

John shut the door, rattling the rusted bolt in place. He

closed the wooden shutters one by one. Maria's heart raced. She worried too about the burning coal in the kitchen and the *kitchuri* boiling over. He would kiss her again like last time, perhaps fondle her breasts. She had breakfasted hours ago, but her stomach still churned in apprehension.

John took long slow steps toward her reminding Maria of the panther in Calcutta zoo. His strong hands held her head steady, her hair bunched in his fingers. His tongue assaulted her mouth with fierce darts. Unable to move her head, Maria's response, try as she might, was absent.

'Come on, do something,' he grumbled. 'A free taster should be better than paying a whore, huh?'

One sharp tug loosened her sari and her blouse gaped open where the buttons had popped. Her tiny breasts were kneaded like dough until she squirmed in pain. She was thrown on the couch reeking of his sweat. Maria gulped, swallowing a rush of bile. John's hands discovered parts of her body that no one else except her mother had touched a long time ago.

She squeezed her legs together, but John forced them apart. Stifled screams swelled her lungs. If the neighbours heard, her shame would be revealed to all including her father. Maria wished she could close her ears to John's long grunts. She counted ten, but she was sure there were at least twenty thrusts. Pinned down somewhere under his sweaty body, were her aching arms. The strings of her petticoat cut into her ribcage. The underskirt was bunched up high above her stomach.

She tried to exhale to let him in, but every muscle in her body rebelled and constricted making it all the more painful. There was a tear as he entered. Her lips bled from biting down her screams. She would not call out to the Lord in her impure state. The ceiling was cracked in the shape of a sly grin, leering at her predicament. Afterwards, John lay limp beside her for an hour.

Someone knocked on the door, but left after a few minutes. Maria's body was trapped under John's heavy arm. She noticed a snake's head tattooed on his upper arm; slanted eyes stared back, making her shiver. Her sari was on the floor.

She wanted to cover her naked body, but if she moved she would wake him. When at last he opened his eyes, John looked surprised to see her next to him. He shook his head and groaned.

'Get dressed,' he told her, looking at the floor.

Maria rose from the makeshift bed, her trembling hands twisting the sari around her slim frame. She went to the kitchen to wash her face and tidy her hair. The cottage did not have a toilet, only a shared one in the compound. The fire in the kitchen had burnt out, the stew ruined.

'Leave it,' said John 'Go home. I'll buy some *chapattis* at the station.'

He opened the front door, checking to see if any of their neighbours were around.

'Forgive me,' he whispered in her hair 'You'll be safe here, I promise.'

She had wanted rose petals on her bed the first time. Garlands dangling around their necks and the wedding vows still fresh in their minds, they would discover each other, savouring each touch. To have her honour practically stolen from her well before her wedding night, was not what she had envisioned. They hadn't even set an auspicious date for the ceremony yet. The one saving grace was the ring on her finger.

Maria walked towards the river. She could not go home just yet; her mother might sniff out the truth. John's semen was still sticky down her legs, she must wash first, feel cleansed.

A group of laundry women were gathered by the banks. They sang as they beat clothes on a stone. Maria rested her aching back against a tree and shut her eyes. The image of John, naked with his erect penis coming towards her, made her feel sick. Maria put her hands over her stomach. She felt her birth canal burning.

As a girl she came here often, diving into the water in her *salwar kameez*. When she was older her mother forbade her to swim; wet sari clinging to the body was a show of great immodesty. After she had rested a while, Maria lifted her sari and waded into the cool river. She let the river wash away the filth.

The afternoon was almost over by the time she returned home. Pamela was standing at the door, looking down the path.

'Where you've been? Did you fall into the riv-ver?'

Maria went inside to change into a fresh sari. She looked in the cracked mirror to see if there was any change. Her dark skin was a little pale. She pulled the sari end around her shoulders to cover her arms.

'Your father very angry with you,' shouted Pamela from the kitchen.

Half an hour later, John came over. He knocked several times before Maria opened the door.

'We've all been searching for you. Where did you go?' He had even gone to Indira's house to look for her.

'I sat by the river. I was feeling sick,' she replied not looking at him.

'Well, you're safe. I better get back to work now and explain my absence to the station master.' He turned to go.

'Sorry,' said Maria.

The next day she arrived at Indira's house early to steal a chat with her friend before her duties began. Indira came out of the bathroom drying her wet hair with a towel.

'What happened to you yesterday?' she asked.

Maria sat on a stool fingering a long dried leaf she had plucked from a potted fern on the balcony. She was not sure she could tell Indira everything.

'John and I had a fight so I went to the river to calm down. I was upset and didn't want to go home to cook and clean. I just wanted to be alone for a while.'

'What did you fight about? I can't imagine you arguing with anyone, least of all John, whom you worship.'

'John will not go to church. I think he is a *nastik*, he has no religion. They don't have a single picture of Jesus and Mary in their house. When we have children, I want them to be Catholics. What if he refuses?'

'You are running ahead of yourself. There will be plenty of time to change his mind when the children come along. As for you, you can carry on going to church by yourself. No one is stopping you.'

The great unsaid felt like a boulder in her heart, but it was comforting to talk to Indira about her fears for the future.

'What's this mark? Did John hurt you?'

Maria twisted her scarf around her throat.

'Talk to me, tell me everything.'

Indira crouched beside Maria to hear her better.

'It was nothing. He was tired and a bit rough with me. He apologised and promised it would never happen again.'

Indira patted her shoulder. 'His behavior is unacceptable, Maria. Next time it happens, tell your father. Peter will put the fear of God in him.'

Maria wiped her face, despising herself for taking a weak stance. Educated women took control of their lives. She watched Indira getting ready for her coffee morning at the Ladies Club. The silence was broken by a grandfather clock striking ten.

'I better go, Sister. I have to type some letters for your father and catch the midday post. Which sari will you wear today? The pistachio silk looks nice.'

Maria could never tell Indira the truth; she might think her a cheap slut born into a low class family where such things were common. Worse, Indira might report John to the police on charges of rape.

Chapter 7 Rohini

Traffic was backed up for miles along the coastal route to Marine Drive. Rohini's car came to a halt by the stadium where a Bollywood event was being hosted by Sharuk Khan. The doctor's Red Cross sticker on their windshield got them as far as the outer circle; beyond which only VIPs and ambulances were allowed. Hundreds of fans had gathered to see the superstar even those who could not afford tickets. Khaki clad police lined the streets, waving batons and shouting *get behind the barricades*. Security guards pushed back swarming bodies clinging to the gates, like ants clustered around jam jars. Some tried to scale the walls, but were dragged down and arrested. Handcuffed perpetrators of public disorder were pushed inside police vans even as they screamed *Sharuk Sharuk*. The rising chant mingled with the incessant cacophony of horns reminded Rohini of the fervour of Sufi worshippers. Shiv rolled down his window and shouted colourful words at the crowd. Had he known about this madness he would have taken a back route to avoid the chaos.

Rohini arrived a quarter of an hour late for her appointment —tired, out of breath, and with a migraine brewing. She dumped her large laptop bag in the chair next to her. The doctor carried on checking her notes while she explained the cause of her delay.

'Would you say you handle stressful situations with ease Mrs. Chatterjee?'

'If I did, I wouldn't be here, doctor babu,' replied Rohini, sipping some water.

Bose looked at her, ignoring the 'babu' tag at the end of 'doctor'.

'I mean how anxious do you usually get, on a scale of one to ten?'

'That depends entirely on the situation. If it's a work related problem, five or six; if it's personal, I rise to seven or eight. It's hard to quantify emotions, isn't? I mean we are human beings, not robots.' She wanted to say *bloody* robots, but refrained.

Bose's pen scratched across an A4 note pad. Rohini often wondered whether he took down a transcript of their entire conversation or just noted some comments. *Patient in a tetchy mood today; has a problem with authority.*

He paused. Rohini could see his pupils through fashionable black glasses. His eyes were brown. Not a hazel brown but darker. The receptionist was laughing outside, a polite, tinny laugh. The next patient was early. Bose folded his arms.

'Has there ever been a level ten?'

Rohini focused her gaze beyond Bose to the clock on the far wall. There was still a good half hour left of her session. The metal hands blurred. She tried yogic breathing, in and out, in and out, as surreptitiously as she could. A mosquito buzzed around the green hooded desk lamp. The doctor watched, still as a statue sculpted by Rodin, head inclined, hand resting on his chin.

Rohini noticed a ring on Bose's finger, a gold band with a small white sapphire sunk into the middle. Shourav would never wear jewellery. The ring that her father had blessed him with on the eve of their wedding remained in its box. He blamed hospital regulations, but she knew he thought such trappings made men appear effeminate. Bose was anything but. Cultured, wellspoken and intelligent, he had an air of confidence that the ring could not take away.

He tapped the wooden desk with his Mont Blanc pen.

'Sorry.' Rohini stared at her unvarnished fingernails. 'Last year… when I woke up in Ward Seven of Lillavati hospital… I wish I hadn't…' The words came out of her memory, leaking all over the sterile room, unpleasant, unwanted.

'Hadn't what?'

'Woken up.'

'Why were you in hospital, Mrs. Chatterjee? What happened to you?'

'Stress at work. I had a nervous breakdown, I think. I don't remember. Let's move forward a bit and deal with my current situation, shall we? My husband says I have to come here so you can prescribe me sedatives. I am not sleeping very well, I am anxious all the time. I just need something to make me sleep and I'll be fine.'

Rohini fiddled with the gold chain around her neck.

'We need to treat the symptoms with cognitive behaviour therapy as well as medicine. I am not going to just write out a prescription for Valium if that's what you want.'

Rohini stood. She smoothed down her tunic.

'We still have fifteen minutes left, Mrs. Chatterjee.'

'I have finished.' Rohini rummaged through her handbag. An embroidered handkerchief fell out and landed on the tiles.

'It's dirty now!' she cried. 'I can't use it.'

Dr. Bose picked up a box of tissues and offered one to her. 'You-were-in-hospital-with stress,' he repeated the words slowly as if she was a little *baccha* incapable of understanding simple statements. 'Why? You have to work with me to get the answers. I won't let you take a passive stance. Take control of your life Mrs. Chatterjee, think *hard.*'

Rohini pushed back her chair. Steel legs screeched across tiles.

'I won't be bullied.'

'Will you please sit? I need to finish the session.'

'You and your session can go to hell! What joy do you get in upsetting patients like this, huh? Is it a joke with you to get me to confess all? As if a huge catharsis is going to solve all my problems. What's happened has happened. I've made my peace with it and now it stays buried. Understand? I'll ask my husband to terminate these sessions because I have no wish to get myself into a worse situation by opening up old wounds.'

Rohini sniffed. The chair felt cold against her bottom as she sat again. Why he had chosen this minimalist, uncomfortable seat instead of the previous soft-leather variety she did not understand. Perhaps to increase a patient's discomfort. Or it was Polly's choice, his fancy young assistant. All she wanted was to close her eyes for a few moments and shut out the world. The hands of the clock disappeared, everything was spinning.

'The past will keep coming back to haunt you unless you go back and deal with it. Only then can you be free,' Dr. Bose continued in a flat voice. His sang-froid irritated Rohini so much that she wished she could tip the vase of lilies over his head.

Rohini blew her nose, folded the tissue into a neat square and threw it into the bin.

'I've already been to the past. Why revisit a time one has already lived through?' she asked. Her brain was clearing a little.

'To unlock something you've buried there, perhaps unable or unwilling to confront at the time.'

'Pandora's box? I wish my life was as exciting as you make out, doctor, but it is actually pretty mundane. I am an ordinary woman leading an ordinary life full of ordinary failures. Everyone has a few of those.'

'Not everyone comes to me. When ordinary lives become extraordinarily difficult people seek help. They come to me.'

'And you just wave a magic wand and cure them, I suppose?'

'No I help them to cure themselves. The answer to your problem is within you. I just help you to find it.'

'The faithful come to the Oracle at Delphi!' Rohini replied, her sense of humour returning.

'Except, I don't foretell the future, I help people to dig up the past, more like a psycho-archaeologist,' said Dr. Bose closing his notebook.

'You know, it has always been my dream to go to Italy or Greece, and wander around the ruins of ancient sites.'

'The best thing about having a dream is it means we have hope.'

'Thank you, doctor. I am sorry I got agitated earlier.'

'Don't mention it. I like getting my patients agitated.' He smiled. 'I'm sorry I was rough with you. I wanted you to react. That way we can see clearer afterwards.'

'What a sadist you are Dr. Bose. I pity your wife.'

'Yes, Sudeshna is a great partner for a psychiatrist. She remains composed at all times. The other day when I told her that one of my patients likes to run around the hospital ward naked, she suggested I get him to wear an overall with multiple hooks at the back like a bra. That way it would take too much effort to take his clothes off.'

Rohini thought of the laughing Buddha she had at home

exuding *bonheur*. Dr. Bose was not like the oversized idols one sees in gift shops. In his youth he would have resembled the young Siddartha, the prince who renounced his privileged life to seek the truth. But she did not tell him this. It would only inflate his ego further.

And he was right about the past. She would not tell him that either. Something nagged at her daily. It wasn't just depression. Why did Shourav and Kavita exchange looks when she said something? They whispered behind her back.

Rohini stopped at Kathleen's next to the clinic to pick up chicken pasties for dinner and a chocolate cake. She would make a salad with tomatoes, cucumbers, radishes and sweet corn seasoned with chili powder and lemon. A Honda motorbike screeched, swerving past her as she stepped off the kerb. Shiv was waiting for her on the other side of the road. 'Memsaab, *saabdan*!' he yelled.

'These crazy motor cyclists should be caught by the police.' He helped her into the car. 'I forgot Dr. sahib is not with you this evening. Otherwise I could have waited for you in front of the clinic.'

'Let's go home now. Did you get yourself a snack? I hope you had enough money after paying the parking charges.'

'Yes Ma I even have some left over.'

'Good. Keep that for next time. *Achcha*, how is your wife's leg?'

It was nearly seven when Rohini reached home. Kavita hadn't returned from school. Rohini checked her mobile phone. There were no text messages or missed calls.

'Did Kavita come home first before going out again?' she asked Paru.

'No Ma, Kavita -*didi* never even called.'

'Ok, make your *chapattis* now. I'll try her again.'

Rohini tried Kavita's mobile a few times. She hoped she did not to sound too anxious when leaving a message. Half an hour later when she had changed into her comfortable indoor clothes and there was still no message from her daughter she sent a more urgent sms. *Where are you? Please call home. When are you coming back?*

It was eight o'clock. Kavita was never three hours late without contacting home. Rohini had to try something more invasive and bear Kavita's wrath later. She still had telephone numbers of her daughter's friends from when they used to come over for tea.

'I haven't spoken to Kavita for months. She took me off her Facebook list,' complained Priya.

'Sorry *beti*, I'll talk to her. Do you know the names of any of her new friends?'

'Pinky, Ash, Tara and Jag.'

'Is Jag a boy?'

'Yes, short for Jagdish and Ash for Ashok.'

'What kind of people are they?'

'Rich. They all come in nice cars. Ash's father owns a brewery.'

'Do they party a lot?'

'I don't know Aunty. You'll have to ask Kavita.'

Rohini paced the sitting room floor, wearing out the Tibetan rug. Kavita was mixing with a smart set of friends. She envisioned late night parties with drugs and alcohol. It was not a new phenomenon. There had been certain types in her college—huddling around in a circle, smoking pot while Rohini and her friends sat a few feet away, enjoying the Calcutta Inter-College Music Fest. Different worlds existed side by side. One just had to choose the right one. She had never given her parents a moment's anxiety.

Rohini wanted Shourav next to her, calming her down with logical answers. *You are making a drama about nothing. She is young. She is making new friends.*

The doorbell rang. Rohini raced Paru to the entrance. She found Mr. Kapoor leaning against the door frame, half his bulk inside their property. In his hand he had a letter addressed to 'Mrs. Chatterjee'.

'The name is not clear. It looks like Kapoor-ji, no?'

Rohini saw that the letter-headed paper was from Dr. Bose, her bill for the month. It had gone to Flat one-hundred-and-eighty-five instead of one-hundred-and-eighty-four. She would have words with Bose's secretary.

'I opened it by mistake,' he added.

Instead of an apology he was looking at her for an explanation. Bose's credentials in psychiatry were clearly displayed on the top of the letter.

The lift doors opened as Kavita slipped out, dressed in a short denim skirt and a fuchsia top, multi coloured beads bouncing on her chest. Mr. Kapoor's reading glasses slid down his nose as he strained to look above them. Kavita acknowledged their presence with barely a nod and brushed past her mother. Taking advantage of her neighbour's loosened grip, Rohini snatched the letter saying a curt thank you and slammed the door.

Kavita had already retreated into her bedroom. Rohini knocked on her door ignoring the sign in fluorescent yellow saying 'Keep Out'. Above the music emanating from her iPod, Rohini could hear the cascade of water in her shower. At least Kavita was home and unharmed; she would ask questions later, when the mood was right.

When Kavita emerged from her bedroom after nearly an hour, Rohini's anger abated seeing her daughter's face, devoid of lipstick and mascara, damp curls clinging to her cheeks.

'Did you have a good time with your friends?' Rohini tried a less accusatory tactic. Kavita flicked through TV channels, a blur of soap operas and news bulletins.

'Yep. Did your visit to the doctor go okay?' Kavita replied with a question, picking up a handful of cashew nuts.

'Yes thanks. We are making some progress I think. I was worried about you. You didn't even call or leave a message.'

'Forgot. Sorry. I went to my friend's house to study for our test next week and we had some snacks,' Kavita answered, preempting her mother's questions thereby killing all three birds at once—where were you, what were you doing there and have you eaten anything?

Rohini was not fooled by the information volunteered, but admired her daughter's new found confidence in handling her parent's interrogation.

'I rang Priya. She said you were out with some new friends?' Rohini played her trump card.

'*What*? Why did you call her? Mummy, you are impossible!

You treat me like a child.' Kavita's tone changed to angry teenager, a phase Rohini knew better than complacent young adult.

'Well if you acted responsibly and called me I wouldn't have to ring your friends.'

'Don't talk to me about behaving responsibly. Do you always act as you should, huh? Your pill taking and other things are not the behavior of a responsible adult.'

When Rohini spoke her voice was still a little shaky. 'I'm trying to seek help for that. You know I work hard and have to look after everybody's needs. One day you'll find out what it's like being a mother.'

Kavita put her feet up on the sofa and hugged a cushion. 'At least I'm not like Mona.'

'Who's that?'

'You know Aunty… Never mind. I'll listen to music in my room.'

Kavita got up dropping the silk cushion on the floor.

'Which Aunty's daughter? Not Champa's, is it? She's a wild one. But I don't think her name is Mona.'

'Mummy, forget it.' Kavita slammed her bedroom door.

Rohini set the table. The pasties had gone cold, the salad limp. She smacked the plates down. Kavita came out of her room.

'Next year I'll be in University so you won't be able to control my movements.'

'You'll go to Mumbai College, won't you, and stay at home?'

'No, you don't listen! I want to study Politics in Delhi Uni.'

'A bit far, isn't it darling? Although, we have family there.'

Kavita stormed back into her bedroom. The music was back on, louder. Shourav called to say he would be another hour. As Rohini munched through half a dozen celery sticks she took stock of the situation. Her daughter was still an innocent young girl underneath her trendy new image yet it did not alter the fact that she was mixing with the wrong crowd. Something must be done.

This time Rohini opened the door without knocking. Kavita's bed was covered in party dresses of all kinds, shimmering sequined tunics, a silk kimono and faux leather trousers. Rohini did not recall buying her these.

'What's going on?'

'It's Ash's birthday this weekend. He's holding it in Taj Hotel in a private function room. The band Hot Ginger is going to play. And... Mummy you won't believe this, Aamir Khan is going to drop in! You know the actor from The Three Idiots. He orders a lot of beer from Ash's father. We're going to be picked up in a limo from Ash's place and be taken to the hotel. Isn't it fantastic? I don't know what I'm going to wear. I'll go shopping with Pinky. Zena lent me these clothes, but they're a bit big for me.'

Rohini sat on the edge of her daughter's bed. Her teddy was still tucked behind her pillow. She would have to pick her words carefully or lose Kavita forever.

'Darling, your new friends are from a very different social world. How are we going to compete with them? We are welloff, but not millionaires. Your birthday is going to be at home or in a restaurant. We can't afford to hire celebrities. What about gifts? What on earth do you give to people who have everything?'

Kavita sat next to her.

'You worry too much. My birthday is months away. I'll think of something. As for presents, the rich people give each other joke gifts, something cheap and tacky. We are buying him a pair of green bell-bottoms. It's hideous! A tailor in a slum is stitching it. Jag ordered his driver to sort it.' Kavita gave her mother a hug.

'I know what I am doing. I totally fit in. My friends respect doctors like Gods. Plus we are high class Brahmins. If they meet Grandma they'll think we are aristocrats. They may have money, but we have class.'

Kavita kissed her mother. Rohini looked at her daughter—confident, luminous and hopeful. She did not want to take that away. Sometimes she wished Kavita was a baby and she could put a discreet black *kajal* dot on her left temple to protect her from the evil eye.

Chapter 8 Maria

As the weeks went by, Maria tried to get John to talk about himself. There was so much she wanted to know about the man she was going to marry. She started by questioning the cobra tattoo on his forearm, the one that haunted her every time they made love. It was a talisman, he said, to protect him from demons that plagued him when he was young. Things got a lot worse after his father disappeared for the first time. The villagers talked. Some said the cruel old man had shacked up with a woman in town, throwing his family in the path of Saturn's misfortune. First their cow Chandra died; then someone stole their goats. Few days later John dropped an axe on his foot.

That would explain the limp, thought Maria. John took his shoes off to show the full extent of his injury. The digits were sliced at an angle at the top. His toes were black where the flesh was missing. John put his socks back on. Maria averted her gaze. She understood why John chose to wear shoes and not sandals even in the heat of summer. She had never seen his bare feet.

'They didn't heal properly although Ahmed's wife put *tulsi* paste on them daily. I couldn't work for days.'

John smoked a cheroot blowing circles of smoke into the air. Maria covered her face with the end of her sari. She settled on the charpoy next to him, folding a *paan* in her hands, something to chew while she listened.

'I was sixteen when Father left us. All the trouble we had that year was the bastard's fault. Hassan Ahmed took over the land. He let me work in the fields for a few rupees and some food. Some days we only ate rice with a slice of aubergine or bitter gourd. How is a man to survive on that?'

John mashed tobacco leaves on his palm.

'I thought he died of TB,' said Maria.

'A bad wind was blowing our way. Singh-ji's wife told me of a spiritual healer, Babaji. The locals thought he was a blood-drinking monster, a *rakshash!*'

John laughed. Maria had heard of yogi men like that. She was too afraid to approach them in case they put a curse on her.

'Curse, *na*. He showed me his book of tattoos. I chose the serpent's head. Babaji laughed. *The design chooses the person, he said. Sala* was right. I wanted peace, but I returned with Shakti, power. My life changed after that.'

Maria shivered. They were sitting in the blazing sun. A long shadow fell across the courtyard. It was only the man selling sweets, two pots balancing on a pole. His shout for wares *laddoo-rasgulla-chamacham* made her jump.

Later, when it was just the two of them in his hut, John asked her to trace the dark lines with her finger. She thought it aroused him and complied. The serpent's eyes, returned her gaze with malevolence. The scales grew larger in size close to its head. The hood descended into a point of an arrowhead. The forked tongue leered at her with disdain. In death its spirit was preserved for eternity in indigo. Some ghosts stayed with you forever, taunting, playing with your mind.

It happened again when Joy was in Palashpur, visiting her cousin. John asked Maria to stay the night. She told him it was improper, but he would not listen. The lie to her parents was harder, telling them she was at Indira's. When the moon slipped behind dark clouds, Maria entered the cottage, wearing a black shawl around her head and shoulders.

John insisted they lie down on Joy's bed. He began playing with her breasts. Maria tried to respond, but her inert body was trapped between him and the wall. Her lover soon dispensed with gentle foreplay and pulled off her sari. Maria helped him, afraid he would tear her clothes.

Afterwards, John fell into a deep sleep. He was breathing hard, his body twitching and convulsing. Sometime in the early morning he sat up. It was still dark outside.

'He is here.' He pointed to the door.

'There is no one. Go back to sleep.'

'I've killed you once. I'll kill you again,' he roared.

John got up and pushing aside the table, lumbered towards the door. Maria coaxed him to come back to bed. She wiped his brow. His body was soaking. She forgave him for violating her during the night. She ached from his deathly grip on her.

Unhappy spirits haunted the living. He would never be free.

Maria crept out of the bungalow at dawn before the neighbours were up. She bathed by the tube well. Jugs of ice cold water barely washed away her sins. The reverend was surprised to see her at the church so early in the morning, wet and shivering. He did not ask questions.

The sun was high when Maria did her chores for the day. There was a pile of laundry. She cried out dropping a bucket full of water by the well. The clothes remained unwashed. Maria came home and lay on the floor. Pamela filled a muslin bag with herbs. She warmed it on the coal bucket oven and placed it on Maria's back, just above the waist. Women's troubles, she had them when she was young, comforted her mother. Besides, anyone could see that Maria was working like a slave in John's household.

'Your mother-in-law-to-be is a lazy woman, making you do all the work before you are even married,' said Pamela.

What Maria wanted was a few days rest, but that was hardly likely. John expected her to shop and cook while his mother remained sequestered in her room all morning. Most days she rushed back from her job at the Bannerjee's to arrange lunch for John. She was getting smarter now and cooked for both families at the same time; serving John first then racing across to her home carrying her father's lunch in a tiffin carrier.

Maria was not afraid of hard work and knew it was a temporary situation. Soon they would be married. That made her anxious. The rough love-making would become a nightly ritual. But what worried her most was John's struggle with his inner demons. He brushed away her questions.

'Who are you so afraid of? Whom do you fight with in your dreams?' she asked.

John got agitated, threw things around. Once or twice he raised his hand to her face. She cowered but persisted. If Maria was to spend the rest of her life with him, she must have answers.

Later that week Maria arrived at John's house a little past two in the afternoon. It had been raining all day. She folded her unruly umbrella, blowing inside out in the wind. Sharp darts of rain had soaked the bottom half of her sari. Maria leaned over to wring out the wet border, *the par*. Her head swam. She had been sick all morning. Pamela, rousing herself from her habitual comatose state had made her daughter a herbal drink. It tasted foul. A monsoon virus, she stated. Maria agreed quashing her own fears. She would broach the subject of marriage with John.

Maria was relieved to find John asleep on the couch. All she wanted was to lie down for a while. John's mother was in her room. Maria unrolled a mat and curled into a crescent with her head facing the wall and fell into a deep sleep. She woke choking. John's hands were squeezing her slim throat. Her screams came out in a painful groan.

'Die, you beast!' John was saying to her, his eyes glazed.

Maria felt life slipping away from her body. She prayed— Forgive him Father, for he knows not what he does. Just as the room disappeared in a grey mist, a shadow loomed over them. John's mother struck her son with a carved wooden stick, *thwack* diagonally across his spine.

'Let her go, son! Wake up Jammi, wake up,' Joy cried clawing at his fingers.

John crumpled into a heap on the floor, his head in his hands. Joy squatted beside the broken body of her son, trying to calm the shudders with her arthritic hand. She turned her, grey-eyes, hitherto perceived by Maria to be blind, towards her future daughter-in-law.

'Go to the kitchen *beti*, and have a glass of water. I'll put some arnica on your bruises. Wrap the end of your sari around your neck when you go home tonight.'

Maria noticed a purple mark where Joy's headscarf had slipped in the struggle.

'Why did he do it Ma?' Maria asked Joy. 'Does he hate me so?'

'No sweetheart. He hates himself.'

'Why?'

'Maybe he will tell you that one day. My son is wracked by demons. They have chased him for a long time. I have seen five ghost priests. He wears a moon stone I bought for him with all my savings, cleaning up to three houses a day and cooking for two families. But nothing works. I thought he will have peace with you. But God knows why he always has these fits. Anyway, I'll look after him tonight. You go home. Don't be afraid of him. It's not John who is trying to kill you.'

Maria did not know whether to be reassured by the cryptic words or to be more afraid than ever. Whose spirit possessed John? She would seek help, but not in this village. She did not want the whole community to talk about their dramas.

'I like you nickname for him.' Maria was tidying up her sari preparing to leave.

'What's that?' A frown etched Joy's forehead.

'Jammi, you called him Jammi just now. It sounds nice.' John was sleeping, his gentle snores emanated from the bedroom.

'His name is John. I don't know why I should call him by any other name. He was baptised at Kishoregung Church with his father present,' Joy retorted, her voice rising by a fraction of a decibel.

She picked up a broom and brushed the floor vigorously. Little clouds of dust rose into the air. Maria covered her mouth trying to stifle a cough.

'Sorry Ma, I must have misheard you. I didn't mean…'

'I am not your Ma yet so you can call me Aunty from now on. Taking liberties is not what decent girls do. When John marries you in church you can come and live here, but until then you better stay away. It's not right to be eating and cooking here and spending afternoons in this bungalow with John when I am at the mos… church. Gods knows people gossip about anything here. I don't want John's future wife to be insulted.'

Maria left the hut clutching her cloth bag. She stopped to rest under an Ashok tree. Not many people were about in the heat of the afternoon sun. Maria took out her rosary necklace, passing the beads through her fingers. Saying ten Hail Marys calmed her. In fact that was the only bit she knew well. The rest were just a jumble of the Reverend's words. She kissed her cross.

A crow stood on one foot, his head cocked to one side, inspecting her with his dull eyes. His voice was raw and hoarse as he called over and over again. An emaciated girl appeared around the corner, sniffing back a little rivulet of snot running from her nostrils. She shooed the crow with a stone. The crow flapped his wings, but refused to budge. He knew her threat was empty. She knew he would rise and perch in another spot nearby and continue to annoy her.

'Look what I found under the bush.' The child held out a mud streaked palm on which sat a twenty-paisa coin, dirty and sticky with some unknown substance.

'It's mine.' She closed her fist and pulled back her hand towards the hem of her torn dress.

'What's your name?'

'Jharna.' Waterfall.

'Buy some sweets with the money,' said Maria.

'You can't have it.' With a free hand Jharna wiped her nose smearing yellow catarrh across her cheeks.

'It's yours. Don't let anyone have it.'

Maria tilted her head and rested it against the tree. Her temples throbbed, she felt nauseous. Perhaps her period was due. She would have to check the calendar. The sun was low in the sky. Her body sagged into a hollow in the dry unyielding ground. Thick roots spread all around her, gnarled fingers gripping the soil. She would stay a little longer under the cool shade of the Ashok tree.

A burst of colour swept into view followed by loud clucking by a group of boys. A gaudy kite swerved past Maria knifing into the ground before being jerked up by its expert owner.

'*Chaal chaal chaal*,' they urged the kite flocking into the narrow alleyway leading to a field.

The girl stared at this delicious new treat, breaking into a run to join her friends and brothers.

'Wait for me,' she shouted.

Maria saw the penny drop as the girl's hands let go of one prize in the hope of securing another. She sat for a long time, until the sky had turned violet, and the birds had sung their evensong. If she were to marry John she must learn to tame his inner beast.

*

One afternoon, while getting water from the well, Maria heard the ladies talking about a witchdoctor in the next village. Bimala had cured one lady's infertility and another's madness. It was a dangerous method and sometimes resulted in terrible consequences. Still, it could be worth the risk. She would need something belonging to the victim, some object he was close to.

Maria had remarked on a pendant John wore with Arabic writing on it; an unusual thing for a Christian to wear.

'A holy Islamic man, a *pir* used to get the Kharagpur Express regularly. He had a bad leg so I always helped him on to the train and made sure he got a seat. One day he blessed me with this pendant. He said I had a kind face. See, it's my name written in Arabic.'

The locket was rather beautiful in the shape of a crescent moon. Maria had to find a way to get John to give it to her for a day. Perhaps she could offer to polish the brass ornament for him.

Maria asked the women in her village for help. They agreed Pamela was possessed. A wicked spirit had scrambled her brain and her soul was in a disturbed state. Maria listened patiently to their advice and swore them to secrecy. The ladies told her the way to go. There was an hourly train to Palashpur. Bimala lived in a hut behind the Kali temple.

John refused to have the pendant cleaned. He had not taken it off for years; he would die with it on. In the end Maria told him a half-truth. She was worried about his health. She was going to see an *ayurvedic* doctor who could sense the patient's state merely by touching an object belonging to him.

There was no fooling John. His mother had tried everything to cure him: witchcraft, homeopathy, astrology— nothing had worked. He gave Maria his moon stone ring instead.

Maria held out the ring to Bimala. The old lady closed her eyes and fingered it for a long time. The craggy map of her face was lit by yellow light from a kerosene lamp. Most of the room was in shadows. Bimala muttered a mantra. Her head dropped. She threw the ring across the floor as if it had scorched her fingers. She was staring at something in the distance, through mud walls into another world. Maria could hardly breathe.

Bimala was shaking, her right arm in an uncontrollable tremor. She panted like a dog. Maria worried that the old lady might faint. She got up to support the frail woman, but was pushed aside with such violence that she fell back against the charpoy bed.

Bimala collapsed in a heap. Maria touched her with trembling hands. Was she dead? She shook the old lady roughly. The lamp was no longer flickering. Maria called out her name. At last there was a movement. The witch doctor sat up. She pushed her hair back from her face. Leaning forward, she put her lips in Maria's ear.

'It is too late. You cannot get rid of him now.'

'Who is he? Why does he possess John?' demanded Maria.

'How do I know? I just feel the power surge through me. Oh, he's a nasty one. Stay away from him or he'll be after you too, my girl. Put the money on the table over there. Can you pour me a glass of water from the pitcher? I am so thirsty. Now go, I need to rest.'

Maria bent over to pay her respects to Bimala.

'Bless you my child, no need to touch my feet. If you haven't married him yet, don't bother, he is damaged goods.'

On that portentous note Bimala saw Maria off at the door.

Chapter 9 Rohini

It was spring in Mumbai and although the temperatures were already in the high 30°s, Rohini was reluctant to have the air-conditioning as last month's electricity bill had been a shock. Being alone in the apartment, she had the ceiling fan on instead, rotating at high speed above. It reminded her of the hot summers in childhood sans AC. A sheet of paper, an essay, fluttered dangerously in her hands, threatening to blow away at the slightest loosening of her grip or a minor distraction. The phone rang; an insistent tinkling that irritated her during the minute it took her to rise from the sofa and reach the telephone. It was her mother. Rohini had missed the weekly call to her parents, but it was unlike Indira to telephone, simply to complain about her daughter's lack of filial piety.

Rohini waited for the initial '*how are you*' to end, to hear the real reason for the call—Baba has had a fall, Aunty Maria was in hospital, or someone in their extended family had died. Her first anxious enquiries about Baba's health were quelled by Ma's vigorous reassurance. Yet Rohini detected a faint tremor of something different and disturbing. She was prepared for a gradual revelation of news: not good, not bad, just a minor concern such as might arise from a little ascent in the blood pressure meter.

She was wrong. It was in fact, joy. Rohini was as astonished by the news that unfolded as by the timbre of her mother's voice, girlish and excited. Indira was naturally reticent, loath to display her emotions even to loved ones. Her volubility therefore made a refreshing change. She reminded her daughter of a *mynah* bird, words tumbling out of her mouth. Rohini listened to her mother's voice growing in strength with every sentence. The invisible dam she had built around her for so many years had broken at last.

'I have some news. 'Janani' has been awarded the best charity organisation in India. I am holding a letter in my hand, from the President.'

Rohini dropped the essay. The breeze swept it under the cabinet; she would retrieve it later. The marking could wait.

'Ma, that's brilliant news! You've worked so hard.'

'We couldn't believe it. You know Bakul and Parul, the Bannerjee twins. You met them last year in Calcutta Club.'

'Yes, yes, I know them.'

'They gave me the letter on Monday when I went in to supervise the auditors. Even the paper is of such fine quality. I read the letter several times—first with my glasses on and then off. It says *The President of India Mr. Harish Khanna would like to present you with The Best NGO Award in recognition of your tireless service in helping destitute single mothers*. We have been invited to go to New Delhi to collect the award. I don't think the real President will be there, maybe a senior civil servant, but still.'

Rohini heard her mother take a deep breath. She ceased this opportunity to offer her congratulations.

'Everything happens with God's grace Ma, *Ishwar's kripa.*'

'That's true dear, but I always feel that we make our own luck. All these years of going to 'Janani' in sunshine and rain have finally been recognised. During the floods we even fashioned a bamboo raft to get to the hostel. The residents collected rain water in a bucket on the roof. We couldn't get any drinking water from the submerged tube wells. Our volunteers threw together rice and lentils to make *khichuri* in a giant pot. The ladies were so grateful.'

Rohini remembered the floods, wading through knee-deep muddy waters with Raja after school. Maria was waiting anxiously at the doorway, having already sent Bibhuti to look for them. Maria made mugs of steaming Horlicks to warm them up. As per ritual, a story followed, rich with memories, laden with danger: riots, snakes, giant spiders, men with sticks, shouting and chasing. They were never calming tales and yet Raja and Rohini gobbled up those large chunks of life they had not yet lived.

'I hated you leaving me. Aunty Maria used to say what a fine lady you were, like Mother Teresa.'

'Well, it was a worthy cause. I didn't like leaving you and Raja, but I trusted Maria to take care of you. Most mothers I knew left their children in the care of maids while they played bridge. Shocking manners the children picked up, not befitting people of our class, if you know what I mean.'

Rohini agreed. You could not accuse Maria of vulgarity. She used to haul Bibhuti over the coals if he so much as said *sala* in front of the children. Raja got smacked once for saying *sooanr ki baccha, pig's baby*. It had sounded innocent enough, but he knew it was swearing.

She remembered the motherless days—early evening trips to the park, playing cricket with Raja, Aunty Maria singing lullabies, *ghoom parani mashi pishi*, calling the sleep aunties to come to their house, sitting on Maria's lap eating hot puris, listening to ghost stories. Rohini would cross her fingers repeating a mantra in her head: these were just stories, the ghost man did not exist, he was not real.

One afternoon, Rohini watched Maria washing dishes in smooth even strokes, using a steel sponge dipped in wet ash. Rohini picked up a plate; she could see her face on it clear as a mirror. Pots and pans were stacked up neatly against one another, glasses in a row, plates fanned out.

'Let me have a go,' Rohini pleaded.

When her mother found her in the kitchen with ash smeared hands, she was dragged out of the room and scolded soundly for wasting time cleaning dishes when she should be practicing spellings. Indira and Maria exchanged angry words.

'Every girl has to learn some housework,' said Maria, defensive.

Indira stood ground. 'Right now she needs to work hard in school so she marries well and never has to do such jobs.'

It was only fun, thought Rohini. It's not like she wanted to clean dishes for a living. No, she would become a dancer, *thakita thakita, tha*. Ma walked in as Rohini glided around the room practicing *Kathak* steps. It was one of the few times that Ma had slapped Rohini. Her cheek burned for ages. Rohini could not understand why Ma was so angry that day. Later her mother brought her a bowl of jelly, long after she knew the ten spellings by heart and her cheek had stopped hurting. Ma put her arms around Rohini and kissed her hair.

'Was that nice?' she asked.

Rohini nodded her mouth full of strawberry dessert.

'You'll make a beautiful dancer one day and get a first class degree in Mathematics.'

Rohini did not want to disappoint her mother. 'What if it is in English? I'm not so good at Maths. Raja is the clever one.'

'So are you dearest. Raja is different. He is a born scholar. Your brother knows his times tables at the age of five!' Ma stroked her hair. 'But you are clever too. You have so many qualities. You can dance and sing. You act. I love to see you in school plays. If you want to study English that's fine with me. That story you wrote the other day about the prince rescuing the little girl was magical.'

Rohini did not feel the need to explain Maria's part in her inspiration. It was nice to hear Ma talk about her. Ever since Raja started school last year it had been all about him, his brilliance. He was a *poordigy*, whatever that meant.

Long after Rohini hung up the phone to her mother, she sat staring at the Buddha on a corner unit, serene yet sad. Almost twenty five years and it still hurt like a raw wound. The pain would never go away, she thought. The image of Buddha blurred. Raja's voice 'Didi, sister, listen to my sitar' played in a forgotten part of her brain. She turned to look at a black and white photo of her brother on the eastern wall, an auspicious position. Dead flowers hung around his neck in a handmade garland and a sandalwood dot on his forehead remained in blessing. It was his birthday last week; he would have been forty two, a middle aged man.

In early April Indira called to say the whole team of volunteers should go to Delhi for the NGO Awards ceremony. The following week she decided to decline the award in a gesture to indicate they were not seeking glory. The eminent Bengali poet, Tagore, had rejected knighthood for nationalistic reasons. Two days later she thought it would be churlish to refuse such an important award. After all it was a competitive world and even charities needed publicity. What did Rohini think?

'Ma, this is a special recognition and you should go. You are their leader. They would want you to represent the charity and receive the honour.'

Ma had a request. 'Would you create a Facebook page for us? Explain the meaning of the charity's name, Janani, Mother in Sanskrit. We'll be linked to other charities in the West. I believe with internet anyone in the world can view our page.'

'Of course, I'll do that, but not this week Ma. I have a lot of assignments to mark on King Arthur and the legends. The kids are not inspired by the medieval subject.'

'Will you come with me Rohini? Maybe say a few words about me? I am so nervous.'

'Mmm?' *Sir Gawain* not *Gwen and the Green Knight, Rohini corrected. Whatever would the unknown medieval poet think of the modern spelling and its gender reversal?*

In order to make the subject more relevant Rohini was teaching her Class Twelves 'The Lady of Shallot' and asked her students to research Arthurian stories.

Indira repeated her request.

'I'll be delighted.' Rohini pushed aside her work, she would tackle it later. 'When is the ceremony?'

'October fifteenth. It's a Saturday.'

'We can all come. Shourav and Kavita would like to see you receiving the prize. What about Baba? Will he be able to travel?'

'No, it would be too tiring for him. He'll be fine at home with Maria.'

'Why don't you go ahead and book the tickets? I'll send over the money.'

'We can stay at Kanika's house, your father's sister. I'll call her today. Start looking at flights. Don't leave the plans for the last minute.'

'Ma, it's only April. The thing is, it's term-time for me, so I'll have to ask the Principal to arrange a substitute teacher. Kavita will also have to take special leave. The Diwali break is later, after Durga Puja, but I am sure she will be permitted to attend her festival.'

Her paper marking was completely forgotten as Rohini contemplated a far more enticing future.

'We'll stop in Kolkata first. It's been a while since I've been home for Durga Puja.'

*

Rohini had plenty to do before her autumn break. As President of the Bandra Bengali Club, she was in charge of the two day cultural programme to celebrate Bengali New Year in April. They met twice a week to rehearse the musical. While the young people worked with the choreographer, Rohini and others discussed the organisation of the event.

Rohini had chosen Shakuntala, a play written by Kalidasa, a love story between the beautiful daughter of a hermit and King Dushmanta. The two met when the king went hunting in the forest. Dushmanta wed Shakuntala and promised to return to take her back to his kingdom. But a curse from a sage made him forget his love. After many years apart, Dushmanta remembered Shakuntala when he was shown a ring he had given her. The lovers were reunited at last.

'It's a bit corny,' Kavita had said, looking at the script.

The role of Shakuntala went to Kavita. Rohini read out the names of the actors she had chosen for the various roles. Pritha, a committee member, remarked on the lack of discussion before casting. Rohini said that every year there was too much discord over who should play which role. Therefore this year she felt it would be easier if as President, she chose the parts.

'Kavita doesn't have classical training in Bharatnatyam or Kathak. Are you sure she can manage the steps?' asked Champa. 'My Piya has trained for seven years.'

'Tagore songs require light footed, elegant moves free of the rigours of classical steps. So I think Kavita would look more natural as Shakuntala, a fair maiden brought up in the forest.'

'Kavita is quite fair-skinned, unlike you. Who does she take after? Not Shourav as far as I can see.'

Champa was chewing a scented betel leaf. The diamond on her nose sparkled. Rohini shifted in her seat. Her posterior was getting numb sitting on the hard plastic chair. She looked Champa in the eye. *It had been many years since someone had asked the same question.*

'So? I don't look like my mother either. At least Kavita is not dark like me.'

'Ah, but you captured Shourav with those big-big eyes, like

a lost deer. Kavita has your eyes. Piya is dark but she is quite pretty, no?'

Champa's daughter was on stage flirting with King Dushmanta, a shy teenager with acne, who was trying not to look down her blouse. Her large eyes were enhanced with aubergine khol, and her lips were painted a deep auburn. Piya was attempting to draw a moustache on Tilak's upper lip holding his chin firmly by her two fingers.

'I'm sure Piya and the other girls would make beautiful *apsaras*,' said Rohini.

Champa shook her head; large curls bounced on each side of her round face.

'Your daughter is brought up in the jungle and mine is a heavenly prostitute. What great roles we have chosen for them. Why not a more suitable play like, Chitrangada? A warrior princess, surely she would have been a more inspirational character?'

For once, Champa made a good point, but Rohini stuck to her decision. The thing about management was to be sure of oneself.

'There are more female parts in this one. Listen, Champa, I want you to play the flute, you'll be a fine accompaniment to my voice. I am going to sing Tagore's song about *biraho,* the agony when lovers part.'

'Shourav is just over there fixing the lights. You are not pining for him are you? Or is it someone else?' Champa leaned over and whispered the question.

Rohini clucked like a hen, thankful for her dark skin hiding the warmth on her cheeks.

'Your head is always full of mischief, Champa. Now, come on we need to decide on the menu.'

Rohini spoke rapidly, driving the conversation away from dangerous grounds. For a moment she felt she was back in Shyamnagar.

'I was thinking of using Haldiram as caterers this year. Last year we did too much. We can't afford it. I am cutting out *paneer.* Cheese is too expensive. I was thinking of something a bit more traditional Bengali. How about pea *katchuri?* I remember my mother making crispy pancakes stuffed with spicy mashed peas.'

'That's a great idea. So we need just one dish of potatoes to go with that, dry *aloo dum* with extra asafoetida. Proper Bengali fare.'

'And for dessert, sticky *zelabies* or dry *barfis*?'

Champa thought for a moment. '*Barfis* I think, *zelabies* are too syrupy.' She looked down at her notepad with two lines written in so far.

'Our food tray was very popular last year. Do you think the people will think this year's menu too shabby?'

'Well, we didn't get enough donations to cover the cost. If they want more elaborate food, they'll have to dig deeper into their pockets. I think that's it. If you could type up the minutes of the meeting, I'll distribute it to the rest who could not be bothered to show up. They just drop off their kids and go!'

Rohini packed up various things she had brought for the rehearsal, a brass pot, silk scarves, her harmonium. She would need Shourav's assistance to take the things to their car.

'We need more men to help set up the stage. Is the musician coming to Saturday's rehearsal? We really need to practise with the music. Otherwise the actors won't know their cues.'

'Yes, yes, don't worry. He's in Pune today. He'll be staying with me from Friday until next weekend's show.' Champa stuffed another *paan* in her mouth.

'And the costumes? I've got Kavita's one stitched. We should see the tailor on the way home to hurry along with the rest. I must make sure they fit one week in advance.'

'It'll all be done. Every year we do this, and every year, you get anxious. Relax! We've been practising since January. We don't want you to have another nervous breakdown, do we?' Champa's voice was kind, yet Rohini stiffened.

'By the way, don't mind me saying this, but your voice cracked today on the high notes. Take a lemon and honey drink for a few days with a little bit of ginger juice.'

Rohini cleared her throat. 'Yes it's a bit scratchy. The air conditioning is too strong at home. Maybe I'm getting a cold. *Chalo*, let's go home. I'm tired.'

Champa patted Rohini on the back. 'You're doing a great job, but you need to stop worrying. Get a good night's sleep. You work as well. I'm lucky I don't have to go to work. Ta ta!'

'I don't *have* to. I like working,' replied Rohini, raising her voice, but Champa had already left the room. Her silk sari rustled down the corridor.

Rohini did not know why she let Champa get her riled. Today she had boasted of her daughter Keya's marriage proposals. She was a Marketing student in Mumbai University and an attractive girl. Not quite as vivacious as her sibling, but Rohini knew she had just as many boyfriends. A good Brahmin family had approached them. Their son was an architect. Champa bragged about his salary using all her fingers. They had a big house in Malabar Hills where the rich and famous lived.

'I guess you haven't received any offers for Kavita's hand yet. There is time. But you know the good ones are always taken young. They ask about Piya but I say no, we'll wait until she is in college.' Champa pushed back an invisible suitor with her open palms.

'Oh we have offers. Just the other day, a lady showed interest in Kavita. Her son is studying medicine in Vellore.'

It wasn't exactly a lie. Last year at a wedding party a lady had remarked that Kavita was pretty. Rohini was sure that they would be inundated with offers once Kavita was a certain age.

On the day of Naba Barsha, Rohini was rushed off her feet. She went to the florist in the morning to collect the floral arrangements for that evening's show. It was almost ten and the garlands were still not ready. Rohini stood under the awning away from the back-burning sun. They would have to keep the garlands in the fridge and the flowers in buckets of cold water. A later pick-up would have meant risking not having the right stuff.

'Where are the bamboo stalks and ferns I need for my forest?' she demanded of Ali, who was deaf in one ear.

'Everything will be ready in five minutes, ma'am, not to worry. Would you like a cup of tea or a cold Fanta?' It was a big order and as a good customer she was entitled to refreshments.

Rohini declined, not trusting the water they would use to make the tea or wash the glass.

'Bring Madam a chair,' Ali yelled to one of his young helpers.

Forty minutes later, two young men piled the fragrant blooms onto the backseats of the Honda. Rohini would have to sit next to Shiv in the front passenger seat. She could not have the flowers crushed in the trunk. Rohini asked the driver to switch on the AC. She gave five rupees to each of the boys and drove off to Haldiram's. It was too early to pick up the food, but half the balance would have to be paid now and the rest on delivery.

By the afternoon Rohini's feet ached and she desperately needed a lie down. Kavita came in to her bedroom.

'The blouse is too tight, Mummy. I can barely breathe.' Her daughter's voice had turned into an irritating five-year old's whine.

'Why didn't you say so at the time of the fitting? Go see if Paru can move the hooks further down. I'm too tired. I must rest or I won't be able to cope with this evening's show.'

Rohini turned over in her bed. Paru was sleeping so it was Rohini who had to make the alterations at the last minute. By four it was done and she rushed into the bathroom to have a quick shower. She emerged a few minutes later, wrapped in a bath towel. Her long hair was wet, so she stripped off her towel to dry her hair. Her back was to the door as she bent over to twist the strands into a turban. She heard the door open and swung round quickly.

'I though the door was locked,' she said, grabbing a scarf to hide her body.

Shourav shrugged and shut the door, securing the bolt. He opened the wardrobe to find his kurta suit. Rohini put on her underwear and slipped her blouse and petticoat on. Her face was still warm from Shourav's eyes on her naked body. There were extra folds and sagging parts that were fairly new. It was so long since he had seen her fully undressed that she wondered what his look meant. A mischievous glint would have been good or a cheeky remark. She was glad there was no revulsion. Although, what she noticed hurt her even more. Indifference.

Shourav's phone jangled, Deep Purple's Smoke on the Water filled the air. Receiving a fierce glare from his wife, he took the phone to the bathroom.

'Who is it now?' Rohini asked when he finally came out, showered and dressed. 'It's nearly five. We have to get ready.'

'It was a patient. I'll be ready in five minutes. You girls better hurry up.'

'You shouldn't be dealing with patients on your day off. Let the doctor on duty take care of that. Honestly you are too nice sometimes.'

Rohini thought she would never ring Dr. Bose at home. Sipping a scalding cup of tea she began to get ready. All the ladies were wearing the same *garad* sari, ivory silk with red and gold border, suitable attire for puja and Bengali events. She caught Shourav looking at her.

'*Ki?*'

'Nothing.'

'Do I look nice?'

There was a pause before he replied, 'Of course.'

Rohini groaned as his mobile rang again. Shourav was in the en-suite shaving. Sometimes she wished she had married an engineer, who did not have any lives to save. She wondered whether she ought to answer, but Shourav rushed out of the bathroom his face full of foam and punched the answer button.

'Yes?' he asked in English. 'No, not possible. Okay, will talk later.' This time he took the phone with him. He said *me too* softly as the door closed.

A few minutes later he approached Rohini, who was throwing things into her handbag. A *kajal* pencil went flying.

'Before you crib, Dayal wanted me to go in to see a patient. I said no.'

Rohini snapped her purse shut.

All the way to the hall Kavita kept up a steady chatter. She was excited about her first proper role in drama. Last year she had only been a group dancer. Shourav looked out of the window. Rohini stared straight ahead. She took out her speech and read it over. The words on the paper were jumping all over the place refusing to build paragraphs. Her hands shook a little. She repeated *Hare Rama Hare Krishna* several times in her head to calm her nerves.

The hall was packed. Rohini could not feel her legs as she stood to read the speech, which lasted an eternity. Quarter of an hour later, she was glad to be back in the green room. She went past Shourav busy with the lights.

'You know phones have to be switched off during the show,' she reminded him.

'Why are you giving me so much hassle about my phone calls today? I get them every day. There, it's switched off now. Happy?'

Shourav shoved the phone into his back pocket and turned his back to her.

The music for the play began. Rohini watched from the wings. Her daughter was ethereal, floating between the trees. The first few songs were to be sung by other ladies. It was a democratic decision in order to involve everyone in the Board. Rohini felt a wave of heat rise from her toes and suffuse her face with warmth. The lights from the set were shining down on the stage casting a warm glow everywhere. She fanned her face with a programme. Her chest felt compressed.

Champa came in from the stage.

'Rohini, are you all right?'

There was a ringing in her ear.

'Get her a glass of water, someone. She looks like she is about to faint.'

'What happened?' asked Pritha.

'I don't know. I found her like this, sweating and breathing heavily. Shall I call Shourav? He is doing the lights though.'

Rohini motioned with her hand, asking them to stop. Champa sat next to her.

'You are on in ten minutes. I can get Pritha to take your place. She knows the song.'

Rohini closed her eyes. The room began to swim.

'Have a *barfi*. Perhaps you've worked too hard today. Some sugar will help,' suggested Champa.

Rohini bit into the pistachio sweet and sipped a glass of

cool water. She breathed in and out slowly.

'I don't think I can sing today. Sorry!' she gasped.

'It's okay. Pritha has been practising. We are always prepared to step in just in case someone falls ill. You just stay here and relax.'

Rohini looked at the stage where her daughter was sitting on a log, lost in a dream, her chin cupped in her right hand. Pritha's voice floated in pure and clear.

> *Dear friend, what is the meaning of this disquiet?*
> *Dear friend what is the meaning of this agony?*
> *You tell us day and night of love*
> *Dear friend what is the meaning of love?*
> *Is it always this full of anguish?*

Rohini watched her daughter's face turn slowly towards the left wing searching for another voice. Her hands weaved delicate moves and her steps were light as she swayed to the melancholic notes of the flute.

Across the stage on the other wing, Shourav was on the phone, his mouth close to the receiver. Rohini had taken a Valium as soon as Champa left. She closed her eye to meditate, clearing her mind of all thoughts, sweeping them clean. What had she promised herself a long time ago? She would not let anyone hurt her. She was strong. She would picture a happy image—an ice-cream van, a glorious sunset, cool waves tickling her feet. Her mother calling her in the morning, *wake up Rohini dear wake up*. Her breathing evened. She would sing tomorrow.

Chapter 10 Maria

Maria slung an arm over her face blocking out the early morning sun. It was impossible to sleep through the incessant chirping of a bird. Through the window she could see a *shalik* perched on the branch of a Seesham tree. The infiltration of her father's snores through the thin wall was the final straw. With considerable effort she dragged her tired limbs out of the warm bed. Her head spun as she stood. Grabbing a chair she sat for a while, her head in her hands. When the room stilled she folded her bedroll and pushed it under the sofa, a hand-me-down from Indira's house.

Maria unbolted the front door, gulping in the fresh morning air. The courtyard was empty. With a tired wave she shooed the *shalik bird* away, a harbinger of bad luck. It should fly out of sight or find a pair. A pair was good. One for sorrow, two for joy.

Maria barely made it to the tube well before she vomited over the cement floor. Her emaciated form shuddered as bouts of dry heaves followed. The *girja* clock struck five. Not many of her neighbours were around. A turban-headed *sirdarji* passed her by on his morning walk, taking no notice of the sick young woman. Maria washed away the waste and rinsed her mouth. A large splash of water revived her a little. Her head was reeling. A bitter metallic taste filled her mouth and she could feel the saliva rising again. A half hour or so elapsed clutching the slimy wet column of the tube well. Maria felt the heat of the rising sun prickle the back of her neck.

As the nausea passed, Maria's head cleared. She must see a *dai*, but not in this village—somewhere where they did not know her. John was in Kharagpur for a day; she could not afford to lose this opportunity. Later at Indira's house, she raced through Bannerjee babu's filing, stopping now and then to wipe the perspiration on her face. Her stomach rumbled. Maybe she should eat something to get her strength back. She rested her head on the cold metal of the filing cabinet.

'Are you all right dear?' asked Indira's mother stopping at the door.

'I didn't sleep well, Aunty. Mother was ill again.' Maria

prayed her God would forgive the little white lie.

'Why don't you go home early and get some rest?'

'*Accha*. I will finish the work tomorrow.' She did not get paid for days off, but needs must.

'Call us if you need to see a doctor.'

'No, no, Aunty. I'll be fine. It's just that I am tired.'

Maria hurried to the station and checked the timetable. There was a train in half an hour to Jainagar. Where she would go from the station was still a question. She did not know a soul there. This time she avoided Palashpur where Bimala the witchdoctor practised. It was bad karma. Besides Joy's sister lived there. She could not risk being spotted by anyone she knew.

The twenty-minute journey seemed to take hours. Maria held the end of her sari across her nose and mouth, and breathed in deeply. The odour of sweaty bodies squashed against baskets of rotting cabbages caused her stomach to churn. Luckily her insides were empty after earlier bouts of vomiting. She uttered the Lord's Prayer to quell her nerves and calm her mind. Maria hopped off the train as soon as it stopped and rushed to find a bench. A few minutes rest under the shade of a tree settled her stomach. She looked around for inspiration. Where to start?

The station *chai* shop was run by a garrulous young man who called out *hot chai, garam chai* to passengers getting off the train.

'Sister, Uncle, Aunty,' he shouted, 'Come and get a cup of *garam chai* at Ramu's stall, the best in the village.'

Even if he knew the directions to a midwife Maria was loath to ask him. She did not have vermilion in the parting of her hair like Hindu married ladies. It did not matter that she was a Christian.

A young woman passed by dragging a toddler in her wake. Maria peered closely at the skinny sari-clad figure. A waif of a girl, she was holding a baby to her breast. She paused after every few steps waiting for her little one to catch up. *Jaldi, hurry*. Maria followed her discreetly until they came to a quiet dirt track road.

'Excuse me sister,' Maria approached the young stranger. 'I

am looking for a *dai*. Can you help me?'

The villager looked her up and down and then rested her gaze on Maria's stomach.

'Depends. Do you want to get rid of it?' the girl asked with no curiosity in her flat voice.

'No, maybe not. It's not for me. I want to check… if someone I know… is with child.' Maria felt her neck flush.

'For that, you need Mira. She lives over there.' The girl pointed vaguely towards the village. 'But she'll need to see the person. She is not a magician,' she added with a smirk.

The baby was whimpering. The girl jiggled the infant, shouting at the toddler not to wander so close to the pond.

Maria dug out a few coins from her purse.

'For your sweet children, God bless them. Will you show me where she lives exactly?'

'Follow me,' said the recipient, tucking the coins away in the folds of her sari. Maria tried to keep up with the girl's sudden increase in pace. 'We go past the schoolhouse and Mira Aunty's *bari* is next to the *neem* tree.'

Maria pushed open the wooden door to a hut. A woman lay on a *charpoy*.

'*Ki chai*?' she asked. What do you want?

Maria explained. She was asked to lie down on a mat. Mira felt her stomach, kneading it like dough. She got a brass conical cup from a shelf and placed it on the abdomen.

'How long?' she asked.

'A month I think. Is it too early for you to tell?'

'I can feel a baby's presence before the mother does. It's not all science you know; it is instinct. I look at your breasts and I see the baby.'

Maria flinched as Mira leaned forward to examine the glands in her rising chest.

'See me in three months and I will check you properly to make sure the baby's moving. My fee is fifty rupees today and one hundred for delivery. First time births are complicated so you pay for safety—of you and the baby.'

Mira jabbed a finger at Maria's abdomen. The midwife's dark face loomed over the expectant mother. There was a mole on her left cheek. Shining coils of hair, reeking of coconut oil, were tightly wound up in a bun on top of her head.

'Do you want it or not? Sitala gets rid of them, not me.'

Maria looked back at her blankly. She stood, holding on to a stool. Her destiny swam before her. Weeks of uncertainty and fear had now been confirmed. She was going to be an unmarried mother, an outcast, if John did not marry her. The room was getting darker. She heard rumblings of thunder. Maria sank onto the floor, her eyes closing in fatigue.

'*Otho otho*,' shouted Mira. Wake up.

Maria felt herself being shaken like a rabbit. If this was the kind of treatment she would get at the hands of a *dai*, she would prefer to do it alone. Maria paid Mira extra for a glass of lemonade and some sweet meats. Judging Maria to be a wealthier prospective client than her regulars, Mira's manners improved.

'Lie for a while,' she said, 'I'll close the shutters. You've had a bad shock. No father, I can tell. You are all alone in the world with a baby coming. Not to worry. God will provide. You just rely on Mira.'

A heavy downpour drenched Maria. She shivered as the train rocked through green fields towards her home. Coming out of the station, she covered her head not wanting anyone to see her and ask questions. That evening, she counted the hours until John was due to return. He did not come. She went to bed, crying softly into her pillow, stuffing her mouth with the torn bed sheet, to stifle sobs. Dreams of headless babies followed, their hollow cries filling the room. She was rushing from cot to cot looking for her child.

Maria woke resolved to break the news gently to her man. He loved her. Surely he would take care of her. Early that evening, she walked into John's cottage and made a start on dinner.

'Another *paratha*?' she asked John, fanning him, swishing the flies away.

Joy looked on with pursed lips. Maria heard Joy mutter comments in the kitchen, *she is back in the cottage with John as if they are married already. Shameless girl!* Maria had to do what was needed to sweeten the blow. After dinner they would take a walk by the river. She would tell him the news, standing next to the same frangipani bush where he had proposed to her.

The river had swelled after the recent spell of rain. The water was muddy. All sorts of debris floated past them: ebony branches, newspapers, used sanitary towels, a dead rat. Maria stood in front of John, blocking his view. She was wearing a pretty colour, a cornflower blue printed sari, the end demurely tucked into her slim waist. Her hair was twisted into a bun circled with a jasmine garland.

'John,' she began, coming closer and touching his arm.

She traced a line along his lower arm, over the tattoo of a dagger. This one was new, the ink still fresh and glistening.

'What?' he asked, trying to light a cigarette with his other hand.

'When shall we get married? I would like to start a family soon and settle down. I am not so young anymore.'

If they married soon she would not have to tell him the truth of her situation.

'No rush. I'm not sure I want a family yet. I can barely afford to feed us. With you at home there will be three of us. You'll need to find a proper job.'

'Why on earth did you propose to me then, leading me down a false path? My father would have found a husband for me. Now it's too late. No one will have me.'

Maria pulled out the end of her sari and wept into it. The conversation was not going as planned. She had vowed not to cry, to use reason instead of emotions.

'Come on, stop crying. We still have a future. We just need a bit of time to settle down first. You can find a job in the city as a typist. We'll save up and then perhaps...'

'There is no time for that, John,' Maria sniffed. 'I am pregnant. So, will you marry me or not? If you don't, I swear I'll jump into that river and end it all.'

She sat on the thick roots of the Krishnachura tree. John slumped on to the ground, next to her, shoulders touching. Neither spoke for a while. Maria cast a sidelong glance at her lover's face and it frightened her. His vacant eyes were far away. His shoulders trembled occasionally, as waves of involuntary reaction surged up and down his body.

'What is it, my love?' she asked more tenderly. 'Talk to me. We'll manage. I'll go out to work until the baby comes. We'll have a simple wedding in the church.'

Still he did not speak. His lips moved. He shook his head from time to time, continuing to stare past the Kangsabati River, over the corrugated roofs and palm trees to the cornfields on the opposite bank. She had to move closer to hear him.

'I didn't tell you everything Maria, about what happened when the day the bastard, my father, came back. I heard the shouting even before I reached the courtyard. She stumbled out of the hut, her sari half-undone. Her face was covered in blood. He followed her out calling her a whore. Everybody must have heard, but no one came out to help.'

John's hands were shaking. For a moment Maria thought he had stopped.

'I grabbed Amma tight. 'Jamil, run *beta* she said. He will attack you next.' He roared like a bull when he saw me, calling me a useless *langra*, a cripple. He snatched her away from me and held a scythe to her throat. 'Where is her gold? Give it to me or I'll kill you both.' I ran inside and took out a tin box with her wedding jewellery in it. He let go of her, looking through the few things she had saved for my bride. Something happened to me, white-hot rage, I don't know, but I picked up an axe and lunged at his back. He dropped to the ground, instantly. Amma screamed, *hai Allah*, asking for forgiveness. I put a hand over her mouth, 'we *must run before they find out.'* We took the jewellery and cut through the woods to the station. We changed trains several times. I bought Amma a niqab so they wouldn't remember what she looked like. We bribed an official and crossed the border at night.'

Maria's head hurt from clenching her jaw, to stop the tears. She clutched John's cold hands and rubbed his arms, trying to get some life back into him. Her lover closed his eyes and rested his head against the gnarled trunk of the tree. Suddenly, he looked ten years older.

'We changed our names, Jamil to John, Jamila to Joy. We were a Muslim family; Abbas was our family name. Christian names gave us a different identity.'

Maria saw defeat in his eyes.

'I'll never be free. He is after me. His spirit is looking for revenge.'

He paused, looking around.

'Can you not hear him, Maria? The wind carries his threats. He will get me in the end. I can hear his laughter.'

Maria shivered. She put an arm around John. 'Shh, there is no one here. He is dead. He cannot harm you now.'

'Maria, I can't marry you. I killed my father. Now you know why I don't want a child. He will be just like his grandfather, or worse, like me, a murderer.' John squashed the cigarette butt into the damp ground.

'You are wrong! It was an accident. You were saving your mother. You don't have blackness in your heart,' she cried.

'My father did. He was evil,' said John, getting up.

Maria sat by the river, alone and with child. The setting sun cast a glow around the banks, a fire burning a body to ashes. Tugging at fistfuls of grass she pondered over all options. The reverend would know of an orphanage. She pictured the moment when she would have to hand over the baby, giving up her flesh and blood to a stranger. Perhaps she could find a job in another town and pretend to be a widow. Indira would help her with some money to have the baby. An unpalatable alternative emerged, Ganesh, the deaf and dumb milkman. If Mary could find Joseph in her hour of need, Maria too must find someone who would wed a pregnant woman, someone desperate enough. Ganesh liked her.

The stars came out one by one. Maria dusted down her sari. Her parents would wonder where she was. On the way home, she passed the church. The light was on. She looked inside. No one was around. Maria lit a candle and knelt by the altar. Jumping into the river was still an option, although it was a sin. She hoped God would forgive her.

Chapter 11 Rohini

Rohini woke early with stomach cramps. She had been queasy since daybreak. Paru's rather zealous, early start on the fish curry did little to help as the pungent spices smoked out the sleeping members of the family. Rohini ran to the bathroom and leaned over the marble sink, staring at the expensive grained design she had chosen at a specialist warehouse. Her painful heaving caused a small amount of orange bile to splatter on the oval basin. Last night's carrot *halwa* was only partly digested. She took a couple of Gelusil tablets. The white chalk-like pills dissolved in her mouth coating her rough tongue with a peppermint film. Rohini swallowed her saliva once or twice to get rid of the slightly unpleasant aftertaste.

'What's the matter?' asked Shourav, putting on his shoes.

'Nothing, just acid indigestion,' said Rohini, taking tiny sips from a glass of water.

She changed into a baggy *salwar kameez*, discarding her former choice of a batik sari. The tight waistband of the petticoat would only aggravate her digestive difficulties. Trousers were out of the question with a bloated stomach. She hoped her sickness would not develop into a full-blown gastroenteritis.

'Come on Kavita, we are ready. Where are you?' Rohini called out from her bedroom.

Kavita emerged in a pair of torn jeans and a crop top. Her iPod headphones were stuck in her ears. Rohini uttered two clipped words, 'Go change,' pointing to the door of her daughter's room.

'But we're going to be late,' cried Kavita, her shoulders slumped in exaggerated despair.

'I don't care. You are not going to school in that outfit. Wear a long skirt and a decent blouse, and *jaldi*! Shiv is already downstairs, waiting for us. Go, before your father sees you dressed like this.'

Kavita eventually left home in an ethnic print tunic and leggings. Rohini was still dubious about the formality of the ensemble, but there was no time to argue.

*

Rohini cleared her throat before starting her lesson. The class of forty stared back at her; some openly yawned, others played with their phones. Yet she thought she detected a gleam in the eyes of a few. She had recently become one of the more interesting teachers, prone to breakdowns and therefore ripe for teasing. Even in a big city like Mumbai, the circle closed in. Champa's daughter and Pritha's son were students in her school, though thankfully not in her class. At least Kavita was in a different school, away from gossip surrounding her mother.

Rohini's heart beat a little faster at the beginning of each lesson, waiting for a prank question or some silliness that would get out of control. Years of experience had taught her to stick to the lesson plan, get through the day's work and keep them engaged. It did not help that the subject she taught could often prove to be dull to the unliterary minds.

'The Love Song of Alfred J Prufrock...' she began.

A loud rustling of pages, whispers and the clatter of pens followed a collective groan from the class. Rohini folded her arms, watching the class, waiting for them to settle.

'Let us go then you and I,

When the evening is spread out against the sky

Like a patient etherised upon a table.'

Rohini's hand shook as she pretended to polish her glasses —a welcome pause.

She saw Raja lying on a hospital bed, tubes sprouting from his veins. A heart monitor emitted shaky green lines. 'Wake up, you silly boy,' she wanted to say, 'pick up your sitar.' When the beeps stopped, they wheeled him away, placed his still body on a cold slab. Rohini screamed. Her mother did not even cry; she sat in the empty room, staring at the vacant space where the bed had been, until they brought in another patient.

Rohini bit her trembling lips, looking out of the window, away from her pupils—same age as Raja when he died. Gradually, the leaves of the trees came back into focus. She turned around. The class looked at her expectantly. Would she start crying? Would she faint? Rohini placed her head in her hands.

Another bout of nausea threatened to overwhelm her. She rummaged in her handbag for *ajwain*. Chewing the seeds brought some relief. Closing her eyes, she took slow lung-filling breaths. A vomiting incident would be the spectacle they were waiting for. Rohini uttered the Lord's names in her head—just five this time, then a string of *shanti, shanti, shanti,* calling on peace to calm her troubled body and soul.

The class had clustered in whispering groups. Paper planes were tossed aimlessly. A couple of boys stood by the window, whistling at young women from the college next door.

Rohini took a stroll down narrow aisles, picking up hastily written notes, copies of best sellers, smart phones. She returned to her desk with the booty and picked one up at random.

'The Arrow Head,' she read. The cover of the book was that of a stone wall.

'What is it about, Sanjay?' she asked the owner of the book.

'It's about an ancient burial site where a treasure is hidden. Some modern day explorers find archaeological evidence of loot stored at the bottom of a well. They are chased by a gang who wants to steal the secret map from them.'

'And kill them afterwards?' asked Rohini.

'I presume so.'

'Same old, same old.'

'But Ma'am, if you read it you'll see that the author has really researched the historical evidence and is using modern day technology to track down an ancient site. It's cool.'

'Okay, I get it. Rita, your little note here says *let's bunk Maths class and go to see* Sheltered Life. I am curious, what's that about?'

Rita rose from her chair looking sheepish.

'It's a good film, Ma'am, about a young girl who leads a very sheltered life, but then has an affair with an older man. She realises afterwards he is just using her for s…' Rita stopped.

'Sex?' prompted Rohini.

'Yees. So she tries to break it off, but he is really persistent and stalks her. She goes to the police to report him. They come to her house to take further statements and there is a *beeg hullah* when her parents find out.'

'What happens next? Do they disown her? Is she ostracised by society?' Rohini was beginning to take a genuine interest in the plot.

'Yes Ma'am, they kick her out on the streets. So she has no choice but to become a prostitute, which is worse really. One day a businessman takes her to his flat and he listens to her story. She starts living with him. Okay, so it's not a completely happy ending, but at least she is safe and off the streets. He seems to love her, but she knows that he will never marry her.'

'No bunking classes,' said Rohini wagging a finger. 'Go to the cinema in your spare time.'

Rohini returned the smartphone to Radhika with the warning that it's usage during school hours would result in permanent confiscation. On her way back to the desk she passed Sangeeta, a khol-eyed teenager chewing gum. Rohini took a piece of paper from her and tore out a little square.

'Spit,' she commanded.

Sangeeta obliged. Rohini folded the paper and threw it across the room and into the bin. The class applauded.

'Two page critical review of Prufrock. Hand in tomorrow.'

'One page, please Ma'am. We have Maths test,' Sangeeta pleaded.

'Fifteen-hundred words due Wednesday morning, first thing in the staffroom.'

'Yes, Ma'am.'

Rohini returned to her desk and hitched her bottom on one corner.

'As far as I can see, all of you like a good story, something that captures your interest. Be it a film or a best seller it's essentially a story. Why, then, don't you want to study the classics? They have stood the test of time. Hands up if you would like to share your opinions.'

'Boring' and 'old-fashioned' were the objections that stood out most.

'Why can't we read contemporary works like Salman Rushdie's *Midnight's Children* or Vikram Seth's *A Suitable Boy*? Both are set in the recent past during an important part of our Indian history. Why are we still bowing to the West?' demanded Kumar. The class cheered. He took a bow.

Rohini put her hands up silencing the dissenting individuals.

'Let's not get too political about this. I will pass your feedback to the Board. Hopefully one day they will include some of your suggestions. But think about it, you say that Thomas Hardy's novels are old fashioned. A young village maiden being ravished by a nobleman, isn't that similar to *Sheltered Life*? Tess has to live with the unhappy consequences of her rape. She is innocent, but society and her true love would not accept her past because she is no longer a virgin. These stories are still relevant to this day especially in traditional societies like ours. They may seem as if they are from another world, but the works of Jane Austen, Thomas Hardy and certain classics have longevity. Besides, if we don't explore the past how will we discover the present? Isn't that what your book is doing, Sanjay, discovering clues from the past? I am sure there is more to that story than making money from buried treasure. It is tapping into the reader's interest in the past, of ancient arrow heads, vase and jewellery.'

Amidst the buzz of numerous voices expressing discontent or exchanging views, Rohini continued to read Prufrock aloud. As her voice rose gently above the rest, the class's attention was turned for the first time to T. S. Eliot's composition. Rohini smiled as she read,

Let us go through half-deserted streets/ The muttering retreats/ Of restless nights in one-night cheap hotels.

The class fell silent, caught in the spell of the words, trapping them in another time. Their souls had risen above the grey room and entered Eliot's world, foggy and bleak, where endless life was played out in limitless melancholy.

It was nearly six when Rohini finished her day at the school. There were papers to mark, but first she desperately needed a break. Shiv had already picked up Kavita and they were waiting for her in the car.

'Shall we go the bazaar Kavi? I haven't been to Chowk bazaar in months and I really want to look for some cheap saries and blouse pieces for the maids. There is always such a rush at puja time.'

'I hate Chowk bazaar. People push you and touch you. Why do you want to go there?'

'But sweetie, I need to get a few things and it's cheaper in the bazaar. I'm not going to buy saries for the maids in Westside Mall, am I?' As soon as she uttered those words Rohini wished she could bite them back. 'They do some nice bangles and stuff you can look at,' added Rohini to sweeten the bitter thoughts.

'Okay, if you promise to let me buy stick-on tattoos,' negotiated Kavita.

Rohini acquiesced, hoping her daughter would have the decency to wear the tattoos discreetly.

'Papa mustn't see,' said Rohini, adding a condition.

They had an agreeable hour visiting stalls. They bought a couple of printed synthetic saries, a pinch at three hundred rupees, plus matching blouses. Both the ladies agreed it was a bargain, having knocked the price down from five hundred. Their cleaner, Namrata, was of indefinite age, somewhere in between forty and fifty. The yellow sari with red print would be just the ticket for a married woman. The gardener's wife, Leela, kept the paths clear of weeds and was seen every evening, watering the plants. Strictly speaking she was not under Rohini's employ, but the young wife always had a friendly word for all. Occasionally she helped Rohini with her shopping or filled in when Paru was absent. Rohini chose an intense blue with a green decorated border for her. The body of the sari was covered with little white flowers.

Kavita flitted from stall to stall picking up rainbow coloured Rajasthani bangles and long earrings. A little bell sounded. It was *sandhya* puja, evening prayer, and Rohini quickly did a little *pranam* with her hands.

'I'll just be a minute,' she told Kavita who was engrossed in choosing a tattoo.

The shop owner had his eyes closed as he performed *arti*, encircling the deities in his shrine, three times with a stainless steel plate of offerings. Thin spirals of grey smoke rose from incense.

'*Prasad, Ma?*' he offered Rohini a piece of a sweet cake

when he had finished.

Rohini opened her eyes, jolted back from her brief meditation.

'Thank you brother,' she said. 'What do you sell?' she asked looking around his tiny kiosk not finding any apparent ware.

The walls were plastered with flyers of Baba Ramji, but other than that it was bare. She would be the *bouni* not perhaps the first sale of the day, but of the evening. Whatever it was, she would buy it, she thought. It can't be anything expensive a prudent voice in her head told her.

'I just spread his good word, Ma. Baba Ramji entered my life and it changed everything. My wife was suffering from cancer. My business was failing. I was a rickshaw-wallah. Then I met a man who asked me to go to Baba's ashram. I went every day for two months for the evening prayers. I sold my business and started selling fans. I made profit in my first year. With that I could get my wife better treatment. Three years now my Sukhi has been well. It is all Babaji's blessing. Here is a leaflet, Ma. I can't read very well, but it is all there. Come to the ashram. See for yourself. You'll find the peace you seek,' the man joined his hands in Namaste.

Rohini looked at the garish picture of a holy man in a saffron cloak wondering: *Is this a scam? What does this man want from me?*

'Here,' said Rohini fumbling in her handbag for a few rupees. She gave the man a fifty-rupee note. After all he was due a cut for his recommendation.

'No Ma, give to the ashram. It runs on donations only. Thanks to Babaji's blessings I make my earning from the fans, Kanti's Electric Fan Store, on Raja Dev Street. I keep my shop open all day and come here in the evenings. But always, first thing in the morning, I go to ashram.'

Rohini was restless that night, tossed in half-dreams and mouth-drying wakefulness. The image of Baba Ramji with his right hand held up in blessing was like a beacon to her. She did not share her thoughts with her daughter or her sceptical husband. She was in no mood to be laughed at. It was a free world after all. If she wished to go to an ashram to pray, what business was it of others? Bose would mock. His was not the only therapy that healed. Rohini was doubtful of her long-term improvement in the hands of an allopathic psychiatrist who dished up anti-depressants and delved into the past. She needed more than that. Spiritual healing would be the next medicine to try. She would go to the ashram tomorrow. With this resolve firmly in her mind she drifted peacefully into sleep through the rumblings of her husband's snoring.

Few days later, Rohini instructed her driver to take her to Babaji's retreat after school. Shiv raced his mistress through narrow streets spilling with cycle rickshaws, bullock carts, mopeds and people. The smell of raw sewage and sweat seeped in through the air-conditioning. Why had Mataji chosen to come to these god-forsaken back alleys of Mumbai? Shiv grumbled. Rohini was hardly old enough to be his mother, but she liked him calling her Mata-ji, like the Latin mater. It showed respect. His tone sounded less respectful soon after when Rohini heard him muttering to himself, 'what a shit-hole.'

'*Bhaisaab*, where is the Ramji Ashram?' Shiv asked a passing brother whose head was wrapped in a yellow turban.

He had chosen the wrong man. He was a Sikh, not a Hindu, but the kind passerby pointed to a *paan* stall to enquire there. The driver and mistress tried to note the rather complicated directions involving turning left several times and a sharp right next to a Kali temple. They passed a mossy pond and a school where uniformed children stopped to stare at the smart visitors entering their modest neighbourhood. They had never seen a vehicle this size and at a shout from a ring leader the little gang ran alongside stroking the gleaming surface. One boy had a stick in his hand and Rohini worried that at any moment there would be an expensive scratch on the car's body.

A few minutes later, a rather tired looking white house came into view. The black wrought-iron gate had a sign saying 'BABA RAMJI KA ASHRAM Open to all Bilivers. Live shoe outside.'

Rows of tattered leather sandals were piled up against the

gate where a guard sat on a stool. Despite his threatening presence, Rohini did not dare leave her expensive leather shoes outside so she slipped them off and placed her feet gingerly on the muddy ground. Next time she would wear her cheap Kohlapuri sandals. Raising her sari high, and showing her calves indecorously, she made her way along the muddy drive to the temple.

A man was collecting donations at the entrance. Rohini placed a one hundred rupee note on the plate. She rang the shining brass bell above and found a corner to sit. A white cloth covered the floor. It was streaked with dried mud although a bucket and jug had been positioned just outside the door to wash one's hands and feet. Rohini tried to relax by inhaling the aroma of incense and flowers.

Hey Ram jai Ram jai jai Ram! The people around her swayed and chanted in unified melody. After ten minutes of repeating the same line over and over again Rohini felt calm. She began to clap to the chant like the others. Closing her eyes she let the world disappear. All she focused on were those seven words praising the Lord. The prayer finished an hour later. There were other *bhajans*, holy songs; she did not know the words of. A group of singers accompanied by brass cymbals, an oblong drum and a harmonium sang the glory of God, of Radha and Krishna's *leela*, of Ram's victory.

Just when Rohini was wondering when Babaji would appear, the crowd cheered as the monks removed a screen to reveal the presence of the holy man. He had been there all along, but hidden. It allowed the congregation to reflect on God and not be distracted by His messenger, he said. Dressed in saffron cloth and forehead marked with three horizontal lines of sandalwood paste, Babaji looked the epitome of holiness. When he spoke it sounded like a low murmur, but each word was clear.

'What are you looking for?' he asked his followers. 'If it is peace you seek, then you have come to the right place. If it is just money then you will find plenty of it out there. I can show you the way to happiness. Follow God's path. Keep Him in your heart and await His blessing.'

It was nothing new, nothing earth shattering. Like the cure

for baldness, many promised, but few delivered. Rohini knew that happiness was an ephemeral thing. What she wanted above all was peace. Would she find it here? She was not sure yet, but when Babaji touched her head in blessing and she bit into the *prasad*, a sweet *peda*, she knew she would come back.

Chapter 12 Maria

The moon was up when Maria walked home after seeing John. Pockets of silver light were juxtaposed with shadows. Turning a dark corner she almost collided into a lamp post situated to the eastern side of the empty courtyard. She stood for a moment outside their cottage before opening the fortuitously unbolted door as quietly as she could. A pungent waft of Pamela's chicken *jhal* made Maria cough. Peter glowered at her tardy entrance, scolding with his mouth full. His cheeks puffed up like two *rasgullas* and the circus-ringmaster moustache danced. Even though her heart beat a little faster under her father's scrutiny, Maria wanted to laugh at his silly face.

'Why you are so late? What you and John do hiding in bush-es? Sooner you get married the better,' he belched.

'That's what we were planning, Papa,' Maria replied quickly. 'We'll speak to the Reverend this week.' She needed to buy time with a diversion.

'Sit down and eat,' ordered her father, waving her to a wooden stool.

'I can't. I'm going over to Indira's house now. A rich Calcutta family is coming to see her tomorrow. The groom-to-be is a doctor. Bannerjee madam wants me to prepare Indira for the bride visit.'

It was not entirely a lie. Maria hoped she could steal five minutes of her friend's time for a chat.

'At this time of night? It's dark and the roads are not safe. You are not going out like a wild shameless girl of no morals. You can go there in the morning.'

Her father stood tall in the middle of the room, his bushy head touching the lights.

'I've been there at night before,' Maria persisted, throwing away her timidity.

'*Chup*, no back-chat, or I lock you in the kitchen like when you were little girl. Don't think I can't do it now. While you under my roof you do as I say. You been sneaking off to Indira's house or God knows where all night. No more, 'til you married.'

'But Papa, I'll take the main roads, *na*? I'll be there in twenty minutes.'

'*Ya*, the main roads, where all the business men drive by looking for easy girls like you. When they know you not professional and no one to protect you, they take it for free and throw you by the roadside. You want that to happen? Hein? Say something Pamela, you the *muth-ther*. Lord, have mercy. What a fool I married.'

Pamela rose from the table and bolted the front door.

'It's late. Neighbours will think you work the streets. *Chalo*, go in the morning. Clear the table after you eat. I'm going to bed.'

Pamela sailed off to the bedroom, her torn kaftan flapping in the draught from the upright fan.

Indira was in her bedroom getting ready when Maria walked in early the next morning.

'What's the matter? You look like you've been running through a hurricane,' said Indira looking at Maria through her mirror. 'Is everything okay?'

'Yes, sister,' replied Maria tilting her head. 'I just came to help you get ready. I was running before the storm comes.'

'What rubbish! It hasn't rained for a week and it's not going to today.'

Maria took out a bottle of hair oil to smooth down Indira's long thick hair. She would wait until after the bride visit to disclose her secret.

'No leave it, Maria, I'll shampoo my hair. I want it to look shiny, not greasy.'

Maria thought it unwise to look like a fashion model instead of a demure bride-to-be, but kept her counsel. For her plan to work she needed Indira to marry well and have her own source of money to help her friend in distress. Maria mixed a combination of gram flour, cucumber juice, *malai*, cream off the top of milk and sandalwood paste, stirring the contents rapidly with a metal spoon. Indira wrinkled her nose at the bowl offered to her.

'I don't want to put it on. It won't make any difference.'

'Sister, it clears the skin and gives it a glow. Come on; lie down. I'll tie your hair back. Leave the mask on until it dries completely. I'll fetch a bowl of warm water to steam your face afterwards.'

Maria busied herself with Indira's needs. She applied a thick cream to Indira's face following the mask. An hour later, Indira inspected her image in the mirror. She conceded that her skin did indeed look clearer and more luminous.

'Do you think the doctor will notice?' she asked, stroking her face.

'Of course, sister. He will definitely say yes, *zaroor hain bolbay.*'

'Is this the sari you are wearing?' asked Maria holding up a stiff cotton *tangail* sari, pale blue with orange flowers. 'It's not formal enough. Wear silk. I'll choose one from your wardrobe.'

'No Maria, I'm too hot. Ma made me bake a cake this morning. I need to cool down. Silk makes me sweat. You can help to flatten the material. You know how *tangail* balloons up.'

Yes, thought Maria, *it makes you look bigger, accentuating the curves.*

Later, Maria kneeled in front of Indira ironing the pleats with her slim fingers. The *anchal* had to be pressed down in front and over the shoulder. Maria fixed the sari material with a coral brooch. Indira picked up her mother's pearl set, draping it round her smooth neck.

'You shouldn't wear a sleeveless blouse,' said Maria frowning. 'You are meeting these people for the first time. They may become your future in-laws. You must show respect.'

'Phsh! This is the style nowadays. We are in the sixties, not stuck in the previous decade. You know what girls are wearing in the West? Mini skirts!'

Maria shook her head. *'Besharam,* shameless fast girls.' Her cheeks were warm. Unwed mother, who was she to judge? She held the comb in mid-air for a split second to centre herself before meticulously untangling Indira's long hair. The tresses were piled high in a bouffant and secured with a stone encrusted barrette at the back.

'Put some lipstick on sister, and draw *khol* lines around your eyes, pointing them upwards like Sharmila Tagore. I'll draw a *bindi* on your forehead.'

Maria carefully drew a pale orange disc on Indira's forehead using her lipstick and then drew a charcoal line around it with her *khol* pencil. Finally, she stood back to inspect her handiwork.

'Perfect! You look lovely,' said Maria, smiling at her companion.

Indira's mother came in. 'Come my dear, they are waiting downstairs.'

Maria watched the party from the hallway outside the sitting room. She helped in the kitchen from time to time, making sure the cake and samosas were arranged correctly on the tray.

Indira came in to collect the snacks. She rolled her eyes at Maria. After tea, Indira and the young man withdrew to the balcony.

Later that night, the two friends gathered in Indira's bedroom for a post-mortem of the events. Maria was right. After the guests left a downpour heralded by thunder and lightning washed away the dry heat. The sky was clear once more and the moon floated behind a solitary cloud.

'Well?' asked Maria. 'What did you think of the young doctor *Saab*? I only saw his socks and shoes and they were all right.'

Indira laughed, loosening her hair. She stared at the mirror with an inscrutable expression.

'Bipesh said he would cure me of my madness.' Indira smiled at her reflection.

'What madness? What did you tell him?'

'We were talking. He likes Bach.'

'What is this *Bak tak*?'

'Western classical music. Anyway, after a while he asked me what was wrong. I said, 'nothing,' He said there is something I am hiding, something that saddens me. When I saw Dr. Roy I knew he was the one, but I was worried that once he knew the truth about me he would walk away. Ma and Baba said it is better for him to know before. So I told him. Maria, my heart was pumping so fast I could hardly breathe. He understood.

He said he will cure me. He held my hand and I let him.'

Maria had not seen Indira this animated for a long time, not since the circus came to town. How excited Indira had been to see the wild animals perform. Maria shivered, crossing herself at the tainted memory of how that night the bastards stole a young girl's smile.

'What kind of proper doctor cures *paglami*? Is he a ghost chaser, an *ojha*?'

'No silly, he is a psychiatrist. He treats people with mental disorders.'

'He looks after *pagols*?' Maria slapped her cheek. 'No, no it doesn't seem safe to be working with madmen. You should marry a normal doctor.'

'Trust me, he is completely normal. You'll like him,' said Indira spinning Maria around.

'Sister, he must be a good man if he has accepted your past. Not all men are kind like that. You should marry him. He will look after you.'

The moon was pale in the sky by the time the two finished discussing Indira's future. Maria did not have the heart to tell her friend how bleak hers looked in comparison.

The next day the Roy family called expressing their approval of Indira.

Mrs. Bannerjee asked her daughter, 'What do you think? Shall we say yes?'

Indira bowed her head, bashful. Her mother took her shy silence as a yes. The marriage date was set for February, less than a month away. Dr. Roy was posted in Nepal and the young couple would travel to the highlands almost straight after the wedding.

So soon, thought Maria. She would have to act quickly.

Mrs. Bannerjee made Indira nervous scuttling around the house with long lists. The telephone was constantly engaged —orders for flowers, priests, caterers and jewellers jammed the line. Mr. Bannerjee hid in his study, doing the accounts. Maria flitted between the two, lending a hand wherever she could. The wedding would take place in their big house. The ink on the invitation cards had not fully dried before Maria posted the lot to hundreds of guests.

Indira asked Maria to join her on a shopping trip to Calcutta. Her friend declined saying she was not feeling too well. Indira did not ask her what was wrong. Every time Maria wanted to speak to Indira alone, she was with someone, a friend, an aunt, her mother.

One morning Maria walked to Indira's house. She was tired when she arrived. The maid said the parents were out inviting people for the wedding, only Indira-*didi* was upstairs.

'Sister?' she called out.

'I'm here. Come up!' Indira's disembodied voice floated down from her room.

Maria ran up the flight of stairs, waiting at the top for a few minutes to get her breath back. Gently, she told herself. Indira's room resembled Aladdin's cave. Saries of all kinds— silk, embroidered, printed, tie-and-dye were spread on the bed. Several sets of jewellery had arrived from Calcutta, pure gold studded with seven jewels, pearl and rubies. Her cheeks hurt with smiling.

'Sister,' said Maria fanning the dying embers of her courage. 'I need to talk to you about something really important.'

'So talk,' said Indira, trying on a new *salwar kameez*.

'Not here. We can meet somewhere outside the house. This afternoon when everyone is asleep can you come to the Pipal tree by the Kali Temple near my house? Bring a tray of flowers, so people will think you are praying before your marriage.'

'You are being very mysterious Maria. What is it? I'll shut the door. No one will disturb us here.' Indira walked towards the door.

'No sister, let's do as I said, please. Even the walls have ears.'

Indira nodded commenting for the first time on the dark circles under her companion's anxious eyes. 'You look tired, my dear.'

That afternoon at three, Indira arrived in a rickshaw, carrying a plate of flowers. Maria was waiting.

'Shall we go to the temple first?' asked Indira.

They gave the offerings to the priest. He put a *tilak* on Indira's forehead blessing her. She rang the brass bell and then joined Maria at the foot of the steps.

They sat on a circular bench girdling the tree.

'This is where John and I used to sit when we first started seeing each other. This is where he told me he loved me.' Maria traced a design on the cement seat. In fact, he had answered her question 'do you love me?' with a question 'do you need to ask?'

'Six months ago. So much has changed since then.' She paused to look up at the sky. 'I think it's going to rain, sister. Did you bring an umbrella?'

Indira shook her head, looking at her wristwatch. Dark clouds had completely obliterated the late afternoon sun. A breeze rustled through leaves above their heads, whispering secrets. Maria stared at the temple.

'I wanted to tell you before… but you were busy. I'm in big trouble sister. John has been mixing closely with me. I tried to say no, but he wouldn't listen. And now…' Maria could not go on. She laid her head on her young mistress's shoulder and wept.

'Maria, no!' cried Indira covering her mouth with her hand. 'You're not! Oh dear God. What will you do? You must marry straightaway, then no one will know. They will think the baby came a bit early that's all.'

'It gets worse. John will not marry me,' sobbed Maria.

'We'll make him.' Indira's dark eyes glinted. 'I'll speak to my father.'

'Oh no, I'll die of shame. It's no good. John's mind is made up. Anyway, I've seen a *dai* in another village and I'll have to get rid of it.'

'Maria, these village midwives are not medically trained. I'll take you to a private clinic in Calcutta. No one will know. I'll tell Ma I'm going wedding shopping with you and use the money for the abortion.' Indira stroked Maria's back.

'Truth is Sister. I want this baby. I want a home and a family. If not, I'll never have another chance in the future. Who will have me if John doesn't marry me?'

'Let me talk to John. Why is he behaving this way? I

thought he loved you.'

'He does. I haven't told you everything yet.'

Indira sat very still as Maria revealed John's past.

'Oh Maria! Why is life so complicated?' Indira picked up one of Maria's limp hands. 'If you have the baby, you'll never see your parents again. You'll have to leave town and disappear forever. Who'll take care of you? You are as naïve as a little girl. If you have an abortion you can live life normally. Someday you'll find another man who will marry you and give you a home.'

'Whoever marries me will find out I've been with another and throw me out.'

'You'll find a good man who will accept you despite what happened. It would be all in the past.'

'If I was rich and educated I could find a man who would perhaps accept me. But for the poor there is no easy way out.' Maria blinked several times, fighting to gain control of her voice. She had decided marrying Ganesh was not an option. Not yet.

When Maria looked up at last, Indira had gone very quiet. Her palms were squeezed together, fingers interlaced as if in prayer. She was staring at a bird dipping its beak into a puddle, desperately thirsty. It bobbed its head up and down, up and down, sipping minute globules of muddied water each time. Indira's long throat rippled in the middle as she tried to swallow some saliva to lubricate her parched gullet. Her long held breath expelled through her mouth in a faint gush.

'Indira-Sister, I'm very sorry. I am not thinking straight right now. Forgive me. Forget what I said. I did not mean to insult you. You never look down on poor people like me. I'll go to the church today and say a prayer for both of us.'

Indira covered her bare shoulders with her sari.

'We all have troubles Maria, rich or poor. Think carefully about your decision. Either way it will change your life.'

'Or, I could put a noose round my neck and throw my luckless self into the river over there!'

'Stop it. That is not an option. How could you think your God would allow it?'

'My God has left me to my Fate. I don't know what to do

sister, which way to turn. I just hope in the coming weeks John changes his mind. If not, I'll have to do something.'

A stray cat brushed against Maria's legs. She picked it up and stroked its fur, dirty with neglect. Indira warned her not to touch it, in case of germs or disease being carried by the animal.

Maria kissed the kitten's head. 'Poor little orphan thing, nobody to look after you. You can stay with me. Would you like that? I'll call my little girl, Munni.'

'I have to go, Maria, sorry. I want you to have a good think about this. Life as an unmarried mother is not going to be easy. You will be treated like an outcast. We can meet here again and decide what to do. In the meantime, talk to John. See if you can persuade him. Are you listening? *Oof* you're impossible. Rickshaw! Rickshaw!'

Maria did not reply. The cat purred in Maria's arms. Munni's heart beat in a steady rhythm, *dhuk-puk dhuk-puk*. Soon Maria would hear another. She held the animal close. Grey fur tickled her face. Maria knew the pet had found her for a reason. It was a sign to keep the baby. She reminded Maria of Bibi, her grandmother's cat who died soon after her mistress's demise. Jane Meera had been fond of her quiet, hard-working granddaughter.

'Don't let your father push you around. Stand up for yourself,' she often told Maria.

Somewhere in the other world her grandmother had sensed her dilemma and sent a stray cat to show her the way. Maria sat with Munni under the Pipal tree long after Indira had gone home.

Chapter 13 Rohini

After school Rohini rushed to Baba Ramji's ashram to catch another glimpse of the Holy Father. She arrived when the *sandhya arti* was almost over. The crowd had overflowed on to the porch. Rohini squeezed past packed bodies to a spot near the doorway. Her knees rubbed raw against the hard cement floor. The thin muslin of her *salwar kameez* offered barely any protection.

Cymbals clashed and bells chimed, rousing the worshippers into a fever pitch of devotion. Rohini found it difficult to concentrate during evening *arti*. She flicked through leaflets advertising yoga classes at the ashram. The person sitting next to her, recommended Hatha Yoga preferring its slow moves to aid relaxation. Using elaborate hand gestures and mouthing words the lady managed to sell the course above the prayers. During the weekend, Baba-ji also gave talks on Hinduism and Philosophy, she added. Rohini felt that the path to her spiritual well-being could be found right here.

After the prayers, Babaji rose to withdraw to his room.

'Kindly, let him pass.' Uniformed guards prodded the crowd with batons.

Rohini pushed aside a few devotees. 'I must speak to him,' she cried as Babaji's saffron cloak melted into the mass of men in white *dhoties*.

The congregation dispersed gradually. There was an air of flatness, as if a fun fair had left town. The floor was strewn with petals.

Rohini approached the guard at the door.

'Please, could you tell Babaji's people that I wish to make a large donation and would like to see him in private? I will wait here for your answer.'

Minutes later she was being escorted into a room filled from top to bottom with dusty ledgers. A bespectacled man entered.

'Namaste,' he said, before clearing his throat of thick phlegm.

A prolonged coughing spasm followed. Rohini covered her

mouth with her scarf. The man spit into a cracked mug. He looked her up and down before speaking to her in English.

'Yes, how much you wish to pay?' he asked, a golden pen poised over a receipt book.

'Ten thousand rupees, but I would like to see Babaji in return.' Rohini held on tightly to her handbag.

'We receive many donations madam, much larger sums. Babaji does not see his followers privately.' He closed his receipt book.

'I'm just a school teacher and this is a lot of money for me, but I can donate some more later. Please. A man in the market said Babaji cured his wife with prayer. I would like his personal blessing. I am in such mental distress. Please sir, can I see him for just a few minutes?'

The bookkeeper counted the bills, twice, before locking away the cash.

He pushed a receipt towards Rohini. 'Wait here,' he said.

After about twenty minutes Babaji appeared. He waved away the accountant telling him to leave the door open.

'What is it my daughter?' Babaji asked, grey eyes resting on her face.

Rohini could not speak. She had an inexplicable urge to cry in front of this holy stranger.

'Are you in trouble?'

'I don't know what's wrong with me. I am sick. I am unhappy all the time. I don't even know why. A doctor treats me with medicine and he talks to me. But I would like your blessing so I can find peace.'

Babaji stroked his beard. 'Bring a glass of almond drink!' he instructed one of his minions, hovering in the shadows.

The drink arrived in a cool stainless steel glass.

'This is made from fresh cow's milk in the ashram grounds. Come during the day and I'll show you my gardens. We have goats too. Milk, almonds and honey will soothe your soul. I'll give you one of our *bhajan* tapes. Rise at five am. Pray to the sun god. Bathe. Then listen to the songs and do your puja. At night, put the CD on just before you go to sleep. Clear your mind of all ugly, painful, worrisome thoughts. Close the lid on them.'

It all seemed achievable except the rising at five. She would have to negotiate that.

'I will show you some simple yogic breathing exercises.'

Baba Ramji sat on the floor cross-legged with such ease that Rohini was embarrassed at her own clumsy effort to do the same.

'I've had years of practice,' he said with a twinkle in his eyes. 'Besides, all these Western style toilets ruin the flexibility of our joints. The old fashioned squatting style was good for our knees. Okay, so, breathe in through your left nostril, hold and then breathe out. Then do the same with your right nostril. This is Pranayama yoga.'

Babaji's breath whistled through his nose, pumping and emptying the lungs. Rohini was shown a few more breathing and stretching exercises. The Holy Father told her to do each set for at least fifteen minutes. After about half an hour, her body felt light, free of chains.

Rohini bent down to touch the yogi's feet. He placed his palm on her head.

'Try this for three months. Come to my ashram regularly. Let me know how you are getting on. Remember, this will not free your *life* of problems. It will free *you* of problems because you will be able to deal with them.'

'Thank you Babaji. You have given me hope. For the first time in a long while I feel at peace.'

She would not share her experience with Shourav or Kavita. Rohini made some excuse about her lateness and they sat to dinner. She could do the exercises in the morning claiming she was trying to get fit. There was a channel on TV showing Pranayama Yoga. She would listen to the tapes with her headphones on.

'What's this, Mummy? *Baba Ramji's bhajans*?' Kavita held up one of her CDs.

Her eyes danced as she looked at her mother, trying to snatch the tape back.

'Where did you find that? Have you gone through my handbag? It's private!' said Rohini grabbing the CD.

'Sorry, you borrowed my khol pencil yesterday so I went to

look for it. We shouldn't share things if you want to be pr-i-vate!'

'Do you know why they are called fakirs? Because they are fakes!' Shourav added joining in the mirth.

'You lot are disrespectful to me. It's my business whom I seek guidance from. So stop making fun.'

Rohini went her bedroom and slammed the door shut.

'We were only teasing,' shouted Shourav.

Rohini switched on one of her new CDs at full blast, dispensing peace at ear shattering volume. *Hare Rama Hare Krishna Hare Rama Hare Hare.*

Rohini did not expect any more reverence from Bose. Whether as an act of defiance or a desire to provoke a man of science, she had decided all along to be frank with Dr. Bose about her adoption of a parallel method of healing. She believed that Babaji's way was having some positive effects on her life. She rose earlier these days, at six forty-five am. After a quick salutation to the blazing sun, she watered her plants in the balcony and retreated indoors for bath and yoga.

Even her potted plants were doing better. The hibiscus had bloomed five blood red flowers. She would use the *jaba* flowers for Kali Puja next month. She fed and watered her gods uttering a simple prayer, asking for strength, Shakti. All the time her CD player emitted devotional tunes filling her with calm. Rohini sat on a rug on her bedroom floor and tried doing the yoga exercises that Babaji had shown her. She was still at an early stage and she rushed through them, finishing in a third of the recommended time. Her mind wandered, but it was a start. Shourav no longer laughed. She had followed the routine strictly for two weeks now.

The following Thursday Rohini stepped into Bose's room and took her seat. He asked her how she was.

'Very well, thank you.'

'Any side effects from the drugs?'

'No.'

'Well, well, we seem to be going in the right direction, don't we?'

Bose beamed, benevolent Buddha style.

'Yes we are, thanks to my new treatment.'

'I'm glad to see how positive you are now. You had doubts about the medication before.'

'Yes, I was sceptical about your allopathic drugs. I have now found a spiritual healer. Through yoga and meditation I have achieved this calm. In fact if it works well I will stop taking your medication. They are poisonous to the body. I want to feel pure and clean.'

Bose yanked his reading glasses off and leaned over the desk.

'Mrs. Chatterjee, I don't know who you are seeing, but *do not stop taking the medication. Do you hear me?* This man is not a physician. He cannot heal you. He is just filling you with false confidence. You *will* crash if you put a halt to the medical treatment. How could you think doctors like me would give poison to our patients? They have been tested.'

'On animals,' replied Rohini, straightening her sari folds.

She was prepared for battle. No one could enforce treatment without the patient's cooperation. She could walk out of the office and never see him again. There was no law against that. Thanks to Baba-ji's influence, Rohini felt calm, for the first time in months. One of his songs played in her head. It had the desired effect of shutting Bose out.

The doctor was on the phone. Ten minutes later the receptionist came in with a tray of coffee and cakes. Rohini stopped humming. The pastries were from Kathleen's next door, renowned for their exceptional fare. A three-layered chocolate gateau was her favourite. As part of her yogic healing she was following a diet high in fruits and vegetables and low in carbohydrates. They did look good. Rohini reached out and then stopped.

'You're just trying to bribe me with these. Baba Ramji encourages a healthy diet. I do yoga every morning and eat only fruits for lunch.'

'What else does he tell you to do?' Bose reached for a large Viennese roll and took a bite.

The cream remained on his lips. Rohini smiled and indicated the smear to him. He licked it clean like a content cat.

Rohini talked about her new regime—waking up early, saying a prayer, listening to devotional tapes and performing breathing exercises. She laughed when she told him about Babaji being able to contort his body into all sorts of difficult yogic poses, which were beyond her ability at the moment. *He blames the western toilets*, she said.

Bose tapped his pen on his pad for a while. Rohini knew he would not believe in Babaji's methods, but she did not care. It gave her comfort. Let him ridicule her if he wished. She had learnt to ignore mockery from others.

'I never thought I would say this Mrs. Chatterjee, but I think from what you've told me following a healthy diet, doing exercises and meditating cannot be harmful. In fact it complements our treatment. *But* you must carry on with the allopathic medication and counselling. I am glad you've told me about Baba Ramji. If there are any other strong influences in your life, I need to know as it affects my treatment. Are we agreed on this?'

'I suppose so.' He was a tyrant.

'Your new regime may be making you feel a bit better, but if you stop taking the medicines you will feel a lot worse so don't stop the medication!'

Well, Rohini thought, *at least Bose had not disallowed Babaji's treatment.* She would bring him a *prasad*, a holy offering from the ashram. This time next year she would get Bose and Shourav's infidel knees down on the ashram ground chanting Lord Rama's praise. She chuckled as she left the clinic.

Chapter 14 Maria

A week after Maria broke the news to John she decided to pay him a visit. Surely he would have accepted her pregnancy by now. She had waited seven days for him to turn up at her door, jumping at every footstep outside their hut, but there was no sign of him. He had disappeared like a stone cast into a pond. When enquiring discreetly about his whereabouts Anjali informed her that John was in Kharagpur and would be back by the weekend. Never was Maria so glad of her portly, *paan*-chewing, neighbour's habit of snooping.

'He'll be back soon my dear, don't you fret.' Anjali's voice was comforting yet alert to telltale signs of lovers' quarrel.

Early Saturday morning Maria took the half-mile walk to John's. She rapped her knuckles on the wooden door. There was a loud rattle of unbolting and whispered questions. Eventually, Joy appeared at the threshold, blocking the view inside. John was asleep, she told Maria. He did not want to be disturbed. Maria heard noises inside, of shuffling feet and something falling. A muffled curse followed.

'Tell him to sleep well. I'll be back.'

She missed his voice, his touch. The rough hands, which so often caused her pain, were now a forgotten sense. Her baby was growing inside without hearing his father's voice.

That night, Peter could not keep quiet any longer. He pounced on Maria when she returned.

'Where is the young bastard? Tired of you already? I'll go and see him. Teach him to take better care of my daughter. Look at you, disappearing under our eyes. The marriage will take place soon, even if I have to put a gun to his head.'

'Stop, Papa, please. He is under a lot of pressure at work. I don't want to add to his troubles. I'm fine. I can take care of myself. If God wants me to be alone then so it shall be.'

She hoped this would prepare the path for what lay ahead. Her father paced the floor every day after work, going through a packet of cigarette each time. Indira pressed her for a decision. She too was ready to confront Maria's elusive beloved. Pamela was the only one who waited, serene, for Fate to take control of her daughter's life like it did hers.

When John finally came to see his fiancée, Maria was shocked to see the change in him. He stooped like an old man. Peter hurled questions at him, but John remained silent, head bowed, a man in defeat.

'Have you been hitting the bottle young man? Don't deny it. I can smell it from here. Is this what my daughter's future holds, a life with a morose drunkard? You probably can't even father a baby.' *How wrong he is*, thought Maria.

When the two of them were alone, Maria painted a rosy picture of their future. When he came from work, he would find their baby rocking in a cradle on the porch. His dinner would be ready. If Joy took care of the baby, Maria could go out to work.

John continued to obsess about the malign spirit of his dead father. One day she found him lying inebriated on the couch. He waved an empty bottle of whisky at her, asking for a refill.

'That *shaitan* is coming for me. He'll have to catch me first. I'll see him in Hell. Do you hear me Abba? Leave—me—alone. Leave—us—alone, Amma, Maaa-ria, and the…'

'Shh, He cannot harm us now,' Maria whispered, afraid he will blurt out their secret. 'Our baby will be baptised by Father Jones. He will sprinkle holy water on the infant's head renouncing Satan.'

'It's all a lie. Nothing is true. Your God, my God,' slurred John.

Maria put her fingers through his matted hair. He had not bathed for days. She tried to straighten his clothes, buttoning his shirt, pulling at his trouser waistband.

The door opened with a loud groan and Joy came in, blown in by the wind. Her eyes narrowed as she noticed the pair.

'Why do you let him take this poisonous stuff? He is not allowed to touch alcohol,' she said, snatching the bottle from her son's hand.

What kind of low family has she come from? Joy grumbled under her breath, giving the room a sweep. *Besharam girl.*

*

120

Maria's morning sickness worsened. Most mornings she ran to the outside tap to vomit. Shanti's mother stopped, on the way back from the market.

'You know they had incidents of cholera in the next village. Have you got diarrhoea as well?'

When her retches ceased, Maria explained that it was simply a stomach infection. After listing a number of treatments Shanti's mother went on her way dragging a heavy shopping basket.

Pamela too asked Maria rigorous questions.

'Why you sick all the time? Have you been sleeping with John? You shameless bitch! Don't you know your father will throw you out if he finds out?'

'No, Ma,' lied Maria. 'It's just a virus. I went to see the *kobiraji* doctor and he gave me some herbs to take. A lot of the villagers have it. It's in the water.'

She hardly slept; her appetite was all but gone. Three times in one week she missed work, sending word with a local boy about her ailment. Indira would visit soon if her illness continued and what would she say to her friend then?

One morning Maria woke with a stabbing pain in her abdomen. Her lower back had been hurting the previous evening, but she ignored it thinking it was the result of carrying buckets of water from the outside tap to their kitchen. She clutched her stomach and groaned, holding back the cry that would wake her parents. An hour later it was much worse. Maria doubled up in agony. Pamela noticed her daughter's distress while ambling past her to open the front door. They left it ajar during the day to let some fresh air in.

'No Ma, leave it closed,' said Maria, stifling a moan.

'Why?' Her mother asked frowning.

Maria was crying, cocooned in her bed sheets. Pamela bent over her daughter peering at her restless body for answers.

'Have you got a fever?' she shouted in Maria's ear.

Maria asked to be left alone and covered her head with a pillow.

'We have to stay in our room because you don't feel well. What's wrong with you?'

Pamela pulled back the sheets roughly, revealing her daughter's body. Maria was perspiring heavily and her sari clung to her like a second skin. Another blindingly obvious sign of her condition was discovered instantly by her mother.

'You are bleeding. Is it your time of the month? It's just women's pain. Come on, get up and get washed. You'll feel better once you are in clean clothes.'

Her aggressive urging had the opposite effect on Maria, whose cry had turned to bitter sobs.

'It's all over, it's finished.'

Pamela shook her head. Peter poked his head around the door.

'What's wrong with our fine lady?'

'She can't bear her pains,' replied Pamela. 'Modern girls, hmph!'

'Leave me alone,' Maria screamed.

A few hours later, Maria gritted her teeth and rose. She stood shakily for a while in one spot until the dizziness passed. This is what John had warned her about. The spirit would come to take the infant away. She checked her sari. The bleeding seemed to have stopped. There was no lump of flesh among the folds. Maria barely managed to make her way to the outside toilets where she fashioned a sanitary pad out of torn clean rags and held it against her sore genitalia. Returning to the cottage she stopped her mother packing up her bed. *Leave it*, she said. She was unwell and they would have to work around her.

Later that morning Pamela offered her a cup of sweet tea and a *chappati*. Maria swallowed the food with difficulty. She must eat to protect the baby. For lunch Pamela made *kitchuri*. She held a bowl of steaming food in front of Maria, grumbling that the cause of period difficulties in a woman was lack of children. At her age Pamela had been married and had a baby.

'Enough, Ma.'

It took her two days to recover. John appeared at their door on the third day. Pamela must have sent word.

'What's wrong?' he asked.

He was smoking a cheroot and the smoke made Maria choke.

'Let's go for a walk.'

She led him past the Pipal tree and half way towards the river. She was too weak to go further. There, behind a large camellia bush, she told him about her near miscarriage.

'*Sala,*' he swore. 'I knew he would try to get it.' *Still,* he said, *that would have been a good thing perhaps, a way out of our predicament.*

'How could you say that about our baby?'

John took a deep lung-full of smoke and stared at a cat licking itself.

'I think I'll go away for a while. It'll give me a chance to clear my head. All these troubles are giving me nightmares. I can't sleep. I see him everywhere. Yes, I think I'll ask for a post in Kharagpur.'

'What about me?' cried Maria. 'Soon I will get big and everyone will know. How can you leave me in this state?'

John put a hand on her shoulder.

'Maria don't you see that our only chance is to get rid of the baby? I promise I will leave you alone after that. You get a job, we save up money and then maybe in a year or two we can get married.'

At her response, John swore, telling her to stop her snivelling. Maria wiped her face with her sari. It was time to be bold, for the sake of her child.

'Marry me or I drown myself and our baby in the river. You'll be responsible for the death of two lives.'

Maria, be reasonable, John begged, gripping her elbow.

'You don't understand. His spirit haunts me every day. It is better to kill the infant before it is born. Would you prefer it if he died after you held the baby close, fed him your milk, sang him to sleep? He is cruel, Maria. He will take all that away from us. I can promise to marry you one day, but I don't want any family. Do you understand?' he shook her by the shoulders.

'I understand,' she said, tying her hair up in a bun. 'Now you understand me, John D'Souza or Jamil Mansur Abbas, whoever you really are—marry me or we die. You have until

Friday to make up your mind!'

Maria walked away from him, taking slow heavy steps. She turned a corner, and did not look back. A black cat crossed her path. She kicked it out of the way, sending it flying to a bush on the opposite side of the alley. Maria heard the loud, belligerent meow that followed, hostile and threatening—no doubt cursing the human who had so callously stricken its soft belly for no apparent reason.

Chapter 15 Rohini

Rohini yawned as the plane knifed through clouds. It was a fortnight before the award ceremony in New Delhi and she looked forward to going home in time for the festivities, Durga Puja, the pinnacle of Bengali celebrations. Grey streets of Kolkata were resplendent with ornate marquees housing decorated clay statues of Durga and her four children. For five days the city was transformed from ordinary misery to spiritual gaiety. Every autumn, Hindus welcomed Goddess Durga who descended from her home in the Kailash Mountains to visit her parents. Ma Durga was coming home and so was Rohini.

The preceding weeks had been a hectic flurry of preparation. Most days Rohini rushed to the shops after school to complete her Puja shopping. In Mumbai people were getting ready for Diwali, the Festival of Lights. Sales were on all over town and giddy crowds flocked to the shops. Rohini bought silk *salwar* material for Kavita. The tailor was given strict instructions on stitching the garments on time, before their flight to Kolkata. Rohini had to intervene several times to tone down the cut chosen by her fashion conscious daughter.

'You are not a Bollywood vamp. Your grandmother would be horrified to see you dressed like that.'

Shourav gave Rohini a Mysore silk sari, deep tangerine with a cream border. Rohini held the material against her, envisioning wearing it with her chunky amber set. She discreetly handed Ali a sketch of the pattern of her blouse—low back with zigzagging ribbons. Of course she would cover her back with her *anchal*, but it would give her a thrill to sport such a daring cut in conservative Kolkata society. Perhaps Shourav would notice when they got dressed.

She had been surprised when he walked home one evening with a bag in his hand. He opened the lid of the rectangular box and the orange sari lay in soft tissue. Rohini gasped with delight.

'It's so lovely,' she said fingering the thick rich silk. 'Did you buy it today? I thought you were seeing a patient again.'

Shourav loosened his tie, as if it was strangling him. 'I'm not always at the hospital.'

Rohini smiled. '*Now I know your secret, Mister.* You sneak off to buy your wife expensive gifts! I can't believe you chose so well on your own. Kavita, look, your Papa has developed some good taste. It must be due to watching serials with us, *na?*'

Shourav's neck was red. She had embarrassed him. Rohini was still smiling as she put her new sari in the *almari*. He was back on the phone again, talking in a low voice, so as not to disturb them. What a workhorse he is, she thought, but a generous man as well.

Rohini bought Indira an expensive Tussar silk, which she knew would end up in the ladies hostel at the Christmas raffle. She chose a simple cotton Kota for Maria and her mother; Indira would wear that. Maria did not like silk *saries* and preferred something light.

Ma and Baba were waiting outside Dum Dum airport to greet the family. Time had sculpted their faces, but the joy at seeing their daughter was evident in their eyes. Rohini looked at Ma, black hair streaked with a few more grey hairs; her starched cotton sari stiffened to attention. Maria called her Indira Gandhi, for a reason. Indira stepped forward to greet her son-in-law.

'*Esho, esho.* Come, Shourav, this way to the car. *Sabdhan.* Be careful of the potholes. Rohini help him with the bag.'

After a quick embrace they piled into the old white Ambassador, driven by Bibhuti, who had shrunk since their last visit. A baggy grey shirt billowed in the wind and in the evening sunlight; Rohini could see his thin brown body. He struggled to put the suitcases in the boot, refusing the help of the esteemed son-in-law, *jamai.*

'*Namashker, didmoni!*' said Bibhuti, slightly breathless. He greeted Rohini as *sister* as he had done since she was a child.

'*Toomi kemon accho? How are you Bibhuti-kaka?*' Ma had taught her to be respectful to servants, never calling them by their names, always adding uncle or aunty at the end.

'Kabita,' Ma pronounced her name with a Bengali accent

replacing V with B. 'My dearest, you are so *roga*! How can we find a husband for you if you are so skinny? It is the fashion to look slim, no? Come on now; get in the car. We don't want you to burn your fair skin.'

Kavita did not say much. At home they spoke a hybrid of English, Hindi and Bengali and as long as they all understood each other it worked.

'Kavita's Bengali is not fluent Ma.'

'*Jaani*, I know dear. How will she learn if you don't teach her?'

Rohini bit her lip. Ma was getting old. It was no point getting upset over her critical remarks. She knew there was more. 'You've put on weight. You must be careful not to get diabetes,' or worst of all, 'You have a few more grey hairs since the last time I saw you.' She longed to hear—'How are you my dear? I've missed you.'—but that would be like asking for the moon. This time she did not even get the customary hug: a quick loose encircling of arms, both hands patting her back in a 'there, that's done' manner, but valuable nevertheless on the precarious emotional barometer. She wondered for a moment why she bothered to travel a thousand miles to see her mother who couldn't articulate her happiness. What holds her back?

The car sped down VIP road, the main link between the city and the airport. They went past Salt Lake, a new town built on marshes. Rohini's heart beat faster scanning the cluster of colourful houses knowing this is where Farooq lived. A scrap of paper with his phone number and address hastily scribbled across was safely tucked away inside a hidden lining in her handbag. She had prayed at the airport when an official picked up her cabin baggage and talked for a full two minutes during the brisk search.

'Rohini,' her mother gently tapped her arm. 'We must go and see your friend Sharmila. They live here somewhere.'

'What's the address?' The chance of two college friends residing close to one another was slim. Still.

'I can't remember the address. I'll look it up later.'

'Yes, I'd like to get back in touch with some of my old

friends, those who are around,' replied Rohini, patting her face with a tissue.

Shanti Niwas had aged gently like its owners. There were cracks in the plaster and the white washed walls had now turned ecru. Ma pointed to a green streak on the eastern wall where the water pipe had leaked. The roof needed fixing after the monsoon rains, but the quote given by a builder was outrageous.

Inside, a faint musty smell emanated from faded upholstery and curtains. Rohini wandered around the room touching old tables and chairs. The chatter and confusion associated with an arrival evaporated as she remembered the stylish dinner parties that used to be held in this drawing room; rustling silks and smoking cheroots. Large clusters of people gathered around the mantelpiece admiring the objects d'art, her father's collection of carved elephants.

Rohini and Raja watched from the hallway, crouching behind a filigreed screen. They were not allowed in, except years later when Raja learnt to play the sitar. He was shown off then, in musical soirées. Trays of drinks circulated the room. The smell of freshly fried samosas and vegetable cutlets made their stomachs rumble. A simple dinner of chicken stew could hardly compare to the grand fare offered to the guests. Maria would sneak out a plate of appetisers for the children. A small chunk of Lamb Rezallah cooked in yogurt, a samosa or a crispy *katchuri*.

Rohini remembered the smell, saffron and rose water, evocative of India's rich connections to the Mughal past. No one did biryani quite so well in Calcutta as Shiraz's. The Hindu maids refused to touch food from a Muslim restaurant. Ma sent Dinesh, the gardener's boy to collect the food. Her dinner parties were renowned for fine cuisine. Ma kept the name of the caterers a secret in case some guests did not eat food cooked by a Muslim chef.

Rohini stood in the tiled hallway, taking a moment to look at the ancestral paintings on the wall. The voices from the past faded away stripping everything of glamour; what remained were relics, tired and full of dust.

'Babyrani, you are home!' a soft voice emerged from a cobwebbed corner.

'Maria! I am not babyrani anymore at my age!' she said hugging her old nanny.

'You will always be babyrani to me.' Maria turned slowly to take in Kavita.

Gnarled hands gripped a slim young elbow.

'Let me have a look at my little princess! So big she has grown.'

In Maria's loving embrace, Rohini found her true home. It was a touch she would never forget for it had welcomed her into this world. It was Maria's voice that had sung to her when she emerged from her mother's womb. Her arms had rocked her to sleep.

Rohini dithered for a couple of days before calling Sharmila. The two friends chatted with the ease of college days despite a twenty-year gap. Sharmila had been in Bangalore before with her ex-husband. She insisted Rohini come to her house in Salt Lake for tea. With her husband out working and her teenage son in school, they would have plenty of time to catch up. *Please aie, she said, come.* The only problem was when Ma heard about the invite she said she would love to see Sharmila again so Rohini, hesitant, but unable to refuse, took her mother along.

An architect designed Sharmila's house. Standing in front of the building it could be mistaken for a Spanish *casa*. A blue and white mosaic pathway led to a wide porch. Caned furniture was arranged amidst potted ferns. They stepped into an impressively large hallway bathed in sunshine filtering in through a skylight. Rohini wondered how hot it got in the summer. Statues of Buddha and water features completed the Zen look.

After a couple of hours, Rohini took her leave promising to return. The two ladies would go shopping one day. Ma smiled.

'I'll warn Shourav to hide his bank cards.'

'I have my own money you know.'

Rohini hoped Ma would not take it as a gibe at her.

Although Indira worked hard at the charity, not bringing home an income often made her feel inadequate.

On Friday, Rohini left early to get to Salt Lake before lunch. The plan was to go to the City Centre Mall and grab a bite before attacking the shops. For lunch they opted for Italian. Twisting the spaghetti around a fork, Sharmila came straight to the point.

'Have you contacted Farooq?'

'Farooq Khan?'

'How many Farooqs do you know?'

Rohini bent to pick up her napkin, which had drifted on to the floor. They were sitting by a glass wall. A group of boys were playing cricket on the street just beyond the periphery of the mall. Over the myriad of tiled roofs, somewhere was a house where Farooq lived now.

Rohini fought with her slippery linguini, which fell off the fork several times. She impaled a large prawn, surveying it before deciding whether to wrap her mouth around the whole fish or bite off a piece.

Sharmila put her fork down.

'Listen, *shone,* I met him at a community function a couple of months ago. He told me about Mumbai. He would really like to meet you again.' Sharmila looked at Rohini with a mischievous dimple lurking in her right cheek. 'Just like old times? I used to be your go-between.'

Rohini coughed. The fizz from her Coca Cola had gone down the wrong way.

'No, Sharmi. I'm married to a good man. Last year was a mistake. Even though nothing happened, it felt wrong. I can't see him again.'

She had promised to God that she would not be unfaithful to Shourav, not again.

Sharmila took her hand.

'You are doing the right thing. Shourav has been loyal to you for so many years. You have to do the same.'

Rohini agreed. Privately, she was not so certain about her husband's fidelity, but it was all in the past. She shut her mind to Shyamnagar. No good ever came of visiting that place they had left a long time ago. After all, they had both made a mistake. She pictured her diary and closed the book. Over.

Puja arrived with much drum roll and the family joined in the festivities with gusto. Shourav hired a people carrier for them to do an all-night tour of Kolkata's *pandals,* handmade marquees, which rivalled each other in grandeur. The media suggested this year the city had excelled itself with decorations and light shows. Rohini was afraid it would be too much for her parents, but they were in high spirits. The car was packed with flasks of tea and snacks. They put a few cushions in the back in case anyone needed a rest. Battling through crowded streets was a hazard, but the reward was extraordinary. Temples, Pyramids and The Hanging Gardens of Babylon were some of the wonders recreated in multi-coloured cloth. Inside, the ten-armed Goddess Durga stood resplendent in elaborate attire.

For once, Baba enjoyed street snacks, delighting in the piquant spices. To Rohini's surprise, Ma wore the Tussar sari she had given her. Her elegance wobbled for a moment when it was time to snack. Everyone laughed seeing tamarind juice run down Indira's chin. At one point, when they crossed a busy road, Shourav held Rohini's hand tightly, letting go well after they had entered the *pandal.* Rohini lowered the *anchal* of her sari for the people at the back to catch a glimpse of her fancy blouse. She hoped Shourav would notice it too. Away from Mumbai and work, Shourav was a different man.

A dazzling display of lights fascinated the group especially Kavita. It was her first time in Kolkata during Puja and she had not seen a sight so spectacular. Her father said it reminded him of Las Vegas where he had gone on a medical conference once. Maria joked that every year during Puja she wanted to be a Hindu. Shourav said he was a Brahmin and had the power to make her an honorary convert. Their laughter mingled with Hindi film music, booming from loudspeakers.

Five days of Puja festival sped by in a blur of music, food and worship. On Dasami, the last day of the festivities, images of Goddess Durga were taken down to the River Ganges in elaborate immersion processions, drums beating, bells ringing and cries of *Durga mai ki jai*, Victory to Mother Durga! They watched from the balcony, sharing the sadness of the close of another year's celebrations. Marquees in every street corner were dismantled. Soon these oneiric days would be over and the city would return to normality, a little less colour, a lot less music, thought Rohini, her chin cupped in one hand.

That weekend, when Shourav went to visit his family for a few days, Rohini seized the opportunity to make plans of her own with Sharmila. First they went to the cinema; Ma would want a full report and she needed to explain her absence for a few hours. They watched a Bengali film, which she would not have seen in Mumbai. Afterwards they went for a walk by the Strand.

The ladies floated baskets of flowers on the water as offering to Mother Ganga. The river was dotted here and there with dinghies rowed by emaciated men in dirty white loincloths. The sky was a bright blue with streaks of pale orange and cream, an artist's palette.

They stepped into the old restaurant overlooking the river. Nothing had changed. Rohini fiddled with her gold chain. She regretted saying yes to this goodbye meeting. Farooq arrived shortly after in a white silk suit.

'I'm going to a wedding,' he explained.

Rohini felt anxious the moment Sharmila slipped away. This was all too stressful now. She was not the same person she was last summer before her breakdown. She wished she had asked Babaji's permission. She would not dream of mentioning this meeting to Bose although he wanted an update on any strong influence in her life.

Stirring his coffee, Farooq studied her with academic interest. Rohini looked at his unshaven face and brown eyes and thought of his wife and son. He had shown her a photo of Ayesha his wife, a distant cousin, and their son, Faizal.

'You only have to say and I can leave everything,' he said reaching out and touching her hand.

Last year, in the park, his hands had felt warm, his lips pulsating on hers. Now it was just skin and bones. Rohini tried to enjoy the moment, to rekindle her passion for him. All these years she had yearned for his touch. He was with her now, willing to sacrifice everything for her. She withdrew her hand. It was foolish on her part to think she could enjoy a little innocent holding of hands, a stolen kiss, without consequences.

'You can't do that. It would be cruel to your wife and son. They need you. They depend on your loyalty and love.' She stood, spilling her coke on the table.

'Wait! You don't understand. It was an arranged marriage.'

'No. You don't understand. It is still a marriage sanctified by God. I'm going to be faithful to mine.'

On her way out she threw his telephone number in the bin.

After her encounter with Farooq, Rohini did not feel like going home to face the family. She persuaded Sharmila to take her to Park Street, their college day haunt. They found Kim Wah tucked away in a side street. Rohini managed a bowl of chicken and sweet corn soup. Farooq called from the wedding he was attending with his wife.

Farooq pleaded with her to rethink her decision. Divorce was common these days. They would find happiness after a few years of upheaval. Rohini could find a teaching job in Kolkata. Her parents would have her near.

'Stop!' she whispered into her mobile. 'You are going too fast.'

Farooq accused her of not wanting to give up a life of luxury. He was a journalist and lived with his mother in a three bedroomed flat in South Kolkata. After his divorce it would be less. But what more could two people in love need, other than a shelter above their heads?

Rohini put the phone down. Was it really their lifestyle she was attached to? She thought of Shourav, how he tightened his body into a slim roll and slept on the edge of his side of the bed. Was he being considerate of her by giving her ample space or was he subconsciously moving away from her? He had been distracted of late, either buried in paperwork or on the phone. He had insisted that she see a psychiatrist. Perhaps she was driving him away with her unpredictable moods.

On her ride home, Rohini could not stop thinking of Ayesha, Farooq's wife; unloved. She felt ashamed at being the other woman, coming between a man and his wife. Hadn't that destroyed her once? Shourav's friendship with Sunita during their first years of marriage in Shyamnagar had tormented her. The suspicion that he was being unfaithful to her, that he loved another woman, was intolerable. And yet, had she ever been able to prove it? He denied it, like any man would. So she had paid him back in kind indulging in a fling, a summer romance, one night in a cheap hotel with a visiting tea-taster. What a slut!

It wasn't just lust. She had genuinely felt something for Tony, a friend who understood her, shared her love of poetry. It could have been enough. But no, seeing Shourav with Sunita had pushed her over the edge and when she was certain he was with her, she accepted Tony's invitation to his bedroom. She shuddered to think how close she had been to ruining her marriage. The episode was like having an electroconvulsive treatment, she imagined, bringing her back to lucid consciousness.

She returned to Shanti Niwas with a headache. Only the light in the hallway was on. Bibhuti let her in and went straight back to his bedroll on the sitting room floor. Maria called out to her as she came in.

'Rohini baby, is that you?'

'Yes Aunty Maria. Are you still up?'

Maria went to bed early, taking her dinner in the kitchen.

'Your mother waited for you, long-time. You *didn-ee-vn* call.'

'I was out with Sharmila and didn't realise the time. We had dinner afterwards. I rang Ma at ten.'

The next morning Rohini woke to bed-tea brought in by Bibhuti. She opened the shutters of the tall windows. The smell of old wood reminded her of her childhood: standing on a stool and looking out, waiting for Ma to come home. The air was heavy with the threat of late monsoon rain. It was stifling indoors. Dark rain clouds hid the sun. Still, she bowed to its benevolent presence behind the mist. The golden orb would soon rise burning the fog away.

Rohini put her cup down and hurried across the corridor and up the narrow stairs leading to the terrace. She had not been there for years. As a child, she came here often to read or watch the world go by. In the summer Maria and Ma left jars of mango pickle in the sun to intensify the flavours. She got caught several times tasting the tart slices before they were ready.

Her father's prize-winning potted dahlias were in a corner. Sometimes she wondered if he cared more about his plants than his family. The day's washing was already strung out on the line, flapping helplessly in a gust of wind. Rohini held the end of one of her mother's saries and breathed in deeply. The smell of damp starch brought back childhood memories of running to Ma and crying on her bosom; she would have just taken a bath, her body smelling of Pond's Talcum powder. Rohini could not run to her now—nor would Ma hold her, murmuring words of comfort in her ear. *Let Raja play on your bike. He'll give it back or Pinky didn't mean to push you—she'll be your friend again tomorrow.*

'*Khuki*, are you all right? I am serving breakfast downstairs.' Bibhuti had come to search for his little girl.

'Bibhuti-*kaka* I'm not a *khuki* anymore. I grew up a long time ago. I'll come downstairs in a minute. It is so hot down there. I am just cooling off.' *Khuki and khoka he used to call Rohini and Raja, little girl and little boy.*

It was a mistake to come home. This place was redolent with memories. She felt Raja's presence everywhere. Even after a fortnight she had not been able to visit his room, not once stepped inside those walls guarding his silent sitar.

Chapter 16 Maria

On a moonless night of *Amabashya*, the village was shrouded in an impenetrable darkness. The air was still, and not a single leaf stirred as a blanket of silence fell over the houses like a deep sigh. The long whistle of a goods train pierced through the hush, waking the residents of Rajgarh, wrapped in dreams. Decades later Maria would still remember that sound and shiver.

Was it a scream, or just the whistle echoing through a tunnel under the Kangsabati Bridge? Maria lay awake a long time, stroking her softly risen belly. Sometimes she wondered if she was imagining it. But the midwife had been certain. Maria drew a thin sheet tightly around her quivering body as the night air, cool and insidious, crept in through an open window.

The hoot of an owl resonated in the quiet, *koouk koouk koouk*. The inauspicious sound of a *kala pencha* did nothing to quell Maria's fear for her future. A white owl denoted wealth and good luck; a black barn owl was a harbinger of death. She placed a protective hand over her stomach. If the bird had come to take her unborn infant away, it would have to wrestle with her life. This place was beginning to suffocate her, with ill luck and bad omens. What was there for her in this village? Soon they would find out the truth. They always did. She must leave; but where would she go?

A gust of wind whipped around the cluster of tinned roof houses. A shutter flung open. Maria was too tired to get up to close it. The restless breeze knocked over a vase, scattering half-dead flowers and putrid water on to the mosaic floor. The breaking of glass awoke the cat. Munni opened one eye and realising the accident had not been caused by a cheeky mouse, went back to her sleep.

Later that night a rapping on the door woke them. Maria sat up on her bed, befuddled, lost in a dream. Her father eventually emerged from his room, tying up the waist strings of his pyjamas. Maria squinted in the brightness as he turned on the lights.

'Who the hell is it?' Peter barked.

Maria looked at the clock. It was three am.

'Open up. It's the police!' they heard a man with a Bihari accent say behind the closed door.

Maria tidied her sari, pleating the folds and throwing the *anchal* over her chest and left shoulder. She patted down her hair. They must be looking for a *chor*, she thought. Their little village swarmed with petty thieves at night, snatching clothes, jewellery, watches—anything they could find through open windows.

Two men in khaki police uniform shone a torch into the room, up and down at the bemused occupants.

'Yes?' asked Maria's father, eager to get the enquiry over with so they could all go back to their beds. 'What are you looking for?'

'Can we come in?' they asked, stepping in without waiting for a reply.

Maria folded her bedroll quickly and shoved the bedding under the sofa. They must be looking for a burglar or worse, she thought. Maybe someone had been assaulted. The fear of having a dangerous criminal lurking in the neighbourhood made her cross the room and shut the windows firmly. She was about to enter the kitchen to light the stove for a round of tea for the policemen when one of them called her over.

'Miss, would you please sit down?'

Maria sat on a stool, waiting to be interrogated, wondering what on earth they wanted from her. The older man with a silver-grey moustache asked her father for a glass of water. Peter threw a disgruntled glance at his daughter, and trundled off to the kitchen, muttering *I have to do everything around here*.

'*Beti*, do you know John D'Souza?' asked Constable Pandey, reaching out and holding her hand.

Was John robbing houses to support his future family? Why was the policeman holding her hand? Did John hurt someone? Maria could only stare at the officer's fine moustache. His hazel brown eyes trapped her. If you looked at them hard, you could see all the way in. He reminded her of Lalbabu's tom cat with the same earnest gaze.

Pandey shook her hands as if to wake her from a dream.

'Maria-ji! Are you listening to me? *Did* you know John D'Souza?'

Words tumbled out of the man's mouth, formal words, detached from any emotion. All the while he looked at Maria's eyes. She saw his mouth moving, the moustache dancing, as he delivered the grave news. *John is dead. John is dead. They found his body on the track.* It went round and round her head like a rhyme devised by cruel boys to taunt her. Her body tilted and she hit her head on the cold floor.

Maria was brought back to consciousness by the shrillness of her mother's scream. Perhaps she had died and it was her spirit looking up, not her. A second later, she felt the chill of water thrown on her face by her father and she knew she was alive. A bunch of unknown faces peered over her, all talking at once. At first the people thought she had cracked her head open on the tiles, but on closer inspection they noticed a tiny dagger of glass sticking out of her left temple. Shards from the broken vase lay invisible in the dim light. One by one the faces began to have a name she recalled; Kanti's husband, Nirmala's son, Paltu, the greengrocer.

The first concern was to stop the bleeding. Whispered consultations took place as to whether they should call for the village doctor or take her to hospital. Was a stitch required and if so who would do it at this time of the morning? Maria's father sent a local boy to the Bannerjee household to alert them of the emergency. By then quite a crowd had gathered in front of Maria's house.

It was nearly dawn when Indira's father arrived in his motorcar, a light shawl thrown over his *kurta-pyjama*. He went straight to Maria, lying on the sofa.

'Hello Maria! The doctor will be here shortly. Indira and her mother are getting dressed. They will be with you soon.'

He spoke to her in a gentle voice, sounding quite different, almost paternal. He patted his hand and carried on talking about this and that.

'Is this your cat? Indira told me about her. How is your typing-course coming along? There are some well-paid jobs to be had in the city.'

Maria closed her eyes shutting out the light above her head. Her temple throbbed. Pamela had fashioned a rudimentary bandage around her forehead after pulling out the piece of glass embedded in one corner. The muslin felt wet. Soon Indira came with her mother and Dr. Barua. He had a kind face, but his fingers worked on her wound with ruthless severity, in and out, in and out, four times with a sharp needle. Despite the injection the doctor gave her, Maria felt every prick, falling into a deep sleep only after he had finished.

Several hours later Indira woke her up.

'Maria, dear. It's time.'

She went in Indira's car, flanked by her parents. The Bannerjees followed in a taxi. Walking down the hospital corridor, Maria stumbled several times. A female police officer held her in an iron-like grip.

They saw John's still body through a glass door. Only the next of kin, John's mother, had seen him once and identified him, of what was left of him. The body would be released after the post-mortem. Until then, his corpse lay on a block of ice like a stone statue.

Joy protested vociferously against an autopsy, telling the police and all those gathered that it was un-Islamic. The people stared back, not comprehending the true import of her words. *We are musalmans*, cried Joy beating her chest. The tragedy expelled the long held secret from the depths of her heart.

'We fled from East Pakistan during the war. Islam does not permit suicide. My son was pushed.'

'Who pushed him Sister?' asked a senior police officer, Modi. 'Does he have an enemy?'

'Yes, his father. He was an evil man.'

'Where is he now?' The policeman was noting her words down.

'In Hell,' she spat out. 'His spirit has been chasing him ever since. He wants revenge.'

Officer Modi shook his head and closed his notebook, muttering unholy remarks. However, his assistant Pandey nodded in understanding.

'Evil spirits follow us everywhere, aunty. *Shabdhan, be careful*,' he warned her. His sister knew a witchdoctor Joy could consult. '*She is Highly recommended*.'

Joy ignored him, and rocked to and fro, chanting verses from Koran. *Allah, ever forgiving, most merciful, pardon us. Forgive Jamil. Let him enter Paradise and be with you.*

'What?' she asked in response to the lady police officer's question. 'No, yes; a masala tea with three spoons of sugar please. Bring one for her as well,' she said jerking her head towards Maria. 'She would have been my daughter-in-law. Now she is a widow before she could become a bride!'

Maria heard the last sentence through the dense fog that clouded her brain. She looked up at Joy, who had aged ten years since Maria last saw her. The *anchal* of her sari was askew; her hair fell loosely over her shoulders, uncombed and unoiled. Maria wanted to reach out and touch this frail lady who had just lost her son.

The lady officer came over with a steaming cup of tea. Maria took a quick sip and although it instantly scalded her tongue, she needed the warmth from the beverage. Despite Indira's shawl, she was still shaking. A deep chill crept up from her toes to her face. Why had this happened? Was it really the father's *atma* that took John away or was it her angry words? She grasped Indira's hand tightly as they wheeled the body away for examination. She could still feel him, in the room, watching.

Joy and Maria were asked for detailed statements. By then John's boss Mr. Sarkar had also been summoned from Kharagpur and a few members of staff from the railway station.

Sub Inspector Khan in charge of their local *thana*, addressed the gathering, stroking his pointed beard.

'It is always an unpleasant duty of ours to go over the circumstances of a sudden death, but it is the regulation. I am sure you are waiting to hear what happened to John D'Souza. We had a call at midnight from Mr. Desai, the duty stationmaster. There was a body on the tracks. It has been identified formally as John D'Souza.'

A deep wail rose from Joy. Khan motioned to the female officer to help the lady.

'The Jharkhand Express had been travelling through at great speed. It does not stop here, so it didn't slow down. There was no moon and visibility was poor. Mr. Bhalla the driver said he saw nothing. He felt the body once the train had gone over it and braked sharply. Mr. Bhalla and his assistant climbed down on to the tracks and discovered the body. They informed the stationmaster who called us. So far, according to the sworn testaments, nobody had pushed Mr D'Souza, nobody bore a grudge and nobody was seen on the platform.'

Inspector Khan paused to look at his audience. Officer Preeti Lal had her arm around Mrs D'Souza who shook her head throughout his speech. He sipped a glass of water and continued, in a bland voice.

'The platform has also been checked for the possibility of an accident; for instance, if it was wet or if he had tripped on something. We are satisfied with the current evidence that an accident could not have taken place. Although…' he pointed at the others with his stick, 'we cannot rule it out. People can trip on their shoes when running.

We know that John was seen walking out of the station office with his flag to wave the train through. The next thing his colleagues heard was a thump and a loud screech. It is unclear, but we have heard from one witness that there was a cry before the fall. Another noticed that John had been drinking from a flask. The contents have been examined and we have found alcohol in it. We will wait for the autopsy results to check if alcohol was present in his bloodstream. This could indicate unusual behaviour, perhaps an emotional turmoil; his mother claims that John did not drink. We now know he was a Muslim and this was against his faith. However, his future father-in-law Mr. Fernandez said that John had occasionally joined them for a drink. Perhaps he did so to cover his real identity. We will never know.'

Khan sahib paused to clear his throat and consult his notes.

'Because of the hot weather we have to work extra fast.

Our colleagues from Kharagpur are helping us. The verdict is most likely suicide, but there was no note left by the deceased. Why would he commit suicide? Any light you can shed on this would be useful. My deputy Mr. Pandey will take you to the interrogation room, one by one. Remember, you'll be under oath so do not hide anything or you will be prosecuted.'

'I am very sorry for your loss Madam,' Khan added after a few minutes, looking directly above Joy's head.

The people gathered in the tiny room were squashed against each other on a couple of benches, drooping heads resting on their neighbour's. After Khan's speech they slowly rose and untangled their bodies from each other, yawning and stretching, struggling to stand straight.

Maria was called into the interrogation room first. She was reluctant to tell the police about her relationship with John, least of all what he had confided in her.

'He was worried about money, how he would support us.'

'Did he talk about killing himself?'

'No,' replied Maria 'never.'

'Did he talk about anyone wanting to kill him?' asked the officer.

Maria thought about his father's vengeful spirit.

'No, he had no enemies. Everybody loved and respected him. You can ask anyone.'

'Was he careless about safety? Did he leave cigarettes burning in his house or forget to lock the doors? Did he take care of you when going out alone at night?'

'I first met John when a bunch of *goondas* were attacking me, eve teasing like. I know they had bad intent. John chased them away with a stick. I did not even know him then. Afterwards, he always escorted me home at night. And no, he never left a cigarette burning. Once I left the stove on for a while and he asked me to put it out.'

She remembered that afternoon, when John had abused her, violated her in one of his desperate black moods; she had not been able to put out the fire. Yet even through that ordeal he had reminded her to check the stove.

'Was he depressed?' asked Constable Pandey.

'No.'

Pandey looked at Maria. She could hear the clock ticking loudly. Sweat trickled down her blouse. She wanted to pull her sari around her, but her hands were under the desk, frozen in prayer.

'Are you pregnant? Did you badger him to marry you and he refused? Is that why he killed himself?'

Maria felt her cheeks burn. She covered her face with her sari. How could he possibly know? Her head swam. People had seen her going to John's house, throwing up by the outside tap. They had told the police, *she* did it; *she* had killed him.

'How can you insult me so?' she cried. 'I'm a poor defenceless woman and you are accusing me of my honour!'

He took his glasses off and polished them, looking down for once, away from her face.

'It's all right, Miss. I am a police officer. I ask ugly questions, things that other people think but can't say. When someone dies under suspicious circumstances we always treat the wife or husband as a chief suspect. Pregnancy in unmarried women is a common cause of someone committing suicide. It should have been you, so the theory doesn't fit very well. Don't get upset. I've nearly finished.'

Maria wiped her face. Her hair was plastered to her cheeks.

'Were you seeing someone else and John got jealous? Maybe... the baby was your lover's and John knew. He was so upset he killed himself. Or did your lover push him on to the tracks to get him out of the way?'

Pandey fixed a hard stare on her, peering through the top of his bi-focal lenses.

Maria did not flinch.

'I *loved* him. I am a respectable woman. You can ask any of the villagers. John was the first and last man I have been out with as God is my witness. You have to believe me.'

She would plead if she had to. The police threw innocent people in jail all the time, beating them into confession.

Pandey stroked his moustache while flicking through hand-written notes. Maria could see his temples moving, as he chewed a *paan*, a scented betel leaf. She could smell the *zarda* in it. Was it allowed, taking a narcotic on duty?

The table fan made a clicking noise as it finished each arc. He turned his head towards her, cocking it to one side, appraising her. Maria held her breath as he stared at her in icy silence.

'We can get a medical examiner to check if you're pregnant you know.'

'I want Mr. Bannerjee to be present here and a lawyer if he thinks it is necessary,' she said raising her voice. 'I am not sure why you are asking all this. John committed suicide and you are putting *me* on trial?'

Maria felt a surge of strength pulse through her legs. She stood steadying herself by grabbing the edge of the table.

'That won't be necessary, we have finished,' said Pandey closing his book.

Maria fingered her rosary beads around her neck.

'The Lord knows I am innocent,' she said leaving the room.

And yet, she had blood on her hands. It was her ultimatum that had pushed John over the edge.

Sunlight blinded her as she entered the corridor falling into Indira's comforting arms.

John's mother walked in unaided into the interrogation room. Pandey held the door open for her and even asked a junior police officer to fetch a glass of water for the lady.

'*Ashoon,*' he ushered her in politely. The door closed. Maria wanted to warn her not to give any additional information, but it was too late. About three-quarters of an hour later, Joy emerged, bent into the shape of a question mark. Maria walked up to her and led her to a seat. She fanned Joy's face with a leaflet.

'Are you all right?'

'That policeman asked me all these questions about John. Why did he kill himself? Who was he afraid of? I told him 'John was haunted by his father's ghost.' But he wouldn't stop. What were our real names? Which village did we come from in East Pakistan? He pressed and pressed, but I have held the secret safe for so long I did not give my son away,' Joy replied with pride. 'We have to leave here, Maria. We will pack our bags and disappear. That Mr. Pandey is very suspicious about everything. It has started all over again.'

Indira reached out to take one of Joy's hands.

'Don't worry, Aunty. They will not bother to contact the police in a Pakistani village. It'll take a lot of time and effort. They are saying things like that to frighten you into confessing more. You were strong. You didn't breakdown.'

'I hope you are right dear. Can we go home now? I am so tired.'

It was several hours before they were free to go.

'What about my son? When can I have his body back? We must bury him soon, officer.'

'We'll call you as soon as we have the results, Mrs. D'Souza. In fact we'll send someone around as I believe you don't have a phone line. *Namaskar!*' he folded his hands to end the conversation.

Joy and Maria were greeted by their neighbours when they reached the bungalow. Some had brought *roties* and fried potatoes.

'You must eat something,' they urged Joy.

'No, I can't eat anything until his body is in the ground and he is with Allah.'

'That could take a bit of time, sister. You had a big shock. You need to stay strong.'

Maria knew she must eat for the sake of her baby. Whether or not she decided to keep the unborn infant she must look after the only thing that tied her to John. The roti felt dry on her tongue, but she washed it down with lemonade. She felt dizzy and nauseous. Maria and Joy shared the narrow bed in her room. The shutters were closed to keep the sun out. Joy asked someone to play Islamic hymns on the radio. It lulled them into a shallow sleep.

Maria dreamt of car crashes and screaming birds. Dark winged creatures flapped around her. A siren wailed. Thick tar of rain came down, smearing her with its blackness. But when she looked down at her hands, they were red, fresh, sticky blood. She rose in a panic. Was she bleeding? She ran to the outside toilet. An intense colic lasted a few minutes and she passed watery stool. She washed her hands at the tube well, struggling to pump the handle.

For a long while Maria sat outside in the heat of the afternoon sun. She called out to a passing neighbour to bring her a sari from her house. She would have a bath.

'You must wash your hair and cut your nails,' said Mrs. Mandal. 'It's the custom dear.'

Maria was sure it was a Hindu custom, but obliged. Her stomach churned again and she was afraid she would have to rush outside, but the spasm passed. She praised herself for functioning: eating, bathing, cutting nails. In mourning, such simple everyday tasks had become huge steps.

'Maria! Where are you?' she heard Joy calling.

'I'm here.' Maria sat by Joy's side, stroking her hair.

Later that afternoon Maria went home to pick up a few of her belongings. The door was ajar. Her mother was picking things up from the floor. It looked like everything in the room had been torn to shreds by a tornado.

'What happened?' asked Maria looking around. 'Did someone break in?'

'The police paid us a visit while we were at the station. God knows what they were searching for. Check if any of your things are missing!' said Pamela.

John's letters were gone; along with a tin box where she kept the flower he had given her on the night of the proposal and his moon stone ring.

'Did they leave a receipt for the things they took? Papa, do something!' She sat on the sofa, her legs trembling.

'Don't worry, sweetheart. I'll go to the Bannerjees straight away. If the police think they can treat us like poor victims, I'll show them what connections we have. You'll have your things back by the end of today, my dear!'

Maria sat for a long time waiting for her father to return. Her mother fussed around her, making her a glass of lemonade, talking about mundane things. Pamela had risen from her comatose apathy and was making a valiant effort to console her daughter.

'Where is that cat of yours? *Aie aie, too too too*? Minnie?'

'Munni,' Maria whispered.

'She is not used to her new home yet. You need to go find her and bring her back. I'll pour some milk for her.'

'Later, Mummy, later. I'm too tired.'

'Of course, *beti*. You just sleep. Go to our room and lie down on the bed.'

But Maria was already half asleep. There was a dull ache in her belly. Waves of grief convulsed her thin body. Still there were no tears. Just as she sunk into a deep slumber Maria realised that her options had been greatly reduced by John's death.

They dressed Maria in a white sari as per local custom. Maria braided her hair with a black ribbon to respect her Christian faith. When the Fernandez family arrived at John's house, the sun was shining with merciless intensity on to the courtyard. There were no shadows. Even the betel palm tree standing thin and erect in one corner left no mark on the sterile ground. Maria squinted, dazzled by the harsh sunlight.

What would she tell her child of the day of his father's death?

John was laid out on a white stretcher, his body washed and wrapped in three pieces of cloth, the *kafan*, by a man from the mosque. His head faced towards Mecca, explained Joy. Maria could smell camphor and sandalwood that had been rubbed on his body. The Muslim prayer Salat-al-Janazah was recited by the *immam*. *Admit him to Paradise*.

The Hindu neighbours asked Maria to touch John's feet and put a garland around her fiancé's neck. Joy said they must view John's face. Maria moved forward, tipping head first into someone's outstretched arms. His face was purple and disfigured, nose bent out of shape, his eyes were swollen and cheeks caved in. She could not look at him anymore.

The people gathered around her gasped. Some whispered about the morgue mending his body reattaching the decapitated head found several feet away. The legs were detached from the torso and had been stitched back. Indira told them to be quiet.

John's body was put on a bier. The chanting rose.

'Jammu, my son, go with Allah!' Joy's wail filled the

courtyard.

She beat her chest. The men from the mosque carried John's body to the cemetery. Joy ran behind the hearse, screaming John's name, until she fell. The women were not allowed to go to the burial site. They would mourn for three days.

Maria sat for a long time under a berry tree. John's dismembered face floated before her eyes. She was desperate for a drink to slake her raging thirst. All the moisture had been sucked out of her body; she had not shed a single tear.

Indira put a hand on Maria's shoulder. 'Come back to our house tonight. We can sleep in my room together, just like old times.'

'I have to be with Joy,' Maria said. 'She is all alone.'

Maria spent the night in John's bungalow. The couch where she often fell asleep in the afternoons smelt of his sweat. A few women from the village stayed with Joy. They were mostly Hindus, but it did not matter. They were mothers.

Your father died today, Maria told her unborn. It was almost dawn when Maria woke. She could have sworn she heard someone, footsteps in the kitchen. Had he come to visit her for one last time?

John? Maria whispered.

The wind rattled the shutters. Clutching a rolled up newspaper in her hand Maria crept across the cold cement floor towards the kitchen. What good was a tangible weapon against a phantom? But still, she felt braver with. A stream of pale light filtered in through a crack in the window. *John?* Maria called a bit louder. Nothing. The room was completely empty. Maria jumped as a metal spoon fell to the ground with a clatter. An early morning breeze seeped in through the cracks. She could smell rain in the air. The cracked earth desperately needed water for life to begin again.

Chapter 17 Rohini

After Puja, Rohini began finalising their trip to Delhi, checking things off the list—tickets, accommodation, outfits, speech. She bought Indira a cream *patola* sari for the award ceremony. It would look good on stage, elegant and dignified. For once her mother was amenable to be dressed in a new and expensive outfit.

The speech made Rohini a little nervous, but she was used to addressing the class and occasionally speaking in the school assembly. Preparation was everything. It was useful to have ample material to talk about in case she dried up. 'Who was Indira Roy?' Rohini would give the audience a picture of the real Indira and what drove her to charity work.

One afternoon when Indira was at the hostel, Rohini decided to poke about in her mother's wardrobe to see if she could find anything there to spice up her speech. Her mother was a private person. Rohini knew Indira excelled in sports, music and arts in school, but it was ages since she had seen the yellowed certificates and photos and a couple of silver medals. She opened the old teak *almirah* and spent a few minutes admiring Ma's collection of *saries*: silks, cottons, and chiffons in rich colours, mostly unworn, and folded meticulously in muslin. Rohini wrinkled her nose at the smell of mothballs.

There were a couple of locked drawers, one behind the other, where Indira kept important documents. The front drawer was uninteresting, full of utility bills, but the hidden section in the rear held a plethora of paper paraphernalia, jewellery and old photos. Rohini liked these best, black and white snapshots of a time forgotten. She fanned out the pictures on the bed, trying to make out the shadowy figures.

The door opened and Maria came in with a tray. She put the tea cup on the bedside unit and peered over Rohini's shoulder.

'What are you doing, dear?' she asked, mildly curious.

'Look, Maria, I found these photos in Ma's drawer. Who is that?'

Maria took one photo and held it away from her eyes.

'God knows baba. Someone we once knew, probably dead by now,' she said giving it back. '*Chalo*, I have things to do. Clothes don't mend themselves. Drink up your tea while it's still hot.'

'No, Aunty Maria, stay a little while with me. I want to talk about Ma's life. Maybe you can tell me stories about when you were girls. What was Ma like? Was she just as serious then?'

'Why do you want to dig up the past? I don't remember anything. Talk about her charity work not old stories.'

Maria's brusque manner was at odds with her willingness to reminisce about Rajgarh—how they swam in the pond, climbed guava trees, and stole berries from Das babu's garden; and how on moonless nights, they played Planchette with Kaberi and her older brother. Fingers poised on the wooden board, they waited for the dead to send a message. Maria's ghost stories still made Rohini shiver and look over her back.

'Have you told your mother you are looking through her things and opening the *almirah*? Who gave you the key?' Maria's stern face loomed large over her.

She came near Rohini and stretched out her hand as if she would snatch the keys away.

'Ma left the keys with me. Why should I ask her? I have *saries* in there too and my documents: passports and things. Why are you making such a commotion?' *Hulluh* was the word she used.

The fun was gone now. Her research had turned into snooping. Rohini opened the back drawer with unnecessary force, pulling out the whole thing and spilling the contents.

'Now look what you made me do!' Rohini said crossly, trying to scoop up the papers and stuffing them back.

Maria mellowed a little and said, 'Here, let me help you.'

Rohini shivered as a harsh breeze forced open the half closed wooden shutters. Amongst the pile was Raja's music. She remembered this sheet, the last he ever wrote. His eyes had glowed like two moons when he told her about the score.

'*I was up all night getting the alap right. It's called Kalbaisakhi jhar, the summer storm. The alap has to create the mood of an impending storm, dust blowing, brooding gloom before the raga begins.*'

Rohini shook his voice free from her head. It would not do

to dwell in the past. She got up and shut the window. Masses of paper were still scattered on the bed. She gathered them up into a neat pile. A long slim envelope fell out. Deeds for the house, she thought. It would be useful to know in the future where the document was kept. She pulled out the cream folded sheet of paper gently, taking care not to damage it.

'Probably the *dalil*,' she told Maria, aware of her disapproval of prying.

'Noo-body touches her things,' Maria grumbled.

Rohini opened the crisp paper and read, silently mouthing the words. Minutes later, she sank unnoticed into an armchair, her legs giving way.

'What happened?' asked Maria addressing the slumped form. 'Feeling tired? I'll open the window. It's stuffy in here. No soft easterly breeze today, just a mad wind. There is going to be a *jhar*. It hasn't rained for days. One can't breathe in this humid weather.'

Maria switched on the fan. The air-conditioning was barely functioning. A brash autumn wind teased the paper out of Rohini's loosened grasp and dropped it on the floor. Searing heat emanated from her glands cutting her up with a butcher's knife.

'Rohini baby? What's wrong, darling?' Maria shuffled up to Rohini, her cataract eyes noticing at last the tears, the distant look in her baby mistress's eyes. She felt Rohini's forehead.

'I'll get some ice. Stay there, I'll call Bibhuti.'

'No! Wait!' Rohini reached out to grasp Maria's thin hand blindly, and pulled it towards her, into the shadows of her corner seat.

She picked up the paper and shoved it into Maria's palm.

'What does this mean? I don't understand. It's all wrong. It can't be!'

Maria tried unsuccessfully to read without her glasses and grabbed Indira's instead, lying on the table. One glance was enough to apprise her of the contents.

'Oh my God!' she uttered to herself and sank in to the pristinely made bed next to her.

'Tell me it's wrong,' said Rohini 'tell me they made a mistake.'

Maria sank further into the mattress, a little hump of a female, shrinking into herself.

With shaking hands Rohini opened out the document once more, reading aloud, not trusting her eyes.

'Date of birth, 30 October 1966. Place Rajgarh. Parents, Mr John D'Souza and Maria Fernandez.'

Rohini is unable to see anymore. Check the baby's name; check the baby's name. She doesn't want to listen to her inner voice. Maria is trying to snatch the document away from her hands. Her fingers, rock hard, like rigor mortis, she would not let go. Rohini Mary D'Souza is her real name, given by her mother. Mary, another version of Maria—she had been named after her mother.

'Ma said my birth certificate was lost. She gave me another document with Ma and Baba's names on it and my date of birth. I used it to get my passport when we went to Dubai.'

Rohini's voice rose in a shrill complaint.

Maria covered her face with her sari and shook with tearless sobs.

'Tell me, something, please,' Rohini sat next to Maria, trying to look at her face. 'Is this true?'

Maria took Rohini's hand and placed it on her chest.

'I didn't want you to know. Ever.'

'Why?'

'Shame. I was an unmarried mother.'

Maria stroked her child's hands.

'You must know our history. It is time. How can you understand your mother's sadness, if you don't know what happened, what took her smiles away forever?'

Rohini waited while Maria sat still, not rocking, not crying, just staring at the birth certificate. She passed her fingers over Rohini's printed name, caressing the letters.

'Your mother was sixteen when the robbers attacked her. It was the night of the circus. So excited she was, chattering like a *mynah* bird. We had such fun. When we came home the house was silent, the servants in bed, we thought. But there were waiting for us, the *shaitans*. They knew Bannerjee madam would open the safe if they grabbed the young girl. I hid upstairs. I couldn't help; I was so scared. After that, she did not trust men. She was never the same again. Thank God the life inside her did not survive.'

Maria paused to wipe a tear. Rohini had turned to stone. Her mother's suffering seemed unreal, like an old film one watches without really connecting. Rage was what she felt above all, being cheated and lied to, all these years.

'Roy sahib understood. He would have waited. But then you came along and I knew God would want me to give you to Indira. I was alone and my family would have disowned me if they knew I was pregnant and unmarried. What could I do? *Beti*, I didn't want to lose you.'

Rohini sat holding Maria's hands for a long time. They felt warm and clammy. She wanted to withdraw her hand, but feared it would offend Maria. Her heart had plummeted somewhere far down her body. Everything was clear and yet nothing was clear. Her teeth chattered. The air-conditioning was still on despite the approach of cooler days. The ceiling fan squeaked in its axis. Maria rubbed her hand. Shadows formed in the corner of her eyes, demons creeping back into her life, taking stealthy footsteps.

'Rohini! Rohini! Shall I get you some water?'

Rohini leaned against Maria. She felt as if she had taken opium, sinking into a slow blissful nothingness. A song played over and over again in her head, *jethey daaw amay dekho na, let me go, don't call me back.*

'Durga! Maria! Where is everybody?' Indira's voice floated up from downstairs.

'Your mother is back,' said Maria hastily getting up from the bed and smoothing out the creases.

Your mother—Rohini never thought those two words could hurt so much, a knife in her stomach. She straightened her back to face Indira while Maria pulled out the *mora*, her usual allocated place—a wicker stool; somewhere between the floor and bed, her status in the household defined.

'What's going on here? Who opened the *almirah*? Why have you taken everything out? I leave for an hour or two and look at the mess,' Indira scolded and grumbled, putting things away, locking up the drawer.

'Bibhuti! Can you bring me a cup of tea? Rohini, have you had one my dear? Maria, go see if Bibhuti has heard me! He's

153

deaf as a post these days.'

Maria got up to leave.

'No Ma, let Aunty Maria stay. We need to talk,' said Rohini, with a surprisingly controlled voice.

She said Ma so easily, as if Indira was still her mother, the source of authority. But something had changed; a little shift. It was that tiny change that gave Rohini the power to say *no, let Maria stay; let my mother hear.*

Chapter 18 Maria

The wedding date was set for eigth February. Indira offered to postpone, but Maria insisted the nuptials go ahead. Indira must marry soon for Maria's plan to work.

A few days later, at Indira's gentle insistence, Maria accompanied her to Calcutta to help choose the wedding sari. Indira rejected traditional red, which matched the vermilion on a bride's forehead, in favour of purple brocade embroidered with golden peacocks. The sari, made of Benarasi silk and fine as a spider's net, was woven through with gold thread and weighed three kilos. Indira laughed when the shopkeeper weighed it in his hands; she was not sure she could walk around the fire seven times in that sari, but the colour enticed her. The richness of plum and gold were like the contents of a treasure box. She was confident that Bipesh Roy would find her irresistible in the attire, she whispered to Maria.

A week before the wedding Maria's mind was finally made up. All the procrastinations of the last few months disappeared. Ever since childhood Maria had relied on Indira's advice. 'What shall I do sister?' she would ask, even on trivial matters. Now the tables were turned. She would tell Indira what she wanted to do. It would be asking for a favour, one that would indebt Maria to her friend for life. But now was not the time to prevaricate.

They met again in front of the Kali temple. The leaves from the Pipal tree were tossed to the ground by an angry wind. Its belligerence was evident everywhere—pulling at a woman's sari, taking off with a rickshaw-wallah's *topi*, sending a tin can scurrying across the courtyard.

When the sun was well past the highest point in the sky Indira stepped off a cycle rickshaw carrying a tray of fruits. Maria shook her head at the exotic offering of mangoes, jackfruit, and slices of coconut.

'There is no need to do puja this time. We are just two friends talking, nothing wrong with that.'

'I'm not going to waste all this fruit now,' said Indira,

mounting the steps to the temple.

Maria realised that Indira's long lost faith had returned and she sought extra blessing before the wedding. The priest came down the steps to offer Maria some *prasad*. He stayed to talk to the two ladies, an odd pair—rich/poor, Hindu/Christian.

'Holy men meditate under this sacred fig tree, known as Bodhi or Pipal. They hope to achieve, *Bodhi,* enlightenment like Gautom Buddha. Hindu worshippers do a *parikrama* seven times round it. So you see it's a very special place to meet.' He sprinkled Ganga water on their bowed heads before returning to his holy retreat.

Maria seized the moment. The priest's blessing was a good omen. She could not have chosen a more auspicious spot to ask her favour.

'Take me with you to Nepal.'

'What? Why?' asked Indira, her thick eyebrows knitted.

'I'll be your companion there. Roy sahib would be away for long hours at the hospital. I'll stay with you and help you run the household.'

'Maria, it'll only be the two of us in a bungalow, not a big house like here. There won't be much to do.'

'Still, I'll keep you company,' Maria insisted.

'What are you planning? Is it to do with the baby?' Coal eyes imprisoned Maria's.

In the cold light of day, Maria's courage waned. Was she asking too much?

'What is it?' asked Indira again. *Bolo,* tell me.

'I would like to have the baby. No one would know me in Nepal. You could say I am a widow.'

'And after that? How are you going to explain the baby to your parents, and mine? We can't hide in Nepal forever. We'll come back to visit at least. They'll come to see me. You must give the baby away to an orphanage, Maria. They will find a good home for your child.'

Maria looked down at the parched ground. They had been waiting for a storm all day.

'Yes, I've decided to give the baby away. I've found a good home. They will make wonderful parents,' said Maria.

A bird swooped past them plucking a piece of bread off

156

the ground. The church bells rang five times. Indira's face cleared in understanding.

'Ah, so you've been to see Father Jones.'

'No,' said Maria. 'I haven't told anyone but you.'

'Maria, come on dear, tell me what's on your mind. I have to get back. Bipesh said he would call at six after he returns from the hospital. It costs a lot of money to make a trunk call from Nepal and I don't want to miss it.'

Indira rummaged in her bag looking for a handkerchief.

'Look, my nose is running. It would be dreadful to have a cold during the wedding. The dry month has caused a dust allergy. This morning my eyes were red and swollen. How can I put khol in them? So much to think of...' Indira stopped; realising Maria was not really interested in her condition.

'I would like...'

'Yes?'

'I would like you and Dr Sahib to adopt my baby. I'll look after it. Don't worry. Just give her your name and identity. But you can't tell anyone. They must believe the baby is yours,' Maria finished the last segment of her statement in a rush.

Indira dropped her bag on to the dusty road. Maria saw how beautiful Indira was with her wide open eyes, straight nose and her graceful upright back.

'Say something sister. Please. It's the best solution.'

'It's preposterous! You are utterly mad. I always thought you were a little scatter-brained, but this... this... what you are suggesting is crazy! I am not even married yet and you expect me to adopt your child in a few months? How can you ask this of me?'

Maria had one last clincher; one she had hoped she would not need.

'I am saying *ki* it is the best solution sister. You said how you are afraid to let any man touch you. How else will you have a child? My baby will be yours without you going through *anny* trouble.'

She saw Indira's mouth tremble and would have done anything to unsay those words. Even a hundred halleluiahs would not be enough.

Indira stared at the church steeples in the distance. The sun was sinking behind the tall Devdaru trees. Maria held her breath and prayed. This time Indira would be really angry and not talk to her, ever. It was a long five minutes before Indira spoke.

'I can't help you Maria. You did this to yourself. If you were firm with John, and said no, this would not have happened. I can't tell Roy sahib this. How can we start a marriage with a secret? We will have to lie to everyone we love for the rest of our lives! You make it sound so simple, take the baby, give it our name and *baas*, a nice happy ending to your story. What about the timing? I need to have nine months after the wedding to have the baby. Yours is already on the way. How can we explain that?'

'Babies come early. I'm only six weeks pregnant. I know. I timed it.'

Indira got up and dusted her sari down.

'I must go now, it's nearly six o'clock. I'll have to take a cycle rickshaw.'

The two-wheeled vehicle lurched forward carrying its elegant passenger out of the poorer end of the village towards the other side—where brick walls, guarded by a durwan at their wrought iron gates, protected big houses. The ponds were cleaner and even the cows looked healthier on that side. Flowers bloomed in well-tended gardens. Nobody shat on kerbsides. No one cleaned their teeth with *neem* twigs, rinsing out their mouths by the tube well.

Perhaps she should have just asked Indira for money to go to a new town and reinvent a future as a widow and child, leaving her old life behind and everyone she knew. Maria put her trust in God. He would provide.

All through the long day of the wedding, Maria hung back in the shadows, watching the bride and groom exchange garlands and look at each other under a veil. When Indira's forehead was smeared with vermilion, Maria let out a sigh, quietly, so the sadness would not bring ill luck to the newly-weds. Just like the bride's mother, she would not shed a tear in front of the happy couple. Her life hung in balance; they had decided to leave it to the groom to settle the future.

Chapter 19 Rohini

The day of the award ceremony drew ever closer like the dusk following a short autumn day. Shourav or Kavita guarded Rohini at all times, as if she would run away. Her only escape was the roof to breathe in the smoky air. *She was taking it all surprisingly well*, she told herself. She ate, bathed and dressed on time. Her mind, counted the minutes, measuring out her past and present. If she kept busy she would find a way round this awkward corner. It was only a temporary glitch in her life. The waters would close over it soon.

Rohini abandoned all preparations for her speech. If she did not know who her mother was, how could she present Indira Roy to others? Everything she had known up to this point was false. The mothers did not want to talk about it. Indira sat in the balcony most days shrinking in her armchair while Maria stayed in her room, wrapped in dreams and nightmares. There was no contingency plan. They had hoped all would be revealed only after their deaths, or perhaps Rohini would never know the truth.

One evening Rohini joined Indira in the balcony.

'You lied to me about everything.' Reproach was the only weapon she had to confront the truth.

'I didn't lie. You are my daughter legally and in my heart. I didn't reveal the full truth to save Maria's reputation. She did not want to give you up. This way she could be with you always. Didn't I tell you since you were a child that Maria is like family? That's all I could say.'

Rohini remembers her birthday, her child-self climbing down the stairs, holding Tara in one hand and the banister in the other, Maria crying. What did they say? There had been clues all along that she had not picked up. Little seashells left on the beach by the waves, each containing a secret.

No more secrets. No more lies.

'I must mention this at the ceremony. The truth about my birth and how you adopted me to protect my mother,' said Rohini, her mind made up.

Once the truth was out it would be easier to accept. After all, they lived in a modern world, where birth mattered very little.

'Dear, is that wise? There will be press coverage and so many people will know. Do you really think that you would be able to face the unpleasant attention? They will interview you and question you,' Indira replied.

'What do you think?' Rohini asked Maria, unable to call her mother just yet.

She had been sitting in one corner of the balcony all along, ignored and engulfed in shadows.

'Do what you like. It's too late for me. No one cares about my reputation anymore. My family are all dead. I won't be shaming anyone,' said Maria quietly, 'Except you.'

Rohini was silent. She wanted to tell the world about her mother. She was not afraid of whispers. She didn't mind not being a Roy. Her friends would have to accept her for who she was. A low-caste Christian or a high-caste Hindu, it shouldn't make any difference. True, there were people like Bunty she wanted to impress with her exemplary upper class background and fine education, but real friends would stick by her.

Rohini began writing her speech with renewed vigour. She worked late into the night, crying when the words would not flow, tearing up sheets of paper and screaming at the new laptop, a gift from Shourav. He was concerned about her health and asked her to take it easy.

'Let's call Dr. Bose,' he suggested.

'What for? I can handle this on my own.'

Shourav found her in tears at three am the night before their departure to Delhi.

'Rohini slow down! You've had a big shock. Let it sink in. Your mother said she would cancel her appearance. Her colleague can go and collect the award in her place. Keep the news to yourself until you are sure you can face the consequences, the questions,' said Shourav rubbing her back.

'You are worrying about nothing. Yes, it is a shock, but I'll get used to it soon enough. I have always cared about Maria. I'm glad Ma looked after her.' Rohini dried her eyes. 'I'm a bit tired. I want to get the speech just right for Ma. She deserves it.'

Nothing anyone said could change Rohini's mind. Her father, the psychiatrist had the least effect on his daughter. The party of four, left for Delhi in the morning. Rohini chatted all through the two hour plane journey. She munched on two bags of peanuts and finished a glass of Coca Cola in seconds. They were to stay with her aunt in Chittaranjan Park where all the Bengalis lived.

Kanika Sarkar was Roy sahib's eldest sister. She had married into an aristocratic family and since then looked down her aquiline nose at the common middle class tier of society she had once belonged to. A widow, she lived alone in a large villa with six bedrooms and an equal number of servants including the driver. Domestic staff flitted in and out of the rooms, polishing the already gleaming floors or dusting spotless walnut tables. A well-known Afghan chef had trained her cook, Ram Din.

The Kolkata family installed themselves in their respective rooms. Later that afternoon, Indira took a stroll around the garden with her sister-in-law, admiring the chrysanthemums and roses. Rohini fidgeted with her speech for the following day, rehearsing the words in low tones. She alternated between a state of absolute calm and hyperventilating panic.

Shourav asked Kanika if he could have a glass of whiskey before dinner. Ram Din had prepared a fine feast of seven dishes: crispy fried aubergines, stuffed tomatoes, lentils, cauliflower roasted with cumin, green beans with poppy seeds, prawns in coconut sauce, and finally a dish of tender meat in an eye-watering red sauce. Most of the Kolkata family looked at the veritable banquet with apprehension. There was silence as people played with the food on their plates.

Rohini seemed to have a normal appetite and spooning large ladles of mutton curry on to a mound of rice she seized the opportunity to address her aunt.

'Aunty, I've got some news. I am Maria, my nanny's daughter. Ma and Baba adopted me because Maria was an unmarried mother. I'm going to tell everyone my story at the function tomorrow. Let people learn that charity begins at home.'

Rohini sucked a marrowbone.

Aunty Kanika's face dropped into a long oval. The solitaire diamond on her nose flashed as she poured more dal onto Shourav's plate. He was already on his meat course, but did not dare refuse. Indira opened her mouth to say something, but changed her mind. Rohini hummed as she put the empty marrowbone back on her plate and licked her fingers.

'Ram Din clear the plates,' shouted Kanika.

Rohini had not finished, but looking at her aunt's black face she allowed the cook to take the dish away.

After dinner, the guests washed their hands and gathered in the sitting room.

'Sing us a song, Kanika-pishi, a Tagore song like you used to,' said Rohini.

'I don't sing anymore. You have an important day tomorrow so you should go to bed early,' Kanika suggested.

'I'm not all tired. I'll have a look at your books. Such a nice collection you have here.' Rohini hummed while studying the titles.

'All fiction. Enjoy it! Truth is less palatable my dear!' remarked Kanika opening her silver box to take out a betel leaf.

She smeared the middle with slaked lime paste and added a piece or two of chopped areca nut. The *paan* leaf was carefully folded into a triangle and popped it into her mouth. She snapped the lid down and cleared her throat of betel juices spitting the excess into a bowl.

'So, she is Maria's daughter? Haven't I seen that maid in your house?' asked Kanika, directing her question at a painting of a Mughal princess holding a rose. 'Does my brother know? Or is the child his too?'

'Of course not. How could you suggest such a thing? I asked Roy sahib before we were married and he agreed to raise Rohini as our own. Lots of people adopt babies. There is no shame, sister. Maria had nowhere to go. She is not exactly servant class. They were poor, but a good respectable railway family and she was affianced to John.'

'Respectable! You call this respectable, getting pregnant before marriage? I wonder what kind of morals you have,

Indira. I don't think I know the lady who married my brother anymore. You father was well known to everybody. How did he think he could shame us this way?' Kanika hissed.

'Nobody knew, except the three of us. They might have disowned me if they realised Rohini was Maria's girl.'

'Keep your voice down! You think I want everyone to know? Even the walls have ears! You tricked your parents and us with this subterfuge. If you thought it the right thing to do then why didn't you tell anyone, *haan*? Why keep it in your hearts as a poisonous secret? To find out at my age is very unsettling. My blood pressure is high enough already. Why didn't your cowardly husband call me with the news first? To be told by your daughter, just like that, as if she was giving me an update on the latest soap opera, is the height of insult!' Kanika chewed and spat out the words. Indira flinched.

Rohini faced her aunt with a twisted smile, 'But real life *is* like soap opera, no? Who slept with whom? Whose baby is it? We live theatrical lives. And tomorrow the show is going on stage!' she laughed, throwing her head back.

'Enough,' said Shourav. 'I realise the news is unpleasant, but we all have to make the best of it. I will not have my family insulted any longer under this roof. We'll move into a hotel as we are obviously causing you distress.'

Kanika waved her hands. 'No, no, Shourav dear. I am shocked and angry, but we are family. We'll adapt to it. I am Bipesh's oldest sister. Don't I have the right to disapprove? Anyway, what's done is done. You are not moving anywhere. Indira, take your family to their bedrooms. We have nothing more to discuss tonight. I am tired!'

She turned at the foot of the stairs.

'I am not your enemy. I am only saying today what the world will say tomorrow!'

She pulled herself up the steps by holding on firmly to the banister. Stiffened by starch, her austere widow's white sari sailed behind her like a blank flag.

They arrived early at Bhavna Convention Centre. The intimidatingly large hall was filled with gilded chairs, upholstered in velvet rose. Rohini sipped mineral water from a bottle, shaking her legs. Indira gazed at the frilled canopies flanking the stage. Kavita chatted about inconsequential things: the traffic on the way, the carpet, anything that came to her mind, in a desperate stream of consciousness flow. Rohini fingered her script, every word stamped in her heart. She knew once the lights dimmed and the audience disappeared into the darkness, so would the words. She clung to the sheets of paper like a drowning soul while Shourav paced the floor.

They did not have long to wait. The organisers arrived with ready smiles and went straight to the details of the programme. The other candidates mingled, looking confident. About ten charities were to be presented with awards, 'Janani' being the overall winner.

Half an hour later, the seats filled with a minimum amount of confusion. The audience looked like they had done this all before, shaking hands with colleagues they knew, exchanging greetings and business cards. The press took up their positions in the front. Rohini remembered the circus she had been to as a child where the elephant had opened his bowels depositing large plonks of shit on the stage within a few feet of the front row.

The evening's programme began with a montage of work done by various charities. The audience listened with silent respect, gently clapping after each clip. The President's representative, his esteemed wife, stepped up to present the awards. 'Janani' was to be called up last. Rohini tried a Pranayama yoga breathing exercise. Shourav nudged her to stop. She counted off as many of the names of Durga's avatars as she could remember. *Parvati, Kali, Amba, Usha, Renuka, Bhagvati, Chandika... Janani.* Rohini sat up with a jolt.

'Let me present Mrs. Rohini Chatterjee who will be introducing her mother Indira Roy, President of Janani.' A young lady in gossamer silk beckoned.

Rohini stood with effort and tottered up to the guillotine. The papers rustled under the microphone. The audience waited. *Ma Durga Ma Kali.* Rohini pictured her father, silent, forbearing, unafraid. Her voice came out in a squeak, steadying afterwards.

'We all know the story of Mary, Joseph and the son of God. In ordinary families the same tale takes on a less fortunate twist. A young unmarried woman discovers she is pregnant when her fiancé dies. She approaches her wealthy Brahmin friend for help who takes her in and brings the baby up as her own. They keep it a secret because if the family realises that the baby is illegitimate as well as born to low caste Christian parents there will be scandal. The baby would be stigmatised forever as the maid's daughter.'

Rohini met her mother's anxious gaze and nodded. It will be all right.

'Dear Friends, it is now up to you to accept babies such as these in your hearts and rise above the prejudices that our society has created. A child is a child, born out of love.'

Rohini paused to judge the reaction. There was silence followed by whispers. She sipped from a glass of water. It was now or never.

'I am the baby in the story. My real mother was my nanny, Maria Fernandez. Indira Roy brought me up as her own child. It is only in the last few days I have stumbled upon the truth and tonight, I am very proud to share my story with you.

Indira Roy founded this charity and has worked for forty years giving shelter to young unmarried mothers: finding them work, finding homes for the babies. I would like to thank her for her generosity and hope that many others would be saved from rejection and shame by our society.'

Rohini helped her mother up to the podium. Clad in her cream silk sari, Indira took small steps holding her daughter's hand tightly.

Indira peered at the applauding crowd. Her voice shook.

'Thank you. I am honoured to receive this award tonight. I wish my team was here with me. I could not have done it without them.'

The lights came on bringing the audience into focus. Rohini spotted Shourav's anxious face and smiled. His frown cleared. Kavita was shaking her leg, a nervous habit that she had inherited from her mother.

Before they could join the family, the press asked for photos. Rohini stood beside her mother. The smiling presenter, Nina, came forward to usher them into an adjoining room.

'This way please,' she said. Ah, refreshments at last, thought Rohini. The room was filled with chairs and a long table stood on a raised platform covered with several microphones.

'What's this?' asked Rohini, thinking the ordeal was over.

'A press conference. They have a few questions to ask you,' Nina replied briskly. 'Could you take your seats up there? Aunty, can you manage the steps? Be careful!'

'But we were not told. We are not prepared. My husband and daughter are in the other room waiting.' Rohini wiped beads of sweat from her forehead.

'Don't worry, madam. We'll call them over. There will be just a few questions for their cover story, that's all.' Nina disappeared.

Rohini sat in front of the grey steel objects with black coils. Her stomach muscles had tightened once more.

'Could we have some water please?' she asked a stagehand as the press crowded in. She felt slightly relieved seeing Shourav and Kavita sitting at the back.

The firing started.

'Madam Chatterjee, how did you feel when you found out you were the servant's daughter?'

Just like that. No introductions, no polite lead-up questions about how the charity began, its achievements, straight down to brass tacks.

'That is private,' she stated.

The crowd faded before Rohini's eyes. What had she got her mother in to? Indira was poked, jabbed and so was she. The press were relentless in the pursuit of their story. The pair was pelted with questions they were powerless to dodge.

'Mrs. Roy, what was your real motivation in adopting the baby, to escape the rigours of a natural birth? I understand that rich women don't like to suffer.'

'What was the family's reaction to the news?'

In half an hour Rohini noticed how much older Indira looked. When the press left, Shourav pushed through the departing crowd to help his mother-in-law down from the raised platform. Kavita gave her mother a long hug, holding her tight within her arms, shielding her from the world. They left through a side door even as Nina rushed after them with the award statue they had left behind. Kavita dropped it in her large handbag, not thanking the effervescent young woman with false apologies on her bright lips.

The next day the story ran in all the newspapers, 'A servant's daughter'; 'Charity begins at Home'; 'Maid's baby becomes the Mistress's daughter' and so on. Rohini was glad that they were on the second or third page, not the headlines.

'I hope you are satisfied with the amount of mud smeared on our faces,' said Kanika. 'Couldn't you have just accepted the award and said thank you? Why did you have to go public with our private affairs? Indira, you have given your daughter far too much freedom. Perhaps she takes after her biological mother and lacks moral sense.'

'You have no right to speak about my daughter like that or her mother. Maria is a devout Catholic woman who obeyed her fiancé's wishes. John was like a husband to her. He was a good man, but a tormented soul. That's all I can say, the rest is Maria's story and I respect that. *Chaalo*, Rohini we must finish packing. Our flight back is early tomorrow morning.' Indira left the room.

Rohini remembered a documentary of a Spanish bullfight. The matadors danced around the wounded animal waving their red flag, provoking the anger of the bull. They goaded the creature to a slow, undignified, body-shuddering end. She slid further into the sofa and curled up into a foetus position, turning inwards in the middle of a crisis. She would take several Valiums tonight. No one was watching.

Chapter 20 Maria

Nepal 1966

The road to Indira and Roy's bungalow was uphill all the way. Their little house was perched precariously at the end of a cliff. On windy days Maria was afraid the cottage would be blown away. They were guarded on all sides by snow-covered mountains, rising up to heaven. The stiff peaks reminded her of beaten egg whites. At night the twinkling lights of Kathmandu sparkled down below, a busy city full of people, cows, carts and honking cars. She had been there once or twice with Indira to buy baby clothes. Planning for the newborn's arrival kept dark thoughts at bay. If she was a man or did not have a child coming, she would climb right to the top of a mountain and find a quiet spot to meditate; renouncing the world at a click of her fingers.

Maria paused to catch her breath at the elbow of a winding dirt track road. She found the daily journey to and from the market increasingly difficult. It would not be long now. She had insisted Indira not keep a maid except for the village girl who came to clean the house. The less people knew of their circumstances the better.

Just today, the *paan shopwallah* had asked her, *where is your husband?* He must have noticed a lack of vermilion on her forehead. What business it was of his, she did not know. She was a widow, she replied. He was in the army, killed in border battles in Kashmir. He nodded in sympathy. So many lives were lost in the *fauj*. No wonder the young did not want to join the army. They agreed it was a problem.

'How many Nepalese *gurkhas* had died in the British-Indian army, sister?' he asked. 'So many mothers without sons, so many widows,' he lamented.

Maria's feet were growing numb from standing so long in front of his shop. She asked politely if he had Roy sahib's brand of cigarettes. She could barely hang on to her heavy shopping bag and dreaded the long walk back. Indira wanted to come but Maria would not let her. She would gladly do these little favours for her friend, as long as she lived, in exchange for a home for her child.

Towards the end she was housebound. The baby was a week overdue. Roy checked her blood pressure and it was high. Still, she would not see a doctor. A bed had been reserved for her at Bir Hospital. Early one morning Maria felt a dull pain in her back. It would not go away after an hour or two of twisting and turning in her bed. The flushed eastern sky at dawn had turned into a golden morning. The water broke and she called out to Indira, 'Sister, it's time!'

Throughout the long labour lasting eighteen hours, Maria said no to drugs. She gripped a cotton cord tied to the foot of the bed, pulling it hard each time the contractions came. Not once did she scream. Her baby would not to be distressed. Indira watched, pale and agitated. She bathed her friend's forehead with a cool flannel. *Breathe Maria, breathe.* Indira begged her friend to take some medication to ease the pain.

It was midnight when the baby entered the world, her small face purple with discontent. Indira and Maria held each other and cried.

'A daughter, Goddess Laxmi has arrived,' announced the nurse, gaping with open wonder at the fuss made by the gentle folk of a maid's daughter.

She asked Roy sahib to step in to see the baby, if he wished. Roy came in, unshaven. His shirt was crumpled after trying unsuccessfully to sleep on the bench outside. Too much coffee had made his eyes bright. Nurse Sharma knew the doctor vaguely from his rounds in the small psychiatric ward where her unfortunate colleagues worked.

Roy picked up the white bundle.

'What shall we call her?' he asked the ladies.

'Rohini,' replied Indira, instantly.

'Mary,' whispered Maria.

'Dr. Rohini Mary Roy,' said Roy sahib holding the baby aloft.

'No,' said Indira 'I want her to be a writer, as I had always wanted to be.'

Maria kept quiet. The baby belonged to them now. She wished John was there. Perhaps he was watching over them. He would keep their daughter safe.

*

Maria breast-fed her baby for the first month stopping only when Indira suggested they try a bottle. Her breasts ached with unused milk. She missed Rohini's mouth sucking her nipples; her tiny fingers curled around her little mouth.

Maria's favourite time of the day was early morning when she took the baby out to the park. She crept out of the house while Indira rested after a disturbed night's sleep. The cold air cut through Maria's threadbare coat. The baby was snug in a thick blanket and a woollen cap as they walked through clouds. So many stories she told the baby, about Rajgarh and the circus, of playing with coloured water at *Holi* festival and eating chocolates at Easter. She whispered secrets in the baby's ears, things she mustn't remember when she grew up.

Despite their plans to hide out in the mountains until the baby was older, they were summoned to Calcutta. Roy's mother was very ill and she wanted her son to come home.

Sure enough, the visitors commented on the early birth and the baby's looks.

'She's a little dark,' they said. 'Who does she look like?'

Maria hid in the kitchen most days helping to prepare meals, and thanked God Rohini resembled John.

Indira and Maria took the baby to Rajgarh for a visit. They were given a warm welcome with special sweets brought over from Kharagpur. People came bearing gifts for Rohini's *annaprasan*, rice-feeding ceremony: silver spoons, gold rings, rattles and dolls. Peter and Pamela Fernandez came to bless the baby with a hand knitted cardigan. Maria sat far away on a stool watching the grandparents. They just said what beautiful big eyes she had, just like her mother. Indira and Maria let out a sigh. Privately, Maria's mother told her that the baby was dark and rather ugly, not like Indira at all.

Maria desperately wanted the baby to be baptised. Indira agreed. They took Rohini to a Catholic church in Dharmatala Street well away from Shanti Niwas. Roy, Indira and Maria witnessed the baby being baptised Rohini Mary D'Souza. Her name was entered in the register as Maria and John's daughter.

Somewhere Maria knew she existed as a mother. Her baby daughter was blessed with holy water and an invisible cross was drawn on her forehead. The evil forces could not touch her now.

The official adoption process took a bit longer and when they finally came, Indira and Roy rejoiced at being able to claim Rohini as their own. Maria went to her room and sat in front of John's photo for a long time, grieving the loss of two of her loved ones. But she mustn't cry. She would see her baby grow up in this grand old house, hold her and teach her nursery rhymes. The future held so much promise.

When Indira's mother came to visit Maria made sure she was out of the way. One afternoon she sat in the balcony, playing with Rohini, just out of sight of the sitting room where Indira and her mother were drinking tea.

'You let her spend too much time with the ayah. Look how dark she has become, playing in the sun all the time. If you allow Maria to bring up your daughter she will not only look and dress like her, but speak in that silly Anglo-Indian accent. Maria is a good woman. I've known her since she was a little girl, but Rohini is your daughter, of Roy and Bannerjee blood.'

'Blood isn't everything Ma. She will learn kindness and manners.'

Sipping a cup of masala tea at the kitchen Maria thought over what Mrs. Bannerjee had said. Her child was now of an upper class family. She must not pick up lower class manners from her mother.

Eight years later

Every birthday Maria gave her daughter a cross, a bible, a picture of Mother Mary, or a storybook about Jesus. Rohini had never complained, except on her birthday eight years later.

How pretty she looked in her white organza dress. Maria had embroidered little ducks across the smocked chest. A chain of daisies lined the hem. Rohini's dark curly hair was held back by a silver barrette on one side of her head. The rest fell across her shoulders and tumbled half way down to her waist.

Maria had never asked Indira for anything except that first time. Now she had another wish. It was time for Rohini's First Communion. She wanted a Catholic blessing before Rohini was old enough to ask awkward questions.

Maria spoke to Father Reynolds at St. Thomas's Church and he agreed to Rohini joining the service. Maria's heart swelled with pride, looking at her daughter, pretty in white with flowers in her hair. John would have been happy to witness this moment; perhaps he was there already, casting a protective web over his child.

After the cake had been cut Maria gave Rohini the gift. It was so simple compared to Indira's that Maria hardly knew whether to bother. It should have been a gold cross, but Maria could only afford a set of rosary beads, just like the one she had been given as a child. Maria thought Rohini would like it as a piece of jewellery and later she could explain to her how to use it to pray.

Maria placed the beads on Rohini's upturned palm. She kissed Rohini on her forehead before lightly drawing a cross, pretending to sweep some of her curls. Looking at her daughter's face, Maria knew it was the wrong gift. She wished she could say something to make up for the unwanted gift. *You will have your real present on Saturday, just before the party.* Perhaps she could rush to the shops with her savings and buy some furniture for her doll's house. Then the bitter words came, that had Maria's head spinning—*Why does Maria kiss me like that in front of my friends? Leela says she is a maid and must not touch me like that.*

Maria rushed out of the room without looking back. She ran down the stairs almost tripping over her sari. She sat on her bed, panting. This is the day she had always dreaded, the day when her daughter would call her a servant.

Chapter 21 Rohini

The return flight from Delhi was a mirror image of the one going out. Rohini, like Indira, was silent throughout the two-hour journey—slumped in her seat, eyes closed, and discouraging conversation. The stewardess took away untouched trays of food. Rohini gazed out of her window at the bed of clouds below, wondering if anyone had ever attempted to jump out of a commercial plane. It would be a short fall before losing consciousness, and gravity would do the rest. All her life she has had the urge to jump: from a tree, over a waterfall or into the river, but never quite had the courage to see it through.

As Rohini stepped into the shadows of the entrance to Shanti Niwas she realised that peace, *shanti* had disappeared forever from her childhood home. The gate, where as a child she had waited for the ice-cream cart to come by, squeaked open. Hanging on one hinge, it too looked forlorn. Rhododendron bushes drooped along the mossy pathway. Rohini wished desperately to escape, somewhere she could breathe without choking.

The doctor was called later that night as Ma's blood pressure had risen. Rohini sat on her mother's bed, reading a book while Maria hovered around the patient, straightening the bed sheet over her and wiping her forehead with a wet flannel. Shourav felt his mother-in-law's pulse and urged her to sleep. Baba wandered around the rooms like a lost child. It was evident from the scattered news sheets lying in the drawing room that he knew, although no one had told him.

When Indira tried to tell Maria of the nasty words written in the tabloids, she merely nodded.

'I knew something bad had happened when I heard Roy sahib swearing at the morning papers. I saw your pictures and read the headlines, but couldn't really understand the rest. Never mind, people will forget this soon enough. The dust will settle,' she comforted Indira.

'M-a-r-i-a! The kettle has boiled for Ma's tea,' shouted Bibhuti from the kitchen downstairs.

'I must go,' said Maria. 'You see, how it has already begun.

Bibhuti now calls me by my name. He does not add sister at the end, like he used to. How can I blame him? He thinks I'm a loose woman and do not deserve his respect. Such is the way. I'll get your tea.'

'This too is my fault,' thought Rohini.

'Maria, I'll talk to him. Tell him he must call you Maria-didi.' Indira threw off the bedcover attempting to get up.

'Don't trouble yourself on my behalf, Sister. Let it be. No one can hurt me now.' Maria took Indira's tray away, with half-eaten rice and lentils forming a cold glutinous mess on the plate.

'Tomorrow, I'll make you a light fish curry with green banana. It'll give you strength.'

With Maria out of the room, Rohini moved closer to Indira.

'Shall I read a poem from Tagore's book, Ma?' she asked in a soft voice.

Indira said '*na*' and turned on her side, facing away from her daughter. Rohini sat next to her for a while, listening to her mother's deep breathing, wishing she could be of some use.

Everyone in the house was busy nursing her mother. Rohini spent hours in Indira's room, trying to make light conversation, putting on a tape of Tagore's music or pressing her mother's forehead, but every gesture was rejected. The music disturbed Indira. She was too tired to talk or listen to her daughter's readings. She did not want her forehead massaged. Maria coaxed Indira to eat, put an herbal balm lightly on her forehead and slipped away as quietly as she had come.

'I'm sorry I embarrassed you in front of others, Ma. I should not have spoken about our private life,' said Rohini one morning, determined to make amends.

'Please, not this again,' replied Indira, not looking at her. 'What's done is done.'

Streams of relatives and friends visited them daily on some pretext or another. They looked at Rohini and Maria scanning for similarities. What hurt Ma most was the reaction of her fellow charity workers.

'It was very kind of you, Sister, to adopt a maid's daughter. I am not sure I would have been able. My parents would not even accept a non-Brahmin let alone low caste Christian in the family. You are a brave lady, Indira-didi.'

Rohini manned phone calls from Indira and Roy's relatives. Family members, near and distant, barely said hello before asking to speak to Indira. Her mother was ill and in bed, she told them, but they would not go away. 'How could Indira and Roy do this? Did family honour mean nothing to them?' Their verbal assault kept Indira in bed for another week.

Rohini's friends, mostly from Mumbai, put consoling messages on Facebook. She received private emails reassuring her there was no *shame* in these revelations, caste didn't matter anymore; '*We live in a modern society.*' She had seen how these people spoke to their servants and was not convinced. When others were busing tending to her mother, she went up to the roof several times, psyching herself to jump.

Early one morning, when Rohini went to Indira's bedroom with a cup of tea she found the two of them, Ma and Maria, talking in low voices. She hid behind the door to listen.

'Don't tell her about John yet. See how fragile she is, Maria.'

'What if she tries again? I can warn her. Let me tell her of the demons.'

'Tell her it was an accident.'

'No sister, she must know the truth.'

'If you wish, she is your daughter after all. I just brought her up.'

'She is our daughter, beautiful and luminous like the moon. Shourav brother will take care of her. See how Kavita protects her mother from dark moods.'

Rohini sank on to the floor. What more was there to know about her past? She felt Raja's presence so near, she could almost reach out and touch him. *Didi, sister! Come with me* he whispered in the breeze, but she resisted the urge to respond; Maria had warned her never to say yes when the dead called.

A little later, Maria came out of the room with Indira's dirty laundry and nearly tripped over Rohini sitting in a heap against the door.

'Rohini beti, what's the matter?'

'Tell me about my father, how he died, everything. No more secrets. Don't you see that it is driving me mad listening to you two whispering behind my back? Ever since I was a child I knew there was something you were trying to hide. My adoption isn't the only thing, is it?'

Maria sat next to her and muttered a quick prayer before recounting the events of the past that would change her daughter's perception of her parents forever: John killing his father with an axe, John jumping on railway tracks. She did not tell her of the nights he violated her nor describe the image of his broken body.

Rohini put her hands over her ears; she could hear the whistle of the train.

'Stop! I don't want to know anymore.'

Bibhuti came running. Why was Rohini screaming? Maria waved him away.

'The old man is still out there. You are not safe,' she whispered in her daughter's ear.

Rohini woke to find Shourav sleeping next to her. She lifted the bed cover gently and put her feet down on the cold tiles. Guided only by a thin stream of moonlight she teased out an aluminum foil of tablets out of her handbag amidst tissues, lipstick, chewing gum, and other medications. She knew the shape of each pack. Reaching for her glass of water, she saw a shadow appear before her.

'Sister?' asked Bibhuti in a reproachful whisper.

'What are *you* doing here?' She hissed back.

'Shourav brother put me on night duty. He said to wake him if you get up and take any medicine or leave the room.'

'Go back to bed. I was only taking some headache pills,' she told her sentinel.

She knew he could not read. But Bibhuti would not be duped easily and woke his master. Shourav shook the contents of her handbag out and took away her supply of Valium, aspirins, even her antacid tablets.

'It's for your own good Rohini. You are not thinking clearly. Earlier Kavita found you in a daze. You were rocking

anxiety,
'Exc
coat. Th
'Hov
She
sari? Sh
But
of a wc
with be
differen
compas
was stro
comple
was on
illiterate

She clo
Doctor
adjustir
on suic
She wa
differei
It all m
along a
On
eat the
sauce.
on Roh
in a un
nor m:
crimin:
'Bh
her jail
She
The la
'To
contac

and muttering to yourself, clutching an old doll. I called Dr. Bose. He said to keep an eye on you and see a psychiatrist here. I need to take you back to Mumbai as soon as possible. I can look after you better there.'

The next night, Rohini waited until everyone was in bed. She breathed deeply, feigning sleep. The ayah, who had been hired to look after Ma, slept on Rohini's floor. Bibhuti and the nurse were taking it in turns to keep an eye on her. It would only be a matter of time before Latika fell asleep on her watch. Rohini knew from her hospital stay last year that night nurses dozed off periodically. She watched through the fan of her eyelashes.

How to stay awake? Rohini opened her new laptop, an early birthday present. Keeping the volume button really low she began typing. She wanted to pour out her soul to the world.

A couple of hours later, Rohini saw her chance. Latika had her mouth open. Rohini opened her handbag. An emergency ration of twenty to thirty Valiums was stitched into an inner lining. She had fooled her clever husband. Gazing down her at her secret stash, Rohini hesitated. It had taken days, driving around the pharmacies of Mumbai on her own, to build up her emergency supply. She could take them all and be free of the pain.

Rohini looked at Shourav's sleeping figure, a slim log lying on the far end of the large bed. His chest gently rose and fell, lulled at last into a relaxed sleep knowing his wife was being watched. Could she bear to leave him to raise a daughter on his own? She touched his thin, wrinkled, surgeon's hands. A *paula* ring sat on one his fingers to ward off the evil eye. Kavita was asleep in the adjoining room with her grandmother.

Rohini slipped some tablets back in the hidden pocket. Grabbing a large handful of the rest she gulped them down with a glass of water, choking as they struggled to slip down her throat. She said a little prayer and curled back under covers letting the drugs take their effect. All she wanted was to obliterate the pain for a few days. Perhaps it would finish her

off. Sh
off wit
Rol
wrappe
closing
had fo
Rohini
for her
'Co
He
'R-
Ne
name.
'Co
'Ke
'Co
Rol
floor.
'Yo
He
echoes o
'St
Th
holds o
'Fo
Ro
'M

'Here
came
'H
aroun
Sh
'Tl
whisp
M:
and K
suppc
into

What's your name? Rohini used the familiar form of address hoping to indicate her seniority by age and not status. After all, she could have been sweeping floors in another life.

'Kajal,' replied the lady. 'Don't talk too much. Eat up now and rest,' she added with kindness.

She too used *toomi* to address Rohini, a form villagers used with each other with an endearing lack of formality.

'I've been resting all day. Tell me about your life. Where do you come from? My mother… used to tell me stories about her village,' said Rohini pushing her plate away.

Kajal brought in a bucket and mop. Tucking the corner of her sari into her waistband she began to clean the floors in even semi-circles. After covering half the room, she rested the tall mop against the wall and began to fix her loosened bun.

'I was born in Midnapur jela. We lived in a hut by the temple. Every morning my mother rose at five to do puja at the temple. She took a plate of fresh flowers from the gentleman's garden where she cleaned. She woke us up when she got back and we had to wash before we could eat the *prasad* that was blessed by God Shiva. Oof! The water was so cold in the pond. We swam like fish.

Then we dressed and went to the village school. We wrote alphabets on slates, *o, ah, harshai, dighai*. The village teacher Mr. Ghosh had a cane. He beat the boys if they could not do the sums. The girls had to stand on one foot and hold their ears for five minutes. It was two miles to the school and on the way we climbed trees and ate unripe guavas in summer and berries in the winter.'

Maria was carrying Rohini on her hips. They were going to the market. She could see a park where children played on swings, their laughter floating in the air. Maria put her on the seat chanting a rhyme, pushing her up higher, higher, 'My Shona will go to her in-laws house/ who will go with her?/ The tom cat will go with Shona with a sash tied round his waist'. She had felt safe then, a time before nightmares began.

Rohini opened her eyes. Miniscule daggers stabbed her eyeballs. A pale green door was ajar and through that she could see polished tiles. A maid in a white sari and a mask over her face was squatting in a corner wiping the floors with

180

a red cloth. Every now and then she glanced up and gave the patient a furtive look. *Afraid to catch whatever she had*, thought Rohini.

Kajal had gone. Or had she dreamed their conversation? It was hard to tell. If only someone would make some noise. Then she would know she was in a real world. Sleep, the opium she needed to drown in, overcame her again.

She was not sure how long she had dozed off for. She heard a cough. It would be the evening nurse with her medicine. Rohini struggled to lift her heavy eyelids. A familiar vision emerged above her bed, like a Cheshire cat appearing face first.

'Hello! How are you?' asked a formal voice.

'*You*! What are you doing here?'

'I'm your psychiatrist. Your insurance requires me to be here to make sure they are taking good care of you.'

'As you see doctor, nothing lacking.' Rohini waved to the empty space beyond her room. The drugs had made her tongue heavy like lead. 'I am alive,' she added in a hoarse whisper.

'Yes, luckily you took enough sedatives to be very ill but not to die.' Dr. Bose replied so quickly, she thought he must have practised his remark beforehand. Rage gave her strength.

'Are you insinuating that I just wanted to create a scene, and that I didn't really want to die? It's grossly unprofessional. Get out of the room. I'm ringing the alarm button.'

Dr. Bose moved to her bedside with alacrity and closed his palm over hers.

'Stop! I didn't mean that exactly. I just feel instinctively that you don't really want to die. You need their attention and you deserve it after all you've been through. But can't you see how much they love you? They've been through hell the past year, waiting for you to try another attempt on your life. When you woke up last year in a similar hospital you had forgotten why you ended up there. They thought it wise not to tell you in your fragile state. Depression was named as the cause. You dying would be the worst possible pain you could inflict on them.'

'What about my pain? I can't stand it anymore.'

'Yes you can. You are a brave, strong woman. Inspirational teacher. Loving wife and mother.'

'Sounds like my obituary,' said Rohini, a flicker of life entering her eyes.

'You mustn't give up. I won't give up on you.'

Rohini stared at a painting on the other side of the room. It was an idyllic seaside scene, complete with palm trees and fishermen's boats rocking on the waves.

'Yes, bad for business, isn't it? Patients dying on you after all the philosophical crap you feed them.'

'Very true,' Dr. Bose agreed with a smile.

'Go home now, doctor. It's Sunday afternoon. When they release me from this prison I'll come and see you. The doctor here says I have a lot of rage inside me so hide your fine objects d'art or I might hurl them across the room.'

'Goodbye Mrs. Chatterjee. Chin up, as the English say. I've bought some wild orchids for the reception. You'll love them.'

'Why? Do they need taming like me?'

'Goodnight Blanche Du Bois,' said Dr. Bose touching her arm gently.

A moment later his black suit had slipped through the crack in the door and he was gone.

It was on the third day at the hospital in Kolkata that Rohini remembered where she had spent her birthday last year. Just as Bose had predicted she arrived at the memory herself, found in the deepest recesses of her mind. She recalled racing through dark streets, blue lights flashing, and a plastic tube down her throat choking her. Her plan had been to pass out or die before her brain could record these inane details. The ambulance pulled up at Lilavati Hospital.

Earlier that day, Rohini had jumped to answer the phone knowing it would be her mother. The quiet voice of Indira wished her a long life and a very happy birthday. Where was she going tonight? Her mother asked. They would go to a theatre first, just Shourav and Rohini. Afterwards, Kavita would join them for dinner at the revolving restaurant in The Ambassador Hotel. The views of Marine Drive were magnificent. Shourav had bought Rohini a string of grey

Hyderabadi pearls. She would wear a primrose chiffon sari.

Her mind was on the evening's delights when Indira passed the phone on to Maria. She wanted to say, *let me speak to Baba first*, but she knew the women in the household got priority. Indira's voice floated faintly over the receiver as she held out the handset to her Maria.

'Here, quickly, *taratari*, wish your daughter now. She is getting ready to go out.'

She said *meyey*—daughter, girl—it could have meant either, but something in her voice told Rohini another story. One she had heard a long time ago. Maria's thin voice spoke to an empty space, 'Rohini Rohini dear... talk to me...' Rohini slipped on to the floor in slow motion, the thick Kashmiri rug softening the fall a little. The lights went out. Her chest ballooned with suppressed air. Her head was stuck awkwardly between the chair legs. Just before she lost consciousness she thought she must tell Paru to dust underneath the seats.

Rohini had held the secret for a long time. It was not last year. It was in the middle of childhood she had discovered the truth. Only, it was a puzzle. The words and clues were hidden. Like the quilt Maria had embroidered for her, wild animals dominating the jungle scene, elephants, tigers, giraffes. But there were birds too, little *mynahs* stitched here and there. *Find the birds, Rohini, set them free*. It was their nightly game.

It was her eighth birthday, or maybe nine. She remembered the cake, the unkind words to Maria, being sent to bed. Her day had already gone wrong with an unscheduled stop at the old church. She had hoped to be taken to the cinema or the zoo. She still remembered the taste of the crisp wafer the priest put in her mouth, bland like cardboard magically melting on her tongue. When she asked Maria what kind of a biscuit it was, she was told it represented the body of Christ. Ugh! On the way home Rohini spat out the imaginary remains in the car. To this day she could feel the strange papery texture lurking in her sensory memory. It was an unpleasant reminder of the day that unfolded soon after.

Late at night Rohini woke after a nightmare about Ghostman. She crept down the stairs, clutching Tara in her hand. She must find Maria and climb on to her soft lap.

Rohini wandered down a dim corridor to Maria's room, touching the wall as she went along for guidance, although she could quite easily walk this route blindfolded. The door was ajar. A beam of yellow light streamed out of the narrow crack. Good, thought Rohini, Maria is awake. Perhaps there will be biscuits as well at bedtime. Rohini peered into the room stealthily, her child brain cunning enough to check her welcome before entering. She was surprised to see Ma there. They were talking. Or rather Ma was. Maria was weeping.

'She hates me,' sniffed Maria. 'She looks at me and sees a servant.'

'Now Maria, she is a child. She doesn't mean what she says. You must forgive her,' consoled Indira, stroking Maria's slim back.

'There is nothing to forgive. Rohini says what she thinks. Why didn't I give my baby to you and leave? All these years I've watched her grow up in a lovely home, having a fine education. She talks like a *bhadralok, unlike me.* It was everything that I wished for her. I didn't realise she would grow up to be my mistress and look at me with such *ghenna.* She recoils from my touch. Sister, I have to go. I can't see Rohini growing up hating me, hating her own mother.'

'Enough dramatics. Rohini adores you. This is just a passing phase. Is your mother's love not strong enough to pull through this? I can't do this on my own. Sooner or later your daughter will ask questions. What will I tell her then?'

'Tell Rohini that her mother is dead. She died a long time ago, giving birth to her.'

Rohini trembled as she leaned against the doorframe. It made no sense, no sense at all. They were talking secrets like her friends whispering in the school playground. It was never anything nice. She dragged her tired feet up to bed.

'I'll always look after you,' she told Tara. 'I'll never leave my *meyey.'*

Part 2

Chapter 1 Rohini

Rohini suppressed a cry of pain as the sharp end of a clipper stabbed the soft flesh of her left forefinger. Sensing a current of human emotion, Ghum raised a furry eyebrow and one shaggy ear. A post-breakdown gift, she was only a recent addition to the family and therefore not wholly intimate with her owner's moods. Rohini paused for a moment pressing the injured digit with the end of her scarf to staunch the flow. The autumn sun was fast disappearing behind the clouds. She had been at it for over an hour—snipping the drooping heads of yellow roses draped over her arbour. Their month away had hastened the demise of the flowers, the long summer ending abruptly, much like their holiday.

The fragrant blooms needed care. The monthly fertilising regime—regular pruning, teasing the creeper over the arch, was a true labour of love. Rohini wiped her brow, glistening with sweat. The pain had begun to abate a little. She removed her scarf from the wound to take a look. A few drops of crimson fell on the pale-yellow petals. She sucked the rest of the oozing liquid into her mouth, ingesting her own warm blood, the blood of a low caste Christian; a servant's daughter.

Rohini had seen a picture of the arbour in an English magazine called Home and Garden and instantly fallen in love with it. A carpenter from Bandra was summoned and within weeks the structure came to life with madam's strict instructions. The bench had to be three feet across, with the trellis forming an arch above it. Rohini's lack of native level Hindi or Marathi had made the entire process tedious to reluctant listeners, *aaarch, treeellis, arbourrrr*. Repeating the words slowly did nothing to invoke the romantic visions she had in her mind to the baffled craftsman. In fact to the best of her knowledge, no equivalent in everyday Hindi existed in which most objects were functional and rarely included vocabulary for garden furniture meant for sitting and musing.

Hassan the carpenter was more experienced than others of

his trade, having served the rich and famous. He understood at some level the need for this piece of red wood where madam could sit under the arch covered by creepers. Perhaps picturing his own *bibi* under such a rosy arch made him take up his tools and begin the work of art. He only made one comment, 'This would look better in a garden,' to which his madam replied '*Chup raho,*' be quiet, silencing him and Hassan knew he had overstepped the mark.

Kavita stood poised in the doorway, drawing a question mark with her slim body, her head resting at an angle against the frame of the veranda door, legs together and arms folded.

'Would you like to eat something Mummy?' she asked.

Rohini shook her head.

Ignoring the silent negative response, Kavita continued her effort to tempt her recalcitrant mother to eat.

'Shall I make a toasted sandwich, with potatoes and coriander? I am having one.'

'I am not hungry.'

'What about the cat?' Kavita used the Hindi word for the creature *b-i-l-l-i,* rising and stressing on the first l and descending on the second.

'The cat has a name.'

Kavita withdrew into the shadows of the lounge. Rohini wanted to go after her and explain, but the words would not come. She could only hope that her daughter would forgive her.

She stroked Ghum, digging her long fingers into the soft fur. Shourav had rushed off to Whiskers & Tails in Paradise Mall after reading somewhere that a pet did wonders for patients with depression. Rohini had been dismissive at first, not wanting to be responsible for yet another being. But Ghum's demands were little. She ate, slept and let her mistress tickle her tummy now and then. She reminded Rohini of Kavita as a baby, a content soul.

The faint sound of voices from television emerged out of the open door, a reminder of a world of normality just a few steps away. Rohini squinted in the low sun, inspecting her handiwork.

The clatter of china broke the silence as Kavita placed a saucer on the tiled floor of the balcony and retreated. Ghum opened her eyes, the prospect of food rousing her from habitual somnolence, a tendency that earned her the tender appellation Sleep. Rohini wished she could sleep away the approaching winter—hibernate in oblivion until she could face the world again. Ghum stretched, first elongating, then growing in width and finally in height, creating an arch of smoke-grey fur. Rohini stroked her back, murmuring words of love, sugar coated nothings one reserves for pets. Ghum sniffed the air with feline hauteur and marched off in the direction of the saucer of milk leaving her human mother to continue her worthy task of tidying the terrace garden.

The wrap-around balcony allowed Rohini to bag the eastern corner, which received glorious sun in the mornings. She placed potted herbs and vegetables near the door to the kitchen. The chillies had grown well, but the okra plant had failed to produce the usual fat green fingers, sprouting emaciated vegetables instead.

The arbour needed attention. During the last few weeks whilst the owners were away, the birds had felt free to perch, splattering the wooden seat with their droppings. Rohini pictured herself sitting there, dressed in a flowing kaftan, a book of poems in her hand and perhaps a glass of wine in the other, dreaming away the afternoons; the ebb and flow of the sea yonder and the distant Malabar Hills, purple in the setting sun, creating a perfect backdrop.

Rohini shook her head free of a cobweb of dreams. Living in the city of Bollywood had given her brain fodder for romantic nonsense. The sea was still and grey, the hills were a hillock. She filled a bucket of water from the outside tap and began to scrub down the seat vigorously. This is what she was born to do, clean, cook, and be subservient to a master. Her life as a doctor's wife in an affluent West Mumbai suburb was fake and unreal, a mockery of her birth.

Rohini returned to her sessions with Bose. It was the only place she felt completely safe—free from judgements, of anxious care. When she entered the white room for the first time since her return from Kolkata, she was eager to see if she would feel different. Now that the cause of her troubles had been revealed, would it be an anti-climax? After all, what would they dig about? The secret was out. She was unsure if she wanted to rake over her emotions. What good would it do? Nothing would change the facts. She considered cancelling her therapy sessions and letting life take over.

On reflection she decided to give him one more chance. Perhaps he had a trick or two left up his sleeve. He would have to earn his fees though. There were subjects she bet he had never discussed with another patient.

'Patricide, I thought it only happened in Greek tragedies or Mughal times,' said Rohini straightening the pleats of her sari that divided her lap in two.

'You would be wrong to think that. Believe me, beneath the surface of our civilised society, lies primeval violence. After all, the same passions still run through our veins— jealousy, revenge, tyranny, to name but a few. We've either just learnt to control our emotions better or we fear the consequences,' said Dr. Bose, looking at his patient through black Armani glasses.

'My father killed my grandfather. What does that make me?'

'A victim of an unfortunate circumstance, Rohini. Ordinary lives are turned upside down sometimes by bizarre violent events. Unhappily for you, your family suffered from such an instance. Your father was protecting your grandmother. She may have died had it not been for his intervention.'

'Either way there would have been a killing in the family. I'm sorry. No amount of explanation and theorising is going to erase that ugly truth from my brain.'

Rohini picked up a glass paperweight from Dr. Bose's desk. Inside was a miniature model of the Sagradia Familia. Gaudi's crystallised fruit lay within the glass bubble, twinkling in the room's subdued lighting.

'Your mother and Maria tried their best to protect you from the truth.'

'The princess lived her happy life in a palace only to realise she is Cinderella after all.'

'Now you're suffering from self-pity. Thousands of babies are adopted all over the world. Some grow up and realise they were unwanted babies. In fact, once traced, the real parents often reject the product of their mistakes. They want to hush up a teenage pregnancy or an extra-marital affair, things that would ruin their current relationships. At least your mother loves you and so does Indira. Aren't you happy that you grew up knowing your real mother?'

'I guess so. I know it makes me sound mean, but the truth, uglier than my father's misdeed, is my shame. I thought I was born into a cultured, classy family. The truth about my humble birth upsets me just as much. It would have been different if I had been born into poverty or another social class, but to find out now at my age, is just unbearable. I know my friends talk about me behind my back. My daughter Kavita has been shunned by some of her rich classmates. I didn't like that set anyway, but still, it's difficult for us to adjust.'

Rohini took out a muslin handkerchief from her Louis Vuitton handbag. It was a gift from Paris when Shourav had gone there on a medical conference. He was wasting money like water, she told him. He pretended it was a fake to appease her. But she knew it was the real thing. Nothing delighted her more than the feel of the exquisite leather, the unique design, the elegance it portrayed. She was the envy of the Bandra ladies. No more.

Slippery strands of Rohini's freshly washed hair fell out of her twisted bun and cascaded down her back. She clutched a handful of abundant tresses and tried unsuccessfully to braid the unruly waves. Bose stared at her for a few seconds before searching for his notes.

'It takes time to adjust to such a life changing revelation. Together you will see this through. You are angry now. Anger is a kind of high. The low period, grief, will follow. I'll help you through all the stages until you arrive at acceptance,' explained Dr. Bose, flicking away an errant mosquito, which had somehow sneaked into the room through sealed windows.

'Don't you ever get tired of these text book platitudes you

dole out day after day? Look at you. You are perfect. You went to the best school, St. Paul's in Darjeeling followed by medical school in Vellore. You did your MD in US,' counted Rohini on her fingers. 'You speak English with a perfect accent and dress smartly. You have this tastefully decorated therapy room filled with patients with minor cases of depression mostly due to too much money, too many servants and not enough to do.' Rohini paused to point to a framed picture of the Bose family. 'And *then*, in your private life, you have a beautiful biochemist wife, two sons, handsome and intelligent, one studying to be an Engineer and the other a doctor. Have I missed anything? Oh yes, a luxurious villa, a Mercedes and half a dozen servants!'

'Two servants actually. And your point is?' asked Dr. Bose, unruffled.

'Your life is perfect! Mine's a mess!'

'You have a loving family. You...'

Rohini put her hands over her ears.

'Shut up, shut up, *shut up.*'

'Let me finish. You will get over this. Nothing has changed. You are imagining all sorts of bad consequences, but you still have a great life, a husband, a daughter, and two mothers.'

'You're not listening to me. You are an armchair psychiatrist. You don't understand or give a fuck about me because you live in Paradise and I'm in Hell!'

Rohini stood and hurled the paperweight across the room. It narrowly missed Bose as he ducked. A corner of the glass cabinet door was shattered to pieces. The secretary rushed in to check the cause of the accident.

'Everything all right Dr. Bose?' she asked, looking at Rohini.

Bose sent her away with a discreet wave. Luckily the paperweight had landed on a Russian doll, which, made of sturdy wood, lay on its side, knocked over but intact. A marble pyramid just to the right of the impact was also undamaged. Like its real life counterpart it too had withstood many such attacks.

Rohini sat, shaking. She could not find any word of apology sufficiently humble to excuse her behaviour. Dr. Bose passed his remorseful patient a box of tissues. Caught in his intense scrutiny, Rohini obliged him by blowing her nose diligently.

'I don't belong here—in your, cosy, plush office. I should be out there earning a living, selling my body, selling my soul, whatever. I wish Maria had walked out into the night with me. At least that life would have been true.'

'Rohini, listen to me. At any moment mine or someone else's life could be hijacked by some twist of fate. We have to cope. As human beings we have the inner resources to deal with that. I promise you I'll find a way for you to accept and adjust to your new life.'

'You have no idea sitting on that leather chair with your souvenirs from Barcelona and your shelves full of Freud and Jung. I have *murder* in my family. I am a servant's daughter. The worst that's happened in yours is probably when someone farted in public!'

'Rohini, I am shocked by your language. You are bordering on vulgarity.' Bose's mouth twitched; his pen raced across his notebook.

'I am sorry to shock you doctor, but I come from the gutter and that's how we speak.'

'I do believe you are enjoying the drama at some basic level,' his smile broadening by a fraction.

'You just sit there calmly and come out with pseudo-psychoanalysis, which does not fool anyone, least of all me. And don't think I haven't noticed that you have started to call me Rohini, instead of Mrs. Chatterjee. How's that for a little Freudian slip of manners? You obviously don't respect me as much as before.'

Dr. Bose rocked in his chair a little, staring at his patient's face, his fingers latticed into a triangle over his stomach.

'The reason I switched is to make you feel safer. I feel we've grown to know each other a bit better and decided to relax the formalities. Quite often patients open up more if they are treated as a friend. But if you are offended by the gesture I apologise. I'll revert to Mrs. Chatterjee in the future.'

'You can call me Rohini, if I can call you Pranab,' she countered, meeting his eyes.

'Unconventional, but since you are Shourav's wife, I accept, as long as our boundaries as doctor and patient are strictly observed,' conceded Bose.

'Of course, I am a conventional person. I would not have it otherwise. By the way, I thought it's only fair to point out that our session ended ten minutes ago. You are overrunning, doctor Saab.' Rohini got up from her chair and turned back to look at Pranab adjusting his tie.

'Until next time?' she asked walking towards the door.

Her hair was now tied into a neat braid. A thick black coil rested along her back. She was wearing a burgundy silk blouse with a low cut back and felt the curls scratch against her smooth olive skin.

She caught Bose's gaze and he turned away, scrabbling through his papers.

'Yes, yes. I'll have your notes, urr… typed up.'

'Why?' enquired Rohini, turning round, slinging her bag over her shoulders.

'Just updating patient records, that sort of thing. Routine matter. In case I am away someone else will know what is going on.' Dr. Bose rose from his chair and pointed his left arm towards the door.

'Just because I call you by your name now, don't feel that you have to share everything with me Pranab,' said Rohini sailing out of the door.

The *anchal* of her batik printed silk sari floated past the silent doctor gently stroking his arm and leaving goose bumps in its wake.

'Did the session go all right?' asked Shourav putting a magazine down on the glass coffee table in the waiting room.

'Fabulous!' replied Rohini waving a quick goodbye to the receptionist. 'I'm sorry for the mess,' she whispered.

'Fabulous? What are you in there for, Ayurvedic massage?'

'Don't be facetious, Shourav. Aren't you glad I don't come out crying? We tackle difficult topics and then we resolve them.'

'Sounds like he is a good doctor.'

'He is. But don't tell him that. His ego is like a giant hot-air balloon. I need to prick it from time to time to bring him down to earth.'

'Who is treating whom?' wondered Shourav matching his step to his wife's.

'It's a two way street, modern medicine. You won't understand.' Rohini gave Shourav a dimpled smile.

'Actually, most of the time I think he is a smug, arrogant bastard. Then the cloud lifts and he is human. That's when I trust him most.'

Rohini had seen the doctor's face behind the clouds today. He was a mere mortal after all belonging to the male species. He had noticed her low cut maroon blouse and his face had gone almost the same shade when caught staring. For all his textbook learning he had reacted like an ordinary man, giving into primal instincts, but she would not tell Shourav that.

The following Saturday, a letter arrived in the post, addressed to Mrs. R Chatterjee. Rohini tore open the long cream envelope. Her heart raced. It looked like an invitation to a wedding or a party. The Mumbai circle had embraced her back into their fold at last. Rohini picked up her reading glasses to scan the document. It bore Dr. Bose's letterhead, but it wasn't a bill.

Dear Mrs. Chatterjee,

I regret to announce my decision to discontinue our sessions…

The words blurred, barely making any sense.

'It says in this letter that Dr. Bose has recommended me to see his colleague Dr. Gupta who sits in another chamber in the city. It doesn't say why,' said Rohini.

Shourav snatched the letter away from her and read with his mouth moving in synch to the words.

'I'll call him. It's probably a mistake,' said Shourav, giving Rohini back the letter. 'Why would he pass you on now? So soon after your breakdown, it's not right.'

Rohini shook her head. She could not think clearly.

'No. Leave it,' she told Shourav. 'It says from next month so I still have a couple of sessions to discuss the matter. I'll be in the shower.'

It was a good hour later that Shourav found Rohini in the bedroom clipping her toenails.

'I was watching the cricket highlights,' Shourav explained taking his wristwatch off. It was Saturday. 'Aren't you going to eat? Paru's waiting.'

'Tell her to eat. I'll get some dhal and rice later.'

'What's wrong?' asked Shourav. 'You're not still brooding about the stupid letter. I told you it's just a mistake. I'll call up his office.'

'I'm too much trouble. I threw a paperweight across the room last time. It was a souvenir from Barcelona. How am I ever going to replace that?' sniffed Rohini.

'If the paperweight was so valuable to him he should have kept it at home,' reasoned Shourav.

'He thinks I am a *pagol*.'

Rohini looked at her reflection in the mirror—dark eyes lined with kohl, now smeared after a few tears, black hair plastered around her oval face and undulating down her breasts. She did not look mad, or particularly repulsive. What did Dr. Bose find in her so distasteful that he had pushed her away? Life seemed to take people away from her—Raja, her mother, and now her doctor. Losing fake friends was one thing; it hurt her pride. But losing a true friend was more painful. How would she cope without him?

The following Thursday, Rohini was in Dr. Bose's office well before time. She wore a smart *salwar kameez*, low heels and had her hair tied back. This was her schoolmistress look, business like.

'Namaskar, Dr. Saab,' said Rohini bowing with folded hands.

'Um Namaskar,' replied Dr. Bose, getting out of his chair.

The formality of her greeting had thrown him off balance. Good. Rohini sat and put her hands on her lap.

'How are you?' asked Rohini with a polite smile.

'Fine. Shouldn't I be asking you that?'

'I am feeling very positive today. I was quite depressed a few days ago when I received a certain letter in the post. Feelings of loss and rejection overcame me for a couple of days. I took your pills increasing the blue tablet for one day. Now I am calm. I have accepted that you don't wish to treat me anymore and I am ready to move on,' replied Rohini.

Dr. Bose carefully moved a silver penholder from the patient's side to his. He straightened his tie before speaking.

'Good, good. I am glad to hear that. Dr. Gupta is a very well reputed man, quite a few years my senior. He has excellent qualifications. I have briefed him about your case and luckily he has space.'

'Ok enough of this *bakwaas*. What's your real reason to pass me on after all we've been through?'

'Clearly you are not making as much progress as I thought. So it is best that you try another doctor. You had a breakdown and a suicide attempt during my care. I think that speaks volumes. I couldn't prevent that.'

Rohini rolled her eyes.

'You are not God! I have free will. If I decide to end my life I will. It doesn't mean that you failed me. You need therapy as much as I do if you can't see that.' Rohini's long silver earrings jangled as she shook her head.

'See, this is the problem—the way you speak to me. It's not clear doctor-patient relationship.'

'Pranab, it's important to me, as a patient to know my doctor cares about me. You do, don't you? I am not just a case to you. I know we switched to first names and say *toomi* instead of *apni*. The informality of our address only highlights the fact that we have a relationship. Maybe part friends, part clinical. No one is sitting in on our sessions listening.'

Dr. Bose rose from his chair and went to the window. He fingered his collar. Rohini saw that his neck was suffused with a deep rose colour. He did that when he was agitated.

'You are right. No one is listening. These walls don't have ears. But I probably take home my work more than I should. Sudeshna has told me to stop treating you. She feels we have become too close and this relationship is affecting your care. I am not objective anymore.'

'She is not the psychiatrist, Pranab. You are. I am not supposed to get emotionally involved with my students, but I do. No matter how unruly or rude they are, some of them feel like they are my own children.'

Pranab looked across the room at her. His eyes were on her, but his mind was elsewhere.

'I shouldn't be discussing you at all outside this room, but I find myself talking about you to Sudeshna, to colleagues. As a case, you are not even that unique. Sorry, I mean your case isn't so out of the ordinary that I need to pick the brains of others. It's just that I've come to know you as a person not just a patient so it seems normal to say Rohini said this or did that. Perhaps Sudeshna does not like our friendship. She finds it a threat.'

Pranab stood by the window continuing to look out at the Arabian Sea. A late monsoon storm had churned the grey waters. It was hard to see where the dull evening sky met the troubled surface of the sea. He passed one hand across the back of his neck, wiping away invisible beads of sweat. Rohini watched in silence. She waited for him to speak again. The reservoir of thoughts had not been emptied yet; she could tell by the way his body leaned to one side.

'It's been hard for me too, arriving at this decision. For once I didn't tell Sudeshna that I have grown attached to you. She may feel hurt or misunderstand. There is nothing wrong in our friendship. And yet we are two adults of the opposite sex. Friendship can lead to feelings, which are wrong.'

Pranab took a turn around the room and faced Rohini. He looked her in the eye. He leaned across the desk towards her. Rohini noticed how light his eyes were, soft brown flecked with bronze. A waft of his aftershave filled her nostrils. She had to bite down her lips to stop the trembling. The room felt very small.

'Contrary to what my wife thinks, I am not about to have an affair with you,' reassured Bose, moving away.

Rohini let out her breath at last. 'Good, because I'm not paying you for sex,' she replied with aplomb.

Their crack of laughter after a minute's pause broke the sobriety of earlier.

'I'm sorry,' said Rohini. 'It just slipped out.'

She used the Bengali word *foshkey* for slipped, which captured the action so well, something slippery and naughty escaping out of one's mouth. Dr. Bose tucked away his smile once more and put his hands in his pockets.

'It's just not professional. You could call me from time to time at work. But, you'll probably find that you don't need me anymore. We'll have one more session when we go over the feelings of change. It may turn out to be the best solution for everyone.'

Rohini left her chair. It was her turn to confront him. She sat on his side of the desk, folding her arms.

'So your mind is made up? You are abandoning me to some stranger? How could you do that to me?' she asked.

Bangles jingled as she shook her open palms at him.

'Please Rohini. I'm just your doctor. I am not a special person in your life. The important family nucleus is still around you,' said Dr. Bose drawing an invisible circle.

He had to find a spot next to her round derriere placed on the desk. She heard a tremble in his voice. He would have preferred her to be sat safely on the other side, and not encroaching on his. But she didn't budge. Instead she crossed her legs. Her high-heeled open-backed sandals dangled precariously from her feet. She made little circles in the air with them. One her right foot she wore a gold anklet, a thin rope chain with little bell charms.

'Like my mother and Maria? Who can I trust anymore to be by my side? Shourav and Kavita have drawn closer and I feel like the outsider. My father hardly says a word to me. Everyone walks around on tiptoes around me except you. You talk to me like a normal person. You make me feel strong. At the hospital when everyone spoke to me in tender whispers, you accused me of being attention seeking. Do you know what that remark did to me?

It made me want to sit up, throw off my bed covers and walk right into your office and demand that you explain your attitude. You gave me strength when others made me weak. If you think that's bad for me then fine, I'll try another doctor. But I think you are a coward, bowing to your wife's wishes, listening to your textbook explanations when you should be listening to yourself!' said Rohini jabbing a finger at him.

Her voice broke. If she could not convince him, he would

be gone from her life forever. 'Who runs this practice you or your biochemist wife?'

'I don't have to listen to this. Our session is over, Mrs. Chatterjee.' Bose folded away his notes and switched off the computer.

Rohini was glad she had stirred his emotions. He was angry now, but it was a start to further negotiations.

'We'll continue this next time doctor,' replied Rohini with a smile on her lips. 'I've rattled you today, but next time we'll go over our feelings in greater detail. Could you tell your secretary to move forward the appointment by half an hour please? The evening traffic is a nightmare and I don't want Shiv to cut corners. I'm not planning on taking my last breath on the polluted roads of Mumbai.'

Pranab watched his patient walk away through the door carrying a hint of Evening in Paris out of his sealed office.

Chapter 2 Rohini

The trill of the phone woke Ghum and she tugged listlessly at a black chiffon *dupatta* trailing the Kashmiri rug, trying to provoke a reaction from the still figure on the sofa. *Rohini dear, please pick up the phone. We are all very worried about you. We need to talk.* The disembodied voice on the answering phone implored her absent respondent once more, *speak to me*, it said, then sighed and hung up. The emotional stress on 'very worried' was heightened in Bengali, *otonto chintito*, the soft Ts and the sharp Ns tapping into the intensity of the caller's anxiety.

Three weeks since Rohini's return from Kolkata, the painful revelation of her birth still digging at her ribs and filling every cavity with something toxic; she could not speak to her mother. The lack of their daily conversation stripped her life of vital blood. Each day at five in the afternoon it was an effort not to look at the clock, not to wonder what her mother was doing. She could picture it clearly. They were sitting in the balcony drinking tea. Indira and Maria were having onion *bhaji* with puffed rice, or perhaps *upma*, a savoury semolina dish. They were talking of the weather or the neighbours, while stroking Muniya, the ten-year-old cat. Three weeks was the longest she had gone without speaking to her mother.

At six Rohini finally decided to end the silence with a question. She dialled the Kolkata number. It barely rang twice before her mother answered.

'Rohini, is that you?' Indira sounded breathless. '*Hello?*'

She waited seconds before repeating the greeting, afraid that the crackly old Kolkata line had disconnected her and she was drifting afloat in telecommunications space. Even when raising her voice, the elegance of her diction was evident. Her 'hello' rose in sophisticated annoyance, not commonplace rancour.

'Ok, speak, *bolo*! Tell me everything, but mostly, why? Why didn't you tell me before? I was an adopted child, it happens all the time.'

Indira cleared her voice before speaking. Rohini had to strain to make out the words.

'We didn't want to burden you with all the unnecessary pain.'

'What about my pain now?'

'Be patient, dear. This is such a tangled mess. It will take time to unravel. In the meantime, just carry on as you were before.'

'Yes Ma, I'll do that, pretend nothing has happened.'

Indira did not respond. Beneath the tip of the iceberg, lay a reservoir of secrets that Rohini would have to chisel into, day by day, month by month. But there was one more truth she must know, however painful.

'What about Raja? Where did you find him? Was he really Bibhuti's son you adopted?' Let Ma feel the pain she was feeling.

Indira replied with apparent ease, 'No, no. Raja was ours, mine and Baba's.'

Rohini noticed the maternal pride in her voice, the stressing of mine and ours, a sense of belonging associated with flesh and blood. Even the rhythm of the words 'mine, ours, mine and Baba's' sounded as natural as the flow of the tides. There was nothing fake about Raja. The fact that her brother was born legitimate did little to ease her pain.

'So you ultimately overcame your dislike for men? Or you just didn't try with me?'

'Who told you that? Dear, I wanted you before you were even born, before I knew about Maria. I wanted a baby to hold in my arms, but I wasn't ready, you know, to be touched by a man, be close. After that time... in Rajgarh, I haven't told you all. There was another...'

Indira's voice trailed away into irregular breathing and silence, a white noise transmitting down the telephone wire, mother to daughter and back again with the earth completing the circuit. It was only a fraction of a second, but in that gulf of silence that separated them, Rohini wished she could have unsaid those words, reminding and taunting her mother of pseudo-infertility, of her trauma and the one she lost, so young. She knew all from Aunty Maria already. Why scratch that wound, expecting blood as revenge?

'I know Ma. I should not have said anything. Forgive me.

Forget the past. Murky waters seldom bring up anything good.'

The conversation turned to normal. Mutual exchange of blood pressure results, the rising price of rice and the lack of rain united the two. The subject of servants and their faults would never rise between them again. A progress no doubt into this new century, but a shared habit lost forever. Rohini would, for the rest of her life, cringe at the very mention of that ugly word, *jhi*, maid.

Rohini trundled back to the sofa, a haven of comfort, a receptacle of dispirited souls; a bargain at thirty thousand rupees. She swallowed as many painkillers as she dared hoping to numb the pain. There was negative pent up energy inside her, ready to implode. She put on her favourite CD, an old Simon and Garfunkel number, playing softly from the shadows of green velvet curtains, where Ghum had now retired abandoning their little one-sided game. She followed Bose's advice and visualised happy images—falling in love, seeing an old film, standing at a street food stall with friends having *bhel-puri*, a crispy savoury snack laced with tangy yogurt and tamarind, which left behind a lasting heat of chilies.

She was alone in the flat. Shourav was working and Kavita had gone to see Priya, an old friend. No doubt the smart set in school were out cavorting with people of their own status, laughing at her fall from grace. The only scandal the rich elite accepted were those of smutty love affairs; it showed prowess of a kind. The revelation of Kavita's humble origin was just plain embarrassing. At least that is what she told her mother that morning in between heart rending sobs. Rohini would have hunted down those pack of Levi's wearing snobs and unleashed her wrath, but that was not what Kavita would want, further embarrassment.

Rohini sat up. Lying around and wishing to die was sapping all her energy. The memory of food had awakened her senses a little and she decided to give cooking a try. Flicking through old recipe books, crisp with age and warped with humidity, she found an item that tantalised her dormant taste buds, pea *katchauri*, stuffed fried pancakes.

The spicy pea mixture was best cooked in a round-based *karahi*. Once the filling was ready she began to knead the dough in rhythm to a boatman tune: *Go a little slower my friend, see the green fields drenched with rain, little boys swimming in the river, boatman, go a little slower, see how the fishes glide in the water.*

Rohini paused to wipe her brow. The *katchauries* were a lot of work, but assimilating all the ingredients and creating a traditional snack kept her agreeably occupied for over an hour. Seeing the pancakes puff up in hot oil was reward enough.

The new galley shaped kitchen was built in a unique style, a long dual aspect room hugging the entire side of the apartment. A Swiss architect had designed their block of flats. At one end there was a window opening out to the front, with unobstructed views of the sea beyond the balcony. This formed the actual cooking area with red Formica cupboard units and a stainless steel sink. The other end, where the washing machine hummed, overlooked a square of grass far below, dotted with pretty bushes and children playing on swings.

Rohini glided from one cupboard to another, opening and shutting doors, searching for ingredients for the evening curry to accompany the *katchauries*. The bell shaped sleeve of her navy *kurta* caught round a door handle, snagging the fine linen fabric.

'Fucking thing!' The expletive hissed out of her unpainted mouth.

'Mummy!' said Kavita shocked.

Coming in through the front door she had wandered in to the kitchen following the aroma of cooking. In all her seventeen years she had never heard her mother resort to foul language.

Rohini turned to greet her daughter and in doing so accidentally knocked over a jar of mustard oil. The thick yellow liquid spread sluggishly over the tiled floor. Ghum darted in hearing the crash and tried to lap up the interesting alternative to milk. Kavita pinched a big shard of glass between brightly painted fingernails.

Rohini shouted a warning to both, 'Careful *Shabdhan*! *Hoosh hoosh*, Ghum go, *ja!*' and grabbed a long brush stuck behind a cupboard. As she yanked it free, it fell from her hand and the long wooden handle landed in the oil and glass mixture.

'I can't do this anymore,' cried Rohini grabbing the end of the kitchen table, the shortness of one of its legs emphasised by her body in tremor.

Kavita stroked her mother's back. 'It's only a little accident, nothing to cry about. I'll clear up the mess in no time. You just sit here. I'll make some tea.'

Rohini tried to listen to Kavita chatter about her new friends.

'It's Jennifer's Confirmation next week. Should I buy her a cross or something? We are invited to see the ceremony in church and then to her house for a party afterwards.'

Years ago Rohini had accompanied Maria to see such ceremonies. The incense and chanting in masses were similar to Hindu rituals and yet so alien.

'Should I be baptised?' asked Kavita.

'Absolutely not! You're a Hindu. I brought you up as one,' said Rohini, bristling.

It was Maria's fault. She would rather die than see her family converted. Kavita played with a rolling pin, spinning it round and round, annoying her mother.

'So? You sent me to Catholic schools. I sometimes feel more comfortable with Christianity than our silly puja and stuff.'

'Don't ever speak about our religion with such disrespect, Kavita! We have thousands of years of heritage; the Christians only have two. I respect all religions, but Hinduism is ours. I don't care what Maria believes. This is what I believe.'

'Papa doesn't believe in anything.'

Rohini clutched her head. Kavita words were ringing in her ears, a hundred church bells going off at once.

'Kavi, stop provoking me. You know how sensitive I am right now about everything. I don't want to talk about this subject.'

There was silence as Kavita made masala chai, simmering the tea in milk with cardamom, cinnamon, ginger and sugar—just the way her mother like it. She added a plate of Nice biscuits to the peace offering. While Rohini sipped her tea,

Kavita picked up in the kitchen. She brushed the floor, gathering all the glass in a dustpan. Sitting on her haunches, she wiped the floor with a wet rag. Rohini watched in surprise. When had her daughter learnt to do all this?

Kavita wrung out the cloth hanging it out to dry in the balcony. The dough was beginning to dry. She rolled out the rest of the pancakes and fried them. The stack of hot *katchauries* was covered with foil to keep them warm.

'Do you have a secret mother hidden away somewhere, Kavi, or did you learn all this from Paru?'

How many days had Rohini rested in bed with a headache or depression while her daughter grew up and took charge?

'I learnt while you were in hospital last year. Priya's mum lets us help her in the kitchen.'

Kavita came and sat next to Rohini, addressing the slumped form.

'Mummy, why won't you talk to us? I can't see why you are blanking everyone out! Dad and I had nothing to do with it. *Kuch to bolo*, say something.' Kavita switched to Hindi when emotions dominated the conversation.

Rohini raised her head at last.

'I am ashamed to *speak* to anyone. Do you understand?'

'Not even to your own family, to your mother? Dida has been ringing every day asking about you.'

'She's not my mother. I don't want to speak to either of them. They lied to me about the most important thing in my life. How could they do that? It's cruel. I called today to ask, why? Indira Roy said they did not want to burden me with the truth. That explains nothing. I am not going to excuse their behaviour. I'll speak to them when I'm ready.'

Rohini polished the tabletop with a thick rag. Her strokes went up and down the wood in vigorous motions until her arms ached. One rectangle area was shiny, the rest of the wood, dull.

Kavita changed tactics.

'Listen, Aunty Diya called. She wants to invite us to her daughter's birthday. Everyone will be there, all your friends. If you can't speak to us, can you not speak to your friends? They'll understand.'

'Yes, they'll understand. Why do you think the phone is ringing all the time? They want to hear all the gossip, *na*? Like vultures, they are waiting over my dead body to shred me to pieces.'

Rohini pulled out a tissue from her pocket and blew her nose hard.

'Mum, how can you say such a thing? They are your oldest friends.'

'They also love to gossip. I know that, I've been part of it. When Maya's husband had an affair, we all discussed it behind her back.'

Kavita paused for a moment before asking,

'And last summer?'

'What do you mean?'

'Uncle Farooq?'

'Close the door.'

Rohini sat at the kitchen table picking up her large mug of tea. Kavita leaned against a cupboard, ankles crossed, a hot pancake gingerly held between her fingers. She blew on it, her entire attention focused on the snack as her mother's voice floated above the drilling and hammering sounds coming from their neighbour's flat. Rohini's shoulders slacked, letting the memories wash over her.

Last summer Rohini was surprised to get an unscheduled call from her sister-in-law. Normally Sujata rang every Sunday at five to speak to her brother. 'Hello! How are you? Is Shourav in?' That was the sum total of their conversation if Rohini happened to pick up the phone. 'I'll pass him on' sufficed as a reply.

Working as an editor for India Times, Sujata was smart, ambitious and articulate. She played Rohini like an old fiddle, one to toy with when she was bored. This time she sounded anything but bored. Her voice bubbled over the telephone. Maanik's University friend Farooq was coming from Kolkata to visit them. He would be staying a couple of weeks to attend a conference.

Twenty summers had passed since Rohini had last set eyes on her ex-boyfriend. She still had a fragile copy of Khalil Gibran's The Prophet. It was a parting gift. He was absent at the wedding. He would not see her marry a successful doctor instead of spending the rest of her life with the man she loved, a poor journalist, a Muslim. Her defence, that she could not inflict any more pain on her parents after Raja's death, was not accepted. It was tragic that her brother had died, but why should she have to sacrifice her life? Farooq's reasoning and pleas fell on deaf ears; she had made up her mind to marry a worthy Bengali suitor to appease her family.

The sound of the kettle boiling created a natural pause in the conversation.

'Didn't you love Papa at all?' asked Kavita.

'Of course I did, do. In an arranged marriage love comes after. So anyway, your Aunty Sujata invited us to dinner. She said 'I remember you and Farooq were friends once. It would be a proper Presidency College reunion. What do you say?' Sujata was not asking. She was throwing me out a challenge. I could hardly refuse. On the night of the dinner party, I wore a peach chiffon sari. I slipped an old silver chain with a dove pendant round my neck. Perhaps he would recognise it, I thought.'

Rohini cupped her palms around the tepid mug, looking beyond Kavita, remembering that night.

The square lounge with low style Japanese sofas, embroidered silk scatter cushions, the ornate lamp casting a circle of yellow on the Tibetan rug.

'He was standing in the shadows. When he emerged I saw how he had changed. His chin was dark with a day's growth of beard. There were a few streaks of silver in his hair. A white *kurta* clung to his slim frame above dark blue jeans.'

The cuckoo clock in the lounge sounded seven. Kavita made a face and put down a half-eaten *katchauri*.

'Yuk, I wish I hadn't asked. You sound like a love-sick teenager.'

'Just listen, *na*? After that there were phone calls, meetings in the park. I wasn't sure what Farooq wanted—a summer romance, or something more? I didn't want to think about it too much. I was enjoying a brief moment of being in the presence of an enigmatic man who still adored me. I knew I would not let it go out of hand. One day, we went to Powai Lake. We took a picnic. Neither of us ate much. We sat by the water and watched the kingfishers skim the blue surface. We kissed. I felt alive, floating high above in the clouds.'

'You kissed him,' said Kavita, scandalised. 'I thought you just met him once or twice in a shopping mall. Nita said she saw you with a man in Café Haven, holding hands! That was bad enough. They laughed and thought it cool. I was so embarrassed. But kissing in the park, that's disgusting! You were acting like a couple of adolescents. I hope that has stopped.'

'Yes, Kavita.'

Rohini thought it wise not to mention her last meeting with Farooq in Kolkata. It had ended after all. 'Look, it was nothing. It's over.'

'You had an affair!' Kavita banged the table with her palm. Her Rajasthani bangles jingled. 'Don't ever accuse Papa of anything. What do you think he would say if he found out about your little misdeed?'

'You make it sound like felony.' Rohini was hooked on CSI Miami.

'You make it sound like a walk in the park.'

'It was.' Rohini suppressed a smile. 'Kavita, sweetie, I'm joking. It'll never happen again, I promise. Your Papa's not so innocent either. He was very close to a female colleague once.' At the back end of the comment she remembered her fling with Tony. Kavita deserved better—model parents without a blemish in their past.

'I'm going out with some friends. So I'll see you later!' announced Kavita, picking up her handbag and keys. She was dialling her mobile while exiting the kitchen. 'Chris, it's me. You wanna meet up? The bar in half an hour?' Did she say Le Mur Coffee Bar or Murphy's Bar? The two attracted diametrically opposite clientele.

Rohini followed her out into the hallway where her daughter was twisting her feet into incredibly high heel sandals, 'slutty shoes' she wore to nightclubs. Why couldn't Rohini act like other mothers and ban everything she disapproved of? No night clubs, no parties, no going out after dark. The streets of Mumbai were unsafe; everyone knew that.

'What time will you be back?' she asked, trying to inject authority in her voice.

'Not sure, before dinner.'

'Take the car. Shivu will wait for you. Here, give him fifty rupees for the evening and dinner.'

'I'll get a lift.'

Rohini sighed. She had lost the right to question her daughter's whereabouts being a mentally deranged, affair-having mother.

What she needed was a distraction, something constructive to do with the rest of her day. Rohini emptied out a cabinet chock full of albums. She flicked through one with her childhood photographs. She was not sure whether to set fire to it. It was a fake testament to a made-up childhood, packed with lies and secrets. There was one of her in front of the lion's den at the Calcutta zoo, holding Indira and Maria's hands. Raja was just three then, coming up to her waist, clutching her dress. She remembered being terrified that the beast would leap over the walls and tear her to pieces.

Where was Baba? He was a shadowy figure in her life. He had left the women to bring Rohini up. She did not have a single memory of doing any activity with her father, walking to the playground, reading stories. Perhaps fathers did not do such things. But Shourav was different. He had helped her raise Kavita. She remembered how angry Baba used to be with Raja, his own child. He never lost his temper with her. She must ask Bose that question. Did it mean that Baba cared more about Raja if he showed his emotions?

Rohini began to rip a photo in half. It wasn't as easy as she had envisaged. The black and white picture of her in a frilly dress and Raja in a silly sailor boy outfit bent hideously out of shape, but did not tear. She tried another, a birthday photo. The cake was *Snow White and Seven Dwarfs* themed; it was her seventh birthday, just before the troubles began. A spasm radiated from the epicentre of her body and spread in searing hot circles. Now that she had read the page, the book containing her past would not close.

Rohini picked up a bottle of wine and sat on the sofa. Sula

red trickled down her throat; the faint peppery kick behind the initial depth of plum kept her senses at bay while soothing the ripples of emotions created by the phone call earlier. She had only herself to blame for bringing up the subject of Raja. Why goad her mother now? Twenty-four years on, the wound was still raw.

Yes she missed Raja. The days before his departure remained in her memory sharper than any before. Her mind had stored these images with a keener focus, forcing them to stay and not drift away like autumn leaves. Was it that day they had received the telegram or another? She could never be sure. Rohini sipped her wine and flicked mindlessly through a magazine. The words zigzagged across the pages, images blurred. She clutched one side of her head breathing through the pain.

She remembered his smell. The reek of his greasy hair as she tousled it, begging him to have a wash, had lingered in her hand for a long time, as did the fragrance of almond oil she rubbed into his aching arm. The crazy fool would practise for hours without a break. After he was gone she crept into his room, stuffing his shirts in her face. That was the time she began to take Valium.

Rohini threw the remainder of her wine into a plant pot. The drink tasted bitter. She had a photo of Raja in the wall unit. She took it off the shelf and put it inside a drawer. He was never a brother. In one fell swoop she had lost an entire family. There was a black and white studio photograph taken on her twenty-first birthday with Ma, Baba, and Raja. Rohini held a cigarette lighter to the photo and watched the orange flames curl around the edges. All that remained was a pile of ashes.

Ghum purred at her feet. Rohini placed the creature on her lap, a solid reassuring presence in a shimmering evanescent world. The cat protested loudly against the tight embrace.

Chapter 3 Rohini

Rohini had just mixed a face mask with gram flour and cream when the phone rang. She tried to ignore it, but the caller would not hang up. Her hour of relaxation was meticulously planned. The music tape played Ustad Ali's sitar, the jet spa tub bubbled with scented water. She had poured herself a glass of green apple, cucumber and ginger juice to detox her body.

It was Shourav's sister, Sujata. At once she regretted answering her phone. Since Rohini's past had been revealed she had avoided speaking to anyone in the family especially her in-laws. Shourav's brother Suniel lived in the UK. His wife Nupur was a conservative woman. No doubt Sujata had conveyed Rohini's scandalous drama to their family abroad. Rohini knew they would shun her too. This was the price of truth. She should have just let the phone ring. The bath would have to be delayed by half an hour at least.

The conversation began well enough. Sujata was concerned about Rohini's health. Shourav had told them that Rohini was not in a fit state to speak so Sujata had waited, giving her time to recover. She hoped Rohini understood and was not offended? Not at all, said Rohini. She had not wanted to talk to anyone.

'How are you?' asked Sujata. 'Is the medication working?'

'I think so.'

'I hear you have an excellent therapist. He's a proper psychiatrist, no?'

Their conversation turned to normal topics. Sujata was busy; her efficient maid had left their service leaving her in the lurch. The girl was pregnant. Sujata suspected that she did not know who the father was. There was a pause.

'Come over and see us,' said Sujata. 'I'll cook.'

Rohini smiled, she had never seen her sister-in-law make so much as an omelette.

'Perhaps in a few weeks, I'll ask Shourav to call you.'

But Sujata hung on. Rohini pushed away some albums with her toe to make some room for her to stand comfortably.

'There is one thing. I hate to bother you at this stage,'

Sujata began. 'But I feel that your parents should have told us the truth at the time of the wedding. We are from a high caste Brahmin family and I think our parents were seriously deceived. I'm glad they are not alive anymore to see this debacle! Of course I don't judge people by their backgrounds, but still when it comes to marriage, especially arranged marriage, one has to be honest.'

Rohini wanted to put the phone down. Her voice sounded weaker than she would have liked.

'Sujata, my parents are well respected and honest people. How could you suggest...'

Her sister-in-law cut her short. She snorted like a cow in heat.

'Your parents! Which ones? Fact is my brother was tricked. Such alliances he had from well-known families and we turned them down! There were rich, educated families. The girls were fair-skinned and beautiful. One family was going to send Shourav to England to do his fellowship. Another from Patna had aristocratic blood. After all that, we end up with a low caste Christian family. I hear all sorts of things that make my blood go cold. I could not believe what I read—your father killed his father. My God! What a horrific background. You must be going out of your mind with all this revealed to you suddenly. Did you really not know anything?'

Rohini felt she was lying in the path of a giant bulldozer. She made an immense effort to squeeze out a question.

'How did you know?'

'From you Facebook post of course. How embarrassing to read such scandal on the Internet for everyone to see. How could you be so indiscreet? I never thought you capable of such exhibitionist behaviour.'

Rohini clapped her hand on her mouth. She remembered writing things on her laptop the night she took the overdose. Since then she hadn't opened her Facebook account, afraid to see messages. The memory of unburdening the ghastly truth to all had been effaced from her brain. She had thought to close the account and start a new one. But it was too late. Murder will out.

'I have to be honest with you. I fear this alliance will ruin our entire family. Suniel has a son who will get married in a few years. Your daughter will need a husband. How will we marry them off with such scandal in the family? Rohini, are you listening? Are you even there?' Sujata squawked through the black cord.

Rohini slumped on the sofa, cradling the handset from whence the poisonous words kept pouring out. She could have put the phone down, told her sister-in-law to shut up. After all she was older than Sujata. How dared she speak to her with such disrespect? But Rohini took the hit without a word of protest. She was Draupadi in the court of King Dushashana, being disrobed. In her state of utter humiliation Draupadi had prayed to Lord Krishna to save her. He answered her appeal by making the sari endless. The more Dushashna pulled at the fabric, the more came out. Who would save Rohini now?

Darkness descended around her. She could not face the lights just yet. The doorbell rang. It would be Kavita.

'Mrs. Chatterjee, Namaste. How are you my dear?' asked their portly neighbour Manjula Bhatt. 'I would have come round sooner, but my husband met Dr. Saab in the lift and he said you are still recovering. So pale you look! Sit sit. I got some homemade sweets for you. All fresh. Just pure milk, butter and sugar. They will give you strength.'

Rohini reluctantly let her guest wander into the lounge. Manjula waddled and talked, the words pouring copiously out of her mouth. But unlike Sujata's straight talk, they were coated with honey.

'*Hai, hai* what a *natak!* I watch serials every day, but I tell you there is more drama in real life than on TV. Life is cruel sometimes.' Manjula sat her plump bottom on the sofa, inviting her mute hostess to do the same.

'Who told you about my health?' Rohini asked.

'Oh you know! News like this travels quickly—first in the newspapers, then through servants. Such shocking stories you hear these days. You never know what will happen in your life. My brother in Amristar has just made a bad marriage. The bride is a girl from a low caste family and she wears such tight-

tight jeans and low cut blouses. Shameless! But what can you do? If he doesn't know at his age, what can we tell him, *hain*?' Mrs. Bhatt chomped on a *barfi* talking with her mouth full.

Rohini took a bite of a pistachio *barfi*. Momentarily her senses were fed by the sweet comfort.

'I hear you are seeing a Mental doctor. Your daughter and doctor Saab will take care of you. Mind you, that girl is dressing a bit fancy these days. You need to keep an eye on her, Mrs. Chatterjee.'

Rohini gritted her teeth. She picked up the box of sweets and gave them back to Mrs. Bhatt.

'I am not allowed to have sweets. Doctor's orders.'

But Manjula was not quite finished. She pushed back the container.

'No no, keep for your family. And you look after yourself Mrs. Chatterjee. No more scares like last year. When they took you to hospital by ambulance, my heart was thumping. We didn't know what was wrong! I thought you were dead. I prayed to Hanuman-ji to save you. Seeing your still body on that stretcher was such a shock. To this day if I hear a siren I shiver.'

Rohini stood and walked to the door holding it open.

'Actually Mrs. Bhatt, I am not feeling very well and I need to lie down. Why don't you come another day?' Manjula raised her eyebrows and left the flat, clicking her thick-heeled shoes.

Rohini went straight to her bedroom with a couple of pills and an ice bag pressed to her head. Her temples were throbbing. She could see spots in front of her left eye. For one terrible moment she considered the balcony. How far would the fall be? It would be the end of her for sure, no long recovery in a hospital. No more people stabbing her with words. She looked around the room with a white heat of anger. People were spitting at her and she was living in this tower like an exiled princess. She had handpicked every object in the room: fine Egyptian cotton bedspreads, designer furniture, and expensive tailored curtains. It made her feel cheap. She was not entitled to this life. All of Mumbai knew and they were laughing at her.

She would throw all the trash out. Rohini flung open her

wardrobe and seized her saris, *salwar kameezes*, shirts and trousers at random. She tipped them over the balcony for the Mumbai poor. She could not bear the sight of them.

Paru came in to Rohini's bedroom when she got back. A thick beam of light shone through the open doors. A gentle hand stroked her forehead.

'What is it Ma? Is the pain in your head bad again? Can I make you some lemonade?'

Rohini sat up. 'It's *you*! You gossip behind my back, *na*? How does everyone in the building know about me? Explain that! Leave my house immediately, *ja*, you traitoress!'

She caught Paru's shoulders and shook her like a rabbit.

'Speak! Have you lost your tongue?' She had Paru in an iron clasp.

Rohini would not let the girl slip through her fingers before she had confessed all. She should have known. Paru was privy to all their private discussions. She was a Bengali maid and understood everything they discussed. It was Paru who was spreading the ugly truth. She would ruin Rohini's life.

Paru trembled under her mistress's grasp. 'Ma, I didn't tell anyone. I swear on my mother's life. Let me go, Ma you are hurting me! Help!'

'What do they say about me? *Hain*? I am a servant girl? I am a madwoman? You can tell me, don't be afraid.'

'They know from somewhere, not me, I swear. They read the papers. The day it came out some of my friends showed me the pictures. They can't read English, but their mistresses showed the page. Besides, all the neighbours can hear what you say. The walls in this building are so thin. I tell them you are like a mother to me. So what if your real mother was poor? Look how well you have been brought up by Aunty Indira! Like a fine lady! I tell them, you are so lucky!'

Rohini let go of her shoulders and grasped a bunch of Paru's hair with one hand. She pulled hard, enough to make the young girl cry out in pain. Rohini saw the fear in her eyes.

'You think I am stupid? *Bol*, tell me what you told them and I'll let you go.'

Paru continued to cry and pulled at Rohini's fingers to free herself. Her breath came out in shallow heaves.

'You won't tell? I trusted you, you stubborn little witch!' said Rohini picking up a vase from her bedside unit.

She shook out the dry roses and wielded the heavy vase over Paru's bowed head. This would make her tell the truth. A red mist appeared before Rohini's eyes. She raised the vase higher, threatening to bring it down with all the force in her forearm. Paru would confess, she was sure of it.

The front door opened and Kavita came running in. She rushed into the bedroom snatching the vase from her mother's hands. 'Mummy, stop! What's the matter?'

'Ask her! Ask that little snake! How did Mrs. Bhatt and the people in the building know about me? Paru told everyone and she won't admit it. I'll sack her right now.'

Kavita patted Paru's head and signalled to her to leave the room. She could be heard moaning in the kitchen like a wounded animal.

'I could hear your voice down the hall, outside the flat. You leave all the windows open in autumn when the AC is off. The neighbours' balconies are adjacent to ours. They can hear all our conversations. Why do you think Papa and I speak quietly? You get angry and emotional and you shout at people down the telephone. Your news, at your insistence, was made public in the newspapers. You divulged terrible family secrets on Facebook. At what point did you think you could keep this quiet? Yes, servants talk. But I don't think Paru does. She is different. We are lucky to have her. She treats you like a second mother and today you frightened the poor girl to death. I wouldn't be surprised if she left us tomorrow.'

Kavita fetched her mother a glass of water. Rohini's legs shook. She sat on the bed, urging her daughter to sit next to her. Her voice was hoarse and she had to whisper.

It had started with Sujata's phone call. The words had gone straight to her heart. Then Mrs. Bhatt had come in with her insinuations. Rohini had seen red. She blamed Paru for spreading the nasty gossip. But she could see that perhaps she was wrong. In the heat of the moment she had reacted severely and let her anger get out of control. It was not normal behaviour for her, surely Kavita could see that? She was not a violent woman. This was an isolated incident brought on by stress. She wouldn't really have hit Paru; she was like a daughter to her.

Kavita carried on tidying up the room. She put away her mother's clothes strewn all over the floor. Some were shredded. A glass photo frame was shattered. She stepped outside the room to make a call, no doubt to her father.

Much later when Rohini had calmed down she asked to see Paru. Kavita told her that Paru had gone to bed. She was too upset to speak. Rohini remembered Paru cowering under her wrath.

When Shourav came home, Kavita spoke to him in the lounge. Rohini could hear them talking. She wanted the chance to explain. Shourav looked haggard when he entered their bedroom. Rohini reached out to him, grasping his arms.

'I never meant to hurt her. I am really sorry. Tomorrow I will beg her forgiveness. I was angry, but I would not have hit her with the vase. Don't you believe me?'

Shourav shook his head. 'You don't know what you are capable of at the moment, in a fit of rage. Kavita saw the wild look in your eyes. You were not in your senses. I need to tell Bose.'

He put on his pyjamas and went to the bathroom to brush his teeth. Rohini sat on the bed, twisting the tassel of a cushion. Her family treated her like a madwoman. She would not have been surprised if Shourav slept in the spare bedroom away from a savage being. He took off his slippers and slid under the covers.

'I have spoken to Paru. I am giving the girl a two weeks' vacation. I'll personally drop her off at the station tomorrow. She is too scared to be left alone with you again. I am sorry Rohini, but you could be suffering from paranoia, thinking the whole world is plotting against you. Paru is an innocent girl from the village. What next? Are you going to attack me or Kavita?'

If she could not control her emotions, would he send her away to an institution? Her nightie was drenched in sweat. She rubbed her chest. Should she tell Shourav about her palpitations? Her own family was turning against her. Kavita was lying. She had exaggerated the whole thing to be rid of her. Without her mother around she could do as she pleased.

Earlier, Rohini had heard her speaking to someone on the telephone.

The words were not very clear, but she got the gist. 'Yes Aunty S… I'll tell Papa when he comes.'

Was it Aunty Sujata? Rohini asked Kavita. *No* the girl replied. *Then, who? No one you know, my friend's mother, said Kavita.*

Rohini knew it was a lie. Sujata was setting a trap for her, pushing her towards insanity. She thought it best to apprise Shourav of her version of the events, what had set the catastrophe in motion.

'Your sister said nasty things,' Rohini said in her defence. 'I was very upset.'

'I know. I'll speak to Sujata. She has no right to speak to you like that. These consequences are bound to occur. We'll have to learn to deal with them.'

Rohini blew her nose on a handkerchief. It triggered off a sinus pain. She gritted her teeth waiting for the spasm to pass.

'Then Mrs. Bhatt came. What did you tell her husband? She knows everything. She said servants' talk. That's why I… Paru is Bengali and I thought…' The tassels on the cushion were now twisted beyond repair. Rohini threw it on the floor. 'You're determined to send me to a lunatic asylum. Then you two can build a nice quiet life without me, without any scandal.'

Shourav reached out and patted her arm, dry fingers sending goose bumps up her limb. He was looking up at the ceiling. The fan whirled above. Rohini liked a cool room. Shourav preferred a more even temperature.

'Stop crying, please Rohini. I'm not sending you anywhere. I am worried that you will harm yourself or others. If you had hit Paru on the head with the vase you could have caused a very serious injury, one that could have landed you in court or prison.'

Rohini promised she would never do it again. Shourav rolled over and lay still.

Paru left the following morning without saying goodbye to

Rohini. Sujata arranged for a temporary cook to come by every day, an older woman who would take no nonsense from her employer.

Bose sent a new prescription. He wanted to see her. Her next appointment was three days away. In the meantime he gave her some tranquilisers. He called her several times. She hung up. But she took the medication. She was spiralling down a rabbit hole and like Alice in Wonderland she found herself lost amongst strange characters in a surreal world. Kavita stayed away from her. Perhaps it was Shourav's instructions. The girl was fragile. Her exams were in four months. She needed to concentrate and not be drawn into a theatrical world turning in on itself. Rohini pictured herself stuck in revolving doors trying to get to the other side, but just going round and round.

Chapter 4 Rohini

Rohini sat in Bose's waiting room, knees jiggling against the coffee table; an errant school girl outside the Principal's Office. She stared at the large clock on the vanilla wall, a white square with black Roman numerals. Her hands were folded on her lap; the fingers interlaced so tightly that her knuckles hurt. Shourav and Rohini sat silent, side-by-side. Polly, the twenty-something receptionist, must have taken a hundred calls before the door opened. Rohini watched her mouth, amethyst lips lined with aubergine, open and shut like a delicate goldfish, *Hello Good Evening, Maya Clinic, Yes sir, no madam, thank you, goodbye.*

A middle-aged man in a suit left and Rohini was asked to go in. It was not her normal day. Everything felt disjointed. She did a little Namaste and sat at the edge of her chair. Shourav sat outside waiting to hear the results. She refused to let him sit in in her session promising to be honest and tell the doctor everything.

Rohini wondered if Bose was waiting for her to say something. He was writing notes before she had even begun speaking: *Agitated patient showing signs of violence; Threatened maid; Danger to society.*

'Shourav told me you threatened to hit the maid with a vase. Is that correct?'

She did not have the energy to go over the whys and the provocation from her sister-in-law. The futility of it all and her guilt overcame her.

'Yes, I'm sorry,' she said to Bose after a few minutes.

'Why are you apologising to me?'

'I don't know. Maybe I have let you down. I lost my cool. It won't happen again, I promise on my life.'

'Did you apologise to your maid?'

'I tried to so many times, but they wouldn't let me.'

Bose looked down at his pad. Rohini wondered if his textbooks had answers for every situation or he just made them up. It wasn't like any other field of medicine. There were set treatments for diabetes, heart problems, and liver disorder. His line of work was purely subjective judgement. Although, according to Hippocrates, ill humour—especially melancholy —could be attributed to liver malfunction. Molière had portrayed this condition so well in his play, but Rohini wasn't a misanthrope; she did not quite hate the whole world.

'What should I do? I am angry all the time.'

'I know. You threw a paperweight at me. I should have known then that your anger was getting out of control. You could have injured me.'

'Sorry,' said Rohini again, looking down at her lap. He too was playing on the other field.

'I thought it was a one-off event. We need to address this seriously now before it gets out of hand. I'll give you some new medication, but first I need to understand the cause of your anger. Who are you so angry with?'

'My mother. My situation.'

She felt tired explaining what she had told him already and faltered in her speech, pausing to wipe her face. Bose gave her extra pills to calm her down. He agreed that saying a mantra or listening to Baba Ramji's tapes would be beneficial.

'Will they send me away?' asked Rohini in a voice just above a whisper.

'Not yet,' reassured Bose, 'as long as you keep your temper under control.' He smiled. 'I'm joking. You are a sensible woman who lost control under stress. I know you are not a real danger to anyone at the moment. You gave up the weapon as soon as Kavita disarmed you and you didn't actually hit Paru. I doubt you would have carried out the threat. However, imagine that scene with a pupil. You'll be sacked on the spot and perhaps sued. You can't afford to take that risk. Little things can trigger off an attack. I know you were goading yourself to see how far you would go to search the truth. There is hope for you. Believe me, there are far worse cases. We only institutionalise people who suffer from schizophrenia or other severe cases. You are still well within the safe limits.' He came over and pressed his hand on her right shoulder.

'They don't think so. Will you tell Shourav? He sent the maid away because she is scared to be alone with me. Kavita avoids me.'

He promised he would talk to her husband although he was sure that she was imagining the worst. Counselling the family was part of the treatment. He would speak to Kavita as well. It was important for the others to know how to deal with her stress.

'Truth is, I think it's time I went back to work. I need occupation. Sitting at home receiving people in person and over the telephone is not doing me any good. I have time to brood and get angry,' said Rohini.

'I think it's too early. How about starting a hobby? Singing or art lessons?'

Rohini looked at her hands. They were slim, well-shaped hands. She could not believe she could hurt anyone with those. Would those hands be tamed by art? She was not so sure. There was still a lot of rage in her. She was embarrassed to have her ugly demonic side exposed to her doctor, one who had perhaps admired her a little. No more.

Rohini could return to work after six weeks if she remained stable with no further set back. It gave her a goal. Determined to follow a good behaviour pattern she decided to catalogue her emotions and deal with them in a logical manner. The result was her three-step ERS method.

Emotion- anger

Reason- mother

Solution- talk

Underneath she added an extra note—No matter how angry do not throw things at people or attempt to hurt them. Consequences unimaginable. She underlined this in red. She would laminate this and put up in her room as a constant reminder.

Bose agreed it was a sensible approach.

She left the clinic feeling mildly hopeful. They drove home in silence. She spoke to Shourav briefly in the waiting room about her new medication, but nothing more. He did not prod further. He could easily get the answers from Bose. She was exhausted. All she wanted to do was go home and go to bed. The new maid, Nirmala, had left some *chappaties* and a chicken curry for their dinner. She would heat them up in the microwave.

Rohini stepped out of the lift in Menaka Towers only to be confronted by Mrs. Bhatt. Her way was blocked.

'There you are! I've been ringing your doorbell and no one is home. Is everything okay? The other day there was such a commotion and my maid Bina said *ki*, Madam, Paru has left. Why was she crying for help? What happened? I nearly knocked on your door to see if some intruder was attacking you or your maid. Such troubled times! The other day Ahuja's flat was robbed, *during the day!* The maid let the burglars in; can you believe it? You never know if you are keeping a *chor* in the house. *Accha*, you have to go? Namaste Dr. Saab! Come for tea both of you.'

Shourav inclined his head at Mrs. Bhatt, not bothering to reply. Rohini felt a compulsive need to explain to the quivering backside of her neighbour.

'It was nothing serious, just a minor misunderstanding. You know how dramatic young girls are.'

She did not want the Bhatts to spread rumours about the incident. Who knew when the police would come knocking on the door hearing reports of abuse? Bhatt was hardly in a position to point fingers. Rohini was a model employer compared to that lot.

Later that evening Rohini, dedicated a whole puja hour to do penance for Paru, reciting *slokas*, even prostrating before God, lying on the cold hard tiles for fifteen minutes to pay for her wrathful act. She set aside a pair of gold earrings for the young girl to be offered as a loyalty reward on her return. She would give clothes and rice to the local poor as *dan*, donation to the needy. Perhaps, then, God would forgive her.

Rohini made a trip to the ashram the following week. Baba Ramji was kind enough to allow a private consultation based partly on another generous gift. She had written copious notes about things she wanted to speak to him about, but her mind was now blank in his holy presence.

'What is it my child?' Babaji asked in a gentle voice.

She told him about her birth and the family history of violence. Did a bad spirit possess her?

Babaji stroked his fine white beard for a long time. Rohini

could hear the humming of priests chanting in the main temple. Occasionally a bell rang. Her mind began to clear. In the empty space devoid of words she saw meaning.

'*Sadhana*. The answer is in meditation. Through deep transcendental meditation you will overcome your anxieties. You will ask yourself, who am I? And you will find the answer in your heart. You are Rohini, whatever name they give you in this world, whoever it is who gives birth to you—it does not matter, for you are you. Your *atma* was born and will die. These clothes we wear, our worldly identities, can be thrown away in an instant. If you shed those, will you become someone else? No my child, you will always remain who you are. *God* knows who you are. It is time you make the introduction to your inner self. Shed the outer clothing. Be yourself. Learn to become you.'

Babaji left the room as quietly as he had entered. Rohini went to the temple room and sat on the floor for a long time. She was filled with peace. Lord Krishna's eyes seemed to see through her. She could almost hear his flute playing in Vrindavan, the garden where he played with the milkmaids.

It was the first day after Rohini's long sick leave. Everything seemed changed. The school had been redecorated. On freshly painted walls the students had written quotes from famous people, Gandhi, Shakespeare, and Abraham Lincoln.

There was a shuffle of feet and murmured Good Morning Madams as the class settled down. Rohini read the first verse of Tennyson's 'The Lady of Shallot' aloud.

'Any questions?' she asked the class. No one answered. She tried a different method. 'Okay let's discuss life. Any questions at all?'

Sangeeta raised her hand. Rohini sighed. The student, known for her frequent trips to the Principal's office, was chewing gum again and a new tattoo could be seen on her left arm. Rohini knew it would be a difficult question, something to shock the class, no doubt sex-related. She leaned back against the desk and asked, 'Yes?'

'Madam, did you *reaa-lly* try to kill yourself?' asked Sangeeta continuing to chew.

Black eyes pierced Rohini's with an intensity she found hard to bear. She prayed Sangeeta would not ask the unaskable, *did your father kill your grandfather?* Her life had become a Shakespearean tragedy.

In-drawn breaths were released in a long hiss. Forty heads turned towards the girl. Rohini willed her hands to stop trembling. She focused on a spot just above Sangeeta's head. Palgrave's book of poems fell on the floor with a soft thud.

Heads turned this way and that; there were whispered consultations, unprepared for such a situation.

Kumar walked towards Rohini.

'Here, Madam, please sit. Sharmila, get Mrs. Chatterjee a drink. And you lot, shut the fuck up,' he yelled pausing to say 'sorry,' to his teacher.

By then a few of the girls had gathered around Rohini, stroking her back. 'Sorry miss, she didn't mean it like that.'

Sangeeta could be seen sobbing into another classmate's arms.

'Shall we take you to the staff common room? We'll study by ourselves if you want to recover there,' one suggested.

Rohini shook her head. The mist was clearing a little.

'Could you open the windows? It's suffocating in here.'

Rohini asked the class to read the poem by themselves and prepare a list of questions for discussion in the next lesson. A gentle susurration of voices could be heard rising above the shouts of the workmen outside. She rested her head on the desk, wanting to fall asleep and enjoy a temporary escape.

A cool hand touched her arm. It was Sangeeta. Rohini took one look at the girl's mascara smeared face and felt pity. She was a mere waif in her skinny jeans and a vest top.

'Can I sit with you?' asked Sangeeta.

Rohini nodded and returned her heavy head to the wooden desk. Sangeeta stroked her hair, up and down, up and down, in long slow movements. She bent closer to whisper in Rohini's ear.

'I was adopted too, you know. I found out when I was about eight. I don't know my real parents, but I bet they are servant class and I must have been illegitimate. Once I snatched a lollypop from my cousin's hands and my aunt said to another lady *you can't hide their natures, no matter what nice education you give them. Servant class people are born thieves, they can't help it.* I took out my anger on my poor cousin and hit her with a metal toy car, narrowly missing an eye.'

Rohini sat up. 'I'm sorry, Sangeeta. I didn't know. It hurts, doesn't it?'

'Ya. But Ma'am, at least you know your real mother. I will never know mine. I'll probably have nothing to say to her. I come from such a different social world.'

'Me too. Sangeeta, how does everyone know what happened to me?' asked Rohini, tying her hair into a knot.

'Newspapers, Social network, gossip. They piece together all the juicy bits and make it into a soap opera. No one here knows I am adopted. I trust you with this secret. It's not worth dying over you know, madam. You have a wonderful family. One day I hope I have my own.'

'You will,' said Rohini touching Sangeeta's cheek. 'You are beautiful and smart. Don't let anyone take that away from you!'

Rohini had an appointment with the Principal at five. She dragged her tired feet into Anjali Bhojraj's office. The room was decorated with tribal art. An enormous rubber plant sat in one corner.

'I am worried about you, Rohini. I'll come straight to the point. I wanted to see you today anyway, your first day back after a long break. I only have the doctor's certificate stating that you were suffering from stress and that you needed hospitalisation. But of course word has got around of your attempted suicide. Thank the modern world of Facebook, every private event goes viral.'

Caught in Bhojraj's stare, Rohini did not know what she was supposed to say. Should she apologise, or deny everything?

'Kumar told me what happened in class today. Of course I read the papers and am aware of the incident in Delhi. This is a prestigious school. Parents don't want to see our teachers' names splashed unflatteringly across the tabloids. I had a difficult time explaining to some that I don't judge my teachers by their castes or backgrounds. I do however judge them by their mental ability to handle stress.'

Anjali paced the room seeming to address the plant or her paintings, not looking at Rohini directly.

'They have to be emotionally stable. Teachers deal with vulnerable children who imitate their mentors. What would they say if one of our students took his life? They will say they followed their teacher's example. You see, what a legal minefield you have put me into? Rohini, you are a good teacher and I value your experience. I've known you for a long time, so here is what I propose. We deny the 'suicide attempt'. If anyone asks, you had a meltdown. It happens all the time to teachers. You are seeking treatment. You are fit to return to work. Is that clear?'

Rohini mumbled a form of affirmative. Anjali stood, indicating the end of the meeting.

'You have my full support to carry on with your current workload on the understanding that if things start to get difficult for you, you'll tell me. I can cut back your hours for a while. If another incident takes place I'll have to consider replacing you. I have already had to fight with the Board of Directors to reinstate you. I can't do it twice.' Anjali stood. She touched Rohini's shoulder 'Come, it's not so bad. You are back to work. Things will improve. Life takes us down difficult paths sometimes, but if you hang on to your faith you'll find your way back.'

Rohini thanked Anjali and left. What would her Head teacher think if she knew about the incident with Paru? Do teachers with a history of attempted assault keep their jobs? Rohini did not think so. She would have to step very carefully in her private and public life.

Outside the school building Rohini could see their dark blue Honda. It was empty. Perhaps Shiv had gone to get a cup of tea. A group of boys were loitering in front, looking through the windows. Traffic flowed past in unending waves, horns blowing, tyres screeching, and eddying swirls of exhaust fumes. Rohini stepped out on to the melting tarmac. A crescendo of klaxons deafened her. She felt a rush of wind from a heavy goods vehicle rolling past her.

'*Madam!*' shouted Shiv, diving into the river of cars from the other bank. He held her arm in a firm grip with one hand and halted the approaching wall of cars with his other. She should have called him, he complained.

Rohini told him not to fuss. The bumpy road worsened her nausea. Just then Shourav called the driver on his mobile and said he would be late and intended to take a cab back. She was relieved. They wouldn't have to go miles across traffic to pick him up.

The next day Rohini woke feeling fresh after a good night's sleep. The children at school were chastened following the previous day's drama. Lessons went smoothly for once and she planned the following week's classes. She was going to read out Sarojini Naidu's poems to them. The class had shown an interest in Indian authors. Why not tweak the set lessons a bit and deliver a customised package? She was tired of following rules. She would immerse herself in her teaching profession, bringing back some of that passion she had when she first qualified. Her head was full of plans. She even hummed on the car journey back from school.

When Rohini returned home that night, there was a message flashing on her answerphone. She expected Shourav's voice saying he will be late. A woman spoke instead.

'Rohini, this is Champa. How are you? We've all been very anxious about your health. Listen, Kanaka-di has offered to take over from you and make all the arrangements for Saraswati Puja. I know it is a few months away, but we must start soon. The voting will take place tomorrow for the new President's role. Do come if you feel up to it. We are all behind you. But you must take it easy. We feel we would like to take the burden off your shoulders. Call me.'

Rohini pressed delete. It had begun. She was being gently removed from her position as the President of the Puja Committee. This was the thanks she got after three years of organising New Year festival and Durga Puja. Their events were the most talked-about in Mumbai. It was Rohini who thought of a Facebook page and a blog for their social club.

As long as she was a Brahmin, of priest caste, she was looked upon as a fitting leader. Her current status of being illegitimate and born into a low caste Christian family was not acceptable to the members. She was an outcast.

Rohini stared at a glass-framed picture of Goddess Durga they had bought in Shantiniketan in Bengal. The image was sculpted out of delicate white shola wood. She lowered herself on to the floor and attempted a lotus position. Closing her eyes she began to recite *slokas* from *Bhagavad Gita*, the song of God. She needed to hear the wise counsel of Lord Krishna urging his charioteer Arjuna to overcome his doubts and prepare for the battle against his kinsmen.

That person who excels over all others, who looks with an equal eye on well-wishers, friends, foes, neutrals, mediators, hateful ones, relatives, the virtuous and the sinful.

The practice of meditation performed by a yogi was written in the holy book she had bought at Babaji's ashram. The book recommended sitting on a grass mat, *kusha*, but her embroidered cloth would have to do. She sat erect and still, harnessing her mind to concentrate on the Supreme Self, be free of desires, be self-controlled and rid her soul of any hankering for possessions.

The mind Oh Krishna is fickle... no less difficult to control than the wind itself.

The Lord replied

No doubt, the mind is restless and difficult to control. But Oh Son of Kunti (Arjuna), it can be brought under control through practice and renunciation.

As the clock ticked away the minutes and Rohini's bottom gradually became numb, followed by pins and needles in her ankles, she wondered if Nirvana would take longer to attain. She hoped for inner peace. It would no longer matter who ran the puja club, or who had given birth to her. Although meditation calmed her mind to a certain extent, the question of her mother still troubled her. She finished with *jop*, an intense prayer counting off the various names of Krishna, touching all the lines of her fingers with her thumb bent inwards.

'Who are you talking to?' asked Shourav stepping inside.

'Take your shoes off! How many times do I have to tell you to leave your shoes outside my puja room? Do what you like all over the flat, but this little room is mine,' cried Rohini with her hands still folded.

She turned her head to address the offending shoes. The shoes and their owner beat a quiet retreat.

'Sorry,' she said when emerging eventually from her sanctuary.

It was almost seven. Rohini sat next to her husband on the sofa. Shourav was watching India vs West Indies in Madras. It was the third day of an exciting cricket match. She could not wait for the highlights to finish.

'Champa called. They are voting for a new president of the puja committee. I am obviously a deranged and low-caste person, unfit for the role.'

Shourav put his paper down. 'So? Don't go to the meetings anymore. Who cares about the puja arrangements? It's too much stress for you. We'll go to the South Mumbai puja event instead. The Dases go there, excellent food. They serve goat curry on the ninth day of the festival.'

'Is that all you care about, good food? Your wife has been snubbed by the Mumbai Bengali circle and you just think about who serves the best curry?'

'It's either that, or sex. Judging by your current mood I'm guessing the latter is off the menu,' replied Shourav with a wink.

Rohini chuckled, nudging her shoulders against her husband's, letting some of the tension ooze out of her. She felt a rosy blush on her cheeks; Shourav could be so charming when he flirted.

Chapter 5 Rohini

One morning a letter arrived in the post for Rohini. She recognised the Kolkata postmark instantly and left the envelope on the corner unit to open later. Maria's shaky handwriting was scrawled across the front—Mrs. Chattarji, Monaka Towers, 114 Park Road, Moombay. It was a miracle the letter had reached her with all the spelling mistakes. It meant Maria had not shown the letter to Indira for checking. Rohini waited until her day was nearly over to open the dreaded missive.

She needed her reading glasses to decipher the squiggly letters forming crooked lines across a page torn out of an exercise book. It took a while to translate Maria's English. She threw it in the bin after skimming over the content. Certain words and phrases danced before her eyes, 'I em so shemed. Forgiv me. I love you my childe.' The burden of guilt was evident in every malformed word.

The next morning Rohini called home. Maria answered after clearing her throat loudly. *'Hello?'* she shouted accusatorially, as though she had already repeated the salutation several times without a response from the caller. Rohini held the phone away from her.

'Is Ma there?'

'Are you well?' *Bhalo accho?*

'Yes. Can you put me through to Ma?'

It was imperative to speak to Indira first. Rohini had mulled over the matter the previous evening and it was the only way. Shourav need not be consulted. This was her home as well.

Indira came on the phone, sounding tired. She had had a restless night. Rohini had too, but dawn brought clarity.

'I'll send tickets for you and Maria to come over to Mumbai. We need to talk face to face and sort this thing out. You'll have to buy her some new saries. I'll transfer the money. Something from Bengal Home Industries, nice prints, some silk, some cotton. And blouses and petticoats that *match!* Buy some new sandals as well, and a perfume, something subtle, not too cloying. I'll provide everything else. You two can share the guest bedroom. We have twin beds in there. Is that okay?'

Indira agreed, *thik acchey*, she said with barely a pause after Rohini's offer. She only asked if her son-in-law was happy with the invitation. Rohini assured her that it was her decision and of course he would respect it.

'Practise English with her. Her Hindi is good so that's no problem. Help her read the newspapers, tell her what's going on in the world in case people ask or she has to join in the conversation.'

Rohini felt she was forgetting the most important thing that would give the whole game away, but couldn't quite recall what it was. She was not going to hide the ugly truth, just dress it up a little.

She consulted her list. 'I nearly forgot. She needs a decent leather handbag. Go to South City Mall. Take her with you in fact. She needs to know the prices of things and brands. I think you should get her involved in food shopping as well. God knows how long it's been since she has lived in the real world. She needs to talk about everyday things not just her prayer books and rosary beads.'

'Really dear, you are being a bit harsh on her. Maria knows every aspect of this house. I am giving you my word; she won't embarrass you. She wears simple clothes because she doesn't like to show off. I buy her new saries every year, but she prefers my old ones. She doesn't meet many people in our house, but of course if she meets your friends she must be better-presented.'

Rohini was not as confident of Maria's social skills, but she felt more reassured.

'I'll book a flight for you two. Will Baba be all right for a couple of weeks? I won't be able to put you all up in our flat.'

'Yes, yes. No problem, dear. Bibhuti and Durga will take good care of him. I'll bring Maria's medications as well, but you should warn your doctor in case her diabetes gets worse or something.'

'Oh God, I had forgotten that. Bring plenty of her insulin injections. You better tell me about her diet.'

'You know the usual, no sugar, and not too much fat. I'll tell your cook.'

Rohini rearranged the guest bedroom at least five times with Paru's help. The maid had returned after her vacation to resume her position. Rohini preferred Nirmala's experienced help, but Paru's family needed the money. They put their trust in Rohini and hoped Mistress had recovered from her sickness. Paru suggested an *ojha*, one who exorcised ghosts. For surely Madam had been possessed when she attacked Paru? Everyone in the village believed that. Paru had come back armed with an iron key to ward off evil. She burnt a bunch of herbs every morning to rid the place of any lingering malign presence.

Everything was dusted down, beds were separated, the wardrobe cleared out. The bedside table would double up as Maria's medicine cabinet so that she would have everything ready to hand. Every inch of the room was washed, polished, scrubbed. Fresh towels adorned the bathroom. Rohini remembered Maria's favourite soap, Mysore Sandalwood. Her mother liked Pears. She kept both in the bathroom cabinet, along with a jar of Pond's cream and imported Yardley's talcum powder. A new bucket and jug were placed in the shower room knowing Maria and her mother could not manage the shower. They would bathe in the old-fashioned way. A geyser provided hot water for chilly mornings.

Rohini picked up the two women from Mumbai domestic airport. She told Shiv and Paru that Indira Madam and Aunty Maria were coming for a visit and avoided referring to the latter as her mother. They both knew the real score, but it helped to keep up the pretence. Another realisation hit her en-route to the airport. She would have to talk to Maria. There was no avoiding it now. So far brief exchanges had sufficed. Ma was there to fill in the gaps. But at home, in her territory, Rohini knew it would be rude to ignore Maria's existence. She would have gladly effaced Maria's ghostly presence in her life, a nagging reminder of her birth, but she remembered Ma's upbringing.

'How was the flight?' she asked the ladies.

They replied, simultaneously talking into each of Rohini's

ears. It was Maria's first flight and she had not dared to use the toilet for fear of getting stuck in mid-air. The food was so-so. The potato curry was a bit too rich and spicy. The *parathas* were soft and served hot! Rohini smiled at the way the two women finished each other's sentences.

'I was scared at first when the plane took off. *Bapre*, my stomach went *dhophank* down to my knees. It reminded me of the fun fair rides we used to go to. Remember Sister? Every puja time we went to the Big Rajgarh Mela, with giant *Nakar dolnas*, that swung us round and round, up and down. Coming down was scary as well. *Oof!* I was glad when it was over. But it's so quick. It would have taken us two days by train, no?' Maria's simple chatter filled awkward gaps.

Rohini pointed out the sights—The Taj Hotel, where the terrorist attack had taken place, India Gate, Marine Drive. Maria was awed by the sea.

'Can we go there, sister? It's been a long-long time since I saw the sea.'

Indira agreed. 'Yes, I too would like to see it. Is it Chowpatti Beach Rohini, where it's very lively and there are lots of food stalls?'

It was not an area Rohini frequented preferring Juhu Beach with better crowds. But she would bring them over one day, to savour some street life. They were cooped up in a big old house for months, not stepping out of their time-warped world.

Rohini took a few days leave to be at home to help. Maria seemed at ease in her new surroundings. She and Indira took an early morning walk in the compound gardens. They stopped every few feet to inspect the plants or talk to a gardener. Rohini found it tiresome to go at their pace and finished her brisk walk in twenty minutes. By the time she completed her prayers and shower, the ladies were back, out of breath but full of chatter. Sometimes they would bring a plant cutting and offer it to Rohini for her pots in the balcony. Other times they would stay out later talking to a neighbour. Rohini discouraged them mixing with the gossipmongers, but Indira would not listen.

'They need to get to know us normally not through gossip.'

*

Rohini let the ladies settle down in her home for a few days before arranging a tea party to meet her new friends. For once she had taken Shourav's advice and cut off relations with the old conservative set. She fretted all day about the food they would serve and the conversation that would take place. Menus were planned and scrapped. The sofa and chairs were moved around quite a few times until she was happy with the arrangement. She shut the door to the shrine as the Rotary Club members were primarily Christians.

'These are a new bunch of friends. I want to make a fresh start. Please try to understand and stand by me.'

'Of course,' said Indira 'we'll do everything right.'

Maria nodded her head vigorously. 'Nuththing to worry about, my dear.'

Together the women prepared the snacks: triangular chicken sandwiches, iced cup cakes, a savoury semolina dish and a pot of fine Darjeeling Tea. Listening to Indira and Maria reminiscing about the tea parties in Shanti Niwas calmed Rohini a bit.

The party of five arrived punctually and there was a reassuring murmur of small talk as they introduced themselves to the host family. It was time for Rohini to present her parents. Her heart beat rapidly and her throat was dry as she stood next to her mothers.

'This is my mother Indira. Maria is my real mother, but she was on her own when my father died so my mother adopted me.' Her circuitous explanation of her circumstances seemed to baffle the tea party circle ever so slightly, but they were too polite to probe further.

'How long are you here for?' 'Have you been to Mumbai before?' they asked the visitors and Indira answered on behalf of both.

Maria shifted in her wicker stool. Rohini had wanted to seat her on the sofa next to her mother, but Maria insisted she was more comfortable on the *mora*.

'It's where I always sit, even at home.'

Rohini had relented. If something could go wrong, it would.

Paru brought in the tea tray. Rohini signalled to Maria with her eyes, forbidding her to help. Maria clasped her hands on her lap and looked out of the window opposite. Rohini served the food on delicate bone china plates. Once she had poured the tea, she relaxed. The conversation turned to fund raising activities. Indira had lots of good ideas. The group was interested to hear about her charity work. Maria fiddled with the end of her sari, straightening out the pleats, pressing them flat.

Acharna explained the role of Rotary Club to the new members. Indira nodded, understanding the Club's range of activities encompassing the needs of the community.

'Would you like to attend our next meeting?' Acharna asked Rohini's house guests. 'We meet once a month at the Taj Hotel, where Rotary Club has met since the beginning. I can take down your names to make temporary badges. Security is stringent since the terrorist attack. We need to give the list of members and guests to the hotel before we attend. It's just a routine matter.'

Rohini wanted to catch her mother's eye to dissuade her. She wouldn't be able to guard Maria in a large gathering. But it was too late.

Acharna asked her mother 'Your good name and title madam?' 'Indira Roy,' her mother answered. Acharna turned to the silent figure of Maria.

'And your name Madam, Mrs...' The question hung in the air like a giant mushroom cloud.

Rohini remembered what she had forgotten in her list of things to prepare. A Name. Maria looked at Rohini, panic showing clearly in her dull eyes.

'D'Souza,' replied Rohini, thinking quickly, 'Mrs. John D'Souza.'

'Maria, my name is Maria.'

'So, Mrs. D'Souza, you are Christian like me. Are you Catholic or Protestant?' asked Jenny, the young treasurer.

'Catholic.'

'I'm sorry?'

'Catholic,' repeated Maria a little louder, looking around blindly.

Rohini shared her mother's fear, feeling the tentacles across the room.

'That's great! Me too. We are renovating a church in the Southern district. It's a poor area and the church roof needs repairing. Could we ask for your support? Please aunty. I'll take you to see it one day. It has the most amazing frescoes.'

Rohini caught Maria's eye, a deer trapped in a headlight. She will explain frescoes to her later. 'Of course, you can count on her support. I'll make a donation to the Church.'

'Good. I'll take you there next week Aunty and you can pray for a while.'

Maria's face softened and her shoulders relaxed.

'I'm from Goa and a group of us go to St. Agnes's Church in Bandra. But the masses in Goa are the best especially on Christmas Eve.' Jenny moved closer to the elderly lady.

Rohini leaned forward as far as she could go without tipping her chair over. Archana tried to draw her attention to a leaflet published by Rotary Club. They wanted Rohini to help start a website.

'Yes, yes, okay, let me see,' said Rohini, grabbing the leaflet with one hand, but not letting Maria drift out of her earshot.

She was astonished to see her mother step out of the shadows. Maria was telling Jenny about the church in Rajgarh.

'The ceiling so high, with painting on top. And beautiful statues, Mother Mary *fully* covered in gold... not real gold, but gold painting you know. Once a year at Christmas, Indira takes me to St. George's Church in Khiddirpur for midnight mass. When Rohini baby was little I take her there, but she was sleeping all the time on my lap,' Maria cackled.

Rohini could not remember these nocturnal visits to the church. She must have been very small. Jenny and Maria were chatting away like old friends.

'Then afterwards we could go to Chowpatty beach and have some *pau bhaji,*' offered Jenny. 'You must try the local food Aunty.' Maria looked at Rohini, as eager as a child promised a new treat.

Rohini knew Maria was trying to relieve her of an irksome duty. She could take Indira to the more classy resort of Juhu, without the oppressive presence of her socially unacceptable biological mother.

'It's okay. We plan to go there ourselves. But thanks for the offer. I am sure Maria Aunty will enjoy the visit to the church though,' Rohini added as a concession.

Damn, she had said Aunty. It was difficult to change the habit of a lifetime.

Later that evening, the ladies gathered in Indira's room to discuss the success of their soirée.

'That went okay I think,' said Indira taking off her gold chain and placing it on the dressing table.

Maria was completing her ablutions in the bathroom. She said 'went well' as an echo of Indira's sentence.

Rohini smiled with relief. 'Do you think Jenny was being genuine with Maria or just snoopy?' she whispered to her mother.

The door to the bathroom was now shut. Indira held Rohini's hand.

'Dear, you are being paranoid. You can't protect Maria from others all the time. You have to let her mix with people if that is what you want. In my house she likes to be private.'

'You could have given her the status of a family friend. She was embarrassed because she felt she was a servant.'

'Rohini dear, you don't know what people are like! They could tell she was not our class and would have treated her as a servant no matter what we did. How do you think they would have behaved towards you if they had known? Servant's daughter, that's what you would have become. What choice did I have?'

Rohini winced at the s-word that cropped up so often with relation to Maria's status and thereby her own. Unlike Indira, Rohini could not accept their social differences with such nonchalance.

Maria emerged from the bathroom dwarfed in a cotton nightie that Rohini had bought for her. She shrunk a little seeing her daughter sitting on the bed with her mother. After applying some Nivea cream generously on her face until her skin was completely white, Maria sat on a stool next to the bed. The next few minutes were spent rubbing the cream in. Rohini wished that at some point in their visit they would sit together on the same bed or sofa, side by side, all differences forgotten.

'Have you taken your medication?' Indira asked Maria, breaking the ice. She took the pot of cream and put some on her face. 'We've been here a week and this jar is almost empty. If you're looking for a youthful skin, it's too late dear!'

'Always you joke with me. The winter air is not good for skin.' Maria rummaged through the drawer in the bedside cabinet. 'I just need to take the injection.' She waited with the syringe tucked into her lap.

'I'll go to bed soon,' said Rohini. 'I was just telling Ma that the evening went well. Jenny seems to like you.'

This was one of the first remarks she had made directly to Maria. It felt like a little breakthrough.

Maria nodded with her head down. 'Nice girl,' she replied almost inaudibly.

Rohini felt a little stab in her heart. When did she stop being nice?

'*Achcha*, I am off to bed,' said Rohini closing the bedroom door behind her.

About a quarter of an hour later she reentered the room. Maria was praying by her bedside table where an empty insulin syringe lay next to her bible. Indira was sitting on her bed, reading a book.

'What is the matter?' asked Indira, 'did you forget something?'

Rohini took a deep breath. Maria kissed her rosary beads, at the end of her prayer. She rose stiffly using the corner of the table for support. An evening breeze blew the curtains inside the room almost enveloping her thin frame. Maria closed the shutters, coaxing in the unruly voile. Indira snapped her book shut. She folded her reading glasses and placed them on the bedside table with an impatient clatter.

'*Ki?*' prompted Indira, what is it?

Rohini sat on the corner of the bed furthest from her mother. She fingered the tassels of the bedspread.

'I was thinking perhaps I should call Maria by some other name. After all if I am introducing her to people as my real mother I can hardly call her aunty. I thought maybe Maria-Ma maybe appropriate while you are in Mumbai. In Calcutta we can carry on the same.' Rohini was looking at the mosaic floor, but she looked up briefly to see the reaction.

Maria's cataract ridden eyes lit up. Rohini wondered how long she had waited to hear her daughter call her *mother*.

'One name for people here, one name for people there, it's so confusing. Just stick to one. Keep it simple,' said Indira.

'But you don't understand. Our family and friends in Calcutta know us as we were before; Maria aunty was my nanny. I can't call her mother there, it would be awkward.'

'As soon as you decided to make this affair public, it became awkward. You'll get used to it in time, and so will they.' Indira picked up her book to indicate the end of discussion.

Maria's sitting position had not changed at all, but Rohini thought her back looked straighter as she voiced her opinion, a rare moment of putting herself forward.

'Do what you think is best dear. Think about it tonight. To change a name is hard. If I had to call you by another name I would find it difficult. It takes time to adjust. Maria Ma sounds so nice, but you decide *beti*,' said Maria. 'I don't mind what you call me.'

'Ok, *Thik acchey*. I'll see you in the morning,' said Rohini once more closing the door.

The following Sunday, Rohini took her mother and Maria to the beach. Shourav stayed at home with Kavita, giving the three ladies a chance to bond. Shiv dropped them off at the beach. The sand felt cool under the soles of their bare feet. It was late afternoon and it had been overcast all day. They lifted their saries up and let the wind play around their ankles. Paddling in the sea was refreshing after a sticky humid day. Gentle waves tickled their toes.

'I remember when we went to Puri. The waves were sooo big. Rohini baby nearly fell over,' recalled Maria.

'I was really scared of the waves.'

Her heart beat at a furious pace watching the giant curls coming towards her. She was swung out over the crest by a lifeguard. Thrill overtook fear. The water receded on the wet sand, sliding underneath her

239

feet, an eerie life force. Some day she was sure the waves would carry her away from her mother, to a distant land. She would be lost forever. They could never understand why she cried so much.

'Yes, but once Baba carried you into the sea and swung you over the waves you laughed.'

'Baba played with me? I don't remember that.'

'You were only five. After the holidays he used to take you swimming every Saturday. You would come home with a large lollipop if you stayed in the water for twenty minutes. He spoilt you!'

Until Raja came along, thought Rohini.

'Sister, do you remember the house in Puri, with large balconies? The fishermen sold fresh sardines, which we fried up. Oh so nice, I can just taste that food now.'

Chowpatty Beach stretched behind them polka-dotted with people in all colours: purples, oranges, limes and yellow. The wind scooped up ponytails, braids, *dupattas* and *pallus*. It tossed up whispers, laughter, balloons, and kites. Bright shirts opened up like sails in high tide, saries made upside down bells. The salt air coated their tongues, and matted their hair.

A waft of *pau bhaji* and *pakoras* made their mouths water. Rohini ordered a selection of street food for them to try— toasted bread with spicy potatoes, and *gol gappa* crispy semolina balls filled with chickpeas and dipped in tamarind sauce.

Later, Rohini took them to Paradise Mall. The ladies from Calcutta had not seen a shopping mall of that size and grandeur. The guard at the door looked Maria up and down. Rohini knew that if Maria had come alone she would not have been admitted. They would have asked to see a credit card or something. With Indira and Rohini, she was accepted as a poor relative or most likely domestic help, someone who would carry their bags.

Rohini wanted to show them a sari shop, but Maria did not want to go in. 'It's too grand for me. I'd be afraid to ask the price of anything!' she giggled nervously.

'You can come with me. We don't have to buy anything,

just look,' said Rohini.

She wanted Maria to see her world, where she shopped, where she drank coffee with her friends. Indira nudged Maria along. The ladies pushed open the glass door into a palace of shimmering fabrics. A mist of cool air fanned their faces. They were asked to sit. Maria sat gingerly on the edge of a stool, her back ramrod straight.

'Would you like some masala tea?' the proprietor asked.

'Yes please, one without sugar,' replied Rohini in her haughtiest tone.

Indira looked down through bifocal lenses at a sari labelled 'Murshibad silk' with what appeared to be disdain, but was really thinly disguised suspicion.

'Where is your factory?' she asked.

'Bangalore, Ma'am.'

'Then it is Bangalore silk, isn't it, not Murshidabad?' Indira directed her question at a senior lady sales assistant. 'Murshidabad is in Bengal. I don't think you would sell them here.'

'Urmm, we do sell some Murshidabad. But this one's from Bangalore, you're right Ma'am,' the assistant conceded, not wishing to lose the custom of a classy lady.

'See, it is thick silk. Murshidabad is thinner.'

It was a peacock shade, an enigmatic mélange of purple and blue, intricately embroidered in silver. Rohini looked at the price tag, 'Rs 8500.' a bit steep for an impulse-buy. If it were close to Puja she would have bought it for herself on Shourav's behalf. Besides she felt a twinge of guilt not considering gifts for her mothers.

'What about one for yourself?' Rohini asked her mother in Bengali.

'Absolutely not! At these cutthroat prices? You must be crazy. You bought Maria a few saries already and I still have your Puja gift practically new. Get one for yourself. You go to parties and things.'

'This is one of the cheaper ones in our range. If you want something a bit more special we can show you ones with pure zari.'

Rohini ultimately walked out of the shop with a large bag.

Maria had not spoken a word during the whole time they spent inside the boutique.

'How about a coffee?' asked Rohini.

They walked in to Café Haven and ordered three cappuccinos. Maria marvelled at the creaminess of the hot beverage. They laughed at her milk moustache.

'Hello,' said a liquid voice, penetrating their laughter.

Rohini looked up. Champa stood there, resplendent in an orange georgette sari draped across her large belly, the thin material hiding nothing. Long gold earrings dangled from her ears.

'I thought it was you! How are you? It's been so long,' she said dragging a chair across and sitting down. She clicked her finger at a waiter even though it was supposed to be self-service.

'One expresso please.'

'I am cutting down on fat,' she said looking at their frothy drinks.

Rohini took a large swig of coffee.

'It's a pity you didn't turn up at our meetings. Hope you are better now. We were genuinely concerned about your health,' said Champa resting two plump elbows on the table.

Rohini had picked up a magazine and was staring at a page of glamorous models.

'You must bring your guests to our New Year Festivals if they are going to be here for a while.'

'I am Rohini's mother, Mrs. Roy,' said Indira folding her hands in a belated salutation.

'Oh, *acchha. Namaskar* Aunty!'

'And you Madam? Are you also related to Rohini?' Champa asked Maria.

Champa's bulldog tactics astonished Rohini. 'Yes this is Maria D'Souza, my birth mother. No doubt you have heard all about the *ketchcha* in our family.'

'No, no, I don't listen to gossip. People have nothing to do, spreading nasty rumours. I don't believe everything I hear. It is so nice to meet you all. Mrs. D'Souza, is this your first time in Mumbai?'

'Yes,' said Maria, stirring her coffee.

Champa studied her with an invisible magnifying glass, recording all the details to be reported to the circle later.

'Well, I must dash. Call me!' She sailed out of the coffee shop rustling oversized paper bags.

The waiter came out with her expresso watching his customer rush off into the crowd.

'Let's go home,' said Rohini.

The others murmured their assent. Indira walked ahead with Rohini, leaving Maria behind to stare at shop windows.

'Don't worry about Champa. It's a good thing she has seen us. She can tell the others what she likes. But the fact that she saw us having a coffee together proves there is nothing dirty or ugly we are trying to hide.'

'Ma, you can dress someone in silk saries and pearls, but you can't hide their birth. I am beginning to think the same about myself. I feel a fraud. This expensive sari I bought, is it covering up where I come from?'

'Your snobby friends embraced you into their fold before they knew about all this. People just see the exterior. If I had dressed Maria in fine clothes and sent her to Spoken English classes to improve her accent, maybe we would have fooled people. But they would have still asked questions. Who is she? Where is she from? Why does she live with you? It was better to keep her in the background. If your friends can't accept you, it's not worth having their friendship or respect.' Indira linked her elbow with Rohini's.

Maria lagged behind, lost in window-shopping. She stopped now and then to peer through the glass, holding her spectacles away from her nose to get a clearer view. Indira and Rohini waited for her to catch up.

'Come on, slow coach. We'll miss Paru's dinner at this rate!' Indira tucked her other arm through Maria's. 'Did you see some nice jewellery Maria? It's not too late to catch a boyfriend in Mumbai.'

Indira's laugh was like tinkling bells, thought Rohini. You can't learn such examples of good breeding.

Maria joined in, 'Sister, you are too much joking all the time.' Her voice cracked and she was overcome by a coughing spasm.

Rohini was afraid that Maria would need to spit beetle leaf juice and looked around for a waste bin. It had been a mistake bringing Maria to the shopping mall. It was her quiet retreat, where she met friends. It was where she had been meeting Farooq last summer. A more unsettling thought entered her head. She had worried about marrying a Musulman, giving up her religion, sharing her life with beefeaters. Had she known then that she was of quasi-Muslim descent, would that have changed her destiny? She could have been living right now with the love of her life.

Chapter 6 Rohini

Rohini bumped into the headmistress one afternoon after a string of classes ranging from Standard eight to twelve. Covering for an absent colleague meant an increased workload. She was happy to do it knowing others had done the same when she was ill, but the drain on her energy level was significant. By five, the school corridors were empty of running footsteps and laughter bouncing off the walls. The extra planning and marking had taken a toll on her. All Rohini wanted to do was to sit quietly and sort herself out. Going home would mean distractions and tensions she was not quite ready to face that evening.

There was no one in the library except Ms. Arora, sorting out the index cards. The thick silence was a balm to Rohini's tired spirit. There was a lingering smell of old books—dust, dankness and something she could not quite define. It elevated her mind just to be in this room. Philosophical thoughts captured in scholarly tomes floated in the air like lost souls who had not crossed over, forever imprisoned within these walls.

Her work could wait. There was something deliciously indulgent about leafing through a book of poems. Her affinity with verses had not abated since childhood. She read Coleridge, her mouth moving silently to The Rime of the Ancient Mariner, feet tapping the ground. Her body swayed as she felt the waves; she was being tossed in the ocean.

The words were barely visible after a half hour had passed. Heavy curtains obscured the view of the world outside. Ms. Arora did not look like the sort of person who embraced light. Despite her efforts to shut out nature, the curtains glowed with the burnt orange light of a setting sun.

Rohini yawned. Her hand was cramped where she had rested her head. She needed a coffee to wake up. The librarian did not allow any food or drink in her sacred sanctum so Rohini made her way to the staffroom. It would be empty by now and she could make herself a coffee in peace.

Anjali Bhojraj exited the room colliding into Rohini.

'The coffee machine in my room is broken,' Anjali

explained.

Rohini switched on the kettle. Anjali was still there, hovering by the door.

'Anything the matter? Why haven't you gone home yet?' she asked Rohini.

'Nothing's wrong. With Nalini's absence, I have extra work, which I thought I'd finish in the library. There are just too many distractions at home. It's so peaceful here after everyone has left.'

Anjali sipped her drink, blowing on it now and then. Still she did not go away. Rohini fidgeted with the cap of the coffee jar, nearly dropping it.

'You know, if you have any problems at school, anyone says anything nasty to you, you just tell me. I believe in zero tolerance when it comes to bullying. Are the other teachers okay with you?'

This solicitude from Anjali Bhojraj was surprising. She had not taken Rohini's occasional tardiness lightly and questioned her frequent sick leave. Bhojraj was known amongst the staff to be a disciplinarian. They were wary of the Headmistress— her unannounced visits to the classroom, the insistence on checking each lesson plan, the approved dress codes for pupils and teachers. Progress reports were not just an indicator of a pupil's advancement; they reflected the teacher's ability to teach. Rohini tried to stay under the radar, wearing conservative clothes, and making sure her students achieved reasonable grades. However, recent events in her personal life had catapulted her into pole position of Anjali's attention.

'Leave your work for a moment. Come up to my room,' said Anjali.

Rohini thought about the mountain of paperwork that would not disappear. She would have to work beyond midnight. She had no choice but to accept the boss's invitation. They went up to Anjali's room. The fifth floor room boasted a clear view of the bay.

'It's a beautiful world, no matter how much filth there is,' she said. 'Why are you so despondent? It's a modern world, Rohini. What have you got to be so ashamed about? No one cares about these things, caste or class. It's so old-century.

India is a thriving new country. It has broken its shackles from the colonial world. We are a democracy. We are all equal. I can't understand why you are taking all this to heart.'

Rohini pointed to a tall building on the edge of the bay. 'See that tall tower? Imagine living right at the top. Now look at what is down below—miles and miles of slums in between wealthy suburbs. One day, you jump off that tall building and you fall far below into that world of open drains, latrines and tiny rooms packed in together where ten people live in one. That is how far I have fallen. Have you ever stepped inside that world?'

Anjali shook her head. She was about to say something when Rohini continued her diatribe.

'Let's go to Dharavi one day and see if a top notch, snobbish school like ours can bridge that gap. We should take our students there to help out once a week, teach their unfortunate fellow beings. I was born to parents who lived in such slums, but I was brought up by middle class parents. Now I have to face my origin and it is *bloody* hard. So excuse my language and my long face, but I have a lot to cope with. My mother isn't my mother. Do you know the grief one feels when discovering a fact like that? I didn't think so, Anjali Bhojraj. Thank you very much for all your help and kindness, but I have to fight this on my own. I'll go back to the library now where I have serious work to do.'

They could have been playing statues. By the end of Rohini's speech, Anjali's still silhouette had darkened against the window. She stirred at last roused by Rohini's flight, heels clacking down the stairs. Her words, 'Rohini, I'm sorry,' echoed down an empty corridor.

It was a relief to be in Dr. Bose's office, away from family, friends and colleagues. This was her time to explore her feelings, to vent her frustrations or simply to think. Rohini was early for a change and she sat in the waiting room idly flicking the glossy pages of Femina. The articles 'Ten Ways to Please Your Man' and 'How to Look Good in Skinny Jeans' caught her eye. Judging by the size of the pants, she would never be able to squeeze any part of her body in those. They would suit

Kavita, but Rohini would insist she wore a long tunic top to cover her bottom.

A young man with a faint hint of a beard entered the room. Rohini looked up. Was he a patient? If so, it was a pity because he seemed so normal. He had his whole life ahead of him.

'Hi Polly! Busy?'

Rohini was sure she hadn't seen him on her previous visits and yet there was something very familiar about him.

'Always,' Polly replied with a smile. 'What are you doing here? Finished college already?' Her earrings dangled as she moved her head left and right rhythmically like a doll.

'Vacation. Come home for two months. Is the old guy in there?' he gestured towards the closed door. Irreverent, Rohini liked that.

'Yes, but he is with a patient. And Mrs. Chatterjee's next, so you'll have to wait,' Polly whispered.

'Mrs. Rohini Chatterjee?' He strode, panther-like across the room.

'Yes. I'm sorry I can't remember your name. Were you my student a few years back?' she asked with a tentative smile.

Teachers could be forgiven for not remembering the names of all the students who passed through their lives.

'You don't know me. I am Prodosh Bose. That rhymes. I don't know why they didn't consider that when they named me. Dad's told me a lot about you,' he said.

'I know your father?' she asked, resting her folded reading glasses on her chin.

'Yes. Dr. Pranab Bose, your doctor.'

'*Achchah*!' Rohini recognized him at last from the photo on his father's desk. 'You are studying Engineering in US, no? Or are you the doctor?'

'Guity of the second charge. I'm hoping to be a psychiatrist like the old man.'

'Oh.' Rohini paused, trying to think of a polite way of asking the burning question. 'What did he tell you about me? That I am a mad capricious woman?' she asked, trying to sound nonchalant.

'Oh no nothing like that. We discuss some cases in general.

Of course your confidentiality is completely intact. We talk about patients and symptoms. I don't know which patients have what illness for example.'

'So I could be a raging kleptomaniac or a paranoid schizophrenic?'

'Absolutely, I would have no idea,' he replied with a twinkle in his eyes.

'And you call yourself a psychiatrist?'

Their laughter made Polly turn her head towards them.

'I don't know why your father would talk about me. I am not that interesting really,' she persevered, trying to gauge what it was about her that the Boses discussed. She was sure it was not very flattering.

'If you are trying to trick an answer from me, it's not going to work. I am very good at poker. Don't worry. Baba only mentioned you as his friend's wife whom he is treating. He briefed me a bit about your case. Despite your difficult situation it sounds like he enjoys your lively sessions. Normally they can be quite draining.'

So Bose found her amusing. Rohini wasn't sure that she liked that; it made her troubles seem petty. But she did not share this sentiment with the young man who had innocently revealed more than he should have. What a perfect match he would be for Kavita.

'Your father has a warped sense of humour.'

'He doesn't show *any* humour at home,' replied Prodosh with a grimace.

The subject of their discussion emerged from his room with a patient, a stylish woman in a trouser suit. She shook the doctor's hand and smiled goodbye. Bose watched her leave. For a fleeting moment, Rohini was jealous of the time he had spent with this attractive stranger, closeted in a room sharing intimate details of her life. She had all the attributes that evoked envy in another woman: looks, wealth and supreme confidence. It's a façade, thought Rohini. Why else would she be here?

Dr. Bose walked towards them with a smile.

'I see you two are getting acquainted,' he said. 'I don't have to give any *parichay* to my son.'

Prodosh folded his hands in a polite *namaskar* to Rohini to say goodbye. She returned the gesture. Bose asked Rohini to go in. He would be with her in a minute.

As she closed the door behind her she could hear the doctor asking his son 'What are you doing here?' in Bengali using the more formal *toomi* instead of *tui*.

Prodosh asked his father 'Can I borrow your car? I have to go to the mall. I'll pick you up afterwards.'

'Be careful. You haven't driven in Mumbai traffic for a while. This isn't the US.'

'Clearly. I'll drive like an old lady.'

Bose entered the room shutting the door behind him. A faint line still crossed his forehead. He was not with her yet.

'What do you think about our sessions?' Rohini demanded to know as soon as Dr. Bose sat down.

'They are going fine. Why do you ask?' he frowned.

'It is just that I was talking to your son and he thinks you find our sessions amusing. I'm glad my melodramatic outpourings entertain you. It makes a nice drama, no?'

Rohini used the Bengali word *natak* for drama.

'I'm sorry to hear my son would even discuss your case with you. He is not your doctor, I am. I'll have a word with him later.'

'Oh I'm not angry with him. He's only a young boy, *bachcha chcheley*. He didn't mean to be indiscreet. I just don't like you talking about me. It makes me feel insecure,' sniffed Rohini.

'Naturally, I understand. Believe me anything we have talked about has been very superficial. We discuss cases objectively between two medics. We don't judge anyone. Besides, the fact is, he implied I enjoy our sessions. It's not an irksome task. Surely, that's a good thing?'

'You always know how to put a positive spin on things. Have you considered a career in politics?' Rohini flattened out a crease in her sari. 'I guess I wouldn't have minded if I had a brain haemorrhage and you discussed that with another doctor,' she conceded.

There was a soft knock on the door. Polly entered, going up to Bose.

'Sorry to disturb you sir. I booked us a table for seven-thirty. They are full at eight. Is that all right?'

'Yes that's fine. We'll pack up early tonight. You can finish the reports tomorrow.'

Rohini had never really seen Polly standing up. She was tall and wore a tight silk *salwar-kameez*, the midnight blue matching her long peacock feather earrings. She was wearing a large navy stone on her ring finger, a fashion accessory rather than an engagement symbol. Silver stiletto heels clicked on the tiled floor as she walked back to reception.

'Going out to dinner with your secretary? I'm surprised your wife permits it,' said Rohini.

'We're just going to Otter's Club for her performance review.'

'Of course that sort of business can't be conducted in the office. It's much better discussing someone's work over dinner and wine.'

'Are you jealous?'

'Not at all, why should I be? I'm not your wife. If you want to flirt with a girl young enough to be your daughter, you're welcome to all the heartbreak it'll bring you. By the way, that... girl was being very friendly with your son as well. I don't think she has decided which of the Boses she prefers.'

The doctor threw back his head and laughed.

'She knows Prodosh from US. That's how she got the job. My son recommended her as she had worked as an assistant in a lab and was familiar with medical matters. I am sure she prefers my son's company to my own. Now can we get back to our session?'

Rohini took out a purple journal from her handbag.

'As discussed last time, I have been keeping a diary. I made a short list of key things to discuss each time.'

Rohini passed her notebook to the doctor. He perused it with interest.

'I think it's a really good idea of yours—keeping a diary of main events, positive and negatives. We'll begin with you meeting your friend at the Mall with both your mothers present. How did that encounter make you feel?' He leaned back in his chair, pen poised. An eagle transmogrified into Bose.

Under his keen scrutiny, Rohini hung her head. 'Ashamed,' she murmured. *Lojjito.*

Bose leaned over to catch her answer. Her muted tone had left behind faint eddies of the syllables *lo-jji-to.* He leaned back. His unasked question hung heavy in the air, weighed down in the brocade curtains, whispering in the hiss of the air-conditioning system.

Rohini looked down at the desk; she could see a shadow of her reflection on the polished surface.

'I am embarrassed to introduce Maria as my mother. I've been so used to having a mother I looked up to, one who is elegance itself, that anyone else is unacceptable to me. By accepting Maria I am lowering myself several rungs in the social class. I know how shallow that sounds, but that's how it is. I feel *lajja*, shame.'

Dr. Bose took his reading glasses off and wiped them unhurriedly. He had long eyelashes for a man. Why should she care about his opinion? She bit her nails. With every passing second, she gave herself a ragged manicure.

'You've gone through anger and denial. You have reached shame. The final stage of acceptance will come and you will heal.'

'Truth is—I don't know if I have the strength anymore. The other day, Shiv was driving through slow traffic and a huge bus came up beside us. It kept speeding and then braking. For a moment I wondered whether I had the courage to open the door and jump out and prostrate myself under those giant wheels. I closed my eyes and felt their weight, crushing my body. A more painful way to die than taking sedatives, but my poor miserable life would end. And then, the spell broke and I couldn't do it.' The pencil Rohini was playing with snapped in half. 'Besides, the traffic was slow. I would have ended up with broken ribs only and lingered in a dreary hospital for weeks.'

Bose rose from his desk and came round to his patient's side. He encircled Rohini with one arm. She liked the citrus fragrance he was wearing. His terry cotton shirtsleeve rested against her bare upper arm. She shivered, wishing she had brought her shawl. Bose picked up her right hand and held it firmly in his palm. She could barely breathe. If he kissed her now she would let him.

'Rohini, I promise you I'll help you through this. Just don't ever consider suicide. It would be such a sad waste of a life. You are a wonderful person. You have strength, humour and compassion. Your family would be devastated. Your true friends would miss you.'

He had one foot on the elevated base of her chair. The gunmetal grey fabric stretched across his muscular thigh. A tennis player. Or squash. She withdrew her hand. It wouldn't be wise to let their professional relationship become ambiguous.

'You and I both know I am a wreck held together by the thinnest of strings. Nothing in my life will change. I'll have to bear it the best I can.'

'Bearing is good, acceptance may bring you peace.' He rested his hip on the desk, remaining by her side.

'Do you know I have such unkind thoughts? I think that if she were to die I would be free of this. I used to love Maria. I care about her still and yet her presence in my life is causing me so much upheaval.'

Rohini did not look up for a few minutes. She could hear Polly talking to another client outside. Her time was nearly up. Bose went back to his chair.

'You are shocked by my feelings. It's okay. I hate myself for thinking these thoughts.'

He was right to be repulsed. Any normal human being would. He was staring at his notepad, hardly aware of her presence. She wished she could enter his mind, step into the polished oak drawing room she pictured in his home, with everything in its place, neat and impeccable.

'I would like to suggest something, but you may not like it,' said Bose at last.

'What?' she asked with dread.

These modern psychiatrists had all sorts of tricks up their sleeves, little experiments, games, mental exercises. She was ready to say no. As a patient she had some rights.

'Bring your mother with you next time. Maria, not Indira,' proposed Bose.

'No!' Rohini exclaimed, getting up from her chair so suddenly that her handbag fell on the floor, scatterings its contents.

Earlier, she had left the top unzipped to take a tissue out. Her Revlon lipstick rolled underneath the heavy desk.

'No, this is my retreat, my special private place. She has encroached on my life enough. She has entered my home and invaded my life complicating things between my family and friends. She is not coming here. I know what will happen. You'll take her side and make me feel like the outsider.'

'Don't get agitated. Believe me you'll need to embrace her to get past this. It is the only healthy way,' cajoled Bose.

'*Na, na, na*. I'll fight you on this,' said Rohini picking up her things from the floor.

Bose knelt besides her, teasing out the runaway lipstick with a ruler.

'Think about it. It's really important. You won't make any progress if you don't push yourself to face the next step,' advised Bose. 'I'll call you in a few days. Maybe I could speak to Shourav.'

'Why? Can't I make decisions for myself anymore? My answer won't change. You can call me on Thursday. I finish early.'

'Good. See you next time.' He held out his right hand. Rohini marched past him saying 'namaskar' as formally as she could. She did not even nod goodbye to Polly.

On Thursday evening Rohini came home by five thirty, waiting for Bose's call. She closed the bedroom door for privacy. The last thing she wanted was for Maria to listen in. By the time she had her evening shower and changed into a loose kaftan it was quarter past six. She looked at her phone. It was fully charged. The call setting was on general. There were no missed calls or texts. Had he forgotten? Bose was never late.

She started tidying up her bedroom. The morning's choice of clothes was strewn across the bed: arms and legs of salwar kameez sets zigzagged in macabre positions as if some alien had sucked out the bodies and spat out the remains. She tried to hum a Tagore song, her mother's favourite, *if no one calls you go alone.* She stopped. Indira might overhear and presume that her daughter had forgiven her and all was well. The door creaked as Maria came in.

'Would you like some tea, dear?'

Rohini shook her head and then after a few moments called out after the retiring figure.

'Can you ask Paru to make me a milky coffee?'

She wanted to be alone when Pranab called. There was hardly any privacy in their flat with both the older women drifting in and out of rooms, opening drawers, picking things up from coffee tables and bookshelves to inspect. Shourav would be home soon and listen in to her conversation. Paru came in with a tray. The coffee was strong, not milky as she had asked for, but it soothed her. She nibbled at a biscuit, limp from moisture sipping into the tin on foggy winter days.

At seven the phone rang.

'Yes, hello?' Rohini tried not to sound breathless.

'Sorry I'm late. A patient called.'

For the first time Rohini began to believe that patients do call doctors and perhaps her husband did not lie to her every time he uttered those same words. However, instinct prevailed.

'Why don't you just admit you were working late? A meeting with Polly perhaps?'

'Yes and that as well. Her performance review is up.'

'Another one? You took her out a few days ago.'

'Her mother was ill and she had to leave early that night.'

There was a pause as Rohini digested this piece of news, weighing it for credibility.

'Rohini, what's all this about? I'm busy sometimes. Is this going to be a problem between us?'

'There is no us. Yet. This is a professional call. You said you would ring at six. I may not be a doctor, but my time is precious. Kavita and Shourav will be home soon and I'll have to prepare dinner.' Paru had cooked already, but that was not his business. 'We need to decide if I am bringing Maria on our next appointment.'

'I think it would be a good idea.'

So that was settled. Maria would intrude into yet another space. Like a drop of ink she just spread and spread and no amount of good quality detergent was going to take this stain out.

Rohini hung up and took her reading glasses out. There was a note from the Building Directors in her letterbox. The residents met once every few months to discuss cleaning issues, noise levels, and so on. There was to be a special meeting on Friday evening. It was not time to vote for a new Secretary yet. The last one was still serving her second term.

The next day, Rohini left work later than planned and went straight to the meeting room on the ground floor. There was a hum of voices as they discussed topics on the agenda. A dozen or so other residents were present including Mr. Joshi the chairman and Mrs. Tiwari the secretary. Meena Tiwari was a Gujrati lady of fifty-odd years. Her diamond nose stud flashed whenever she disapproved of a rule. She began by discussing the new cleaner whom she had personally employed after verifying his background and caste.

Ganesh was the son of a potter, not a toilet cleaner she explained. They had fallen on hard times and the poor *bechara* had to do anything he could to feed his family. Every morning she painted *rangoli* designs outside her door. The hands of an untouchable could not tar such auspicious markings. Rohini watched the faces of her neighbours who nodded in agreement. She wanted to say something, but held back knowing it would only lower their opinion of her.

'Mrs. Chatterjee, is your husband going to join us soon?' asked Mr. Joshi.

He expected the head of the household to be present at important gatherings. Rohini told them that Dr. Chatterjee was still at the hospital.

'That's a pity! Still, we must discuss an important issue. For the rest of the people the meeting is over.'

A few lingered by the door hoping to catch some of the conversation. Mr. Joshi waved them out towards the exit. As his wife was present to preserve propriety, he felt it would be all right to shut the door so that they would have some privacy. Even so, he asked Mrs. Tiwari and Mrs. Chatterjee if they objected to the door being shut. Both shook their heads. He cleared his throat and sipped a glass of water before launching into his rehearsed speech.

'Mrs. Chatterjee, we are reading such shocking things in the papers about you. You are the maid's daughter? She is from poor low caste Christian family and an unmarried mother, I believe?'

Joshi stressed on the Un-married in a manner that would intimidate the strongest of people. He waited for a response. Rohini stared back.

'We understand *ki* it is difficult for you. But Menaka Towers is an exclusive residence and our residents do not like such scandals. People are complaining to me of violent disputes with the maid, and attempted suicide by you. All these things bring bad name to our building. It lowers the property value, to say nothing of the social aspect. This is not Bollywood. We have good Brahmin families here who are not comfortable with…'

'People of low caste family like me? Maybe we should make caste one of your criteria for prospective buyers. I can't imagine which century you think we live in Mr. Joshi.'

'Caste issue aside, the noise and the shameful behaviour are too much for us to ignore.'

Mrs. Joshi and Tiwari nodded. 'We cannot tolerate such conduct,' said Mrs. Tiwari. She wagged her sapphire-clad finger stressing on the English word 'conduct'.

'Are you telling us to leave? If so, I'll take you to court for discrimination. In case you are not aware, our Government has laws against caste crime.'

'No madam, you misunderstand. It has No-ththing to do with your caste. I'm merely saying *ki* we should keep the noise down, control the dramas. In some buildings in Mumbai they have only vegetarian residents, some just Brahmins. We do not make an-ny such distinctions between our families. After all, the veg families have accepted the non-veg even though the smell of meat makes them feel sick. We have some good non-Brahmin families living here. Also some Christians?' He asked his wife and Tiwari for confirmation.

They nodded vigorously although lines of uncertainty furrowed their brows.

'But no Muslims,' said Mrs. Tiwari twitching her nose. 'This is mainly a Hindu building.'

Rohini was tempted to tell them that her father had been a Muslim. She left the room, slamming the door behind her, humiliation burning on her face. She was not sure whether she ranked above the cleaner so judiciously selected by Mrs. Tiwari or lower. Perhaps her shadow crossing the corridors prompted the Brahmins to go home and take a bath.

'It's intolerable!' she fumed stepping into their flat.

Indira and Maria were watching the news. Rohini paced the floor, jerkily recounting the event to the women. She did not care if Paru heard. The news would be all over the building by now. 'Mrs. Chatterjee has been threatened by the powers-that-be of the Building. If she does not toe the line she would be forced to sell out.'

She had not told anyone of the little notes in their letterbox. *This is not the place for you, Go back to the slums.* She had burnt them with a cigarette lighter. The recent stress had triggered another college habit she had shed a long time ago. Rohini desperately needed a cigarette, but the mothers would smell the stench on her breath. Since they had come, she had not even touched alcohol. She needed some air.

Rohini stepped on to their eighteenth floor balcony and looked down below. The traffic moved along narrow roads like a thousand ants going home. Her head swam. What if she hurled herself off the balcony? How would Joshi and Tiwari react to that?

The value of the property would certainly plummet.

Chapter 7 Maria

A thin Mumbai mist descended over the horizon, sweeping across the harbour and shrouding tall grey buildings, the colour of anthracite, with a sinister dirty white film—hiding them from view and yet leaving a ghostly trace behind for idle beholders of the sky. Few in Mumbai have the leisure to gaze at the mist much less ponder upon its thickness or thinness, except perhaps Maria who was fascinated by the world disappearing before their eyes.

A warm shawl bought last year in Kolkata's winter fair enveloped Maria's slender figure. The colours were joyous—orange and red bands, one fading into another in an unending sunset. Indira wore a double knit lilac cardigan she had made herself. Why they could not sit indoors like two normal people, she could not fathom. A little later in the day would have been better when the sun was high and the fog gone.

Inside the apartment, Maria felt overwhelmed by expensive rugs, Kashmiri cabinets and whatnots, but here in the balcony, she could breathe. She looked at the violet hills in the distance, tucked beneath the dark clouds, where she was told the richer crowd lived. She could not imagine anything grander than her daughter's flat. It reminded her of a five star hotel, like the one where a crazed gunman had shot so many people. She had felt their souls trapped between the walls. Of course she would not mention such things to Indira. Sister would only laugh at her silliness.

Laxmi, a Marathi lady half her age, cleaned their marble bathroom every morning. Maria did not like to dirty the elegant shower cubicle and so she mopped the floor after bathing. When Paru brought their bed tea, Maria had to control the urge to go to the kitchen and make *moori*, preferring a bowl of puffed rice to crispy buttered toast. It wasn't just that; she was unused to being served. The only time that had ever happened was when she had pneumonia a few years ago. Durga brought her meals to her room. Maria had shaken off the covers and tottered to the kitchen as soon as the fever died down.

She yearned for masala tea with extra thick milk, crushed cardamom and three spoonful of sugar. Paru made her English tea and Maria did not dare ask for anything else for fear of being considered uncultured. Once or twice she had stepped inside that pristine kitchen and it was a world of polished cabinet doors, which swung back and forth like a butterfly's gossamer wings. She was afraid to touch them lest these fragile limbs of the furniture broke off in her hands. Secretly, she felt the presence of a mischievous spook as the cabinet doors shut by themselves and things disappeared in her room. If she told her daughter she would think Maria was accusing the maid of stealing.

A faint streak of lightening appeared, briefly illuminating the eastern sky. God was switching the lights on and off in heaven, thought Maria. It would rain soon and they would have to go in. At first she was afraid to be in the balcony perched high above the streets. Now she was getting used to the height. When they flew to Mumbai, she looked out of the window of the plane and saw the world through the eyes of a bird.

Maria looked at Indira's serene face and decided it was time to ask the question that had been on her mind all night. Her hands were knitted together tightly on her lap.

'Sister, did Rohinibeti tell you about the doctor's appointment?'

'What about it?' Indira demanded, folding the newspaper she was reading.

'She said the doctor wants to see me. I don't know what to say. Will you come with us?' She couldn't look at Indira just yet.

'If Rohini wanted me to come she would have asked me. You go with her. It does not involve me. None of my business.' Indira cleared her throat with a loud and protracted rattle.

Indira's feelings were hurt just as Maria had imagined. In times like this Maria switched to English to emphasise her points.

'She want you to come sister. You, her real mother. She *totally* depend on you. The doctor, he know noththing. He want to see me, for what? What I can tell him? You brought her up,' replied Maria her voice rising up to 'for what?' and then descending, cajoling, on the last sentence, 'you brought her up,' a truth she acknowledged with less and less pain each year.

Maria used the Bengali phrase, *manush korecho, made her into a human being* switching from Pidgin English to Hindi-accented Bengali, her tongue moving as swiftly as her fingers with an embroidery needle. Indira's replies were always in Bengali peppered with a few English words, which Maria would not comprehend in Bengali. For instance she said 'problem' instead of *samashya.*

'But the problem is not with me Maria. It's between you and her.'

'*Ki bolbo?* What do I tell the doctor? I can't tell him about these small small things between Rohini beti and me. She will tell in front of the doctor, she *is not my real mother, I hete her.* Every day I pray to God to give me *mukti* from this shame,' said Maria.

Indira focused on a cactus plant in front of her. For a few minutes neither of them spoke. Maria pulled out a muslin handkerchief tucked inside her bra. She dabbed the corner of her eyes and blew her nose. Indira put down her mug of tea with a loud thump.

'Are you quite finished? I don't like drama. All this *natak you are making now that the cat is finally out of the bag.* Didn't I tell you long ago? You will regret it Maria, the lies we told. No one will know, sister, you said. Ugly truths always leak out bringing down everyone with them.'

Indira picked up her knitting, a sweater for her granddaughter. She surveyed the length and then continued to click away the lines of wool, left to right, right to left. Maria was about to say something when Indira spoke once more, listing her grievances.

'So far you and Rohini have talked about the effects on you. What about me? Has anyone asked me how I feel? Do you know how much sacrifice I made for you, bringing up *your* daughter like my own? I wanted my own child. But I started our marriage with yours—giving your baby all the love and attention that we could. How about Roy sahib? Did anyone ask how he felt? Don't you think he would have preferred to have our own child, born out of my womb, someone bearing his seed?'

Indira paused to breathe. She picked up her heavy handbag from the floor and rummaged inside for her inhaler. Taking two deep puffs she settled into her chair more comfortably, resting her head on the raised back of the wicker chair.

'Sorry, sister. I was young and desperate. I only saw my need. I thought you loved her too.'

Indira stared down at her elegant hands joined together, fingers interlaced. 'Yes I did, I do. Rohini was the daughter I wanted to have. When you held her in the hospital ward, I knew we couldn't give her away. But I always felt she was yours. You were there constantly in our lives. You looked after her every day. It made me feel like a lesser mother.'

'No sister. To her you were the mother, I was the maid.'

'Don't start that again. What is done is done.'

Indira started to pack away her knitting, shoving needles and balls into a small bag. She stopped mid-way to look at the cars far below in the streets of Mumbai. A life in miniature flowed past at a faltering pace, the morning rush-hour traffic stopping every so often with a screech, a hiss and raucous honking.

'As Rohini grew older and started nursery school, I felt I was ready to bear a child. When I held Raja in my arms I knew how you felt. I sensed your desperation, the need to protect. I failed.' Indira's hands trembled and a pair of knitting needles clattered on to the tiled floor.

Maria rose, pushing herself up by the arms of the chair. She put a frail arm around her friend.

'We couldn't keep him, sister. He was special. God took him away to serve Him.'

'Rubbish,' said Indira, sniffing. 'It was that damn motorbike. How many times had I told him not to ride that thing on Calcutta roads? Did he listen to me?'

'The young people, they don't listen, and sometimes they pay heavily for it. It is us who suffer from their errors. Don't cry, sister, he is in a good place. He is at peace.'

'I'm not crying. I have turned into stone, this many years. My beautiful boy has been taken away. Now I am about to lose a daughter. Do you think she will ever love me like she did before? I doubt it. Every time she is in hospital I think of that time with Raja. I fear *Jaam*, the God of death has come to take away another of my child. I knew I should have kept those birth and adoption papers in the bank. She would've never known the truth and we could have all been happier. But no, your God has other plans,' she said pointing her hand upwards.

Maria nodded in agreement. She firmly believed in a Divine Plan, but unlike Indira she accepted it without question. Her friend would fight Fate to deflect Him from their path. Except that summer when Raja was seventeen years old; Fate had the upper hand that day.

'He was special, sister. To me he was like an angel,' said Maria, remembering, the longhaired boy with eyes like Krishna, enormous vessels filled with such light.

When he used to play the sitar, he reminded her of the shepherd god calling his flock. Sometimes Maria could not help but feel envious. Indira could love her child openly, feed him, scold him, and hold him close. All that Maria was unable to do.

'I was always afraid, Maria. I never told you or anyone. There was something about him, some inner glow that frightened me. You know when you hold something really precious in your hands and you fear that you are going to lose it; it was like that. I was never whole again.'

'Why was Roy sahib so hard on him? Poor Raja, he just wanted to be a sitarist. If his father had not scolded him so much that day maybe he would not have left the house so angry.'

'For how long? No, I don't blame his father. All we asked was that he finished his studies before taking up music. How is a man to feed himself on a musician's salary? Raja was gifted for sure, but stubborn too. Sooner or later he would have had his way. You can't stop a river from flowing. I always knew I would lose him. He came to us just for a short while, like a visitor. I wish I had seen him grown up and happy.'

Even today Maria could hear Indira's wild cry as she pushed the police officer away, trying to run out of the house. His mangled body was found against a tree, his motorbike still running. The telegram stating *Programme cancelled* was still in his breast pocket. His father's rebuke was evident in the crumpled paper. It was Roy sahib who read it first and reproached his son for wiring money to the musician in Benares. If only Roy had waited a day or two when Raja's disappointment had lessened, Maria was sure the tragedy could have been avoided.

Indira would not enter his room. Maria often went in there when Sister was asleep, to tidy up and dust around Raja's papers strewn all over. His music notes were like little black birds caught in flight. Maria included him in her prayers every night. It seemed to her that Sister had put all the essence of Raja in a jar and put a lid on it.

'He looked like us, didn't he Maria, with Roy sahib's nose and my eyes? I tried so hard to keep him. But he too floated away into another world. I still dream about him, a young man laughing and playing his sitar. He would have been about forty now, married with a family. I would have had grandchildren, been a *thakurma*. Such dreams I had!'

They turned their heads hearing the staccato sound of heels. Rohini entered the balcony. She was ready for work and had come to say goodbye. Every day she told them what was for lunch and when she would be back. She was early, it had only just gone half past seven. Her blue sari billowed out in the wind. Heavy clouds laden with rain were about to burst. A crack of thunder shook the building. Maria crossed herself. Her daughter's face was as dark as the clouds above.

'I'm sorry I didn't fulfil your dreams, Ma. Kavita is not really your granddaughter, is she? I bet you wished it was me who died that day and not Raja,' said Rohini before walking back into the lounge.

Indira and Maria rose quickly despite arthritic joints and stumbled over the threshold. They squeezed through a narrow gap, not wasting time pushing the patio doors open.

'You will always be my first child and my only daughter,' Indira told Rohini, sitting next to her on the sofa, grabbing her shaking shoulders.

Maria nodded in agreement. A shiver went down her back. She knew about *the other one, conceived with violence, killed before she had a chance to live. Abhaghini, the unlucky one.* The hapless soul drifted in limbo following her mother. Maria said the Lord's name thrice in her head. *Go, little one, go.*

'Of course I will grieve for Raja for the rest of my days, but I am thankful that I have you and Kavita. Raja died young with his whole life ahead of him. I can't forget that. You understand, don't you?' she asked her daughter.

Rohini rested her head on Indira's right shoulder. For so many years Indira hardly ever spoke of her dead son. After a while, she retired to her room, too upset to go to school. They heard her talking on the phone asking for sick leave, again. Indira muttered that Rohini would lose her job at this rate. Maria wanted to go to Rohini, but she could not leave Indira. It seemed disloyal. Always, she had to take sides between Sister and Daughter. She drew her stool closer to the side of the sofa. Her hearing was not so keen these days and Indira's voice was softer than usual.

'Maria, I fear I am losing Rohini, just like the other one, a tiny chunk of flesh washed out of my passage. I called her Usha, because it was at dawn that I lost her. She came into the world with such hate. Still, she was a part of me, a tiny piece of life ticking inside.'

'Don't think about that now, sister. It was so long ago. You were not meant to keep her.'

Indira stared past Maria to the balcony where Ghum was chasing a bird, her body as still as a statue, eyes blank, breathing irregular. Maria wondered if Indira had fallen asleep with her eyes open. Only her mouth twitched.

Later that day, when Rohini was taking a nap, Indira picked up the days newspaper. Maria dusted the magazines on the coffee table, complaining of Paru's lack of attention to detail in a hoarse whisper. She stopped in the middle of a labyrinthine sentence comparing the staff at Shanti Niwas to the ones in Mumbai.

'Your hands are shaking Sister. Give me the tea cup. You must tell Dr. Sahib. I noticed it the other day too when you were helping Rohini set the table. I worried you would drop her nice plates!'

Indira let go of the newspaper she had been trying to read and clutched one side of her head. Her shoulders were trembling. In fact, Maria noticed that her whole body was in tremor.

'What is it Sister? Is your head hurting again? Let me fetch some water.'

'I don't need water. My head hurts a lot, but it's not that.'

Indira's words were garbled, but she shook her head at Maria's misdirected concern. She covered her mouth with her sari. It was then that Maria saw the newspaper on the floor, English paper with difficult words. There was a picture of a young girl, candles and flowers, people marching with slogans that were written in an angry style, black slashes in white. It was her, the one who died recently after the sick incident.

'Every time I read something like this, I think, I think.'

Maria patted her back. 'Sh sh, such brutal things happen to women. You mustn't get upset. You must forget.'

'I can't. I'll never forget,' said Indira.

Maria remembered the night of the circus too. How excited they had been chattering all week like mynah birds. Indira wore a red salwar kameez with mirrors winking all over. When they went home that night the robbers were there, waiting for them. They took Indira. Later, they found her huddled in one corner of the terrace, a rabbit caught in a trap. There was blood all over Indira's legs. Maria turned away and vomited all over a Kashmiri rug.

Indira smoothed out the creases in the newspaper.

'When I read how courageous she was to name her rapists I think what a coward I was, hiding away. I should have identified them and put the bastards behind bars. They did not even conceal their faces. I knew their names. Why didn't I do something? Those *nemek-harams* must have done it again to other helpless young girls.'

Maria sought Indira's hand and covered it with hers. So many years she had kept quiet, not owned up to her cowardice. Indira's words wrenched the truth from her.

'Forgive me Sister. I never had the courage to tell you before. I could have made a phone call. I was in the study. Stupid, stupid girl that I was, I froze. I did not think or act. I could have saved you.' She hit her forehead with her palm.

They held each other. 'I'll never blame you for that. When one is petrified one can do nothing. Come, let's ask Paru for some more *cha.'*

Just like that, Indira seemed to flick off an inner switch. It was a habit of hers. She could talk about something profoundly emotional and then return to normal within minutes, as if nothing had happened. It was this quality that had helped her to cope with so much in life. Maria often wished she too possessed an off button like that.

She had to help Indira to her room. Sitting for so long with her feet tucked under had given her pins and needles. Indira was restless for hours before falling into a deep sleep. The next morning she did not remember anything. Maria thanked her Lord for that.

The next day, Rohini rose early and went to school without saying goodbye. Indira and Maria watched the car leave through electric gates.

'When will she forgive us, Maria?'

'She has lot to think about. It'll take time. Shourav brother is never home. When he is here he is talking on the phone, always busy, no time for her. Kavita has her friends. I feel Rohini *beti* is all alone. She thinks she has lost us too.'

It was nine o'clock when Paru came to see them about what groceries to buy. Indira gave her a list.

Later that morning, Indira took out a bag of wool.

'I'll knit something special for Rohini. It's time to live with the living. Maybe we can take her to see a film, do things we used to do together.'

Maria agreed.

'I'll clear out Raja's room when we go back to Kolkata. Perhaps I can keep his sitar. The neck is bent. While I am alive, it can stay. After that they can throw everything out.'

'Yes we'll keep his sitar. You can listen to his music even though he is not around.'

Maria could hear him. But she was not sure that her friend's ears were keen enough to hear the dead.

Chapter 8 Rohini

Shourav sauntered in through the front door with his phone attached to his left ear. He nodded to his wife, ignored the others and kicked the door shut with his right foot. Placing his briefcase on the sofa, he tugged at his tie continuing to speak, rather utter, affirmatives: 'hmm, yes, I know'.

Rohini tried to catch his eye to send him an unmistakable signal, *hang up, or else*. The night before he had returned well after midnight and now he was walking into their evening as if he was a hotel guest.

'Give it to me,' she commanded in a dangerously calm voice.

Shourav raised his eyebrows and looked at Indira and Maria for explanation. They looked equally perplexed.

'Why?' he asked after a minute's pause. 'Hold on a sec,' he whispered into the mouthpiece before covering it with one hand.

'Because I want to see who calls you day and night. It's a patient, is it? Waiting for heart surgery? Don't give me that bullshit.' Rohini spat out in English. 'Do you take me for an idiot? It's been going on for a year. Only I was too blind to see it before. Phone calls, hanging up. Sleeping with the phone next to you, taking it to the *bathroom!* What kind of emergencies do you deal with, *hain?*' Rohini thrust her flushed face against Shourav's.

He backed away, retreating into the bedroom, muttering something about coming home to a mad woman. The call had ended halfway through Rohini's rant.

'Why won't you show me your phone?' she yelled.

He shouted back from the room 'Because it's my private property. In this public world of theatre you have created, I need to hold on to something that's mine.'

Indira told her to be calm. She could not see why Rohini was attacking her Lord Shiva-like husband, the purest, most decent person she had met.

Maria added, 'He is a perfect gentleman, so polite. A bit busy but...'

Rohini fumed, they did not know the half of it. It was all coming back. Why had she ignored it for so long?

'Go to him,' urged Indira, 'make up. You are just angry with the neighbours and taking it out on the poor man. He has just come back from a long day. He does not need to be harangued by you.'

Kavita came in. She was given a confused account of the argument.

'Your mother is accusing your Papa of all sorts of silly things just because of the phone calls. Tell her to calm down.'

Kavita took her jacket off and sat by her mother, stroking her hair.

'Papa just needs to talk to a friend now and then. It has been a tough year. She is really nice. He didn't tell you because when you met her in Shyamnagar you didn't like her. Her daughter Mona is the same age as me and if you meet Aunty Sunita again you'll see that she is just trying to help us.'

The enormity of this simple explanation stunned the others. The same thought seemed to pass over their faces like the shadow of an eclipse. So, there *was* a person in Shourav's life.

'Sunita?' Rohini whispered in disbelief. 'Sunita Dhaliwal?'

She had buried that ghost a long time ago, or so she thought. It seemed her world was full of them, the past blighting her present.

'She is Sunita Bhatia now,' corrected her daughter. '*Dr. Bhatia,*' she added, with pride.

Rohini could have slapped her. Fury and pain flowed like twin-rivers down her body. Unseen by others, she picked up a wooden Buddha and walked into her bedroom, where her fifty-one year old husband was sitting up in bed reading Mark Tully's latest book.

'Bastard,' she said, hurling the teak carved figure in his direction.

The resounding crash brought everyone to the room. The dressing table mirror had disintegrated into tiny grains of glass. Shourav's right temple had a red gash where a small shard had penetrated his caramel skin. Kavita ran to her father's side with a cry, shielding him from further assault by her crazed mother. Indira mobilised herself to find cotton wool and Dettol in the medicine cabinet. Only Maria stood by Rohini's side, one arm round her daughter's waist, another holding down her daughter's threatening right arm. Paru rushed in with a broom to sweep away the fragments.

In the minutes that followed, Maria managed to lead Rohini to the guest bedroom, muttering soothing words. Would she like a glass of water? Through the wall that divided the two rooms they could hear the voices of others.

'Did she want to kill me? She is crazy,' Shourav complained to his mother-in-law.

Indira reassured him, it was just a fit of temper. Rohini was upset. Indira urged Shourav to speak to his wife and explain matters. It was a misunderstanding, she was sure.

Kavita said, 'Sorry Papa. I thought she was referring to Aunty Sunita.'

It was close to midnight and Rohini had still not uttered a word to Shourav. He put his bandaged head around the door to check in on her. 'We need to talk,' he said, addressing the wall behind her. Rohini told Maria to send him away. She would sleep in the guestroom that night. Maria offered to spend the night on Kavita's floor. No, said Rohini. She wanted her 'real' mother near. Indira could sleep on the sofa-cum-bed in the lounge. When chips were down some instinct drew her to her biological mother; the invisible tie of the umbilical cord.

'How could he do this to me Maria Ma?' she asked, in a daze. 'He promised in Shyamnagar he would not see her again if that made me happy. I was expecting Kavita and we left that town to come here. She went away to Delhi. It's all the fault of this internet, people connecting and reconnecting!'

Maria seemed unsure of the word 'internet'. She had heard it bandied about so often, but never quite grasped the meaning.

'I still don't believe that Shourav would see another woman behind your back. No, dear, you've got it all wrong. Like Kavita said, this Sunita madam is just a colleague. A man needs another woman to talk to when his wife is so ill. Remember for one year none of us knew when you would recall everything and then get sick again. What a worrying time it has been. My diabetes got worse, your mother's blood pressure rose. We were worried Shourav would have a heart attack, he was that anxious. He cares about you. This lady is just a friend, another doctor to talk to. Speak to your husband tomorrow. Clear it all up. You can't get upset like this. It's not good for you.'

Maria made sure Rohini got some sleep. Indira checked with Shourav before giving Rohini a sedative. She noisily cleared out her things from the room before retiring to the lounge. Rohini felt guilty asking her to sleep on the lumpy mattress, but why should Maria always get inferior treatment? Maria was the one who had carried Rohini for nine months and brought her into this world. Kavita did not make an appearance. In the end she slept in her parent's room, keeping her Dad company and giving her bed to Indira who readily accepted the arrangement.

It was two days before Rohini was ready to break her silence. She asked the rest of the family and Paru to leave the flat for a couple of hours. Shiv took the party to Juhu beach for an evening outing. Indira complained about the possibility of the cool sea breeze giving her a sore throat prompting Kavita to pack a few shawls and a flask of tea.

Rohini wore a navy blue *salwar kameez* buttoned up to the neck and swept her hair up into a high knot. They sat in the sitting room. Shourav offered her a glass of wine, which she refused. The clock ticked away the minutes while Rohini prepared to launch into her prerehearsed speech, devoid of melodrama. It did not go according to plan. Shourav put an arm around her shoulders.

Sunita was just a friend, he swore. She was married. So was he. He had been going out of his mind with worry after Rohini's first suicide attempt. He could not tell anyone, not even his sister. It was hard to bear with a young sixteen-year old daughter to protect on top of everything. Sunita had moved to Mumbai and looked him up at that sensitive time when Shourav needed a shoulder to cry on.

She helped out when Rohini was in hospital, picking up Kavita from school and taking her home to spend time with her daughter Mona. Shourav did the hospital run, sitting by Rohini's bedside. Sunita was discreet, not even telling her husband what the real situation was. As far as he was aware, Rohini was ill and in hospital. Sunita even came and tidied their flat and left flowers in a vase and food in the fridge, for Rohini's return. Paru was still too young to cope without her mistress.

Rohini dried her eyes. 'Sunita has come to my home and tidied up my things? How dare she? This is my place and I don't want her crossing my threshold. Over my dead body, understood?'

Shourav nodded, 'She meant it for the best.'

'Don't defend her! You may come up with all these innocent explanations, but you don't fool me. You two had something going on back then and you still care about her. I don't trust you with her. If we are going to move forward, you need to end this friendship.'

Shourav did not answer. Rohini stood. She saw it was of no use. In order for a relationship to thrive, one needed trust. He would have to choose.

'I've been thinking, let's go to England. Your brother is there. He can help us to start. You need to sit your PLAB exam and I will do a PGCE. We'll make a fresh start—forget our past and start a new future. What do you say?'

'You think it's that simple? I'll have to pass a rigorous exam. How are we going to support ourselves until we find jobs? You'll have a harder time to adjust there. Nupur is an old-fashioned woman. The Indian society in London is far more conservative than here. You can't run away from yourself. If you want to escape, you can go! I'm not following.'

Shourav banged down his glass of whisky and took out a cigarette.

'You've made your choice then. It's *Sunita* you want!' She should have known.

'It-has-nothing-to-do-with-Sunita,' Shourav reiterated with deliberate slowness. 'What you are suggesting is a whimsical plan, based on escapist motivations. When will you deal with your feelings? Learn to be a bit more mature.'

He puffed smoke into the air, some of which entered her nostrils. She suppressed a sneeze, scrabbling in her head for a suitable comeback.

'You are behaving like a spoilt five year old girl who stamps her feet and wants everything her way. All this upheaval because little Miss Rohini has found out about her real parents. Deal with it, like a lot of people do every single day. People cope with terminal illness and sudden death. This is hardly that!'

She would not let him see how much his insensitivity hurt her. The ash from Shourav's cigarette fell on to the carpet. Rohini wanted to tell him to use the fucking ashtray, but held back the rash words. If he did not understand her pain now, he never would.

'We could rent out this flat and try England for six months. If it doesn't work we will come back.' It was time to negotiate.

'I'm going to the Club. There is nothing more to be said.' Shourav put on a linen jacket and picked up his wallet.

'Well at least, promise to end your friendship with Sunita.'

'Why? I don't ask the same of you.' He lit another cigarette, knowing she hated him smoking in the flat.

'I don't have any male friends that you would find a threat.'

'How about Bose? You seem to enjoy his sessions a bit more than a normal trip to the psychiatrist. You come out of the room with a rosy smile on your lips, blushing at some compliment. Don't pretend you don't notice his attentions. I saw how he was looking at you the other day.'

'You're talking rubbish. Dr. Bose is my doctor.'

'If you say so. I'm off. Don't wait up.'

Just before he reached the door, he turned around for a last shot. 'And that amethyst brooch you wear? He gives gifts to all his patients after a breakdown, I presume?'

Her cheeks burned under his mocking gaze and hurtful insinuations. Rohini sat in her shrine long after Shourav left. This conversation was going to be about *his* guilt, *his* affection for another. How did it end up being *her* in the wrong?

She was so low after her hospital stay that she did not questioned the propriety of accepting a gift from her doctor.

Pranab knew she liked amethyst. There was a purple crystal in his cabinet she had admired once. That night, when she had shown Shourav the brooch and said what a thoughtful man Bose was, he had just shrugged. He could have said something then, but he had saved the incident as a negative tally on her account.

On an impulse Rohini rang Nupur, her sister-in-law in UK. After initial frosty enquiries about Rohini's health, Nupur told her how busy she was with the Indian Cultural Society in London.

'Ustad Firoz Khan is playing at Albert Hall and he is staying with us. Such an honour! We are a Brahmin family and don't usually entertain Muslim guests, but it's a modern world and we are not prejudiced about people's caste and religion.'

Was this a dig at her? Rohini wished Nupur's son would marry a Christian or a Muslim girl to test the real extent of Nupur's broadmindedness. However, there was no time to tarry on tangents and she broached the subject of going to Britain for jobs and education. Concerned about how much the phone call was costing her, Rohini rushed through the plans, giving Nupur only the briefest of summaries, excluding the part where they might have to lodge free at their house.

Nupur laughed. 'Do you know the cost of university here for foreign students? That's before living costs. Your daughter will not receive any help from the government. You haven't even thought of visas and work permits. What makes you think the UK Government wants you here?'

Rohini hung up. It was no use. She would have to think harder. There must be ways. People went to the UK and US on tourist visas and stayed on.

When Kavita came home, Rohini offered her a bowl of Maggie noodles, her favourite. Over snacks, she put forward her suggestions for a new future. Kids in India were dying to get out of the old fashioned country. Her daughter would jump at the opportunity. Kavita polished off the bowl and answered in a calm, matter of fact manner.

'I'm not going to England. I already have a place in Delhi University.'

'Think of the great campuses, forward thinking students and beautiful libraries.'

'Most of the students are not virgins, Mummy. In order to integrate, I would have to drink a lot of alcohol and sleep with many boys, just to fit in. But I guess drinking and sleeping around comes naturally to you and Papa.'

Rohini could have slapped her daughter. The mothers too urged Rohini to forget these capricious plans. They were better off here. If Shourav was not willing to go with them, how would they manage? Who would support them? Rohini sighed. It would take months of research and persistence to turn the tide.

Few days later, Rohini went to see Babaji. He was distracted by the presence of a large white cat.

'Maharani,' Babaji greeted the feline queen in a tone dripping with affection. 'Did you drink all your milk? Did you?'

The cat jumped on to Babaji's enormous lap. She was lost in the many folds of his orange robe, a tuft of fur appearing now and then amongst the pleats. Rohini waited her turn. Maharani was like Ghum, lazy and cosseted. Rohini could see that she would have to start all over again next time. She doubted the old man would remember what she had just said. Babaji looked up, fixing his grey eyes, just to the right of her. He spoke slowly, hissing the 'ss' in a rather sinister manner. He waved his hand with a ruby clad finger parting the air in front of his face.

'Yessss, I see you crossing water. But there is still trouble on the other side. You'll have a difficult few years, my dear. After that you will find peace in your new home.'

Rohini did a long puja at the temple. She carried a tray of fresh fruits and sweets as offering. After many months she put vermilion, a sacred marriage symbol, on her forehead. Clad in a new sari, crisp white cotton with a red print of Om all over, she felt cleansed. Her mind was clear, like a mountain stream. Babaji's blessing was unequivocal. There was still a question that bothered her, but she could not ask the holy man for an answer, it was too private. There was only one person she could trust.

Rohini sought Maria out one afternoon when Indira was having a rest. They sat in the balcony out of earshot. She spent the next few minutes, pruning the roses, not knowing where to start. She brushed away the dead leaves on the floor.

Maria coughed. The winter evenings were cool, especially on the balcony of the eighteenth floor.

'Are you cold?' asked Rohini.

Maria shook her head. Rohini put her clippers down on the arbour and sat under the rose arch.

'Maria-ma, do you think Shourav will follow me to England if I go? I am not sure if he cares about me as much as he used to. Something has changed. I just didn't realise it, until now.' Rohini spoke in simple Bengali, to help Maria understand the crux of the matter.

Maria did not speak for a while. Eventually, her clouded eyes rested on Rohini's.

'There is no doubt that he thinks only of your welfare and recovery. Whether he will follow you, I can't tell you. It is a difficult thing you have asked him. Give him time. Don't rush into such a big decision.'

Indira was up, looking for them and the conversation ended.

Rohini did not completely yield to Bose's request to see Maria. She would devote half the session to her mother and the other half to herself. There were pressing issues to discuss— her future for a start.

Maria was dressed in her best silk sari. She had her rosary beads round her neck to protect her from the evil eye in the doctor's office. The receptionist gave them a curious look. Rohini stared back. Polly turned her gaze towards the computer, banging away loudly on the keys.

Bose walked out of his office to greet them. He gave the ladies a polite Namaste. Maria dragged her chair a few inches closer to Rohini's seat. She wrapped her shawl tightly around her and sat with her hands on her lap, looking at the wall behind Bose. Rohini could smell Maria's cheap perfume and wished she had said something earlier. After a few minutes while Bose adjusted his seat and rearranged his notes, Maria placed one hand on Rohini's leg to stop the restless movement.

'What shall I call you, madam?' asked Bose in Bengali with surprising deference.

'Mrs d'Souza. That was my father's name,' said Rohini.

'I am Miss Fernandez,' said Maria with quiet confidence.

Shifting through his papers, Bose asked the first question he came across.

'How do you feel now that your daughter knows the truth?'

Maria looked down. If there were a place beyond the floor she would look there. 'Ashamed.'

'Just ashamed? You can tell me honestly Miss. Fernandez.'

'No, I feel happy also. At last my daughter knows me. After years of holding on to the guilty secret, it's a relief. I can look at her and say aloud she is my daughter. But I am sad because it has made Rohini *beti* so unhappy. I did not want that. That's why we kept quiet. I did not want her to know all the ugly stories of her past. I knew she was fragile and would break under pressure. I wanted to protect her. But what is the use? God has other plans.'

For the first time, Rohini felt this whole incident could have been avoided if she had embraced the truth. Would the world have dared to point fingers if she had accepted her identity? At the back of that thought, memories of her speech at the Award Ceremony came flooding back.

'I tried to tell them in Delhi, but they turned it all upside down,' she blurted out.

Bose nodded. He looked once more at Maria. 'What do you think Rohini should do now? Carry on as before or work harder to let her circle accept you?'

Maria twisted her body towards her daughter. 'I want it to be how it was before. I want to remain in the shadows. I am too old to start again. I don't like all these smart people talking to me. Indira is her mother in this world. I gave up my rights a long time ago. I will always love Rohini, but I don't belong in her world. People will forget in a few years if we carry on as before.'

Bose turned to his patient. 'Rohini?'

'I am glad I have found out the truth, no matter how hard it has been. All my life I knew something was not right. I would like to get back to my old world, but it's not so simple. Friends treat me differently. I don't feel the same way about my mother Indira, anymore. I am lost. The future worries me. When it is time for Kavita's wedding, they will find out about my background. How many will proceed?'

Maria looked at Rohini and touched her hand. 'Kavita, will find someone she loves and he will accept her whatever her caste or class.' Rohini hoped her mother was right, but she could not take any chances. She would leave this class bound society forever.

Rohini sat Maria down in the waiting room with a magazine to look at. She looked at the clock. She must hurry.

'I have to discuss a few things with the doctor. You'll be fine here.'

She ignored Maria's scared look and went back to Bose's room.

'Something else has happened.'

'Sit down. You still have twenty minutes.'

Rohini didn't know where to start. This *raga* had begun a long time ago; the notes were still ringing in her ears. Try as she might, she could not escape the two years in Shyamnagar.

'Sunita was Shourav's colleague. But I knew they were more than that. He was always late. They worked their shifts together. Sometimes, he came home early in the morning smelling of her. He denied everything of course. He said I was insecure, paranoid. I decided if he could cheat so could I. I met Sarojini, and she introduced me to Tony. He was a tea taster, an Anglo Indian from England. We met a few times and really hit it off. He was into poetry and art.'

She took a deep breath before rushing out the final sentence, 'One night we went to a hotel.'

Bose's pen had not stopped since she started. She wished she had not been so frank. It was all there in black and white now, a sordid part of her life recorded in her doctor's notes. Some instinct made him tell her. If he was going to be a friend for life, he had to know.

'It was only the one time.'

She couldn't read his face. She wished he would talk, but he just looked at his notepad.

'Then Sunita left town abruptly. Shourav was like a ghost for months. I was expecting Kavita. When she came along we mended matters and have kept it together ever since. And now Sunita is back and I am afraid I'll lose him again. He is always on the phone to her. She is married, but since when did that stop anyone?'

He looked up at last. His eyes had gone a darker shade of brown. Was he judging her?

'Can you trust him?' he asked.

'I don't know.'

Bose put his pad away.

'You'll have to confront this or it will burn you up. Talk to Shourav, tell him how you feel, how his friendship with Sunita is affecting you.'

'And if he doesn't listen?'

'Come back to me.'

He leaned back, chewing his pen. His gaze lasted a minute.

Their session was over. Rohini tidied her belongings. She felt the pressure of Maria waiting outside. She said a hasty goodbye to Bose. In the lift she wondered what he really meant when he said *Come back to me*.

Chapter 9 Rohini

Shourav's snoring penetrated the narrow wall between their bedrooms. For years when she had slept next to him, it had not bothered her. Now that she occupied the guest room, it kept her awake. The first part of the night was worse, when he drifted off to sleep, tired after a hard day at the hospital. She could no longer rouse him by a gentle nudge or, if that did not work, give him a sharp jab in the ribs. She contemplated banging on the wall. Their double bed was aesthetically placed in the centre of the room, so he probably wouldn't hear.

She couldn't blame him for the move. It was her idea. A month after Indira and Maria left, Rohini still simmering from her husband's liaison with Sunita, suggested a change in their sleeping habits.

'Is there any point sharing a room when you creep in at night and then sleep furthest away from me? Then there is your loud snoring and coughing. I can't bear this any longer. I need my sleep to function.'

She was addressing the hunched form hiding behind a large, rustling, newspaper.

'What are you suggesting?' Surprisingly the man behind The Statesman responded, folding away the crisp sheets.

Rohini held his gaze—intense, questioning. For a moment she faltered. Twenty years was a long time to sleep next to a person.

'I mean the guest bedroom is empty most of the time. Why don't I sleep there? Then we both get a good night's sleep and I don't have to prod you awake every time you snore.'

Her voice faded away towards the end. She took a large gulp of tea. All the couples she knew slept together—was this a step too extreme?

'Paru, another coffee please,' said Shourav turning his head towards the kitchen.

He scooped up the rest of the *aloo bhaji*, fried potatoes, with a quarter of his shriveled *paratha*. The fan stirred stale air around the room. Paru came in with a fresh pot of coffee. Rohini was proud of her new Corning percolator. She did not drink coffee herself, but Shourav liked it. He slurped the hot drink, abnormally uncouth.

'Well? Aren't going to reply to me?' Rohini had to get ready for school and she was damned if she was going to let this thing hang over their heads all day.

'Do as you wish. I can't see why you are asking for my permission to move out if it's making your life so uncomfortable.'

'You are making a big *natak* about this. It's not like I am moving out of the house. Just to another room. Lots of people do it, especially older couples.'

'My parents shared a room until they died. Yours do the same. But anyway, it's your choice, Rohini. If it makes you happy, do it. When you get tired of my presence in your life, do let me know so I can move out and leave you in peace.'

Rohini banged her fist on the table. 'I knew you would blame it on me. *Paru, clear the dishes later. We are talking.*'

She followed him into their bedroom.

'It is interesting that you are the one talking about moving out. I wonder what Dr. Bose will think of that? Some hidden Freudian wish of yours, emerging in the heat of the moment.'

'I forbid you to talk to Pranab about this. It's private. Have you no sense of dignity?'

'It's you who sent me to therapy. I have to talk about everything in my life.'

She had played the role of docile wife for too long. Who else would put up with a husband, frequently absent or late without so much as a phone call?

Shourav disappeared into the bathroom. The shower jet hit the tiles with intense force. Rohini picked out a maxi dress from the wardrobe, the only space they shared. A brass Ganesh adorned the dressing table. She remembered when Shourav had bought it for her, knowing her penchant for the elephant-headed God. It was such a long time ago, their first year of marriage—the agonies of loneliness indelibly etched in her brain.

Rohini took out her old diary, hidden amongst her personal things. The leather looked worn, the pages crisp.

1993 Shyamnagar

It is June, the time for monsoon rains. Dark clouds have gathered all day, but the rain has not come. The moon, colour of a ripe peach, plays hide and seek with the clouds. I am alone in the bungalow. The sound of the chowkidar's baton hitting lamp posts should be reassuring, but it fills me with fear. We live on the edge of town, dacoit country. Mr. Das, who lived two streets away, was found strung up on a post, right outside his house. Despite the new metal gate, I am afraid. One day someone will come to rob me of my life, of Shourav.

Except it wasn't a robber in the end, it was Sunita.

Her list of accusations backed up by evidence in her journal, fragmented into disjointed pieces when she recounted them to Shourav. He paused in the middle of towelling his hair to decipher the confused volley of words *when you did this and I felt that*. The *chowkidar's* baton mingled with the Das's tragedy, the gate, and the bolts. He shook his head, scattering away her words dipped in self-pity.

'Why do you dredge up things from the past? It has no bearing on the present.'

'*Au contraire.* It shows how even when I was young and vulnerable you left me alone in the house. Did you have to work late every night or was there someone keeping you company?'

'Not now, Rohini. Please. I have to go to work.'

'Shit! Is that the time? Kavita, where are you? We have to leave in fifteen minutes.'

One of those October nights Rohini lay awake, wishing she had not been the one to suggest separate rooms. After a month of sleeping apart she was still not used to it. Bose had advised her to talk to Shourav. She had bungled it—suggesting a separation before talking about the elephant in the room.

Earlier that evening, they had gone to a party at the Guptas. It was an elaborate affair with enough food to feed a small village. Rohini stayed by her husband's side—nodding at one, accepting kebabs from another. Her head ached with stretching her jaws wide in unwanted smiles. They came home silent. Rohini took off her jewellery and her *payannzi,* onion pink, sari.

'I'm off to bed then,' she announced.

Shourav nodded, taking off his watch, a gift she had given him on his fiftieth. She doubted he remembered. She climbed into bed, tucking her feet under a light sheet. They had come home early despite protest from friends. Tiredness overcame her, but she could only doze.

She heard Shourav's phone ring. It was three am, late for a call. There was prolonged talking. She heard him go to the toilet. Ten minutes later the bedroom door creaked. He was trying to be quiet. She could just let him slip out, but something Maria had said once popped into her head—*never go to bed without making up and never let someone leave the house without saying goodbye.*

'Where are you going? Is it the hospital?' she asked, determined to keep up normal communications.

For once, the usual response did not follow swiftly: *It's the hospital. A patient needs urgent care. I'm not sure when I'll be back.*

She looked at him, hair tousled, shirt askew, trousers barely done up. His eyes drifted to a picture of his mother on the wall unit.

'It was Sunita. Her daughter has not come home. She is very worried. She can't go out to search alone. Her husband is not well, heart problems. So she has asked for my help. They don't know many people in Mumbai.'

It was the separation that had made him open up to her— tell her the truth about how the land lay. Sunita calls, she gets him out of bed, searching for her reckless daughter in the middle of the night through seedy streets of Mumbai—it was more that Rohini could have ever achieved.

'I'll come with you.' Surprise was the best strategy in a battle.

'No, no you rest. I could be hours. I'll have to visit the nightclubs… hospitals.' She noted a faint tremor in his voice.

'Is Sunita going with you?'

'No, she is with her husband.'

'Wait for me. I'll be two minutes.' She pulled on a pair of jeans and a crumpled t-shirt.

'I don't want to worry about your safety as well,' he grumbled.

'As if you ever do. I'm worried about you. Do you know how many gangsters parade the streets? If you are with a woman, they might let us through. You have the doctors cross on the window, that'll protect us.'

If there was to be a tearful reunion in the middle of the night, she wanted to be there, next to her husband, a barrier between Sunita and him.

They tried the top hotels first and their nightclubs. The local ones in Bandra were easier to scour. Then Juhu, Santa Cruz, Worli, the list was endless. Rohini dialled Mona's number over and over again, hoping the girl might answer at some point. The eastern sky was pale. Rohini's eyes closed. Five-minute cat nap, that's all she needed. Shourav's tense body over the wheel reminded her of the night they had rushed baby Kavita to hospital with suspected meningitis. How could Sunita ask this of him when the real father was tucked up in bed? Mona could be anywhere—in the arms of a lover in a flat somewhere.

It was four thirty am. They pulled over in front of Tryst, a smart dance club. Youngsters were spilling out on the streets hailing taxies. Shourav jumped out of the car and ran along the pavement. Rohini craned her neck, trying to get a better view. He grabbed one of the boys by the shirt collar, gesticulating with his other hand. The boy made a call and sat heavily on the steps. Half an hour later a black Mercedes pulled up. A waif of a girl fell out, staggering on impossibly high heels. She keeled over and fell into Shourav's open arms. He dragged her across the cracked pavement, avoiding the slime from recently ejected vomit.

He shook her like a rat. She slumped on the back seat, reeking of something nauseatingly sweet.

'What have you been drinking? Did you take drugs? Tell me the truth. *Saatch bolo.* Your mother has been sick with worry about you. Mona! Wake up, wake up.' He tapped her cheek.

There were just groans. Shourav took out a torch from his pocket and flashed it into her eyes.

'Dilated pupils.' He left her supine on the back seat.

He was talking to Sunita. 'Yes she is here. She was hanging out in the campus area with some college kids. Luckily I spotted Pintu and he knew where she was. She'll be fine, don't worry. If we have to pump her stomach we'll do it. Teach her a lesson... Yes come as soon as you can.' He hung up.

He knew Mona's friends; Rohini tried not to think about that.

'Mona, this is Uncle Shourav. Do you recognise me? Tell me what you had. We need to treat you.'

Again soft moans emerged from the girl's mouth, bubbles appearing in the corners.

'Rohini, I could do with some help. Can you loosen her jeans? Then place your hands under her head and gently put her on her side—in case she vomits.'

Rohini slammed the passenger door and walked over, arms folded across her chest. 'You do it. You're the doctor and the good Samaritan.'

'Why did you come then? You want me to be arrested for pulling at her clothes?'

Rohini grumbled, loosening Mona's belt.

'Decent girls don't go out partying like this. Thank God Kavita isn't like her. What she needs is a strong hand.'

Shourav found a bottle of water in the glove compartment, left there by Shivu for hot drives. He chucked the water over the girl's face.

Mona whelped. 'What the fuck? Leave me alone. You're not my father.' She put an arm across her wet face.

'Just tell me what you had.'

'H-a-sh-ish and vodka. It was cool,' she susurrated, a smile emerging on her face.

Rohini noticed her pretty mouth, caked with an unnecessary amount of pink lipstick. She would be a beauty like her mother when not stoned out of her mind. Mona giggled, and then burst into a shout of laughter.

'How high are you? I'm high as a kite.'

Shourav restrained her flailing arms as she tried to sit up.

'What else did you take Mona? Do you remember?'

'Who are you?' Mona squinted at Shourav. 'Go away.' She swished at an invisible fly. 'So thirsty. Feel sleepy. Take me home.'

'Yes we will. Your mother is waiting.'

Shourav closed the car door and took a cigarette out. Rohini frowned.

'When did you start smoking again? Didn't the doctor tell you to stop?'

'I'm the doctor. Let me think. I have a feeling she has taken other stuff and maybe it's safer to take her to a hospital.'

They heard scrabbling inside the car. Mona had rolled on to the floor and was searching for something.

'There is a snake under the seat. Get it out!' she cried.

She climbed on to the seat and beat against the roof of the car, screaming. Her eyes were bloodshot. Rohini thought she looked mad: matted locks were plastered to her head, mascara streaked her face. She looked around, eyes wide with fear. A crowd gathered outside. Shourav tried to explain to them that he was her uncle and she was ill.

'Look at her frightened face! They are kidnapping her.'

A dozen people surged forward, some clutching and pulling at Mona's clothes, others grabbing Shourav. Rohini felt her throat closing. She prayed for someone to save them.

'*Chchro moojhey*,' Mona shrieked at her saviours. *Let me go!*

Shourav told Rohini in Bengali, 'Get in the car. Call the police.'

Rohini had little faith in the authorities. It would take ages for them to respond. Besides, whom would they believe? In her current psychotic state, Mona could not be relied on to vouch for them or tell a coherent story. Rohini picked up Shourav's phone and dialled Sunita's number with trembling fingers. The voice on the other side was calm, sophisticated. Rohini remembered that tone, one that made her feel inadequate.

'This is Rohini. There is an angry crowd here. Mona is hysteric. They think we are kidnapping her. Can you call the police? *Jaldi*. They are about to attack Shourav.'

She could hear him shouting 'I'm a doctor. She's my niece. We are taking her home.' *Saala, he's a pervert, they swore. They'll pimp the girl.*

Rohini looked for some kind of weapon, an iron rod, an umbrella, anything to fend off the mob. She spotted something orange by the gear stick, a worthy tool. Standing away from the crowd she blew hard on the plastic whistle three times in long sharp bursts. The people stopped in the middle of clumsy strikes at their victim and looked around.

'*Mama,*' they shouted. Uncle: euphemism for the police. They dropped their prey and dispersed slowly, shouting back a threat. A few remained who believed in Shourav's innocence and had taken some of the blows. Are you okay, brother?

Rohini rushed to her husband's side, brushing away the blood with a tissue. He winced and spit out a jet of crimson.

'I've had worse at the hospital when they bring in an injured member of a gang. The rivals come to beat up the doctors, to stop the treatment. It's not like we have the police at our doorstep.'

Momentarily Rohini felt pride in her husband's strength. It was easy to misjudge his fortitude for stoicism. So many times he had taken things in his stride, without a word of complaint; she had seen it as a weakness, an inability and unwillingness to take a stand.

Shourav checked on Mona. Her pulse was slow, fading. Her face had taken on a grey tinge.

'She is deteriorating. We have to go.'

Shourav pulled out of the kerb slowly and made a call to a colleague at Santa Cruz. 'We'll be seen to straightaway. Mallik is on duty. I said she is my niece.'

Mona was wheeled into emergency and attached to a drip. A nurse cleaned up Shourav's wound. Rohini felt faint with tiredness. She could never have been a doctor. It required immense amount of stamina to tend to a patient. They had a coffee from the drink machine—hot but tasteless. It would be a long wait. Rohini closed her eyes, resting her head against the wall. She awoke to clattering feet and hushed voices.

There she stood, twenty years on, an anxious mother. Her white *salwar kameez* was pristinely smooth even after a sleepless night. Dark circles enhanced her almond eyes. A streak or two of grey dignified her charcoal hair. Sunita. Her eyes raked Shourav's face, taking in the damage. She stretched out a hand to check the wound; then stopped. It was natural for a doctor to want to examine a patient.

'Ice the swelling when you go home,' she advised.

Sunita turned like a ballerina. She was doing a *Namaste* to Rohini now, apologising for inconveniencing them and thanking Shouravji and Rohini for their kindness. Shourav found her a seat and a masala chai, all very correct. Rohini felt she had misjudged their relationship. There was nothing to suggest anything inappropriate in their behaviour. The two mothers spoke of teenage children. Dr. Bhatia was not well and could not keep control of their daughter. Sunita was busy with her work. Perhaps she should get an unmarried cousin to stay with them: befriend the girl, keep a gentle eye and report back to Sunita. Rohini nodded. Girls needed care.

The doctor called them in at last, next of kin only. Sunita rushed in. Quarter of an hour later, she stumbled out. Shourav rushed to her side and steadied her. Through a muddle of half sentences, Sunita told them that the medical team had found some cannabis and alcohol in Mona's blood. They also found significant amount of painkillers and so her stomach had been pumped out. Mona often suffered from headaches, Sunita explained. Perhaps she had lost count and taken too many. But her daughter was recovering and would be sent home after a few hours. Sunita grabbed a junior doctor to question him further about the treatment. Rohini and Shourav promised to stay until Mona was discharged.

The morning was bright when a pale and contrite Mona was wheeled into Sunita's car. Rohini and Shourav followed them back to their apartment where a bearded man in a dressing gown answered the door.

'Papa!' Mona cried and rushed into his open arms.

'*Beti*, what have you been up to? Gave us such a fright! Don't ever do it again, my precious.'

Dr. Bhatia was a big bear of a man. Mona's frail frame disappeared into his bulk and he rocked her like a baby. When at last he let go he shook Shourav's hands for several minutes.

289

'You saved my daughter's life, brother.'

Shourav fiddled with his keys. 'We better go. Rohini and I will come and see you in a few days.'

It felt good to be included in this duty visit, no longer a clandestine meeting. Why had she not instigated this sooner? Instead of harbouring resent for so long, they could have been friends. Rohini, feeling charitable, gave Sunita a hug.

They arrived early one evening to see the patient. Sunita greeted them at the door and led them inside. The flat was decorated with Rajasthani art. A tray of samosas, scotch eggs, and *halwa* was handed around. There was no sign of Mona.

'I told her to stay, but she went out,' explained Sunita. 'She has gone to a friend's house, Poppy Khanna. I have their number to check she is there.'

Rohini bit into the scotch eggs. The men were talking about cricket. Sunita showed Rohini around the flat. Her kitchen was small but neatly arranged. They swapped recipes. Sunita loved Bengali food. She had tried some at a restaurant in Kolkata on one of her conference trips. Rohini promised to call them over soon.

There was a wedding picture of Sunita and Dr. Bhatia. She was wearing her sari with the *pallu* draped over her front making her look quite big. Her figure had always been a thing of envy to Rohini when she was in Shyamnagar. *Kolshi* shaped —tiny waist and curvy hips, a perfect water pot.

'We had a simple ceremony, just the family. It's Dr. Bhatia's second marriage. His first wife died in a car crash. He has no other living relatives.'

Sunita could have done a lot better for herself, being young, clever and beautiful at the time. Dr. Bhatia was at least twenty years her senior.

'So that was just after we left Shyamnagar,' said Rohini when she saw the year etched in gold underneath. 'Whirlwind romance?'

'Something like that,' said Sunita, moving away from the mantelpiece.

'This must be Mona.' Rohini picked up a framed picture of a toddler. Sunita took it from her. 'Yes. Let's go to the sitting room. Our husbands are waiting.'

The ladies sat on a crescent sofa. There were paintings on the wall, mostly modern art. Sunita followed Rohini's gaze. 'Mona's handiwork,' she said with pride.

'She's artistic,' Rohini acknowledged. 'She goes to St. Joseph, *na*? My friend's daughter, Nita Das is in eleventh. Which standard is Mona in?'

Sunita looked away, distracted by a remark made by her husband.

'My husband thinks I can't cook and I bought the snacks. The maid is off today, so I took over the kitchen.' She turned to her husband. 'Bhatia-ji, I spent all afternoon making the scotch eggs from a recipe on the Internet. I replaced pork mince with mutton, that's all. Renovate the kitchen and I'll cook every day,' she said pouring some tea into china cups.

Rohini wondered if Mona was a poor student and had missed an academic year. That would explain Sunita seizing the chance to segue into another conversation. Food was always a safe topic. Rohini sipped her tea. The girl was wild and no doubt it reflected in her school results. She was thankful once again that Kavita, despite minor rebellions, had not gone off the track like Mona.

The scotch eggs were spiced with chilies, garlic and chopped coriander. The end product was like Nargisi kebab, but there was no point splitting hairs. It was a tasty snack. She would impress the Bhatias with a Bengali chop, spicy mince balls coated in seasoned mashed potatoes and crumbs, deep fried until golden.

The doorbell rang. Sunita glided over to answer. She held the door ajar. 'You're early!'

'Hello Uncle, Aunti-ji.' Mona did an awkward Namaste. Silver and blue bangles tinkled.

Sunita stood in front of her daughter. 'Mona, why don't you go and freshen up? Uncle Shourav and Aunty Rohini are just leaving.'

Mona pushed past her mother. 'I wanted to say thank you for the other night.'

Long earrings swung as she lurched forward on stiletto heels. She scraped back a wayward fringe slanting across her forehead. Her hair was swept high into an untidy ponytail, loose curls caressing her shoulders.

'I am really sorry to have been so much trouble.' She folded her hands. Each nail was intricately decorated with floral pattern and gems.

Rohini noted the short skirt and ankle boots. A turquoise stud twinkled on her nose. 'Trouble' just about summed her up.

'Do you have to leave now?' asked Mona. Hazel eyes, heavy with eye shadow, rested on the Chatterjees.

'It's okay. We can stay a few more minutes,' said Shourav.

'Uncle, I want to show you something I made.' Holding Shourav by the arm she led him to her bedroom.

Shourav returned holding a rolled up poster in his hand. They unfurled it on the coffee table. It was a painting of a young girl. Her face was savagely slashed. Bloodied knives dangled in the air. A pale sun floated amongst dark clouds. A man standing in the shadows beckoned with an open palm.

'You saved me and I wanted to capture it in a painting. Do you like it, Uncle?'

'Of course, it's very nice,' said Shourav rolling it back up. It would never see the light of day. 'I'm glad you're better. Make sure you stay out of trouble,' he said touching her cheek.

Mona smiled; a crooked tooth, one sitting just above the other, poked out of a corner of her mouth. A *gaunge daanth* was uncommon but attractive despite the lack of symmetry.

In that instant, Rohini knew the truth. Bile rose in her mouth. She had seen that smile before, in the car when the girl was drugged. Even then it was evident, except she had not realized the significance in the dark amidst all that commotion. Something had tugged at her memory then and she had tucked away the thought. Two matching cards. Snap.

Chapter 10 Rohini

The drive home from the Bhatias was quick as the office hour traffic had subsided. Shourav's one-sided conversation above the radio extolled the virtues of Bengali food in comparison with North Indian fare. They would invite Sunita and her family soon. Rohini could them cook *aloo dum* and pea *katchauri, na*? Not deterred by silence from his wife, he hummed to a Four Seasons song *I'm working my way back to you babe,* while parking the car meticulously in a narrow space next to a pillar. Rohini walked towards the lift leaving her husband behind. Two clicks of the car keys followed and then the inevitable ring on his mobile. He was definitely talking to a patient this time. He talked dosage, what and how much to administer. If she had arsenic in her possession she would add some to his nightcap.

All the way up to the eighteenth floor he mentioned what a genial person Dr. Bhatia was and that they might play golf together. Rohini's hand shook as she unlocked the front door. Paru was away. Kavita was spending the night at Jaya's house. Rohini switched on the fan and went to her room closing the door. She took out her diary hidden under the mattress and checked the entries for Shyamnagar.

02 October 1993 Gandhiji's birthday.

Mrs. Bannerjee asked me 'Have you met Dr. Chatterjee's new colleague? Dr. Sunita Dhaliwal. Pretty girl: fine nose and fair skin, such pleasant manners too. Shows class. They work well together.'

It's a national holiday, but my husband is working with a pretty junior doctor.

16 Nov

Last night Shourav was late again, playing cards with Dr. Patel. At one pm I rang their house. Their manservant said Chatterjee babu had left a couple of hours ago. Patel Saab was asleep now. What had happened to him? I couldn't bear to think of him lying on a road somewhere. The route back to Gopalpara, our neighbourhood, was dangerous. Dacoits lay in wait for a nice car to come by. I thought of calling the police. Finally at three am a car pulled up outside our home.

Where had he been? I knew he was lying when he said 'hospital'. I had rung there already. Dr. Kumar was dealing with emergencies. Dr. Dhaliwal and Chatterjee were off. Still it isn't proof of any kind.

23 Dec

I went to the hospital to spy on the two. The corridors were lined with fairy lights. A Christmas tree adorned the foyer. I waited forty-five minutes outside the theatre, hiding behind a pillar. There was smell of death everywhere. Spirits floated in the corridor. At last, they emerged laughing. Shourav undid the ribbons on the back of Sunita's surgical gown. She stepped on the hem of her sari and the pleats fell on to the floor in a heap. Shourav gathered up her sari. She kept her eyes downcast watching his masculine fingers trying to tuck the voile back into place— touching her skin where it covered her womb. Time stood still for these two lovers.

He denies everything. I am imagining things.

3 March, 1994

Shourav came home today looking as if he has lost everything. I wonder if he is depressed.

15 March

Mrs. Bannerjee says the pretty Dr. Dhaliwal has found a job in New Delhi.

May

We are expecting a baby. Shourav is excited. Thank God, the madness has passed.

Rohini closed the diary. Shourav knocked on the door.

'*Ki?*' she called out. Her voice didn't sound like hers—deep bass.

'Is Kavita coming home tonight or shall I lock up?' Shourav came in.

'She is at Jaya's.'

Rohini opened a book on her lap. She had hidden the diary under her pillow.

'What's wrong?'

'Nothing. Go to sleep.'

'You didn't have to go to Sunita's tonight. Why do you dislike her so much?'

Rohini dabbed some cream on her hands and rubbed it in. She cocked her head to one side. 'Let me think of a reason. I hate her because... she slept with you and had your child.'

'God Rohini, please stop. You go a little *pagol* whenever her name is mentioned.'

Shourav left, shutting the door. Rohini leapt out of her bed and pounced on his retreating back, clutching his nightshirt. If he had thought her a little mad before, he thought her insane now. The shock on his face was evident as he clearly expected her to bash him on the head with something.

'Mona is your daughter, you blind fool!' Rohini threw her diary at him. 'I knew it all along. Mona's smile is yours. Can't you see that? She was born in September 1994. Sunita left Shyamnagar in March. She got married in July. I saw her photos and the dates. She looked pregnant. Dr. Bhatia married her, a pretty damsel in distress. Now I know why Sunita was rushing us out tonight. She knew she couldn't fool me.'

Shourav sat weightily in an armchair. 'What are you saying? It's nonsense.'

'Do you still deny having an affair with her?'

Shourav shrunk further into the seat. His answer was inaudible.

There were no tears. An incandescent rage burned inside Rohini's head.

'Were all these years a lie? You've loved her all along?'

Shourav buried his head in his hands. Rohini left him there. By dawn her bed was wet with perspiration. She emptied a large glass of water and felt sick. What is the right medication for being cheated? Valium was not working. She would not die and make it easier for them.

Shourav rose early the next day. She heard him creeping about, trying not to trip over anything. Paru was up. She asked if sahib would like a cup of tea. No, he hissed, go back to bed. Rohini rested her head on a folded arm, elevating it slightly to hear their conversation better. She knew where he was going before work.

Rohini went for a walk throwing a light pashmina over her thick Kashmiri *salwar kameez*. A large circular path girdled the compound. Verdant lawn glistened with dew. Seasonal flowers —marigolds, roses, chrysanthemums, grew in gay circles. She brushed past Hydrangea bushes, the pale blue and pink balls of flowers nodding in greeting. The sun warmed her back. Soon it would be too hot to wear a shawl. Even in winter the midday heat was tiresome.

Rohini was aching to unburden all to a friend. She thought of calling Bose. It seemed a bit sad that the only person in her life willing to lend a sympathetic ear was her therapist. And he was paid for his trouble.

When the anger subsided she felt relief. Finally her fears had been proved right. Shourav would accept his misdeed and ask for forgiveness. She didn't feel grief, yet. There was hope. Lots of couples overcame obstacles. Their marriage would survive this.

Back in the apartment Rohini stuck to her routine: prayers, yoga and bath. She prepared her lesson for the day. The class would be given a free writing project today—one thousand words on a topic—Betrayal. Shivu knocked on the door. Was Madam ready? Rohini picked up her purse.

At six, Rohini told Paru to bring out her exercise books to begin their lesson. In her village school Paru had mastered the alphabet and basic numbers. Now with Rohini's help, she could write a few simple sentences in Bengali. She recognised numbers in English. Next Rohini would teach Paru to do proper sums and read signs. Paru was smart and could calculate a lot in her head—the price of three oranges, a kilo of rice, fish and meat. The vendors seldom cheated her.

Rohini asked Paru to write a letter to a friend.

Dear Kanti, she wrote, I am well. How is your kitten? My mistress has one called Ghum. She is lazy. Paru had to ask Rohini for the spelling of *alosh*. The subject of the letter lay curled up next to Paru's ankle, tickling her feet with soft fur. She was putting on weight.

'What do you feed her, rice pudding every day?' asked Rohini.

'No Ma,' Paru giggled, covering her face with her scarf. 'I give her rice, flaked with leftover fish and vegetables.'

Shourav's key rattled in the door. Paru was about to get up when Rohini frowned at her. 'Get on with your letter.'

It has not rained for days. It is cold in the mornings when I go to pick flowers for puja.

'How many times have I told you the spelling of *sakal*? It's the other *S, dontesho not talabbosho.*'

'*S-a-k-a-l.*' Rohini circled the word for 'morning' in red. She crossed out the palm tree shaped S, adding the more pragmatic square shaped S, Bengali alphabets were not easy to master—looping, intricate designs needing a certain amount of calligraphic skill.

'I'm tired,' said Paru.

There were too many joined up letters for her to cope with. In the word for *cold, thanda,* the n and d were joined and had to be scribed neatly. Her friend's name was not simple either: Kanti, n and t sitting on top of one another.

'Ok stop now. We'll do sums tomorrow. Practise your times tables tonight.'

Shourav was in the bedroom. A gentle evening breeze carried the cricket commentary from his radio to the lounge. India was playing Pakistan. There were threats of trouble at the ground. Gavasker's voice rose to a frenzied pitch as a batsman narrowly escaped being bowled out. Rohini rearranged the magazines on the coffee table, smacking each one down on the glass.

'Have you started the vegetables, Paru?' she yelled towards the kitchen.

Paru appeared at the doorway, her hands covered in flour. 'I'm making the bread. The okras have been made already. Shall I do some dal? It'll only take five minutes in the pressure cooker.'

'Yes. Make Toor dal. Temper with asafoetida and a dried red chilli. I'll check later. No ghee,' she instructed the nodding maid.

The cricket was still on. Shourav's eyes were closed when Rohini came in. The flecks of grey at his temples and lines on his forehead were new. She sat on one end of the bed. He pretended to be asleep. She switched the radio off.

'This won't go away you know. I wish it would.'

'What do you want from me? I am sorry. Ashamed and grieved to have been foolish once, but it was many years ago. If you can't forgive me then we have to think of something else.'

Where was the *begging to forgive him*, *let him stay* scene that she had created in her head? He was giving her a bland choice —forgive and forget or split. She felt heat rise from her toes and flood her face.

'Simple for you isn't it? You have a woman and child waiting for you on each side. It doesn't matter to you. In fact it's more comfortable on the other side because you adore each other.'

Shourav got up. 'All I want is some peace. I realise that I am expecting a lot from you to forgive an affair. But you admitted that you had a fling too. It was a bad patch in our marriage and unfortunately I have a painful proof of that. One I know about now and can't ignore. Dr. Bhatia knows the true identity of Mona's father as well so he doesn't want me to go around. I met Sunita in a coffee shop to discuss things. She wants nothing from me. Mona knows her father is Kapil Bhatia and Sunita wants to leave things as it is. I don't know what to do. You will never let this rest. It's going to destroy our marriage.'

Marriage—a sacred bond that had started with walking around the fire seven times, exchanging garlands and glances, resting their hands on a brass pot as the priest chanted mantras in Sanskrit. When Rohini had committed herself to Shourav her heart had belonged to another. Perhaps he had sensed that and strayed. She would do anything now to bring him back.

'I can forgive with time. You can see Mona, but in order for our relationship to succeed you must give up your friendship with Sunita.' This was fair.

Shourav sat on the bed looking at the spread, a Bengal handloom print—elephants and palanquins. He smoothed out a crease.

'I think it'll work. I am not sure if Sunita will tell Mona. I don't feel like I am her father yet. Kavita is my daughter. I can't switch overnight. But I guess, ultimately, it is my duty to be a father to her as well, especially as she is a little wayward.'

'If Sunita doesn't want to tell her then why not leave things as they are for the moment? But you mustn't have any connection with Sunita.'

'Yes, I'll speak to her.'

His docility surprised Rohini. She was ready for his protests. Could she trust him to be true to his word?

They agreed on a few months trial. No contact with Sunita and Mona. Life would continue as per usual. Rohini thanked God for a second chance. She took a big donation to Baba-ji's ashram and paid her respects without revealing any sordid details. Shourav and Rohini went to the cinema, for the first time in years.

When Rohini entered Bose's office she knew she would tell him the truth. He listened, head cocked, pen suspended in air.

'It was magnanimous of you to forgive him,' he commented.

'You don't agree?'

'It's not for me to judge.'

Rohini was uncertain about what Bose thought of her decision. She had expected approval of her reasonable behaviour.

'I trust him.'

'Of course. That is your prerogative.'

'What do you mean? Why do you talk in a mysterious way? Why don't you just say how you feel? Is he going to cheat on me again and see Sunita behind my back? Am I being a foolish, trusting wife?'

'Rohini, I can't make judgments like that. You know your relationship best. Just don't be blinded by a determination to mend matters. You are doing the sensible thing and giving your marriage a chance. I can't fault you for that.'

'But you think it's unwise?'

'I think you should see another therapist. I am not the best person to be objective in this case.'

Bose got up and paced the floor. He tugged at his collar. She had hardly ever seen him distressed.

'What's wrong?'

'Nothing. Please let's get on with the session.'

Rohini talked about her doubts, about Shyamnagar. Bose tapped his pen, much to her annoyance. It was distracting. She was deep into a story, recounting the day Sunita had attended a party and was standing next to Shourav, their bodies nudging each other. She could not read the clock anymore. Bose knelt beside her, an arm cradling her shaking shoulders.

'I can't let you go through this agony any longer. It's going to cause a setback in your treatment. Rohini, you need someone who cares about you and only you. You deserve to be loved unconditionally and not be second best.'

She wept into his terry-cotton shirt. 'It's all been too much this year. First losing my mother, the one I had known all my life and now my husband. I can't take it anymore.'

'Run away with me! We'll start a new life in a new town. Like fugitives with a brand new identity.'

She smiled. 'I like the sound of that.' She wiped her face.

Bose's hand on her shoulder was warm. Shourav hadn't held her like that for a long time. Was she just desperate for a man's touch or? She blocked the thought. Pranab had revealed his cards despite ethical hesitation. If she ran to his arms, she would find shelter. She was not a poker player and feared that feelings she had long tried to suppress were evident in her face. If she returned his affection, then Shourav would win. She would be just as guilty.

Bose stood. He wrote out a prescription for mild sedatives. 'I'll see you in two weeks. Call me any time before that if you need to talk. In fact, call me. I'd like that.'

Rohini felt a gladness that was hard to define. There was someone who wanted to talk to her, hear her voice.

'Hmm, take the tablets regularly and note down any side effects.'

His professional demeanour had returned. For a few seconds, she had glimpsed another Pranab, a risk taking romantic.

He was holding the door open for her now. It was a difficult question, but she had to ask. Whispering with diffidence she queried, 'Were you serious about us running away together?' Then realising the foolishness of her thought, she added quickly, 'Of course not. Don't reply. I'm an idiot.'

'No you're not. Why don't you have a good think and figure out whether or not my offer was serious? The clues are all there.'

She had goose pimples on her arm. He smiled and gave a quick wink before ushering her out. Rohini's hand shook as she wrote out a cheque for the receptionist.

'You've written the wrong date. It's the eighteenth, not the nineteenth, Madam.'

Rohini murmured an apology and neatly amended her error. The door to the doctor's office closed as the next patient was invited in. As she waited for the lift she turned back hearing laughter. Bose had emerged out of his office. Polly was handing him the notes for his patient, snatching it away just as he tried to grab the file. He looked down at her upturned face with a mischievous grin and tapped her head with a pencil in an admonitory gesture. Rohini slammed the door of the lift, making Polly turn around. Bose had disappeared into his consulting room.

Chapter 11 Rohini

The queue to Baba-ji's ashram was longer than usual. It was the winter festival. Pilgrims lined the path, laden with offerings—plates piled high with fruits of the season, Kashmiri oranges, coconuts, rust coloured apples and bananas. Large blooms of zinnia, marigolds and hibiscus topped the fruits. Poking out from the pyramid of fruits and flowers were incense sticks. Rohini suppressed a sneeze, the powerful aroma tickling her sensitive nose. The children carrying bags of rice and boxes of sweets jostled each other in an attempt to maintain their place in a rather crooked queue. How much longer, they asked?

A wan sun barely warmed the bodies crowding together. It was unusually cold for Mumbai. Rohini wished she had worn a cardigan underneath her shawl. They were supposed to worship at dawn. But no one could tell whether the sun had risen or not. A grey dirty fog smothered the city. The ash skies brightened a touch at five causing a stir amongst the tired worshippers. Most had been waiting for hours. *Darwaza khulia!* Open the doors, they shouted.

At six, the guards flung open the gates. *It's past dawn already*, the people grumbled, washing their feet and entering the holy premises. Each sounded the bell upon entering. Rohini found a spot, a few rows behind the idols, a good place to be. The brass images shone and fresh garlands hung around their necks. She felt the eyes of the deities focusing on her alone. Vishnu's hand was raised in blessing. As the room melded into a mass of chanting and fragrant fumes, she receded into a pastoral world, where Krishna played with *gopies*, enchanting the maidens with his flute and Ma Durga reigned over the world, protecting her children. A young man was playing the *dhol*, an elongated drum. Rohini joined the rest, humming and swaying to the music.

It was a holy day off and schools and offices were shut. Shourav was working for a few hours at the hospital. He had promised to come home early and take the family out to dinner. Kavita wanted Chinese. There was a new continental restaurant at the mall that Rohini was eager to try, although she should follow a vegetarian diet on a festival day.

'Papa, you're late,' Kavita rebuked her father as soon as he walked in through the door.

She had changed into a going out outfit already—a long purple skirt with a white *chikan* top. The broderie anglaise blouse was transparent and showed a vague outline of her bra.

'Kavita, change your top or wear a vest underneath. Everything is showing,' said Rohini.

Kavita made a face at her mother but retreated. Shourav planted himself in front of the TV and was absently flicking channels.

'Everything okay?' she asked, a dull foreboding tightening her stomach.

His rigid jaw answered her question.

'Say something,' she urged.

'Sunita called me.'

Rohini got up. If there were a vase nearby, she would have hurled it at him.

'How dare she? Did I not make it clear about not speaking to her? It's only been three months and you have broken your promise.'

Shourav grabbed her arm and pulled her down on the sofa.

'Rohini, listen to me. It's urgent. Bhatia's had a stroke. He's in ICU. Mona has shingles. She has never had chicken pox before. There is no one else Sunita can trust with her care. She has asked me to watch Mona while she is in hospital, which maybe all night. She begs your forgiveness, but she can't find another way.'

Rohini slumped on the settee. 'Even if you don't see Sunita you'll always be connected to her through Mona.'

'Listen, some couples have children from previous relationships and ex-partners. I am just going there as a father, not reuniting with Sunita. It was a long time ago and I have been faithful ever since.'

Rohini breathed deeply, trying to clear her head.

'What about when I was in hospital? Since she has been back in town you two have been seeing a lot of each other behind my back and Bhatia's. I can see it when you are together, you have a bond. You can't deny that.'

'I'm trying to give our marriage another chance and I need you to cooperate. There will be times like this and we'll ride the rough waves together.'

Rohini went to her room and pulled off the silk *salwar kameez* she was wearing. 'Go, just go to that girl. Kavita and I will get a take-away.'

'Thank you.'

Rohini slipped on a kaftan and walked to the cabinet where the drinks were kept. She poured herself a gin and tonic. Kavita came out of her room. 'Where's Papa?'

Rohini briefed her. Kavita sat next to her mother, resting her head on her shoulder. 'Papa still loves us, doesn't he?'

'He loves you.' Rohini kissed her daughter's head.

'Is Aunty Sunita his girlfriend? You can tell me. I'm not a kid anymore. Nita's parents are divorced. Her father had an affair.'

Rohini gave Kavita a squeeze. She had tried to keep the ugly truth from her daughter. The last thing she wanted was to alienate her affections towards her father.

'Once, a long time ago, your father and Sunita had a relationship. It was when we were first married.'

'How could he betray you like that? I'll tell him what I think!' Kavita sat up, battle in her eyes.

'Hear me out, sweetheart. I was hurt and lonely and I too had an affair, a very brief one. Neither of us is completely innocent. I was attracted to this man. He gave me the attention I craved. But I was so ashamed afterwards. I made a huge effort with your Dad, to get him back. Shortly after Sunita left town, you were born and it made us both so happy.'

Kavita pulled her mother into her slim arms. Nothing could come through those limbs wound tightly against her body. Rohini ached to tell her about Mona, her half-sister. But it was up to Shourav to make the revelation. She was doing exactly what her mother had done: shielding her child, protecting someone else's story. She was ready to forgive Indira.

They could hear Paru in the kitchen.

'Shall we go to my room?' asked Kavita.

It wasn't often Rohini was invited into her daughter's inner sanctum. The cleaner grumbled daily of the things *Sister* would not allow her to touch. The room rivalled Aladdin's cave in treasures—coloured beads sprouted from every drawer and were draped over the dressing table. The wall was plastered with photos. One was of Kavita in a bikini by a swimming pool. Her belly button was pierced. When had she done that?

Rohini straightened the quilt and sat on one end of the narrow bed. Kavita bounced onto a pile of cushions and crossed her bare legs. She was wearing her indoor shorts, just covering her hips. Kavita hugged Arjun, a pungent smelling teddy named after a brave warrior in the epic Mahabharata. It was her first gift from her father.

'Is Mona my sister?' Kavita's eyes, charcoal marbles, were fixed on her mother's face.

A tingle in Rohini's left arm travelled up to her shoulders and down her jaw. She was having a heart attack.

'You're bleeding!' cried Kavita.

Rohini looked down at her hand. When had she picked up Kavita's nail scissors? They were on the bed. She remembered holding them in her palm tightly. Her daughter pressed some cotton wool into her wound.

'I'll get the Dettol.'

'No wait. It's only a small cut.'

The unanswered question hung in silence. Rohini wished Shourav was home.

'They have the same teeth, like tusks. He loves Sunita and her stupid daughter Mona. I can't believe he made me be nice to his mistress, *Aunty* Sunita. If I had known I would have told her what I thought of her, shameless bitch!'

'Kavita, no! Sometimes you can't help falling in love.'

'Mummy, stop being Mother fucking Teresa! Open your eyes. Your husband's a cheat! You need to be more assertive and throw him out.'

In her rage, Kavita started to clear up the mess. Clothes were bundled into her wardrobe, shoes flung onto the shoe rack, textbooks dumped on the desk in precarious towers.

'I can't stay here. I'll go to a friend's. I can't face him.'

The sentences came out jerky. Kavita was trying desperately not to cry. What little happiness they had left was going to be destroyed.

'He's at Sunita's tonight looking after Mona. Stay over with your friend tomorrow. I'll tell him you know and demand some answers,' said Rohini patting her daughter's head.

Kavita collapsed on the bed, curling up like a snail. Rohini closed the door, letting her cry it out.

She called her husband. 'Emergency call. Kavita knows about Mona.' She hung up in the middle of Shourav's rant. *'Why did you tell her?'*

Rohni caught a glimpse of her reflection in the mirror in Dr. Bose's reception and noticed how much weight she had lost in the past few months; a good outcome of a failing marriage. She wore steel grey trousers with a tailored mauve blouse that she had bought from the mall. A paisley silk scarf draped the front of her outfit. An opal pendant rested on her bare neck.

Rohini updated Bose on the latest events. After the session they walked together to the reception area. Bose fidgeted with his tie. The next appointment would be in two weeks. Did she want to come sooner? She could not understand why Bose was insisting on another session. Had she regressed?

'Why?' she asked furrowing her brows.

'Actually let's go inside. I need to discuss the matter further.'

'What about the next patient?'

'It won't take long. Polly, tell Mr. Khanjaria to wait ten minutes please.'

Rohini reentered the room with apprehension. It did not bode well for the doctor to suggest an extra session. She must have said something unconsciously to give the impression of needing help.

'Sit down, please.'

Rohini placed her heavy bag of books on the table. She had come straight from school and was tired. Her blouse felt clammy at the back. She would go home and have another shower.

'What is it, Pranab? Shiv's waiting downstairs, I have to go soon.'

'See, this is what worries me. Your driver's waiting. Your husband and daughter are at home. My wife is waiting for me. It's not going to work. Forget it.'

'They'll wait if I need a doctor's appointment. Do you want to do a double session? I could tell Shiv to pick me up later next time.'

'It seems like subterfuge. It's wrong of me to ask.'

Rohini stared at Bose. He wasn't making much sense. Why would an extra doctor's appointment upset their family life?

'I don't understand.'

'No, I know. I am not sure how to ask this, how you will take it.'

'What's wrong? Tell me. I can take it.'

Still he did not speak. He fiddled with a pen. The minutes were ticking by. Should she call Shiv? It dawned on her that perhaps Bose was afraid to tell her the truth of her condition and the treatment that was required.

'Are you going to try new drugs on me? I'm not going to take any experimental medication. You can forget that. And no electric shocks. My father said that. Is it that bad? Am I entering a manic phase? What is it? Tell me.'

'No, no, calm down. It's nothing like that. It's something more personal.'

Rohini could not think of any way she could be of help to Bose on a personal level. English lessons for someone?

'Rohini, would you like to have dinner with me one day after our session?'

'At your home?'

'No, no, God no.' So, she was not welcome there. His wife probably did not want to entertain insane patients.

'I'd like you take you out to dinner.'

'Why?'

'Good question,' he said and smiled.

The penny dropped. Rohini could only stare at Bose in utter bewilderment. He had gone mad. Finally after all these years of treating patients with mental disorder he had succumbed to the disease himself. Bose leaned back on his chair and looked at the ceiling. His neck was blotched with patches of crimson. Rohini felt a warm flush flooding her cheeks. It was irritatingly puerile. A man had just asked her out. She had no answer, only a blush, worthy of a teenager.

'By your silence I take it the answer is no. Sorry I asked. It was rash and unexpected. Not to mention unprofessional. I'll forget what I said. I suggest you do the same. What was I thinking? We're both still married. And not young. It would have been complicated anyway. A midlife crisis, a dream. I have been thinking about you so much lately, in the shower, first thing in the morning, last thing at night. I see or hear something and I think *I must tell Rohini.* It's crazy, at our age. Forgive me.'

'Stop! I'm glad you said it. I was just so shocked. I had never imagined you had anything more than a little crush on me. I value your friendship. I respect your opinions. But I had never considered anything more. Like you said, we're married. Although if the marriage isn't working, then who knows? But right now, it's too early. Will you be patient with me and continue to be my friend? Let's put this behind us. It would be awkward to continue our sessions with other feelings in place. Let's brush it away until we are ready.'

Rohini bumped into a pillar in the middle of the reception area as she dashed out of the room. Polly shouted, 'Madam, your receipt,' after her, but she was already gone, taking the stairs two at a time and risking ankle injury in her new high heeled shoes.

Chapter 12 Rohini

Two months later

The hum of chanting was soothing. Verses from *Bhagvad Gita* were uttered first in Sanskrit and then in Hindi. The flat was bedecked with white flowers: *rajanigandhas,* lilies, chrysanthemums. Incense smoke rose in tightly coiled circles, above the bowed heads and the large photo of the departed, covered in garlands. Rohini holed herself in one corner of the sitting room. She had only come to pay respects to Dr. Bhatia. Kavita was right. Where was her justifiable fury?

Sitting cross-legged, her posture stooped in apparent grief, was Sunita. Clad in a white *salwar-kameez* the widow's head was covered by a thin veil. For once Mona was dressed in sombre funeral clothes, stark white, devoid of any colour. Other than an Om tattoo on display above ruby red bangles, there was no sign of the rebel. The priest spoke to those present of how the body is just a set of clothes one discards after death. It is the spirit that rises. Mona sniffed.

Kavita had refused to attend the s*radh.* Rohini wanted to leave as soon as the ceremony was over, but Shourav offered to help, so she joined the women circling trays of refreshments. Once, she stood near Sunita, and finding a narrow window of opportunity, said, 'He'll be missed.'

Mona turned around and hissed 'Not by her and her BF.'

Sunita looked at her daughter. '*Chup,*' *be quiet* she said in a threatening whisper. 'One more disrespectful word out of you today and you are going to your room.'

Mona pulled off her headscarf and threw it on the floor. 'I'm going to my bedroom.'

Later, Rohini met Mona emerging from the bathroom. The girl leaned against a doorway, a pair of red make-up-less eyes fixed on Rohini's.

'Uncle Shourav was looking after me when Mummy was in hospital with Papa. He bathed my forehead and put calamine lotion on my blisters. He must be a great Dad to Kavita, no?'

Rohini nodded, wary of falling into the girl's trap and betray her jealousy.

'Mummy said she knew Uncle in a place called, Shyamnagar? They met in a small town by the mountains, just before I was born. And now, here we all meet again. Small world, isn't it?'

Rohini could feel the tentacles of Mona's questions tightening around her.

'We must go now. I just wanted to check you are okay and say goodbye. Your Papa was a lovely man.'

Rohini rushed her sentences, knowing others were within earshot and any repartee would be duly noted. But Mona's mouth just trembled. Rohini put an arm around the girl.

'Be strong.'

Shourav said, 'Bye Mona, look after your mother.' A nod towards Sunita and he walked out of the front door leaving Rohini to do the final *namastes*.

Winter was over and the spring sun, already strong, stole in through cracks in the windows. Rohini flicked a fly off the open pot of jam.

'So the path is free for you to make your move. It's no use us even trying,' said Rohini a month after Bhatia's death.

Shourav chewed his toast. 'That's a bit insensitive, isn't it? She is still in her mourning period.'

'Mourning for a marriage of convenience?'

Shourav left the table. Rohini regretted her impulsive words, bitter as *karela*. They were going nowhere. Like a lot of couples, they lived and ate together, but the relationship ended there. She could name at least ten of her relatives who had marriages like that. Soon age would rob them of any spark. She wanted their relationship to be alive with banter, teasing and romance. Was it too late? She thought of Pranab. When she spoke to him, her blood pulsed through her veins, thinking of witty replies or anticipating another round of friendly insults.

She dialled his number. 'Hi, it's me. Can we meet?'

Rohini's hair fanned out in the gentle evening breeze from the sea. She had recently cut it short, to a more fashionable shoulder length. A steady stream of joggers overtook her. She rarely came to Jogger's park on her own, for fear of being mugged or assaulted, although it was unthinkable in such a tranquil setting. Rohini stood by the sea front listening to the whisper of palm fronds and lapping of gentle waves. She wished she had thought to bring some bread to feed the birds despite a sign clearly discouraging such practice. The park had been built on reclaimed land from the sea and was flanked on either side by the waters.

Rohini watched Pranab walk up towards her. He looked younger in an open collared shirt and jeans. His neatly clipped toenails showed through the complex straps of his sandals. He nudged Rohini towards a bench.

'What happened today?'

'Nothing.'

It was true. Nothing definite had happened. She could not gauge where her married relationship was in the measurement chart.

'He is waiting for her. I am waiting for him. It's crazy! It's time to end it.'

'You've said that before. Are you ready?'

A child's cry drew their attention. She could not see her mother. Her voice held the panic of impending doom until a gentle call reassured her. Could Rohini break up the family, deprive Kavita of two loving parents living under one roof?

'She'll go to Delhi University soon. Perhaps the break up won't be so painful.' Pranab was a man.

'What about vacations? She would have to split her time between the two of us. I am not sure where I'll live, where I could afford to live on my own. England is out of the question now. I don't want to be in another continent on my own. I have half a mind to go back to Kolkata.'

'No!' said Pranab.

The little girl looked up noticing the altered pitch in a grown up's voice.

'No, no, no, no, no,' she mimicked, banging a stick against the sign saying, 'Kindly keep off the grass.'

'I want to be near my parents.'

He hung his head, elbows resting on his thighs, hands joined together. She had not seen this thinking pose before. In his office he tapped a pen, looked at his notebook. Without those professional props he seemed like a vulnerable schoolboy.

Rohini touched his hand. 'You are married. It's complicated. I can't wait for you too.'

'I know. I promise I won't mess you around. I just need a little more time.'

'In any case I need to deal with my marriage first before I think of the next step.'

They followed the circular path back to the car. Evening was approaching and soon the park would become a dangerous place. Parents shouted at children, gathering their toys and prams. Pranab took a car key out of his pocket.

'We could go out to dinner one night, talk things out,' he suggested tentatively.

Rohni shook her head. 'Pranab, you deserve a woman who is free to love you back. I care about you, but my life is a mess at the moment. Let's wait a little. Okay?'

'How did you come here? Shall I drop you off home?' he asked after a brief pause.

Rohini agreed. She had taken a bus and didn't fancy going back by public transport at night. Behind the wheel, Pranab opened up for the first time about his private life. He sat still, staring at the open road ahead.

'Sudeshna and I have grown apart for a long time now. We don't share bedrooms or a social life. She's a good person so we carry on. When I met you I realised what I was missing.'

'Just because you enjoy someone's company and find the person interesting it is no reason for a divorce. I feel sorry for Sudeshna. She hasn't done anything wrong. She is a model wife.'

'So are you. Why then, is Shourav leaving you for Sunita?'

'Don't compare the two of us. Sunita is an exotic bird, a temptress who has had her painted claws into my husband years ago. She was determined to have him. I never even looked at you in that way.'

'I know it's not your fault. A man can fall in love on his own volition. I see no reason to stay in a marriage out of pity. Sudeshna would not want me to treat her with indifference. She does not deserve it. We have independent lives. Even though she has her own income I'll give her a settlement, make sure she is all right.'

Rohini shivered, not wanting to be a part of this conversation, discussing the end of a relationship with cold-blooded frankness. How could she be sure this would not hurt Sudeshna as much as Shourav had hurt her?

'Pranab, are you sure this is not just a midlife crisis? You don't know me as person, only as a patient.'

'I'm a psychiatrist. I know everything about you.'

'Still, I don't want to be the third in a relationship. She'll come after me with a frying pan and hit me on the head when you tell her. You know the saying, 'hell hath no fury than a woman scorned'.'

'She is a calm lady. Besides I won't tell her about you. I'll say we have grown apart and it's time we went our separate ways.'

'I'm not sure. Let's take it slowly.'

It bothered Rohini that unlike Shourav and Sunita, who had clearly loved each other for a long time, she wasn't even in a proper relationship with Bose. But then, if Sunita hadn't left Shyamnagar in a hurry, she was convinced Shourav would have ended their marriage soon after he met that woman. Perhaps, all you need is a gut feeling and courage.

Bose started the engine, the sudden revving making Rohini jump.

'I know it's going to be tough, but we need to take back control in our lives.'

With those words he accelerated and for one moment Rohini thought they were going to hit a bus, bearing down towards them from the opposite direction.

When he dropped her off outside Menaka Towers, Rohini did not care who saw her. She waved goodbye to Bose saying loudly, 'I'll call you.' Mr. Kapoor was right behind them, walking his dog. He would have seen her with a man in a black Mercedes.

Chapter 13 Rohini

Mumbai six months later

Rohini reached in her handbag to grab her phone. The tone reverberated through her brain cells. She rummaged among lipstick, notebook, coin purse, sunglasses and a pack of medicine, eventually locating a smartphone. It was Shourav. Why was he ringing her at this hour?

'Yesss?' She hissed.

'Where are you?' he demanded. 'Kavita couldn't reach you at home or on your cell.'

'I am not at home,' she enunciated with care.

'Clearly. Where are you? Please tell me you are at a friend's house.'

'Okay. I am with a friend,' Rohini obliged with a stifled giggle.

'What's all that music?'

'I don't need to be accountable to the family twenty-four seven. Tell her I'm all right.'

'It's two am. We are worried about your safety. It is dangerous for a woman to be out on her own this late. Kavita says if you can't look after yourself she will quit Delhi University and come back to take care of you. Do you really want that to happen?'

'No.' Rohini felt soberer. 'I'm in the bar in Taj Hotel.'

'I'll be there in twenty minutes. Don't go anywhere else.'

Rohini turned to her newly found friend Rajesh. She squinted at him.

'How old are you?'

'Nevver mind. Another G&T?' he slurred.

'Better not.'

'Who was that?'

'Nobody. A concerned pain-in-the *ass*.' She laughed at her American twang. Rajesh clinked her empty glass.

'Here's to those interfering nobodies. I wish I had one. No one really cares where I am. My wife left me a year ago. *I'm free! Free falling!*' Rajesh crooned.

He rested his head against a pillar to support himself. An untidy fringe fell over his left temple. In the mellow light, he looked like a young Shashi Kapoor, her matinee idol of yore. She wanted to kiss him.

Soon, they heard heavy footsteps. Shourav appeared, unshaven, dressed in jeans, trainers and a Nike T shirt—Sunita's influence.

'There you are. Come on, let's go home.'

Rohini grimaced.

'My ex.' She crossed her forefingers to show a large X.

'Good evening sir,' Rajesh bowed.

'Come on, let's go. I left the car parked by the entrance.'

Rohini waved goodbye to Rajesh whose eyes were almost shut. She had a quick nap while Shourav drove her home. He opened the door with his key.

'You still have it,' she said, her proprietorial instincts alert.

'Of course. Until everything is settled in court I have my rights.'

Rohini lumbered towards the spare room.

'Why don't you sleep in the main bedroom?' he asked.

'Why do you think? Full of ghosts, that room. You can go now. I'm fine,' she replied, kicking off shoes and pulling at her clothes.

Shourav waited in the lounge, flicking through medical journals while she changed into a nightie.

'You should really have someone staying with you full-time. I can hire a maid for you.'

'Your generosity floors me,' said Rohini. She missed the bed and fell on to the tiles, laughing hysterically.

Tears followed soon after. Darkness was closing in. She could barely breathe. If she closed her eyes, the nightmares would begin.

'Open the windows,' she gasped.

Shourav obliged. He helped her into the double bed, putting a sheet over her trembling form.

'Where do you keep your medicine?' Shourav opened and shut drawers.

'Babaji said allopathic medicines are poison. I don't take those anymore.'

'Does Bose know? When did you stop?'

'Two days ago. It's none of anyone's buzziness. Not Pranab's, not yours. I can look after myself.'

'Maybe it's best to avoid medication on top of alcohol and God knows what else you've taken,' Shourav muttered typing a message on his phone. His predictive texting was slow, accompanied by much cursing.

'Go home to your mistress,' she said. 'I don't want you hovering over me like a long faced funeral director.'

'I'm texting Kavita to let her know you are safe. She wants me to stay the night.'

'Soon we will be divorced. You will no longer be legally responsible for me.' All those *lls* in that sentence were difficult to pronounce so she spoke slowly.

Rohini buried her face into a pillow. She had held herself together for so long—now her world was crashing around her. Shourav didn't know. Kavita did, hence the concern.

'She says you've had some bad news. That I must stay with you. What is it?'

'None-of-your-business. Stop pretending that you care.'

Shourav put a hand over her forehead, a doctor's habit.

'I've always cared about you despite…' he switched on the bedside lamp.

Rohini closed her eyes, shutting out the yellow light spreading across her face, baring all her emotions.

'Why don't you tell me what's wrong? It's okay. I'll stay with you. Sunita wouldn't want me to leave you in this state.'

Rohini sat up, feeling a surge of current rise up through her spine. She folded her hands.

'Tell her 'thank you' from me. She cares about me, *na*? She has taken my husband. As if that wasn't enough, God is taking away another loved one from me. Soon I'll be totally alone. All this bad *karma* has happened because of you! Bad things happen in threes. First I find out about Maria, then I lose you to Sunita and now… full circle.' She drew a large round shape with her hand and fell back into her bed.

She rolled again to the side, perilously close to the edge. Shourav pushed her limp form back to the safety of the centre.

'Rohini, Rohini, wake up.' He slapped her face a few times —sharp taps to bring her back to consciousness.

She hadn't really fainted, just drifted into a world where things were suspended, nothing changed, a world without colour. She had not told Shourav what Rajesh had given her; something soft to help cross the deep waters. He had understood her pain.

'So, what is it, Rohu?'

'Don't call me by that name. You no longer have the right.'

'What's the bad news?' Shourav persisted—his tenacity to question as strong as a lawyer.

Rohini sat up. The room was still spinning. She was on a merry-go-round.

'Ma is dying.'

Earlier, a phone call had come from Maria, whispering the news in three simple words, over Indira's loud protests.

'Brain tumour. Too large to operate. It's like a time bomb, ticking, ticking.'

Shourav scooped up her shuddering body and rocked her. They sat like that for a long time. Rohini noticed his glistening face.

'Let's go to Kolkata, the three of us. We'll postpone the divorce. I'd like to see her.'

Rohini rested her head on his shoulder. Perhaps Ma's news would reunite them.

'She was never my mother. It was a lie. God is punishing us and taking her away from me so that I can accept my real mother.'

Shourav shook his head.

'No, it's just life. I see it every day. Death. Loss. The unfairness of it all. It's like Russian roulette.'

Only Bibhuti came to meet them at the airport. He stooped over the barriers, his face cracking into a smile when he saw the family. Shourav insisted on carrying their bags to the car. The white Ambassador was brown in places where the paint had chipped. The seats were hard and the covers gaped here and there.

'How is she?'

317

'Not good, *didi.*'

Rohini had prepared herself to see Ma. No matter what, she would not cry in front of the patient. Indira was always strong. Now was the time to share the strength. Despite her determination, she could not help a small intake of breath when she laid eyes on her mother for the first time since her illness. She had never seen her mother ill.

Indira had shrunk since spring when she left Mumbai. Her body covered in a soft blanket hardly created a mound on the large bed. The pale morning sunlight shone on Indira, highlighting her hair, now totally white. Rohini sat on the bed and carefully lifted her mother up to a sitting position. A strong wind would blow Ma away, she thought. Indira motioned to Rohini to fetch her jewellery box.

'Later, Ma. We've only just arrived.'

'No, now. I don't know how long I have.'

Indira's fingers shook as she picked up a string of pearls. Underneath were necklaces in gold and precious stones.

'This is all for you and Kavita. Give my saries to charity, minus any that you like. My wedding sari is for Kavita. If you have a granddaughter, cut it up into a dress for her naming ceremony.'

'It's bad luck to cut up a wedding sari,' Rohini protested.

'I've run out of luck. Sometimes I wish you didn't know the truth and my soul would have water from the hands of my true daughter. But then, I am relieved to have the truth finally out in the open. I can now leave you in the hands of your real mother. That's why the secret came out, because I was going to die.'

Rohini enfolded Indira in her arms, feeling her heart beating against her bones.

'I'm glad I know. There are no more lies, no more shadows between us.'

Maria walked in with a tray. Tea with honey and cinnamon —a cure all.

'The headaches are the worst. I can't remember anything afterwards—what I ate for lunch, what Roy sahib was talking about just before the pain. It's hard for them too. Maria is not in a fit state to look after me. I tell her the nurse will take care of me, but she insists. She says it is penance for her crime, bringing her ill luck and her daughter into my life. It's you that saved me, my sweet. Through the dark days with Raja, I held on to you. I lost one before that, you know, a long time ago.'

'I know, Ma. Maria told me. Don't think about that now. We are here for three weeks. Let's make the most of it.'

'Be kind to Maria,' Indira whispered.

'Of course. I'll look after Baba and Maria.'

'What about you? Can you not take Shourav back? I don't like to think of you spending the rest of your days alone.'

'What, you don't think I can catch another husband?'

'I never knew you had a sense of humour,' said Indira, smiling. They held each other and laughed until it hurt Ma's chest.

Shourav wandered around the house like old times, supervising his mother-in-law's care and discussing medical matters with Roy sahib. Rohini felt safe. They were a normal family again. Perhaps the crisis had passed and he would come back to her.

Indira's face lit up a little whenever her son-in-law was near. She drew Rohini aside while the men talked.

'It's so nice of Shourav to come. He spent a long time by my bedside last night. He apologised for what he did to you. I have forgiven him. These things happen although I don't like to see you hurt.'

Maria was not fooled by the doctor's charm. She banged his teacup down on the table. 'Dr. Dutta says Indira must have rest.'

'God does not forgive cheats,' Maria could be heard muttering as she left the room.

'I should talk to her,' said Shourav and followed her out.

Maria's voice rose against Shourav's quiet explanations. Rohini smiled.

The household was busy with the patient and visitors. A constant stream of friends and relatives arrived daily. Some took the opportunity of catching up with Rohini, others were curious about their marriage break-up and the cheating husband. Most cared about Indira deeply, which was why Rohini let them in, tolerating the gossips.

One afternoon she went looking for her father. He had been neglected of late. Roy was in his study.

'Rohini, dear, come here.' He was in an armchair by the window.

'See that Bel tree opposite? Right on top, there is a crow's nest. The mother is feeding her babies. She flies back with twigs in her mouth to mend the nest. When I go to the roof to tend to the flowers, the mother pecks my bald head, afraid I will hurt her infants. Such is a mother's love.'

Rohini held her father's hand. He was staring out of the window, beyond the Bel tree. Black clouds, their edges dipped in gold, covered the western sky. It would rain later.

'When I met your mother I wanted to possess her and never let go. But she was unattainable like the moon. Slowly, slowly, she let me hold her. Every night I put her to sleep like a baby. I thought I would go first. I was jealous of you and Maria. How she loved the two of you. You didn't need me.'

Rohini kissed the bare patch on her father's head. He smelt of tobacco and Nycil powder. As far as she knew he had stopped smoking a long time ago.

'I wanted Raja to be a doctor so that we could talk medicine and exclude the women.'

'Baba, we needed you. You gave us strength. When we were ill, you looked after us. Ma also has a lot of respect for you. She doesn't say much, but she never does anything you would disapprove of.'

Roy's hands were crossed over the head of a cane.

'Dahlias are hardy flowers. Water them once a day in winter with strained tea and they'll flower like big stars. My hands shake, so your mother takes care of them. She grumbles but she does it. Who will look after them now?'

Rohini hoped her father would not turn around. A long curl stuck to her damp cheek. They could hear busy feet tapping around the house, entering and leaving the patient's room. She heard her name being called.

'Maria, Durga, Bibhuti, your house is full of people. Your cousin from Alipur comes to visit Ma every day. She has a daughter, Diya, who is keen to help. Soon she will go to Brabourne University like Ma. Maybe they could stay here for a while. Aunty Meena is a widow so she only has her daughter to look after.'

Roy leaned over, placing his face right next to her. She could see his wrinkles. His pupils were dilated.

'Your mother will fight this. I'm not going to end up in an Old People's Home when she is gone. Do you hear me? They abuse the elderly there. It's your duty to look after me.'

She gripped his arms.

'Baba, I won't send you away. I'll come and stay with you for a while.'

He was satisfied with that. She did not tell him that soon she would not have a home of her own. She may indeed need to move back into her *baperbari*, her father's house for a while, to find her feet.

The brief winter days shivered and then they were gone, leaving behind a vague memory of shawls and mists. Indira's health worsened. Rohini returned to Kolkata once more after managing to finish the autumn term. Her mother could no longer feed herself. Maria was unrecognisable, a shadow by Indira's side.

Baba installed himself in the room, muttering about flowers—zenias, marigolds, double-petal *dopaties*. Why was the rose not flowering well? Bibhuti, have you watered them yet? The manservant, older than Baba, crept around the house, dusting house plants, watering dead roses in vases. Without Indira's directions they were lost children wandering round empty rooms. The curtains were not pulled back unless Maria reminded them. Durga the cook, fairly new at fifteen years of service, made regular meals, light dal soup, chicken broth served with Dehradun rice. The patient's tray went back to the kitchen barely touched.

Indira's mind wandered most of the time. She thought Rohini was still at home.

'Time to go to college, dear. Eat up your breakfast. You'll be late.'

And always, her mind dwelt on Raja. *He has bought a ticket for me, First class to Kathmandu. I must go. Maria, let's go, it's time. The baby is due.'*

In lucid moments she scolded her friend for looking so thin and haggard. *Go to bed Maria or you'll drop dead before me. Has Roy sahib eaten? Make a chorhcori with pumpkin and radish today.*

When the pain returned the nurse injected her with morphine. Then her face relaxed into a peaceful expression, looking younger.

Rohini began a monthly commute to Kolkata. The overnight journey, negotiating luggage at Mumbai's Victoria station at one end, and Kolkata's Howrah station at the other, brought back childhood memories of trips to the seaside. She slept on a bunk bed in the Ladies compartment, making friends with the working class with whom she had lost touch. It was a physical and financial drain, but she wanted to see Ma as much as possible. The school arranged replacement teachers whenever she needed to go home. They knew the end was near.

If it hadn't been for Pranab she would have collapsed under the strain. He called her every day, met her in the park when she was in town and watered her plants when she was away. It made the wait bearable. In between phases of dealing with the sick she found hope of a future with a man whom she could depend on. These days her heart beat a little faster when she saw his number ringing hers. One more happy conversation before the inevitable.

The dreaded phone call came early one morning.

'Come quickly, it's not long now.'

Rohini called Kavita first. Her Year One examinations were on the following day, so it was impossible for her to make the trip. Shourav offered to accompany his wife, but Rohini declined. The news of their impending divorce had spread. It would be inappropriate to be seen together. The gossip would distract them from the grief. Rohini flew this time.

Her mother was lying on the hospital bed. A small head protruded from white cotton sheets. Tubes were attached to her nose and arms. Rohini touched her mother's face, tracing the wrinkles, remembering the other time with Raja.

Indira slipped away that afternoon with her family gathered around her; the same ones who had watched Raja leave the world. Rohini hoped he was there now, waiting to take his mother away. The doctors and nurses left the room, switching off machines. Deep blue blinds dulled the strong sunshine outside. The air-conditioning hummed with an occasional splutter. They could hear the sound of metal trolleys pushed down the corridor, wheels squeaking in protest.

Baba sat on a chair next to the body, her still hand in his. He was whispering *slokas* from Gita. Maria bowed and crossed herself, touching Indira's forehead, pushing away tendrils of hair. The three of them were like segments of fruit, no longer a whole. Rohini touched her mother's feet in *pranam*. They felt like *papier-maché*. How quickly the spirit escapes the body.

Rohini followed her mother's wishes. They would not have a religious s*radh* ceremony. This angered the relatives. Instead, a memorial service was held and excerpts from Gita read. Indira's charity workers flooded the place—all the women she had helped came out of their retreat to face the world ensemble, paying tribute to the woman who had given them shelter.

Ghat brothers carried Indira's bier to the banks of Ganges where she was cremated. In place of her son, a cousin lit the pyre. Rohini gave them money and clothes as custom dictated, to thank them for their kindness. A simple vegetarian lunch was offered to the guests—*potol*, greenbarrelled vegetables cooked with *paneer*, homemade cheese, gram lentils with shredded coconut and *radhaballavi*, fried flat bread with *urid* dal filling. A mountain of sweets arrived from her mother's favoured confectioners, triangular silver leaf topped *barfis*, dark *kalajams* swimming in golden syrup and thick rice pudding.

People murmured that the food was too much, samosas and sweets would have sufficed, but Rohini saw their content faces and knew it showed respect for the dead. Her mother had been a good hostess.

That night, after the guests left, Rohini sank into her mother's bed. She was too exhausted to cry. Dozing off eventually, she drifted in and out of dreams—she was chasing birds, her mother was tying her hair, feeding her *payash*. Her voice was calling her, shaking her, *Rohini, Rohini.*

Maria stood over her.

'Have some dinner, dear. It's past nine o'clock. You haven't eaten all day. There is no need to *uposh* today. We didn't have any religious ceremony. The servants won't eat unless you do.' Maria said *kajerlok*, the workers—a term Rohini preferred.

Today of all days, Maria could not be persuaded to wear the sari that Rohini had bought her. She stubbornly wore her mother's old *Dhakai* sari, white, embroidered with little orange and black flowers. Rohini had chosen a new ghee coloured *tangail*. 'Too stiff,' said Maria. The Dhakai was no better, yet she clung on to her friend's old clothes, which smelt of her.

Rohini looked at Maria, her remaining mother, and she wanted to attack this frail uneducated woman—*bring my mother back*! Maria's breath smelt sour, her sari was limp with perspiration. She had been shuffling around all day, hither, thither: seeing to the ceremony; Gitapath; readings from the holy book and offering food to the guests—servile, unassuming, not making any conversation or eye contact. *She would always be a servant*—the poisonous words blocked her airways. Unreasonable, inexplicable hate replaced the love she had just lost. It was Maria's fault; Rohini was supposed to have been Indira's daughter.

'I'm not hungry,' she replied turning over.

'I know, I miss her too. But we have to stay strong. You have a daughter to live for. I know how much you loved your Ma. I can't take her place. One day the wound will heal and you'll remember the good times.'

Despite Rohini's rejection Maria continued to remain by her side. After dinner Rohini went up to the terrace to watch the stars. It was a warm night. She asked for a bedroll to be sent up. Bibhuti laid out the mattress, mumbling that the household had gone crazy after Ma's death. Rohini stretched out, gazing at the night sky. Maria climbed up the narrow steps. She paused at the top, holding her side.

'You'll catch a cold when the morning dew falls.'

Rohini pulled a sheet over her head.

It took three days for Rohini to make the transition from anger to pain, just as Bose had said, in emails and texts. Calls from Pranab, Shourav and Kavita only exacerbated her feelings of loss. She was alone in her sorrow. Like a child in a tantrum she sulked and grieved. Prayers were on hold until she was ready to forgive God for robbing her of unconditional love. Maria, buffeted by her daughter, was steadfastly loyal. Her duty was to take care of the remaining family members. Rohini felt ashamed at neglecting Baba, but she just did not have the strength to prop him up. Maria did.

Rohini was sure Baba was losing his mind. He seldom made any sense. Years ago they had a cat named *Baghini* because of her tiger stripes. He called to her now.

'Ai ai too too too. My little Baghini, where are you hiding?'

Muniya appeared instead, licking his feet.

Maria visited father and daughter, chatting, fetching tea and food—urging them to eat, bathe, read the newspapers.

'Leave me alone,' Rohini barked at Maria who had once more become her nanny. 'When will you stop being a servant?'

Maria's hands dropped to her sides. She was dusting the furniture.

'I'm not educated like your mother. What else can I do?'

'You can read and write. Why don't you read a book? I'll buy some simple ones. Or embroider like you used to.'

'My eyesight isn't good.'

'Get proper glasses. I'll take you to the opticians. Listen to the radio or watch TV. Talk to Baba, he needs your company. I am not going to be around forever. You two will become silent once I've gone. Listen to Bangla music, Tagore songs. You can go to church. Take a rickshaw to St. Giles.' Maria nodded like a docile child listening to her mother's instructions.

By the end of the fourteen-day mourning period Rohini was talking to Maria. Her first word to her was 'sorry'. Maria dropped the broom she was holding and grabbed Rohini's hand, murmuring conciliatory words. Despite the lack of religious rituals, Rohini had followed a vegetarian diet for a fortnight, eating fish only on the last day—Ma's favourite, *hilsa*. She sat with Maria and Baba at the table, sharing a family meal at last. They watched a TV show together. Maria updated Rohini on the Bengali soap. Baba nodded from time to time asking questions.

Going through Ma's clothes was painful. Rohini was comforted by Maria's embrace. Women from 'Janani' came to collect a pile of Mrs. Roy's saries, grateful for the clothes and the memories they brought.

Rohini gave Ma's gold necklace and bangle to Maria. She protested vehemently until she was persuaded to accept souvenirs from a woman she had loved for many years. Ma had left Maria a substantial amount of money in her will— enough for her to be independent.

'What will I do with all this?' Maria looked aghast at the amount in her Bank passbook.

'You could live by yourself in a small flat. That's what Ma wanted.'

'And leave your father here all alone? No way. Can you help me make a will? I can't read legal documents. It's better to do it now. Before, I had nothing.'

Rohini agreed. She too had a tidy sum to help her live as a single woman. She put the rest of Ma's jewellery in the vault for Kavita.

One morning, as Rohini organised her packing to leave Kolkata, Maria came in, looking stronger than she had in many years. She put a little box in her daughter's hand. A gold cross, decorated with rubies and sapphires, twinkled at Rohini.

'Maria-Ma, why? You shouldn't have.'

'I've always wanted to give you a gold cross, ever since First Communion. Now thanks to your mother's money, I can. Did the jeweller do a good job? I can't see very well. I mentioned Indira's name and he showed me such respect.'

'It's beautiful.' Rohini put it round her neck. Few years ago she would never have accepted a Christian religious symbol.

'You'll have to show me how to count your rosary beads.'

Maria beamed. Rohini wished she had made this gesture years ago.

Epilogue

Rohini checked the time. She had one hour. The last of her bags were packed. She had taken only the bare essentials, saving the rest for the day she would move into her new home. Ghum sniffed around her legs, getting in the way. A basket was ready for her in the hallway. Rohini looked around. All the furniture was still in place, but something was missing. The place resembled a lifeless corpse.

They had decided that Kavita would keep the flat. She would have a home of her own during the holidays. Rohini did not want her to feel rudderless, like children of divorce.

The job in Pune was a godsend. It enabled Rohini to start a new life elsewhere without the encumbrances of Mumbai: broken marriage, scandal and rumour. She was now Rohini Mary Roy. The role of Assistant Principal would be challenging, but Rohini was looking forward to teaching in a Christian school. There would be hymns every morning and bible study.

She promised Baba and Aunty Maria that she would bring them over for a holiday as soon she was settled into her two-bedroomed flat, all she could afford on her new salary. Baba would have one room and she would share the other with Maria. With a pang Rohini realised Ma would not see it. She was determined to keep Indira's memory alive by working for a charity.

Mrs. Barua, the landlady, was putting a coat of paint on the walls, primrose yellow. The flat would be ready in a week. Until then she would stay at a quiet B&B off the main street. Rohini opened her diary to check the address once more.

The train was at five. Rohini heaved the bags into the boot of the taxi. Shourav had offered his help, but she refused. As they approached the station, she felt a momentary twinge of panic. She searched her purse for her medication. Pranab had packed extra. He would bring some more when he visited her at Diwali.

A coolie placed her luggage on the racks. Rohini gave him extra *bakshish* as the bags were heavy. She found a seat by the window. The platform was packed with travellers and visitors who had come to see them off. She took out a book to read, Anita Desai's Clear Light of Day, a parting gift from Pranab, along with a glass paperweight with a white stone Taj Mahal inside. A message attached to the present read 'Not to be used as a missile.'

A porter entered the compartment laden with suitcases. He was followed by a man. She could tell by his polished black shoes. Rohini avoided looking up. She did not want to enter into a conversation with a fellow passenger for a journey of only two and a half hours. It simply wasn't worth it.

'Is this seat taken?'

Rohini gasped. She raised her face to see Pranab grinning.

'There aren't any good psychiatrists in Pune. So I'm coming with you,' he said with a slow wink.

He leaned over and gave her a kiss. The lady across the aisle glared.